"Natasha, we have to face reality."

But reality was precisely what Natasha no longer wanted to face.

Sergei cleared his throat. "Things have been too intense between us lately," he said abruptly. His words hurt although they were only a confirmation of what she had suspected for days.

"How can love ever be too intense?"

Sergei shook his head. "I expected you to say something like that."

"Sergei, please explain what's happening."

"You're made for grand emotions, Natasha, and I'm not. You take life too seriously, and when I'm with you I also take it too seriously."

"Tell me the truth." She was in a rage now. "You're tired of me, right? You got what you wanted, you got me to dance in your ballet, and now you're ready to move on. You're leaving me, aren't you?"

"I just think we need some time apart, to think things over."

"How long? A week? Six months? A lifetime?"

"I think I should move out and you should get your own apartment."

"And then?"

"Then I'll go on choreographing ballets for you. We can keep working together, just like before."

"Did you ever really love me?"

"Of course I loved you; I love you now for that matter." He chucked her under the chin as if she were a child. "Come on, smile." And because she couldn't refuse him anything—not even now—she actually smiled. Later that smile was a bitter memory, a piece of self-violation that made her feel ashamed whenever she thought of it.

ABOUT THE AUTHOR

MARY MACKEY, born and raised in Indiana, is a professor of English and a Writer in Residence at California State University, Sacramento, where she teaches creative writing and film. Ms. Mackey, who is related to Mark Twain, frequently reviews novels and nonfiction works on ballet. *A Grand Passion* is her fourth novel.

A Grand Passion

MARY MACKEY

BANTAM BOOKS
TORONTO · NEW YORK · LONDON · SYDNEY · AUCKLAND

This low-priced Bantam Book
has been completely reset in a type face
designed for easy reading, and was printed
from new plates. It contains the complete
text of the original hard-cover edition.
NOT ONE WORD HAS BEEN OMITTED.

A GRAND PASSION

A Bantam Book / published by arrangement with
Simon & Schuster Inc.

PRINTING HISTORY
Simon & Schuster edition published April 1986
Bantam edition / August 1987

Lines from "Among School Children" by William Butler Yeats. Reprinted with permission of Macmillan Publishing Company from *The Poems* by W. B. Yeats, edited by Richard J. Finneran. Copyright 1928 by Macmillan Publishing Company, renewed 1956 by Georgie Yeats.

Bantam Books are published by Bantam Books, Inc. Its trade-mark, consisting of the words "Bantam Books" and the por-trayal of a rooster, is Registered in U.S. Patent and Trademark Office and in other countries. Marca Registrada. Bantam Books, Inc., 666 Fifth Avenue, New York, New York 10103.

PRINTED IN THE UNITED STATES OF AMERICA

O   0 9 8 7 6 5 4 3 2

FOR MY HUSBAND,
CHARLES

Acknowledgments

I owe a special debt of gratitude to novelist Sheldon Greene, who read every version of this novel in manuscript. His suggestions and criticisms were invaluable. Special thanks also to Nolan T'sani, artistic director of the Capitol Ballet, who shared with me his memories of eight years of dancing with the New York City Ballet; to Aleksander Chapkovsky and Irina Zaytseva, who corrected my Russian; and to my agent, Barbara Lowenstein, her associate, Eileen Fallon, and my editor, Patricia Soliman, for their unfailing encouragement. Mark Berger, Charles Dalton, Lily Hill, and Misha Mirkovitch helped me tirelessly with the research, as did librarians at the University of California, Berkeley; California State University, Sacramento; Mills College, Oakland, California; and the Performing Arts Research Center of the New York Public Library. Finally, I would like to pay special tribute to the dedicated artists whose performances inspired this book: the dancers of the American Ballet Theatre, the Kirov Ballet, the Oakland Ballet, the New York City Ballet, the Royal Danish Ballet, and the San Francisco Ballet.

Dusha:
a Russian noun meaning
soul, heart, essence, the inner fiber
of one's being.

O body swayed to music,
O brightening glance,
How can we know the dancer
from the dance?

—*William Butler Yeats*

New York, 1974

Lincoln Center was at its best: the great, three-storied windows of the Met gleamed in the last rays of sunlight like the facets of a giant, exotic jewel; because of an optical illusion the figures on the priceless Chagall paintings appeared to float out into the courtyard like angels announcing that some new glorious era was at hand. As Natasha slowly made her way across the plaza on the arm of her eldest daughter, Winn, she felt, for the first time in years, all the excitement of an opening night.

At seventy-nine, Natasha Ladanova still had a special aura about her that made people turn and stare. Her pure white hair was twisted in a soft loop at the back of her neck the way it had been over a half a century ago when she had danced the last performance of *Swan Lake* ever given in Imperial Russia. Hers were still the dark, mysterious eyes that had charmed a Grand Duke, her body as balanced and compact as it had been the first day she met Sergei Maximov, whom she had loved so much and whom she had not seen in more than twenty years.

Now, by one of those odd quirks of fate that a woman gets used to during the course of a long life, Sergei was launching her granddaughter Alysa's career tonight in his new ballet *Tristan and Iseult*—not out of any misplaced loyalty to Natasha herself, but because Alysa was simply one of the most promising young dancers he or anyone else had seen in a long time.

Inside the Met everything was red and gold, so different, she couldn't help thinking, from the classical blues and creams of the Maryinsky Theatre in St. Petersburg, but appropriate perhaps to the changes that had taken place in ballet over the years. Actually, it was too bad Alysa couldn't make her debut in the State Theater just across the plaza. Natasha had been told that the stage was criss-crossed with soft pine and padded with foam rubber. How many nasty falls such a stage must save, and the leaps Nijinsky could have made on it! What a pity he didn't live long enough to dance his incomparable *Spectre de la Rose* on such a marvel of modern technology.

"Mother, would you like a program?" Winn was bending over her, solicitous as usual, making sure she was settled in her seat. A good child, Winn, as reliable a daughter as anyone could wish for. Winn was in her fifties now and fashionably thin, but Natasha couldn't help still thinking of her as the chubby little girl who could never go to sleep without a nightlight. Tatiana, her youngest daughter and Alysa's mother, had been completely different. She had had the passion and soul of a real Russian, a complete unpredictability that Natasha had always secretly preferred to Winn's good-natured obedience.

It still pained Natasha to think of Tatiana—so much talent wasted, such a terrible, unexpected loss. Even now, sixteen years later, part of Natasha continued to grieve quietly for her. Sometimes she wondered what would have happened if Tatiana had married someone else, but then relationships with the wrong men were, when Natasha thought about it, a kind of family specialty, like ballet. Winn—who had made a solid marriage, who had never showed the slightest interest in dance—was obviously the sanest of them all, or perhaps, Natasha thought with secret amusement as she accepted the program from her daughter, only the least imaginative. Still, Winn's blunt honesty had its virtues; it was a reliable trait, one that didn't produce tragic surprises. There was probably no getting around the fact that the more ordinary you were in this world, the more likely you were to survive to a ripe old age. A career in ballet exacts a hefty price, more than you could ever imagine when you were young and just starting out. It was probably a good thing dancers couldn't see into their own futures.

Settling back in her seat, Natasha surveyed the audience with a practiced eye, picking out the famous and the talented: George Balanchine, whom Diaghilev had introduced her to more years ago than she cared to count; Peter Martins; Merrill Ashley; Clive Barnes of The *Times*; Sandra Atwood covering the event for *Dance* magazine; even Estelle Deveau from *Le Monde*. *Boje moy!* Much as she hated to admit it, when Sergei did something, he did it right.

Her thoughts shifted to Alysa, backstage warming up,

nervous no doubt the way a good dancer was always nervous before a big performance. Natasha pressed her lips together, sharing Alysa's tension by proxy. They were so much alike, she and this beautiful granddaughter of hers, as if their hearts had been strung on the same string. They thought alike, they felt alike, and, despite the over sixty years that separated them, they even looked alike. Most of all, both Natasha and her granddaughter had discovered early in their lives something about ballet that other people never seemed to notice: it was more than just an art or an entertainment.

At the age of eight, Alysa had told Natasha that when she danced she felt as if she were creating everything around her, right down to the boards on the floor. These childish raptures would have seemed ridiculous to a nondancer, but to Natasha they had been almost ominously familiar. Ballet—as she had learned the hard way—wasn't a job, or even a vocation. If you were any good at all, the very act of dancing became an obsession with the power to make your life or wreck it completely.

Natasha glanced at her watch; ten minutes to curtain. The dressers would be bundling Alysa into her costume by now, touching up her makeup. It would be complete chaos backstage, with scenery being shoved about and Sergei yelling at everyone as usual. What a temper that man had, and from Alysa's accounts the passing years had done nothing at all to mellow him. She only hoped his yelling wouldn't upset Alysa tonight, but then Alysa was probably used to it by now.

Natasha crossed herself furtively with two fingers—a habit she'd learned as a girl from the peasants of Archangel—and breathed a short prayer in Russian: *Let my granddaughter Alysa get through this evening; please, God, let her do well.*

Ridiculous as it seemed, she was getting more nervous every minute, as if she and not Alysa were making a debut. Well, what had she expected? After all, she hadn't watched a member of her own family dance for a good twenty years—not since Tatiana's last performance. No wonder the very sight of the stage was unsettling.

Planting her feet solidly on the floor, she took three slow deliberate breaths and forced herself to imagine every muscle of her body relaxing—a trick she had learned from her first ballet teacher. She had expected that there would be memories this evening, powerful memories, pleasant and unpleasant, all mixed in with the anticipation of seeing Alysa dance, but she hadn't anticipated how vivid they would be.

To her surprise, as she leaned back against the softly padded seat, she discovered her first day at the Imperial School of Ballet in St. Petersburg emerging unbidden in her mind like a developing photograph. She hadn't thought about all that in years! What a foolish old woman she was, living in the past, as if the present were somehow a poor second. She was tempted to ignore the image, and yet there was something charming, even innocent about the memory, something that made her feel unaccountably light, almost girlish.

Even now, if she closed her eyes, she could see the sunlight streaming in the great French windows of the school, and hear Madame Laurier, dead these many years, clapping her hands to call the class to order. Anya, her first real enemy, was there, next to Katyrina, her first real friend. And soon, if she let herself go on remembering, Grand Duke Alexis would come in, and then Sergei, and that whole dear, dead world would be resurrected out of the vortex of history, and she would be sixteen again with her whole life spread out before her.

Book I

NATASHA

1

St. Petersburg, 1911

Cold spring sunlight streamed through the great French windows of the old baroque palace on Theater Street, flooding the main practice hall of the school, bringing welcome warmth to the fingers and toes of the fifteen young girls who clustered around the barre waiting for their teacher to arrive and begin the morning instruction. The floor of the hall, which slanted at exactly the same angle as the stage of the famous Maryinsky Theatre, was made of bare wooden boards worn smooth by the feet of the hundreds of young dancers who had passed over them in the last century and a half. In the time of Tsar Paul the building that housed the Imperial School of Ballet had been a royal residence, and there were still huge rooms paneled in precious woods, but in this hall, where the world's best students spent every morning learning from the world's best teachers, everything was as spartan as a monk's cell.

Yet there was nothing monkish about the girls whose high excited voices could be heard half a block away. For three mornings in a row they had discussed with animation the recently published list of gifts that ballerina Mathilda Kschessinskaya had received on February 13 when she celebrated twenty years of dancing on the Imperial stage: the gold chest, the elephant with ruby eyes, the sapphire diadem, the diamond eagle mounted in platinum that the Tsar had given the great dancer in memory of the days when she was his mistress—all had been gone over with loving care. But this particular morning the girls suddenly had a new topic, one that eclipsed Kschessinskaya's presents entirely. Something absolutely unprecedented had happened: there was a new girl in the class.

There were never new girls. A student entered the Imperial School when she was nine or ten, worked for seven years learning the classical technique, and, if she were lucky, graduated to the stage of the Maryinsky Theatre as part of the regular corps de ballet. If she were very lucky indeed, she might become one of the great ballerinas of Russia, worshiped by the people, lionized by the nobility, sometimes even honored by the Tsar himself. But *no one* was just admitted out of the blue—especially not into the advanced class.

For six years these girls had lived together, worked together, fought and made-up, intrigued, confided in one another, shared their dreams of being famous dancers; in short, they'd gotten to know one another as well as fourteen human beings reasonably could. They were a family, and now all at once they had a new member: a slender, dark-haired girl of sixteen whom no one had ever seen before. Her name, they had learned, was Natalia Yakovlevna Ladanova. She was from the northern city of Archangel, and it was clear already that she wasn't the shy sort. She stood solidly against the barre, her feet firmly planted on the oak floor, a friendly expression on her face, as they examined her with unfeigned curiosity.

The girls, like most people who saw Natasha for the first time, found themselves thinking that there was something wild about her, a bit of the taiga perhaps. There was a hint of Tartar to her cheekbones; her luxuriant hair had escaped from the pink ribbon that bound it, framing her face with a halo of unruly curls. Her eyes were so black as to be almost colorless, her skin as delicately colored as a rose petal. It was obvious to their practiced eyes that she was well on her way to growing into a classic balletic beauty: slender, high-breasted, fine-boned, and yet at present there was something so supremely healthy and unself-conscious about her that all the girls warmed to her at once—all of them, that is, except Anya Belinskaya, a small blonde whose braids surrounded her head like a crown of sunshine. Anya, acknowledged to be the best dancer in the class, was wary, if not to say jealous. What right did this total stranger have to seem so at ease, lounging up against the barre as if she owned the place. She should at least have had the good grace to be intimidated in the presence of fourteen of the best ballet students in Russia.

Although Anya had no way of knowing it, Natasha *was* terrified, but she was determined not to show it. Having grown up on her own with only a distant relation to look after her, she had developed an independent facade that sometimes got her into trouble. At present she was grinning boldly as she described how skating on the Dvina River back in Archangel was rather like dancing.

"Are you related to someone important?" Anya interrupted abruptly.

"No," Natasha said frankly. "My Aunt Marya used to be a seamstress, but she's been pensioned off for years. My parents, rest their souls, died when I was a baby." Natasha crossed herself with two fingers in the peasant fashion, obviously unconscious of how quaint the gesture appeared.

Anya's lovely face froze into something unpleasantly close to contempt. "Then, my dear, *how* did you manage to get admitted to the Imperial School?" Anya asked, taking in the room with a graceful sweep of her arm. "If you were the daughter of a Count, say, I could understand it. But how does the niece of a poor provincial seamstress manage to walk into the most exclusive ballet class in Europe, tell me that?"

Natasha saw none of the poisonous barbs Anya was flinging in her direction. "I'm not sure how I got into this class," she admitted with disarming simplicity, pushing her curls off her forehead. As Anya eyed her with increasing rancor, Natasha went on to explain that she had been dancing ever since the age of five when a teacher in Archangel had offered to give her free lessons. The teacher, it seemed, had fallen ill; just before her death she had written a letter and told Natasha to take it to the Imperial School of Ballet in St. Petersburg. To Natasha's surprise, and the surprise of her Aunt Marya, the Board of Governors of the school had read the letter, given her an audition, and admitted her to the advanced class on a full scholarship.

"What was your teacher's name?" Anya demanded.

"Madame Rochina." Tears suddenly welled up in the depths of Natasha's dark eyes and threatened to spill down her cheeks. "She was a wonderful teacher. I loved her very much."

There was a stunned silence. Outside the windows carriages could be heard rolling over cobblestones.

"Not Maria Nikolaevna Rochina?" Anya said at last. There was awe mixed with the envy in her voice.

"Yes." Natasha wiped her eyes with the back of her hand. The girls' silence puzzled her. "How do you happen to know her name?"

"*Everyone's* heard of Maria Rochina," Katyrina Gorina said. Katya was a dancer of only moderate talent, but her father was a distant cousin of Grand Duke Alexis, one of the patrons of the Imperial School. Katya's round face colored with excitement. "Why Maria Rochina was one of the greatest ballerinas who ever lived."

"There was a scandal," Anya said in a dramatic stage whisper. "Rochina was at the height of her career and then, all at once, she disappeared and no one ever heard of her again. Some people say she was pregnant and refused to name her lover. The Tsar himself was suspected."

There was an excited "ah" from the girls.

Anya looked at Natasha with new respect. "Now I know why you were admitted to the Imperial School. Oh, I wish I could have seen Madame Laurier's face when she opened that letter from Rochina! To think that Rochina was living in Archangel all those years."

"Look out!" Katya said suddenly with a hiss. "Here comes Madame Laurier!" There was an excited scrambling as the girls rushed toward the barre. Within seconds fourteen pairs of eyes looked straight ahead, spines rigid, hands barely touching the polished rail, feet planted firmly in the first position. Natasha, unfamiliar with the morning routine, was slower than the rest. She barely had time to adopt the proper posture before the door opened and a tall, raw-boned woman with a chignon of auburn hair and a pair of quick blue eyes strode into the room wearing a black practice tunic and a pair of silk tights.

"Good morning, *mes enfants*," the woman called out briskly.

"Good morning, Madame Laurier," the girls chorused—in French, of course, since French was the only language spoken by civilized Russians on such occasions.

Natasha felt a moment of panic. All her life, ever since she could remember, she had wanted to be a dancer, and now she was being given the kind of chance she had never dreamed possible. For the last two weeks, ever since it became obvious that she was actually going to be admitted to the Imperial School, she had been practicing constantly in Aunt Marya's tiny rented room, unsure of her own talent, terrified the Board of Governors might have made a mistake, afraid that at any minute they would throw up their hands in disgust and write her a note ordering her back to Archangel.

Now she was actually about to take a lesson in the very hall where some of the greatest names in the history of ballet had begun their careers. As she stood at the barre, she was as nervous as a thoroughbred racehorse about to start an important race, yet her body, perfectly trained, gave no hint of anything but the classical serenity of ballet.

"Please," Natasha prayed under her breath, "don't let anyone see how nervous I am."

Madame Laurier clapped her hands to signal the start of the lesson. Behind her Mademoiselle Balasova, the pianist, had already settled down on her stool, her fingers poised over the keys.

"Please," Natasha prayed, crossing herself furtively, "let me get through this lesson without making a fool of myself."

The first half of the class was an exhausting series of *pliés* and *battements*. Gradually, as Natasha repeated the familiar postures over and over, some of her nervousness subsided. Although she had never danced with such talented students before, it soon became obvious to her that Madame Rochina had taught her well. Each time she looked up, she saw Madame Laurier watching her, but the ballet mistress offered no corrections.

They had been working for about half an hour when the door opened suddenly and a tall, distinguished-looking man strode into the room. He was in his early thirties, above average in height, with finely chiseled features and a shock of dark hair that gave him a romantic, dashing look. His suit was expensive, of some unfamiliar foreign cut, his gloves the softest gray kid Natasha had ever seen, his shoes polished to such a gleam that she couldn't help staring.

"Your Imperial Highness." Madame Laurier, suddenly transformed into a blushing, fluttering girl, ushered the man ceremoniously into the room as Mademoiselle Balasova's piano fell silent. Natasha realized that for the first time in her life she was looking at a real live member of the Imperial family.

"It's Grand Duke Alexis," Katya whispered out of the side of her mouth. "Oh, isn't he simply splendid! He's one of the patrons of the school, a real balletomane. All the girls are in love with him."

"He has a wife and two little children," Anya whispered, "and he never betrays them. Give up Katya."

Katya giggled. "Oh, I'll never give up on him. Someday he'll notice me."

"You mean he'll notice *me*." Anya giggled. Clapping their hands over their mouths, the two girls bent forward in paroxysms of silent laughter.

Natasha looked at them, impressed. Imagine being able to discuss a Grand Duke so intimately. Having been raised among the God-fearing peasants of Archangel, she would have never considered cherishing romantic notions about a married man—especially one so high above her on the social scale. Still, Anya and Katya were right about the Grand Duke being handsome. Just looking at him practically took her breath away.

"Natasha," Katya whispered, "do you know what he's here for? Oh, it's such a thrill. He's going to help Madame Laurier choose a girl to dance part of a *pas de deux* in *The Buccaneer*. Just imagine, whoever he picks is actually going to get to dance an important role on the stage of the Maryinsky. Oh, I do hope he picks me."

"Give up, Katya," Anya taunted. "You know it's me he's going to pick."

"It's true," Katya whispered dejectedly. "Anya's the best dancer in the whole class. He'll pick her. I haven't got a chance."

"If only I didn't have to dance with Maximov," Anya moaned dramatically. "Ugh."

"Who's Maximov?" Natasha asked.

"A stuck-up, spoiled, rich little brat. I've danced with him before; he always yells at you when you make mistakes."

"You're just jealous," Katya interjected. "You're afraid he's better than you are."

"Girls," Madame Laurier said sharply, "silence, please." Anya and Katya immediately froze into statues. Natasha at once felt forlorn and a little frightened. It was hard to get used to the rigid discipline here. She bit her lower lip nervously and tried hard not to catch Madame Laurier's eye.

Madame Laurier examined the girls in a way that, to Natasha, seemed formidable. "As you know," she said, planting her hands on her hips, "today we are scheduled to select a girl to dance in *The Buccaneer*. Since His Imperial Highness has graciously offered to assist us," she nodded at the Grand Duke who nodded back, "we will now begin—without further waste of time—in the following fashion: I will call you onto the floor one by one, and each of you will dance a brief segment from the piece we have been working on for the last two months."

Natasha breathed a sigh of relief. Since this was her first day in class there was no way she could be expected to know the audition piece. She could relax and watch the others. In the far corner the Grand Duke had settled into an armchair. Pulling a wafer-thin gold watch out of his pocket, he flicked open the case with his thumbnail, consulted the dial, then tucked the marvelous device back into his vest. How elegant. You'd never see anything like that in Archangel. He caught Natasha looking at him, and she blushed and looked away quickly.

"Anya Belinskaya," Madame Laurier said.

Anya glided to the center of the floor as Mademoiselle Balasova launched into a tinkling rendition of a selection by Tchaikovsky. Poised airily on one toe, Anya performed a series of dazzling *fouettés*. She was so good, Natasha couldn't believe her eyes. Why, Anya was better at sixteen than any of the adult dancers in the provincial ballets that Madame Rochina had occasionally taken her to. Natasha watched entranced as Anya glided across the bare floor in her short white skirt, as light and feathery as a seed pod drifting across a summer meadow. When Anya sank into her final bow and the music stopped, Natasha was overwhelmed by a feeling of inadequacy.

So *this* was the standard of the Imperial School. She'd never be able to come up to it, not in a million years. She had no idea what she looked like when she danced, but she knew she didn't look like Anya.

For over an hour one girl after another danced to Mademoiselle Balasova's tinkling rendition of Tchaikovsky. To Natasha's relief none of them was as good as Anya, but they were still superb dancers. Didn't they ever make a mistake? Why, it was practically inhuman the way all of them managed to dance exactly alike, as if they were not fourteen different dancers, but one dancer in fourteen different bodies.

Actually, after she got over the shock of so much technical brilliance, she had to admit it was just the slightest bit boring to see the same thing repeated so many times. Madame Rochina had always been a great believer in a dancer expressing herself as much as possible within the classical format. Natasha realized with a pang of anxiety that she herself had never danced the same piece exactly the same way—although that was obviously what Madame Laurier would expect of her. Was she even capable of repeating herself? She wasn't sure.

She was so busy fretting over this new proof of her insufficiency that she hardly saw the last two dancers. It was only when Mademoiselle Balasova's piano fell silent that Natasha realized the auditions were over.

The Grand Duke fingered his watch chain and shook his head dubiously. Madame Laurier frowned and shrugged her shoulders. "None of them is really good enough," she said and sighed. "*Tiens*, my dear Grand Duke, I feared as much."

"The little blonde might do," the Grand Duke offered encouragingly after a moment of silence.

Madame Laurier brightened considerably. "You mean Anya Belinskaya?" Anya flung Katya and Natasha a triumphant look.

"Yes, perhaps she might just be able to hold her own," the Grand Duke continued, "just barely. She has a strength, a purity of execution that would make her the equal of the Maximov boy if it were sufficiently cultivated."

Anya's face fell, and Madame Laurier threw her hands up in despair. "But my dear Grand Duke, the performance is less than a month away."

The Grand Duke surveyed the dancers lined up at the barre, and Natasha felt his eyes linger on her. She focused on her *pointe* shoes, wishing he would stop staring.

"What about that little beauty over in the corner?" she heard him say. Looking up, she found he was actually pointing at her. Natasha blushed to the roots of her hair. No one had ever called her a beauty before. "I haven't seen her dance yet," the Grand Duke continued. "In fact, I don't believe I've ever seen her before at all. What a lovely girl. How could I have possibly overlooked her? Who is she?"

"Natalia Yakovlevna Ladanova," Madame Laurier said, "a new pupil."

"A new pupil?" There was frank astonishment in the Grand Duke's voice. Natasha cringed inwardly. Perhaps he would object to her presence in the class, have her reassigned to a lower level or insist that she be asked to leave the school altogether. "Pardon, Madame, but how could a new pupil possibly have been admitted without my knowing about it beforehand?"

Madame Laurier touched the Grand Duke delicately on the arm, led him out of earshot, and began to whisper in rapid French. All Natasha caught were the words *Maria Rochina*, *sad case*, and *letter*.

"So Rochina trained her in the classical style," the Grand Duke said loudly.

"To perfection," Madame Laurier said. "Cecchetti himself couldn't have done better."

The Grand Duke turned and gazed at Natasha, his eyes flashing with obvious excitement. "A student of the divine Rochina here among us, how remarkable!" He strode across

14

the floor toward Natasha. His presence was so overwhelming she had an impulse to move away from him, but instead she forced herself to stare straight ahead as he looked her over. After a few almost unbearable moments, he turned and rejoined Madame Laurier. "I simply *must* see her dance."

"Ah, well," Madame Laurier shrugged, "if you insist. But I can't promise anything. Natasha, please come here."

Natasha's nervousness turned to panic. She couldn't dance; it was impossible. She'd need months and months of practice to look like the other girls. He couldn't know what he was asking. At best she'd make a fool of herself before everyone. Oh, why couldn't he have just picked Anya and been done with it.

"Natasha?"

She had two choices: she could run out of the room, or she could try to get through the next few minutes as best she could. Madame Rochina had always said you could find strength in yourself when you least expected it if you just imagined yourself doing what you were afraid of. Taking a deep breath, Natasha forced herself to imagine that she would dance for the Grand Duke as perfectly as Anya. The trick worked—a little at least. Some of her panic subsided. She wouldn't be a coward, not in front of all these Petersburg people; she's just do her best and pray.

Natasha checked her body to make sure it was centered, and then, before she could think any more about the consequences, she launched herself across the great wooden floor of the hall toward Madame Laurier and the Grand Duke. The white chiffon of her skirt rubbed against her legs, and she could feel the solidity of the floor through the thin leather of her *pointe* shoes. It seemed to take forever to cross the few feet between the barre and the piano. She concentrated on keeping her legs straight, on balancing her head gracefully. At least she wouldn't look clumsy any sooner than she had to. When she reached the Grand Duke she stopped directly in front of him and sank into a deep curtsy.

"So you studied with Maria Rochina," the Grand Duke's voice was kind, but that didn't make her any less nervous. Natasha kept her eyes fixed on the toes of his boots. Sometimes in Archangel she had skated out on the river and the ice had begun to crack under her, but this was infinitely worse.

"Yes, Your Majesty."

15

"The Grand Duke is addressed as 'Your Imperial Highness,' Natasha," Madame Laurier said.

Gospodi! She hadn't even gotten his title right. Well, how was she supposed to know these things? She hated making a fool of herself, but most of all she hated the stupid way she blushed in front of strangers. Tears of embarrassment sprang to her eyes.

"I want you to dance for me, Natasha," the Grand Duke said quietly. At least he wasn't laughing at her. Fiercely she brushed away the tears and found her voice.

"I'd be happy to dance for you, Your Imperial Highness, but I haven't learned this particular piece yet." There, now perhaps he'd see that it was ridiculous to ask her to perform.

"It's true," Madame Laurier said. "The other girls have been working on the Tchaikovsky since the end of last year; since this is Natasha's first day with us, she doesn't know the piece at all."

The Grand Duke took Natasha by the hand and she felt the cool strength of his palm. There was something calming in his touch, as if he were on her side after all. "What pieces do you know?" he asked.

She thought a moment, discarding several of the recital numbers Madame Rochina had had her students perform at the annual Christmas festivities in Archangel. They were so simple she could do them in her sleep, but common sense told her they were not worthy of a student of the Imperial School. No, if she were going to dance at all she would have to do something really good—her very best, most complicated piece. A few months before Madame Rochina died she had taken Natasha aside and given her a series of intense, private lessons, as if she knew that time was running out. The subject of these lessons had been one of the great performance pieces of classical ballet. Although they had never spoken about it, Natasha had understood that these lessons were a gift of love, prompted by the faith her teacher had in her. As she sorted through the possibilities, Natasha knew instinctively that this piece was the one she should dance.

"My teacher, Madame Rochina, taught me part of the Swan Queen's *pas seul* from *Swan Lake*." She was amazed at how firm her voice sounded, but now that she had actually made the decision most of her nervousness had disappeared.

The Grand Duke smiled as if greatly amused. "But my dear girl, that's a ridiculously difficult role. You couldn't possibly do justice to it at your age."

16

Natasha jerked away, stung by his words. "I didn't say I knew all of it," she flashed, "but I can dance part of it."

The Grand Duke laughed and Madame Laurier threw her hands up in despair. "*Tiens*, what a little fire-eater. My dear Grand Duke, I apologize for her rudeness. You must remember that only recently has Mademoiselle arrived from the wilds of the taiga."

"So you want to dance a great ballerina's role, do you?" the Grand Duke said with a chuckle.

"Yes, Your Imperial Highness," Natasha said. "Please, I do know it. And I'm sorry if I was rude."

"*Ma foi*, I should think so," Madame Laurier chimed in.

"Never mind her rudeness," the Grand Duke said, "never mind. She has spirit; that's what counts in a dancer." Natasha was so grateful to him for taking her side she could have kissed him. What a wonderful man. He smiled a dazzling smile that made him look more handsome than ever. She smiled back shyly. "Go ahead," he said, "dance the Swan Queen's part if you insist. I presume Mademoiselle Balasova has the music?"

"Yes, Your Imperial Highness," Mademoiselle Balasova said as she nervously rummaged through her sheets of music. She drew forth a large, tattered book. "Here it is."

"Good," the Grand Duke said as he settled into his chair, "then we're all ready."

Natasha's heart leapt up in her throat and her whole body tensed in anticipation. She walked quickly to the center of the floor and assumed the opening position, clearing her mind of everything but the words Madame Rochina had said the last time they worked together: *Man has always wished to fly, Natasha. This ballet that you have studied so diligently demands more than mere technique; it dramatizes the love relation in terms of limitless flight. At every instant you must be the Swan Queen. At every instant you must be pure love dancing.*

As the music began, Natasha forgot her nervousness, forgot even that she was performing for the first time at the Imperial School. Her feet and hands moved of their own accord; for a few exhilarating minutes she was no longer Natasha Ladanova, the new pupil from Archangel, but the Swan Queen, enchanted by an evil magician, able to take human form for only a few hours. Only a Prince who would love her and marry her could lift the spell. Overlapping her hands, undulating her arms like great white wings, elongating her neck, she danced forward, beating with her free leg on either side, poising on *pointe*, sustaining a long, perfect *arabesque*.

A few times she faltered, but she danced through her mistakes and the magic held. When she jumped, it seemed to her as if she drew the floor up with her, and this sense of flying, of seizing the whole world and rising with it, moved her almost to tears. The emotion communicated itself to her legs, and she danced on past the part she had learned, then stumbled to a stop. There was a long silence.

As if waking from a trance, she realized that everyone in the room was staring at her. *Boje moy!* How badly had she done? The fall at the end had hurt her leg a little; automatically she reached out to massage the muscle. No doubt about it, she'd been clumsy at one point, mixed up some of the steps. Natasha looked at the Grand Duke, wondering if she'd performed so poorly that he'd suggest she be dismissed from the school. She'd seen so few real ballerinas. Was she good or terrible? She didn't have the faintest idea. Not until he took her by the hand and led her over to Madame Laurier did she realize that her performance had been a success.

"Most remarkable," the Grand Duke said. Natasha looked at him, unable to believe her ears.

"She made a number of technical errors, of course," Madame Laurier agreed, "but still. . . ."

"She made the piece come alive."

"Exactly," Madame Laurier looked Natasha up and down as if she could see through to her very bones. "Only she's a bit unpredictable, wouldn't you say."

"Rochina had that quality, too—as if she was always on the verge of exploding into something totally unexpected. As you no doubt remember, Madame, that's what gave her dancing its passion." The Grand Duke put his hands behind his back and gazed at Natasha thoughtfully. "You must admit, my dear Madame, that this young lady has potential."

"Anya is, of course, the better dancer."

"Of course—for the present. Mademoiselle Ladanova lacks the polish that only a great teacher of the Imperial School can impart." Madame Laurier colored with pleasure at the compliment. "Yet I wouldn't be at all surprised if she outdanced Mademoiselle Belinskaya some day."

Natasha looked up and saw Anya glaring at her with undisguised bitterness. Oh, dear, now she had an enemy and probably no amount of apologizing would make Anya feel friendly toward her. Anya's envy made an unpleasant stain

18

on her happiness. Why couldn't dancers cheer each other on instead of always being so competitive? It had been the same way back in Archangel: when the lists were posted for the Christmas recital, the girls who were passed over were always left in tears. But Anya hadn't been passed over. It was clear the role was hers.

"You may return to your place, Natasha," Madame Laurier said.

Natasha walked obediently back to the barre. "Show-off," Anya whispered as Natasha passed her, "you're a rotten dancer. You're—"

"Anya."

Anya's face was suddenly transformed into an angelic wreath of smiles as she curtsied to Madame Laurier. "Yes, Madame?"

"His Imperial Highness and I have agreed that you will dance with Sergei in *The Buccaneer*." The Grand Duke touched Madame Laurier on the arm and they conferred for a moment with their backs to the class. "Darya."

"Yes, Madame?" Darya Denissova, a lively brunette from Moscow, hurried forward and bobbed a quick curtsy.

"I presume your ankle has healed completely."

"Oh, yes, Madame."

"No trouble with it at all?"

"No, Madame."

"Then you will be Anya's understudy."

"Thank you, Madame."

Well that was fair, Natasha thought. Darya was obviously a talented dancer. She wondered what had been wrong with Darya's ankle. Dancers were always getting hurt, but unless the injury was very severe indeed they were supposed to pretend nothing had happened and go on dancing.

"Natasha."

"What?" Natasha was so startled at the sound of her own name that the blunt word was out before she could recall it.

"His Imperial Highness has suggested that since you are new to the school it would be a good idea if you were permitted to attend the rehearsals for *The Buccaneer* so that you can absorb, as it were, what Anya and Darya have to offer."

Natasha heard Anya gasp, but this time she didn't care. She was actually being given a chance to watch a piece being created for the famous Maryinsky Theatre. If she hadn't been trained by Maria Rochina, she might have leapt around the practice room out of pure joy, but instead she sank into a low curtsy. This absolutely had to be the best moment in her whole life. She was almost speechless with gratitude and happiness.

"Oh, yes, Mádame. Thank you Madame."

"Good," Madame Laurier said matter-of-factly. "That's settled then. I'll go get the Maximov boy. He and Anya might as well start rehearsing together as soon as possible." She motioned to Mademoiselle Balasova who obediently launched into a heavy-handed rendition of a Chopin mazurka. "Anya will conduct the class in my absence."

Anya stepped to the front of the room and shot Natasha another bitter glance. It was obvious she resented the prospect of having Natasha at the rehearsals. "Mademoiselle Ladanova," she called out sharply, "fifth position, if you please, not third."

Natasha humbly repositioned her feet, resolving to do everything possible to win Anya over.

The piano tinkled on and on, and the girls, freed from Madame Laurier's critical eye, went through the routine exercises without enthusiasm. After the excitement of the last hour, there was something soothing about the humdrum nature of it all. After a while Natasha stopped worrying about Anya and started concentrating on stretching out the sore muscle in her leg. It was a relief to think about her body in such an intimately practical way.

She'd just worked most of the stiffness out when suddenly the door opened and Madame Laurier reappeared, accompanied by a tall, aristocratic-looking boy dressed in a white Russian tunic and high black boots. Natasha turned at the sound and her mouth nearly dropped open with astonishment. The blue-eyed, golden-haired boy was the most beautiful creature she had ever seen in her life. She looked at him standing arrogantly in the doorway and felt an odd, excited emotion in the pit of her stomach, as if someone had let loose a swarm of butterflies inside her.

"Sergei Maximov," Madame Laurier said to the boy, "this is the girl who will be your partner in *The Buccaneer.*"

The boy smiled and moved confidently toward Anya Belinskaya, who stood in a stray shaft of sunlight, her gold curls glowing like a halo.

"Charmed, as always, Mademoiselle," he said, bending gallantly over Anya's hand.

"And this," Madame Laurier said, "is Anya's understudy,

Darya Denissova, whom I believe you have also danced with before on several occasions." Darya's thin face colored as Sergei bent over her hand, muttering some polite compliment. Madame Laurier put an arm on Natasha's shoulder and firmly propelled her forward. "Also I have the pleasure of presenting to you Natasha, who will be observing the rehearsals. Natasha is a new student from Archangel; she only joined us today. Natalia Yakovlevna, Sergei Fedorovich."

Sergei looked Natasha up and down as if she were a horse and he was thinking of buying her. Ordinarily she would never have tolerated a boy looking at her that way, but he was so like an angel out of one of Aunt Marya's icons that instead of being offended, she suddenly found herself filled with shyness and a desperate desire to please him. Timidly she stretched out her hand.

"How do you do."

The boy looked right through her as though she didn't exist. Natasha felt the shock of his rejection; her face grew red, and she drew back her hand.

"How do you do, Mademoiselle," he said coldly.

Natasha took her place back at the barre, considerably confused. Why in the world had he been so unfriendly? Katya, seeing her distress, edged closer.

"Don't mind Sergei," Katya whispered. "He won't give anyone the time of day unless he thinks they're important."

"Katya and Natasha," Madame Laurier called out sharply, "an extra hour of practice after dinner today for both of you for whispering in class."

"Oh, bother," Katya mumbled, "I always catch it." She smiled gamely at Natasha. Well, at least I have one friend around this place, Natasha thought.

2

Natasha sat completely unnoticed on a straight-backed chair in the corner, feeling as invisible as she ever had in her life. Out on the practice floor Anya, Darya, and Sergei had finished warming up and were waiting for Mademoiselle Balasova to launch into the music from *The Buccaneer*. Already the three of them had the feeling of a team, one from which she was very obviously excluded.

Still, it was wonderful to have an opportunity to watch Madame Laurier work. During the first hour Madame coached Anya, Sergei, and Darya separately in the complex sequence of steps that would ultimately comprise the heart of the short *pas de deux*. Anya went first, performing the unfamiliar movements unsteadily at first, then adequately, and finally with a tentative suggestion of feeling. Darya, too, was a quick study, although Madame Laurier naturally took less time with her.

But it was Sergei on whom Natasha's attention was riveted. His first leap caught her completely by surprise. She had seen male dancers in the provincial ballet troupes that occasionally came to Archangel, but not one of them had Sergei's self-assurance. He was still young and unpolished, but he moved with a liquid, catlike grace; every step, every posture of his body very nearly perfect. Natasha knew how much relentless practice it took to achieve such perfection. Why, he must have been working for days on this. Her respect for him grew, and she watched spellbound.

When Sergei finished, he made a short, breathless bow to Madame Laurier. There was an uncomfortable silence during which Natasha heard Mademoiselle Balasova cough nervously and rattle several sheets of paper together.

"So you've already learned the piece?" Madame Laurier said at last.

"Yes, Madame. Several weeks ago I took the liberty of

22

asking Monsieur Nikalukin to instruct me. Monsieur Nikalukin once danced in *The Buccaneer*."

Madame Laurier seemed slightly annoyed. She tapped the ends of her fingers together and surveyed Sergei critically. "And how did you know you were going to be chosen for the role?"

"Frankly, Madame," Sergei said, grinning impishly, "who else could you choose?"

The arrogance of that boy. Natasha could hardly believe her ears. Yet there was something so pleasant and winning about the way he said outrageous things that it was impossible to take offense. Anya and Darya giggled, and even Madame Laurier, after a brief effort to control herself, broke into a smile. "Sergei, you're impossible."

"Yes, Madame, I agree."

What an unusual person he was to stand up to Madame Laurier like that. Where did he get the guts? For the rest of the rehearsal Natasha couldn't take her eyes off him. He was obviously more interesting than any of the boys back in Archangel, and such a fine dancer that she was almost inclined to forgive him for being so rude to her yesterday. When he lifted Anya in the *léves*, Natasha found herself imagining that she, not Anya, was his partner. What would it be like to dance with someone who had such a good sense of timing, and was so very good looking to boot?

The thought intrigued her so much that that evening, and every evening for the next two weeks, Natasha returned to the empty hall after dinner to practice the steps she saw in the afternoon. Having an extraordinarily good memory, she was usually able to recall most of the sequences, although of course without Madame Laurier to coach her she missed some of the subtleties. She worked until she was covered with sweat and exhausted, and then she sat down, rested for ten minutes, and worked some more even though she knew there was no chance in the world she would ever perform the piece, or even have an opportunity to dance it with a partner.

There was something silly about doing a *pas de deux* alone, but the truth was that, despite Katya's kindness, Natasha was lonelier than she had ever been in her life. And long ago she had learned that when she worked she hardly noticed her emotions, having the unique ability to let her body take over completely. So she danced in the great empty, silent room not only to learn the steps but to lose her own unhappiness; at first her efforts had no effect, but after a few days, to her relief, the dancing became absorbing enough that she felt less lonely—at least for a few hours at a time.

"My God, Natasha, have you heard!" Katya's round, tear-streaked face appeared above the history book Natasha was reading.

"What's wrong?" As Natasha put the book down she realized the entire study hall was strangely empty. Outside the door there was an excited buzz of voices. There were so many strikes and political troubles these days that her first thought was perhaps the Tsar had died or President Stolypin had been assassinated.

"Anya is being suspended for six weeks." Katya wiped her nose on her sleeve, and then broke into another gust of helpless tears. "She was caught sneaking out of school with a b—b—boy. Anya says he's her cousin and they were only going to Conradi's for chocolates, but Madame is livid, and the Board of Governors has already been notified, and Anya is to have her things out by tonight."

"But that's the most ridiculous thing I ever heard." Natasha stood up abruptly, dumping her notebooks on the floor. "Come on," she grabbed Katya by the arm, "there has to be something we can do."

Katya pulled away timidly. "But you don't understand. The rules are so strict, and they never make exceptions. Last year a girl named Elena was expelled outright. We all liked her a lot, but it didn't do any good. Why, even when you get to be a dancer in the Imperial Ballet you have to ask the management for permission to marry."

"Don't be silly, Katya, morals around here aren't as strict as all that. Why, it's common knowledge that the stars of the Maryinsky take lovers from the nobility. Look at Kschess-inskaya—she was the Tsar's mistress for years, and now everyone knows that Grand Duke Andrei has taken over where the Tsar left off."

"Natasha," Katya said, shocked, "you mustn't say such things."

"The pack of hypocrites. It's rotten of them to suspend Anya just for sneaking out for chocolates with some boy who probably wouldn't know what to do with a girl if he had the chance—and I've got a good mind to tell Madame Laurier so myself." Natasha plunged out of the study hall, taking the stairs to the dormitory two at a time. She found Anya sitting on her bed on a disorderly pile of clothes, Darya beside her, an open trunk at their feet. Both girls had obviously been crying. Natasha forgot any enmity she might have felt toward Anya. Injustice had always enraged her; it was unfair that Anya should be so harshly punished for such a minor thing. Her first impulse was to sweep Anya up in her arms, carry her off to Madame Laurier, and demand justice.

"Anya," she said abruptly, "I just heard. I'm so sorry, and I want you to know how rotten I think it is of Madame Laurier to—" The look in Anya's eye stopped her cold. It was a hard, unforgiving look, full of such bitter hatred that she involuntarily took a step back.

"So Mademoiselle from the provinces couldn't wait to run up here and gloat," Anya said. "Well, go ahead—dance on my grave you little ghoul."

This was all a terrible misunderstanding. Natasha tried to protest but Anya wouldn't let her. "I hate you," Anya said rising to her feet with dignity, "and Darya hates you. You came in here, hovering around like a vulture, looking for a chance to take a good part away from someone else. Well, you won't get your wish because Darya's going to dance in my place."

"I didn't intend you any harm," Natasha said.

"Well, you did a good job of it. Madame would never have suspended me this close to the performance if she hadn't known you were waiting in the wings to be Darya's understudy."

"I wasn't even thinking about the part," Natasha said, "honestly I wasn't."

"Oh, of course, and I suppose you weren't thinking about Sergei, either."

"Just go away," Darya said. "Just leave us alone."

For three days Darya pushed herself through rehearsal after rehearsal as Natasha stood by watching. Natasha's emotions during those days were a mixture of admiration and resentment: admiration for Darya's dedication, resentment that Darya ignored her so thoroughly. It made her sad to think that a girl who under other circumstances might have been a friend so obviously thought of her as a dangerous rival, and she came to hate the competitiveness, petty intrigues, and jealousies of the Imperial School more than ever.

Then, on the morning of the third day, everything suddenly fell apart. In the main practice hall the music dwindled to a stop as Madame Laurier strode out onto the floor frowning.

In the full-length mirrors her frown was magnified and multiplied until it seemed to fill the whole room.

"Darya, what's wrong?"

"Nothing, Madame."

"You're landing too heavily."

"Yes, Madame."

"And stop anticipating the music."

"Yes, Madame." Darya smiled gamely and pushed a stray hairpin back into her braids. For several minutes she danced well, even beautifully. Then without warning she faltered again, missing a beat, landing so awkwardly she had to grab Sergei for support.

Madame Laurier motioned for Mademoiselle Balasova to stop playing. "Darya, is your ankle acting up again?"

"Oh, no, Madame; my ankle is fine." Darya danced a few steps, and then turned gracefully on *pointe*. "You see, there's nothing wrong."

"I think we should have a look at it nevertheless. Come here, my dear." Taking Darya's left foot expertly in one hand, Madame Laurier untied the silk ribbons and pulled off the *pointe* shoe, exposing a badly swollen ankle. Natasha caught a quick glimpse of Darya's toes, blue and ugly as if they had been dipped in ink. *Slava Bogu* how had she walked much less danced all this time with such an injury?

Madame Laurier sighed and shook her head. "Darya, why didn't you tell me sooner?"

"But it doesn't hurt, Madame, honestly it doesn't."

"You may have done permanent damage to yourself." Bursting into tears, Darya hid her face in her hands. "Come now," Madame Laurier said, "courage *mon enfant;* it isn't the end of the world."

For a moment Natasha felt Darya's disappointment as if it were her own, then a rush of joy at the realization that she was the only person left who could dance the *pas de deux* with Sergei. The thought that she was somehow rejoicing at Darya's misfortune left her thoroughly ashamed; she was no better than the others. Natasha tried to subdue her exhilaration without success. In less than two weeks she might actually be dancing on the stage of the Maryinsky Theatre in front of all of St. Petersburg. *Gaspodi*, how could she help but be excited?

Three hours later Natasha was summoned back to the practice hall. As she walked along the corridor past the classrooms, she tried not to think of what was in store for her; the excitement was too much, too sweeping. Suppose something went wrong. Suppose Madame Laurier decided that the *pas de deux* should be cut altogether.

She found Sergei and Madame Laurier standing near the barre deep in conversation. At the sound of her entrance, Sergei wheeled and inspected Natasha angrily. "You mean to tell me that *this* girl is to be my partner in place of Mademoiselle Denissova?" For a moment his anger washed by without touching her; so she was to be his partner, have the role after all. A sense of relief flooded her, so overwhelming she wanted to dance around the room like a perfect fool.

"I do not see that we have much choice in the matter," Madame Laurier said sharply. "The performance is, after all, less than two weeks away, and I happen to know that Natasha has been practicing the part on her own for some time."

"Well, I won't have her." Sergei turned to Madame Laurier, eyes flashing angrily. "She's no one. How do I even know she can dance? She hasn't been trained in our school. I beg your pardon, Madame, but I'm not going to risk being embarrassed on the Maryinsky stage by some provincial amateur. No, she won't do, she won't do at all. Just look at her."

Natasha hung her head, on the verge of tears as all the pleasant anticipation and excitement suddenly drained out of her. Sergei's words stung. He was right, of course; she didn't have the kind of training the others had, but it hurt to hear him call her provincial.

"Why she stands like a cow," he continued relentlessly, "and her feet are all wrong. You can see at a glance she'll never be any good. Why don't you let Katyrina Gorina take over the role. I'm sure she's a hundred times better. Or, better yet, call Anya back."

How ugly and ungenerous to say she looked like a cow; how insensitive to compare her to Katya, even if it was true that Katya was the better dancer. Natasha's humiliation turned to anger. Her breath burned in her chest; she tried to say something back to him, to deny his terrible judgment of her, but her tongue stuck to the roof of her mouth. Turning abruptly, she ran out of the hall and hurried down the corridor that led to the girls' dormitory.

The room fortunately was empty. Throwing herself on her cot, Natasha sobbed bitterly with rage and wounded pride. She would ask Aunt Marya to take her out of the school. She hated St. Petersburg and everyone in it; she didn't give a damn if she danced at the Maryinsky; she hated the competitiveness, but most of all she hated Sergei Maximov.

After a while, when she had exhausted herself with crying, she went over to one of the iron washstands by the windows and splashed cold water on her cheeks. When she looked up, she caught sight of her own face in the mirror, swollen eyes, puffy red lids. What a sight she was. Was it possible she was as ugly and incompetent as that arrogant boy had said? Was it possible she really was a clumsy cow with no talent? Was she, as Anya had charged, only a rank opportunist?

Everything in Natasha revolted against the verdict. She did have talent! She knew she did. Madame Rochina had told her so. She would show that Sergei Maximov, and Darya and Anya, too; she would show them all. She would practice and practice until she was the best dancer in the Imperial School, the best dancer in all of Russia.

Natasha sat down on her bed, put her arms around her legs, and rested her chin on her knees, feeling homesick, angry, and confused all at the same time. It was so terribly lonely here. She looked around the unfamiliar room: the rows of iron beds, the wooden desks, the curtainless windows. In Archangel she'd had down comforters covered with bright cotton, a bearskin rug on the floor, a red wooden bed shaped like a sleigh. Everything at this school was so practical and somber; she wondered if she'd ever be able to get used to it.

The memory of Sergei's words stung Natasha again, and she bit her lip to keep from crying. Why had he been so rude? Anya and Darya had cause to be jealous, but what was his excuse? Had he seen some lack in her that she couldn't see in herself? He was, after all, an older, more experienced dancer. Was it possible he was right after all.

No, it wasn't possible.

Yes, it was.

The argument in Natasha's mind went on and on until she was exhausted. That night at dinner she ate almost nothing, and when she finally fell asleep her dreams were restless and disturbing.

The next morning as he was arriving for his first class, Sergei Maximov received a message from Madame Laurier requesting that he come to her office at nine-thirty. When Sergei read the note he grew pale and stuffed it quickly into the pocket of his jacket. Twenty minutes later he was standing in Madame Laurier's private office with his cap in his hand, looking as meek as he could under the circumstances and dreading what was to come next.

Madame Laurier tapped the metal tip of her pen against the brass inkwell and glared at him over the top of her huge oak desk as he'd never seen her glare before. "Sergei Maximov," she said abruptly, "come here."

He took a few steps forward, feeling more apprehensive with every inch. There was something commanding about Madame Laurier that none of her pupils failed to notice; not that she was stern-looking or harsh or spoke loudly, but Madame Laurier had a talent for fixing her eyes on her students in a way that convinced them she could read their thoughts. Sergei found himself squirming guiltily under her gaze.

"Sergei Maximov," she said sternly, "you should be ashamed of yourself."

"For what, Madame?"

"You know perfectly well for what. Your treatment of Natasha yesterday afternoon was totally unacceptable. Natasha is a new girl, and I expect you and every other student in this school to do your best to make her feel welcome among us. Moreover, she is an extremely talented dancer who has agreed to take over a difficult role at the last minute, and she needs all the support and help we can offer her. Are you aware that she was trained by Maria Rochina?"

"No, Madame." Sergei could hardly keep his amazement from showing in his face. He began to have a nagging suspicion that perhaps he had been too hasty, and the fine speech he had been prepared to make to Madame Laurier— the one in which he diplomatically pointed out to her the folly of selecting an untried dancer to replace Darya—dissolved into a confused jumble at the back of his mind. Maria Rochina as a teacher; why hadn't someone told him? He blushed, remembering suddenly he had given no one time to tell him anything.

"You were not only rude to her Sergei," Madame Laurier continued relentlessly, "you acted like a barbarian from the steppes. No *French* gentleman would ever address a lady that way under any circumstance. I realize that St. Petersburg is a long way from Paris, but I was under the impression the same rules of behavior applied throughout the civilized world."

Her words stung, and Sergei hung his head ashamed. He was almost morbidly sensitive to the slightest suggestion that he was somehow less than European. His Uncle Gregor had

29

once told him that foreigners often thought of Russians as uncivilized, and now, it seemed, he had proved it to be true. Turning pale he made a slight bow in her direction.

"I beg your pardon, Madame," he mumbled, unable to meet her eyes.

Madame Laurier was not to be so easily mollified. "It's Natasha's pardon you should beg, Sergei, not mine." She put her pen down next to the inkwell, took a deep breath, and leaned forward slightly. "And furthermore I feel you should be made more thoroughly aware that no amount of talent in the world can make up for a dancer who is difficult to work with." She paused. "I know at least three young men in this school who would jump at the opportunity to dance with Natasha in *The Buccaneer*, and who no doubt could be trained in the role even at this late date. Do I make myself clear?"

Sergei was caught so off guard he nearly panicked. Surely she couldn't seriously be considering taking the role away from him. He searched his mind desperately, looking for the right words to defuse her threat. He needed that part in *The Buccaneer* to prove to his mother he'd been right to devote so much time to ballet. The Countess, widowed and in poor health, constantly objected that Sergei's classes at the Imperial School kept him away from her for too many hours a day. Only the fact that her late husband, the Count, had been a devoted balletomane had persuaded her to permit her son to continue to indulge in a career so demanding and so beneath the dignity of a Maximov. Given this turn of events his mother might insist he give up ballet altogether, and even if she didn't, if word got out that he was temperamental and hard to work with, he might have to wait years to get another chance to dance a major role at the Maryinsky.

Madame Laurier's voice grew kinder, as if she sensed he was suffering. "You're a fine dancer Sergei, but you must learn humility."

"I'll try, Madame." He really meant it. He'd do anything, treat the girl like a princess if they wanted him to. He could feel those three other young men pushing and shoving at his back, trying to walk over him.

"When you see Natasha this afternoon you will, of course, want to apologize immediately." Madame Laurier's face softened a little, and she leaned back in her chair.

"Of course, Madame." Sergei's mind raced, making endless plans to secure his position: when he saw Natasha, he'd do more than merely apologize. He'd be friendly, charming, ingratiating; he'd not only make her forgive him, he'd make her love him. And he'd never, never be difficult to work with again—at least not when Madame Laurier was around. Crossing Madame was much too dangerous. He wanted that role more than anything, and if it took being humble to get it, why, he would become the humblest dancer in the Imperial School.

3

Natasha was so keyed up she could hardly breathe. She had arrived for this first rehearsal with Sergei a good hour early so she would have plenty of time to warm up, but although she had been doing one limbering up exercise after another, her legs still felt like two pieces of lumber. A few minutes ago Mademoiselle Balasova had come in, mumbled a perfunctory greeting, and settled down at the piano bench, but Natasha had hardly noticed her.

Taking a deep breath, Natasha tried to relax as she bent into a deep *plié*. She was just about to repeat the exercise when the door opened, and Sergei strode in accompanied by Madame Laurier. Unconsciously clenching her fists at her sides, Natasha turned to confront him.

"Good afternoon, Natasha," Madame Laurier said pleasantly, waving a sheet of music she held in her hand by way of greeting.

"Good afternoon, Madame." Natasha smelled the scent of rose water as Madame Laurier walked quickly past her, her silk tunic billowing softly over her well-muscled legs. Sergei turned without a word and threw off his heavy blue cape. It was an odd cape, shabby as if it had actually been worn by a soldier in some long-ago battle, vast and cavernous, studded with impressive brass buttons stamped with the Imperial Crest. Under it he wore a white practice tunic, silk tights, and the same heavy black boots Natasha remembered from previous practice sessions. Silently, he pulled off the boots and began to put on his ballet slippers.

So he was going to ignore her. She should have expected it. Over in the corner Madame Laurier was deep in conversation with Mademoiselle Balasova, their heads bent over the music. Perhaps, Natasha thought, she should go over to Sergei and have it out with him right now.

"Ready, children?" Madame Laurier walked briskly to the center of the room. "Sergei, have you warmed up?"

"Yes, Madame, I just came from an extra lesson with Monsieur Nikalukin." His whole manner was unexpectedly subdued as he took his place beside Natasha at the barre.

Madame Laurier smiled kindly at Natasha, "I believe Sergei has something he wants to say to you before we begin."

"To me, Madame?" What could Sergei Maximov possibly have to say to her? Natasha braced herself for some new insult. Sergei cleared his throat, and took a few steps forward. Why he looked positively nervous!

"Mademoiselle Ladanova," he said with quiet formality, "I was very rude to you yesterday, and I'm terribly sorry." He smiled at her, an absolutely dazzling smile that made his eyes look three shades bluer. "I was distressed at the loss of Mademoiselle Denissova as a partner and I'm afraid I spoke out of turn. Please forgive me. It will be an honor to dance with you."

Natasha was won over, seduced, rendered almost speechless. Not only had he not ignored her, he had actually apologized.

"You do forgive me?"

"Oh, of course, yes." She hardly knew what she was saying. He smiled again and there was such a friendly, pleading quality in his eyes that Natasha would have had to have been much older and much more experienced to have resisted him.

"Good," Madame Laurier said, "then we can begin." She made two chalk lines on the floor. "Natasha, you start here" she pointed to one of the lines, "and Sergei you over here."

Sergei faced Natasha, and shrugged as if to say, "Ah, well, my dear, now the real work begins." It was a natural, friendly gesture, surprisingly intimate; he seemed to be implying that he and Natasha were now a team. Natasha felt herself glowing with pleasure. She had misjudged him.

Sergei grasped Natasha's hand firmly, his palm warm and alive, his skin like no skin she had ever touched, elastic, charged with energy. As their two arms formed an arch, a current ran through Natasha, a quick sharp pulse, electric and exciting. What was going on? The hair on her scalp prickled, and her skin tingled in a way that was both pleasant and distracting.

"Natasha, are you listening?" Madame Laurier was waiting impatiently. Natasha mumbled an apology and forced herself to concentrate, but as the hour went on things only got worse. Every time Sergei touched Natasha, new feelings overwhelmed her. When he raised her in the *levés*, his hands seemed to penetrate the thin silk of her bodice, his fingers brushing against her flesh, sending ripples of excitement down her spine. She was suddenly possessed by the feeling that she could fly, that she could do anything no matter how impossible as long as he was there to watch.

She had never abandoned herself to anyone before, but now she let him turn her and move her, instinctively following him, adjusting her rhythms to his. As a result, since Sergei already knew the piece, she danced exceptionally well, performing the correct steps instinctively, matching his skill with her own.

"Ah," Madame Laurier said, "it was a stroke of genius to put you two together." Her voice jarred Natasha back to reality. Sergei was already across the room putting on his cape and boots. Surely the hour wasn't up yet; surely he couldn't be leaving. Natasha watched him, confused. Part of her wanted to go on dancing with him forever, yet at the same time she was uneasy. What had he done to her? Or rather what had she done to herself? Why did she feel such strange things when he touched her? Perhaps she was getting sick. But she didn't feel sick at all; she felt wonderful.

"Good-bye," Sergei said, buttoning up the last button on his cape. Winking at Natasha, he jammed his cap down on his head and strode out of the room. Instantly Natasha realized it would be a whole day before she would see him again. She felt desolate, miserable, abandoned, and her stomach was definitely upset. Slumping against the wall, she began to untie her slippers listlessly.

The orchestra of the Maryinsky Theatre blossomed into the overture of *The Buccaneer,* filling the air with a liquid harmony that made Natasha's very bones vibrate with pleasure as she stood in the wings half wild with nervousness and anticipation. Through a small opening in the great blue and gold curtain she could see the tiers of cream and blue rococo boxes, the gilt bas-reliefs, the huge crystal chandelier lit with a hundred sparkling lights. In the royal box, high above a sea of faces, sat the Empress Dowager and her daughter, the Grand Duchess Xenia, resplendent in diamonds, wearing the most elegant dresses Natasha had ever seen. To their left Grand Duke Alexis occupied another box with a woman, who must be his wife, and two little girls, who Natasha guessed were his daughters.

The sight of the Grand Duke was reassuring. Natasha breathed a sigh of relief; at least she would know one person in the audience. She wished again that Aunt Marya had been able to afford a ticket, but they were terribly expensive and almost impossible to get—handed down, Madame Laurier had explained, from one generation of the aristocracy to the next.

"Please, young lady, move aside," a man in a blue smock was motioning her to get out of the way so the last of the scenery could be lowered into place. For this particular performance two real sail boats had been suspended from invisible cables over an enormous cloth painted to represent the sea. As the curtain went up a hundred soldiers from the Tsar's Finnish Regiment would stand under the cloth to make the mock ocean toss and heave as if a storm were brewing. The soldiers were coming on stage now, looking slightly amused as they jostled for position under the cloth. Madame Laurier had remarked casually that it was costing over 500,000 gold rubles to stage The Buccaneer—a sum so impossibly huge Natasha could hardly imagine it.

To the left, just behind Natasha, the great ballerinas Trefilova and Preobrajenskaya were doing their last minute warm-up along with the regular corps de ballet. Fokine—a master choreographer who, it was rumored, was on the verge of leaving the Maryinsky altogether—was having an involved discussion with a tall elegant-looking dancer in a stiff classical tutu whom Natasha recognized instantly as Mathilda Kschessinskaya—the famous prima donna who before the Tsar's marriage had been his mistress, and, some said, his only true love.

Natasha touched the bare wooden boards of the stage with the toe of her shoe, hardly able to believe that soon she would actually be dancing on them. The wood itself seemed to vibrate with history and tradition. She thought of the first Russian dancers: serfs who had performed to entertain the nobles on their remote estates. Perhaps like her, the serfs had felt they were entering another world when they performed.

Sometimes, she remembered, that entry had proved permanent. Every young dancer had heard the romantic story of

Pauline Kovalevskaya, the peasant girl attached to Count Cheremetieff's corps de ballet. Seeing Pauline dance, the Count had fallen in love with her and under the suspicious eye of Catherine the Great (who intended the Count for her own granddaughter Augusta) he had married her. And then there was Taglioni, the great Italian ballerina, who caused such a sensation when she performed in St. Petersburg that a group of balletomanes purchased a pair of her shoes for 200 rubles, made them into a broth, and solemnly drank it at a banquet in her honor.

Elena Andreyanova, Virginia Zucchi, Pierina Legnani, Anna Pavlova—Natasha invoked the names of all the glorious ballerinas who had performed at the Maryinsky. *I want to be one of them,* she thought.

"Get back everyone, clear the stage," Teliakovsky, director of the Imperial Theatre, gave the signal as the great curtain began to rise, and Natasha scurried back into the wings to watch the first act. At the sight of the boats and the tossing ocean, the audience broke into thunderous applause. Suddenly the entire stage revolved to reveal a luxurious tropical garden complete with perfumed fountains and banks of orchids and gardenias. Live peacocks strutted across an imaginary lawn, pairs of love birds hung in gilded cages from the trees. The corps de ballet entered: Trefilova performed a brilliant solo; Kschessinskaya was dazzling.

As she watched the performance, Natasha's admiration increased. As always, she could see that the dancers were straining every muscle in their bodies, yet the total effect was one of airy effortlessness.

A warm hand slipped firmly into hers. Natasha turned and found Sergei dressed as a pirate, his blue eyes looking out through an unfamiliar mask of stage makeup.

"Nervous?" he asked.

"A little."

"So am I." He squeezed her hand harder. "You look beautiful." Her tutu was spangled with gold coins that caught the light at unexpected moments, and her black hair flowed down her back, constrained only by a circle of pink rosebuds. Leaning forward, Sergei kissed her quickly on the lips. "For luck." He gave her a gentle push. "That's our cue; now go out there and dance like an angel."

For one brief instant as she crossed out of the shadow of the wings into the blinding light of the stage and saw the blurred mass of faces raised toward her expectantly, Natasha

36

wanted to turn and run, but as soon as she began to dance her fear dissolved. Without missing a beat, she moved across the stage, and then suddenly Sergei was moving with her and together they turned, touched, paused as if linked together by a network of invisible threads. As he lifted her in the adagio, she discovered she no longer knew where her body ended and his hands began. Their feet danced automatically through the familiar sequences; when he seized her, her arms fell into graceful curves of submission; her hands against his shoulders were as light and boneless as feathers.

He was the pirate, she the princess. In a moment that seemed to last forever, they played out their roles. With one arm outstretched in the direction of the imaginary sea, Sergei pleaded mutely for her to come with him and share the life of a buccaneer. Surrendering to him and to the music, Natasha ran back, turned evenly on *pointe*, and ended the *pirouette* by throwing her arms wide as if embracing everything he offered her. But even as she did so, the music shifted and, with a presentiment of the disaster to come, she, the princess, drooped and faltered gracefully.

At that moment Natasha lost all sense of performing. As the long slow lament of the violins ran up the back of her legs and exploded at the base of her spine, she became aware that there was no longer an audience, or even Sergei, only a vast, glowing hollow space that was the interior of the Maryinsky devoid of anything human; in the back of her mind Madame Laurier's voice offered a single, lucid thread of advice: *Never forget that this is a ballet about the compulsiveness of love mingled with fear; dance, Natasha, dance obsession and passion*. Clinging to the words, Natasha made them come alive. A mutter of approval rose from the audience and drifted over the footlights, but she was deaf to it.

Suddenly, from behind, Sergei brushed down her imploring arms, seizing her, breaking the flow and line of her body. *The pirate abducts the princess; without conscience or mercy, perhaps even without love*. As he raised her over his head in triumph, and swept her toward the wings, Natasha had the strange sensation that Madame Laurier's words were prophetic. Then the performance was over, the audience applauding, Sergei exiting breathlessly holding her in his arms.

"We did it!" He set her down on her feet and gave her a breathless hug. "You were fine, perfect! Not a single mistake."

Madame Laurier came hurrying up to them, smiling broadly.

"Very nicely done, *mes enfants*." Behind them on the stage, *The Buccaneer* was still in full swing and Preobrajenskaya had just made her first entrance. More scenery was being swung into place; through a haze of happiness Natasha watched the stagehands secure a large grove of wooden banana trees, and begin to spread white sand from wooden barrels across a piece of blue canvas. Grand Duke Alexis threaded his way between them carrying three enormous bouquets of pink roses.

"You danced beautifully, my dear," The Grand Duke said, piling some of the flowers in Natasha's arms; she was overwhelmed with their scent, delighted by such prodigal abundance. "From our winter garden in honor of your first appearance on the stage of the Maryinsky." He took Sergei's hand and shook it as if Sergei were a grown man. "Sergei Fedorovich allow me to present my compliments on a first-rate performance." Sergei colored with pleasure. "You have quite a talented pair here," the Grand Duke informed Madame Laurier. He beamed at Natasha and piled the rest of the roses in her arms until she thought she might smother under them.

"If they continue to do this well," the Grand Duke observed putting one arm around Sergei and another around Natasha, "next winter we just might have to promote both of them to the corps de ballet. And now, *mes enfants*, a treat. I've arranged for you both to have dinner at the Theater Restaurant—under the watchful eye of our dear Madame Laurier. I'm told their new gypsy orchestra is quite good. And the *zakouski* are the best in all St. Petersburg."

The *zakouski* at the Theater Restaurant were not only good, they were so splendid Natasha gasped when she saw them. Along the wall stretched a huge table, swathed in white linen, groaning under smoked salmon, wild mushrooms in cream sauce, Beluga caviar displayed in a vast silver and crystal bowl set squarely into the back of a swan that by some ingenious means had been carved out of ice. There were pickled cucumbers no bigger than her little finger, a French salad made of several kinds of greens she couldn't identify, imported hams, sausages, whole glazed ducks, patés enveloped in crisp crusts, quail eggs floating in aspic.

"The sturgeon is rather good, I'm told," Madame Laurier said thoughtfully, gazing at the heavy, embossed menu she had taken from the hands of the seemingly endless stream of white-coated waiters.

"Ah, pardon, Madame," Sergei offered, "but when Uncle Gregor and I dine here, we always have the sterlet." Natasha looked at Sergei in awe. Was there *anything* he didn't know? On a small stage at the front of the restaurant a gypsy orchestra played plaintively as a heavy, passionate-looking woman in a red kerchief sang one love song after another. Natasha felt complete happiness close around her. She was in one of the best restaurants in St. Petersburg, sipping the tastiest bowl of consommé she had ever had in her life. Best of all, she was with Sergei.

Dinner took the better part of two hours. When they finally finished the last crumb of the chocolate torte and emptied three tiny cups of fragrant, bitter coffee apiece, Madame Laurier summoned the waiter and paid the check with splendid abandon, piling the ruble notes the Grand Duke had given her on the table without even counting them. Rising, she motioned for Natasha and Sergei to follow her to the grand walnut-paneled cloakroom near the front entrance.

As Natasha slipped into her coat she turned to say something to Sergei, something trivial and pleasant about the dinner, but the words froze on her lips. He looked pale, distracted, almost ill. "What's wrong?"

"Diaghilev."

"What?"

"It's Diaghilev and Nijinsky coming this way" Sergei pointed to two men who were hurrying into the restaurant. One was large and walrus-shaped with a bushy black mustache, the other—dressed in a shirt of some soft material open at the neck—was young and vaguely exotic-looking with a sensuous mouth. Natasha instantly recognized the younger man as Nijinsky—already quite simply the most famous male dancer of the century. Katya had three pictures of him tacked above her bed, and she was forever mooning over him and lamenting that he was no longer with the Imperial Ballet. A few months ago Nijinsky had had the audacity to perform *Giselle* at the Maryinsky without wearing the customary support under his tights, scandalizing the Empress Dowager and her daugher, the Grand Duchess Xenia. He had been dismissed on the spot. Katya, who had hoped to dance with him some day, had been inconsolable.

Diaghilev was more of a surprise. From what she had

heard, Natasha had expected him to be tall, slender, and vaguely ominous-looking. He was, after all, the great impresario who, in 1909, had first introduced Russian ballet to the Parisian public, staging productions that thrilled and scandalized all Europe. It was Diaghilev who had made Nijinsky and Pavlova world famous, given the great choreographer Fokine a free hand, and hired Stravinsky when he was practically unknown. At the Imperial School of Ballet the instructors, who had once adored him, now called Diaghilev a decadent and a revolutionary and accused him of trying single-handedly to sabotage the classical tradition.

"Madame," Diaghilev waved his cane rather as if he were hailing a cab. Madame Laurier turned, her face expressing anything but pleasure. Diaghilev paused in front of her and made a strange, formal bow, holding a large linen kerchief over his mouth. Natasha remembered one of the girls telling her that this so-called revolutionary was so terrified of catching something that he wouldn't even ride in an open carriage for fear of being exposed to the horses. "Madame," Diaghilev said, "what a charming coincidence to find you here. I was just telling Slava how much I would like to speak to one of your pupils, Sergei Maximov, and now *voilà*, all things are possible."

"Monsieur Diaghilev," Madame Laurier said, "this is hardly the time or the place...."

He waved away her objections. "I know, I know. Not proper etiquette and all that. I should apply to Monsieur Teliakovsky, director of the Imperial Theatres, for permission and wait three weeks for his formal refusal. You know, of course, what terms Monsieur Teliakovsky and I are on? You know, of course, that he considers me one step below an anarchist bomber. But I must insist, Madame. The performance I just witnessed at the Maryinsky was truly remarkable. Such charm, such grace. Why, I haven't seen a male dancer with that much potential since Slava." Nijinsky smiled at the reference. "How terrible," Diaghilev went on earnestly, "to see so much talent wasted on a ponderous melodrama like *The Buccaneer*."

Madame Laurier stiffened visibly. "I think we have heard quite enough of this nonsense. If you'll excuse us, Monsieur, it's getting late and I must get these *children* back to the school."

Ignoring her, Diaghilev planted himself in front of Sergei, took his hand, and shook it vigorously. "Good-bye Monsieur

Maximov. It was a pleasure to meet you. I enjoyed your performance so much." He smiled at Sergei jovially through his mustache. "You'll be hearing from me."

"Natasha, wait." Katya came to a breathless halt beside Natasha, looked her up and down, and sighed. "What's troubling you these days, anyway?" she asked, pulling a chocolate cream out of her coat pocket and taking a small, meditative bite out of one corner.

"What do you mean 'what's troubling me'?"

"You look so glum. If I was in your shoes I'd be dancing on air."

"I'm fine."

"Fine, ha. I can spot the symptoms a mile away." Katya clutched at the front of her coat dramatically. "Pierced by Cupid's arrows. Another victim to Maximov's charms, dying in her prime." She made a gasping sound and pretended to keel over backward.

"Cut it out Katya."

"Why do you let Sergei get under your skin like that? He's just a stuck-up boy." Katya took another tiny bite of chocolate. "Come on confess. Pretend I'm a priest."

"I'm afraid Diaghilev's going to offer Sergei a place in his company." Natasha ducked her head into the fur collar of her coat and hunched her shoulders miserably.

"So?"

"So if that happens he'll be leaving St. Petersburg."

"Good riddance if you ask me."

"Katya!"

"My dear, have you ever got a bad case." Katya grinned. "Listen, if it's any comfort to you, I just happen to know that Countess Maximov, Sergei's mother, is some sort of invalid. There's not a chance in the world Sergei would leave her and go running off to Paris, believe me—Ballets Russes or no Ballets Russes. Everyone knows she's got him permanently tied to her apron strings."

"Really?"

"Really."

Natasha grabbed Katya and gave her a bear hug that lifted her off her feet. "Katya, you're absolutely the best friend a person ever had."

"Easy there, Ladanova. You just seriously endangered one of Conradi's best chocolate creams." Katya straightened her

41

black velvet beret and contemplated Natasha with sudden concern. "You really care about Sergei, don't you."

"I'd walk through fire for him."

"How does he feel about you, if you don't mind my asking?"

"Oh, he likes me well enough," Natasha paused, but she was too honest to leave Katya with the impression that Sergei returned her affection, "but I don't suppose he cares about me the way I care about him."

"Rotten luck. I'm glad I never cared about a boy. I suppose I will some day; everyone seems to. But as far as I can tell, this love business is nothing but trouble." They walked toward the chapel in silence for a few moments. "You know," Katya said at last, "you're really silly to moon over that boy so much. And what if he does leave? I'll still be here, and so will the rest of your friends."

Natasha forced herself to smile. She was ashamed that Katya's friendship was so little consolation for the prospect of never seeing Sergei again, but she was in the grip of a full-fledged obsession that grew worse with every passing day. Ironically, the anxiety she felt made her performance in *The Buccaneer* better than ever.

"Your dancing is becoming more sensitive, more mature, Natasha," Madame Laurier said, never guessing the price Natasha was paying for this new maturity. The Grand Duke, too, was pleased, and told Natasha with some pride that she was attracting favorable notice.

"Natasha, I've been looking all over for you." Putting an arm around her waist, Sergei drew her behind the flats. It was the last night of *The Buccaneer*; sets for the next ballet already piled against the wall, dangling half-finished from cables; the musty air smelled of damp canvas and fresh glue.

Natasha sneezed and put her hand over her mouth, hopelessly embarrassed. What an unromantic thing to do at such a time. Fortunately Sergei hardly seemed to notice.

"Monsieur Diaghilev's invited me to join his company and I've decided to accept." His words struck Natasha and sank to the bottom of her like a stone. She had known this was coming, worried about it for days, yet she wasn't prepared for the force of her own emotions. Sergei's eyes were bright; he tossed his hair off his forehead with a quick, nervous movement of his neck, like a stallion champing at the bit. "Monsieur Diaghilev says the Imperial Ballet is behind the times and everything really exciting in dance is happening abroad. He says that in his Ballets Russes there'll be room for adventure, experimentation, real creativity—that it's a place where a talented young dancer can really make a name for himself. He even says he wants to start grooming me for principal roles as early as next fall. Isn't that wonderful?"

"Wonderful." It took every bit of courage Natasha could muster not to start crying. He was so happy. Surely if she really loved him she should be happy, too. But she wasn't. She clung to him, feeling her own selfishness, knowing that if there were any way she could prevent Diaghilev from taking Sergei she'd do it instantly. It didn't matter at all to her how great an opportunity all this was for him; she wanted him for herself—she wanted him to stay in St. Petersburg and dance with her, not partner some strange girl in Paris.

"What about your mother?"

"Oh, it's all arranged. She's going to come live in France; Maman's always loved Paris, and our Russian winters aren't good for her health anyway. Monsieur Diaghilev's made all the arrangements."

So the last real barrier to his leaving had been neatly set aside. Natasha felt tears spring to her eyes. Embarrassed, she started to turn away, but before she could escape Sergei suddenly pulled her close and kissed her full on the lips. Natasha was so surprised she stopped crying. His lips were warm and hard against hers; he ran his hands over her body soothing her, petting her hair, running his fingers along her arms. Pulling off one strap of her tunic, he touched her small firm breasts and her nipples hardened under his palm until it felt as if they might burst. She knew she should stop him, but she didn't want to. She wanted him to touch her and go on touching her until she dissolved or exploded, for she felt herself dissolving and exploding at the same time as he bent her backward still kissing and touching her. He gave her another long kiss, feeling out the corners of her mouth with his tongue until every inch of it tingled. Then he stepped back, and looked at her with triumph in his face.

"You won't forget me?" His voice was playful; he might, she thought, have spoken the same way to a puppy or a small child.

"Never." She was trembling, unable to meet his eyes.

Sergei laughed and kissed her again, quickly this time. His face was flushed and his cheeks glowed as if he'd been drinking vodka.

"Will you write to me?" She knew she shouldn't beg, but she couldn't help it. He *had* to write to her. If he disappeared and she never heard another word from him it would be intolerable.

"Of course, if I have the time." Sergei smiled pleasantly. "Look, I'll be leaving in three days and I don't imagine Madame Laurier will want me around once I tell her I'm off to Paris, so I guess we'd better say good-bye now." Placing one finger under her chin, he tilted her face toward his, and gave her a final kiss that took her breath away. "*Dosvydanya.*"

He was leaving, turning away. Natasha tried to think of some reason to call him back, some excuse to go after him, but nothing came to mind. He had every right to go. Just before he reached the edge of the wings Sergei stopped, and waved to her with cheerful insouciance. Then he disappeared.

For a long time Natasha stood looking at the last place he had been, wondering if she would ever see him again. A great sadness came over her, and she suddenly felt abandoned, as if she'd lost a member of her own family. Slipping behind the trunk of one of the large plaster trees, Natasha sat down on the cold wooden floor, put her head between her knees, and cried silently, clapping her hands over her mouth so no one would hear her. Katya was right; she was a fool to care so much about Sergei. But she did care, and there seemed to be nothing she could do about it except wait out the pain and hope it would pass.

4

12 February 1914
Rue de la Paix, Paris

My Dear Natasha,

What a spring season we're going to have! I suppose you've heard about the break between Diaghilev and Nijinsky over Nijinsky's marriage. Everyone tries to reconcile them, but D. is out for blood and has taken up with a new choreographer—a strange fellow with enormous serious eyes named Massine who is being given all sorts of numbers to work on. Still, even though I'm desperately jealous, I have to admit this Massine has talent. Where does D. keep finding these golden boys of his?

Ah, and we have further scandal. Richard Strauss (who's composed a lovely new ballet for us) was so annoyed by the unpunctuality of our dear undependable French orchestra that he went into a towering rage and called them a "degenerate race" to their faces—a phrase immediately seized on by all the newspapers. For a while it looked as if the entire program might have to be canceled, but fortunately for us the Gallic memory is as short as the Gallic temper is hot, and D., with his usual diplomacy, has managed to settle things—greasing a few palms in the right places I suspect.

What a pity you're still stuck in Petersburg. I'm to dance the leads in Les Papillons and Midas and then it's off to London again. You have no idea how pleasant it is to feel that one is at the center of the world instead of stuck in some half-Asiatic backwater like Russia. Right now, for example, from where I am sitting I can see Cocteau bustling about on the stage and Marcel Proust—another of D.'s devotees—who, having recently been

45

*abandoned by his male secretary, is leaning up against a
pillar, a perfect picture of misery.*

*From time to time I run into someone from home who
invariably regales me with terrible rumors of strikes and
riots in the streets and all sorts of unpleasant Russian
political melodramas. I do hope you aren't wasting your
energy and talent by so much as reading a newspaper.
Remember: a dancer has no business thinking of anything but dance.*

á bientôt,
Sergei
•

Natasha folded the thin sheet of light blue paper, slipped it
back into the envelope, and placed it carefully in a small
lacquered box with the rest of Sergei's letters. As always she
wished he had said something more intimate, and, as always,
she was grateful he had remembered her at all. Weighing the
slim packet between two fingers, she thought of the hundreds
of notes she had sent him, written in moments stolen from
practice, scribbled when she should have been studying geog-
raphy or the history of dance. By now, she thought ruefully, he
must have a whole bale of her letters—provided he saved
them. More likely he just read them and threw them away.

Over the last three years Sergei had written back to her on
the average of once every six months: a postcard from Monte
Carlo, sent a few weeks after he left St. Petersburg, bragging
that he had already danced in the tableau of the undersea
kingdom from Rimsky-Korsakov's *Sadko;* a brief excited letter
describing the scandal Nijinsky had created by performing
obscenities in *L'Après-Midi d'un Faune;* a telegram congrat-
ulating her on her promotion to the Maryinsky corps de
ballet; a long complex essay—postmarked Buenos Aires—in
which, for some incomprehensible reason—much to her
distress—he discussed all the reasons why a dancer should
have no personal life (later she discovered he had written it
shortly after Nijinsky became engaged to Romola de Pulszky).

Natasha closed the precious box of letters, carried it to the
dresser, put it carefully in the lower-left-hand corner of the
bottom drawer, and then sat down, straightened her spine,
and contemplated herself in the mirror. What would Sergei
think if he could see her now? Over the last three years she
had changed dramatically, growing from a pretty girl to a
willowy, self-possessed young woman who sat squarely over
her hipbones with the perfect balance of a trained dancer.

Her luxuriant black hair was braided smoothly around her head and her cheeks glowed with good health. A pair of flashing dark eyes looked out from beneath exceptionally long lashes. Nineteen now, Natasha had already begun to develop a fiery, passionate beauty that made strange men turn in the streets to stare after her.

Critically inspecting herself in the mirror, she decided she would do. Sergei would probably find her attractive, although no doubt he was surrounded constantly by attractive women. She was a fool, of course, to keep caring about him all this time. There were at least half a dozen boys at the Imperial School who would have been perfectly willing to court her if she had given them the slightest encouragement, but because she never flirted during rehearsals like the other girls, she had earned a reputation of being cold and unapproachable. But she wasn't cold, not in the slightest. At night she often lay awake longing for someone to touch her and love her, but when she tried to imagine that someone's face it was invariably Sergei's.

If she could have controlled her own feelings, she would have forgotten Sergei Maximov long ago, but feelings, it seemed, had a stubborn life of their own. Why couldn't she love someone who was here in St. Petersburg? She, who was so sensible in all other respects, had never imagined unrequited love would be her specialty.

"Natasha." The sound of her own name startled her so much she turned too quickly, knocking a pile of books off the dressing table. The books fell to the bare wooden floor with a thump. Anya Belinskaya stood in the doorway, her hands on her hips. Time seemed to be leaving Anya untouched. She was still the same slender, golden-haired sylph Natasha remembered from her first day at the Imperial School, but inside that deceptively delicate body was a titanic stubbornness and enough ambition for any three people. Coming back from her six-week suspension, Anya had worked so hard and so long to make up for lost time that Natasha for one was inclined to respect her, and would have even made new overtures of friendship if Anya had been open to them. But Anya had never forgiven Natasha for dancing in *The Buccaneer*, and although she was formally polite on all occasions, there was a distance to her that Natasha found impossible to bridge.

Anya began to step into the room and then seemed to think better of it. "Madame Laurier wants to see you in her office," she said.

Natasha scrambled for the books and piled them randomly on the dressing table, embarrassed to have been caught staring at herself in the mirror like an idiot. "What does Madame want?"

"In case you haven't noticed, Madame doesn't confide in me. You'll just have to go down and see." There was an edge to Anya's voice, as if she suspected that some kind of promotion might be in store for Natasha, something she, Anya, had been passed over for. Natasha, through no fault of her own, was always edging Anya out of things, and now that they were both performing in the regular corps de ballet, the competition between them was worse than ever. Both of them were superb dancers and it was obviously only a matter of time before they were given more important roles. Unfortunately Anya seemed firmly convinced that if Natasha succeeded she herself would be left behind.

Natasha found Madame Laurier sitting behind her desk drinking tea from a glass encased in silver filigree and sorting through a pile of papers. Beside her a large brass samovar steamed vigorously next to a small jar of strawberry preserves and a plate of thickly sliced black bread—she had not even waited to finish her breakfast before sending for Natasha.

"My dear," Madame Laurier said, "I'm afraid your aunt has fallen ill." Picking out an envelope from the stack on her desk, she handed it to Natasha. "One of her neighbors sent word this morning that she was running a high fever. Although no doctor has seen her as yet, I gather all the symptoms point to typhoid."

"Typhoid?" Natasha echoed the word stupidly, unable to think.

"Try not to get too upset, my dear," Madame Laurier said firmly. "It may be something else entirely. I'll call a cab for you at once."

Typhoid. Natasha's mind rejected the word. Nonsense, it couldn't be. Half of Aunt Marya's neighbors were old peasant women who still believed in the evil eye. What did they know about sickness. Aunt Marya'd be lucky if they didn't try to dose her with garlic and enemas.

Ten minutes later, as Natasha stood anxiously in front of the school waiting for the cab to arrive, she found herself trying to recall everything she knew about typhoid. She herself had had a mild case as a child, but she could remember nothing about it. Sometimes, she knew—although she could hardly bear to think about it at present—the disease was fatal. There had been a boy named Ivan one form ahead of her in school who had actually died. Why hadn't those idiotic neighbors called in a doctor at once. Why hadn't. . . .

The sound of a honking horn interrupted her fretting. Looking up, she saw a magnificent car pulling to a stop a few feet away. Huge and white, it dominated the street, glittering like the ice statues children used to make back in Archangel; trimmed in brass and gold with great polished headlamps, it had real glass windows and an adjustable roof that could be rolled back in case the weather turned fair. A liveried chauffeur with a formidable black beard was busy opening the door for a tall, handsome man in a dove gray suit. It was Grand Duke Alexis, the perfect picture of good health and self-contented prosperity, stylish fur coat draped rakishly over one shoulder, head bare despite the biting wind.

"Mademoiselle Ladanova," the Grand Duke caught sight of Natasha and his face broke into a wreath of smiles as he strode over to her. "What are you doing standing out on the street in this cold?" He examined her with pleasant good humor. "Shouldn't you be inside rehearsing with Anya and the others?"

"I'm waiting for a cab, Your Imperial Highness."

"A cab? What nonsense is this?"

"My aunt is ill."

"Seriously ill?" He instantly became all concern.

"I'm afraid so. The neighbors seem to think it's typhoid." The fear she had felt ever since Madame Laurier's grim announcement washed over her again, and she bit her lip and turned away, tempted to cry. Undoubtedly the Grand Duke had better things to do than to listen to her personal problems. Natasha struggled with her emotions. "Apparently she's running a high fever," she said with a calmness that amazed even her.

"But you must go to her at once." The Grand Duke motioned toward the street. "And a cab is simply out of the question."

"I beg your pardon?"

"The drivers in this damned city dart through traffic like demons, especially once they get out of the center. Besides, they always take the longest route. I must insist that you take my car."

49

"But Your Imperial Highness," Natasha said and gaped at him, stunned. "I couldn't possibly."

"Nonsense, my dear Mademoiselle Ladanova, you can and you must. Misha," he called to the chauffeur, "drive Mademoiselle where she requires to go."

"But. . . ."

"No arguments. I won't hear of it. Now come along."

The Grand Duke helped Natasha into the backseat of his car and settled the sable rugs around her. "If you need anything more don't hesitate to contact me. I should be here at the school for the better part of the day, until three let's say." She thanked him profusely. "It's nothing," he said quietly, "please don't mention it." With a wave of his hand he caused the great white car to pull away from the curb.

The Grand Duke's car rode so smoothly it was like standing still, but Natasha was too upset to appreciate its luxury. Her mind buzzed with a hundred plans; she would have to build up the fire, make sure Aunt Marya was bundled warmly and out of drafts, make some broth for her to eat, get a doctor. It would all cost money, of course, but Madame Laurier would probably be willing to loan it to her, and if she had to she'd even humble herself and beg Anya, who received a large allowance.

But when she burst through the double doors into the apartment and saw Aunt Marya lying unconscious on the daybed, all her plans evaporated. Except for two unhealthy red spots on her cheekbones, Aunt Marya's broad face was deathly pale, her breath rasping, the front of her neat white nightgown soaked with sweat.

Natasha brushed the fever-soaked hair out of her Aunt's eyes, straightened her pillow, and then hurried over to the stove, stuffed in a few logs from the meager pile of wood, crumpled some newspapers, and lit a smoky fire. She knew she should send for a doctor immediately, but she was almost numb with worry, and besides, she had the horrible feeling that if she let her aunt out of her sight for even a minute she might die.

Finding a pot, she filled it with water and mechanically started some tea. Why hadn't Aunt Marya told the neighbors to send word to the school sooner? She probably hadn't wanted Natasha to worry. That tiny mark of consideration was so like her aunt it brought Natasha to tears. Wiping them away with the back of her hand, she located the tea, measured out two spoonfuls and dumped them into the pot. The water was too cold and the tea leaves floated uselessly on the surface. Swearing to herself, Natasha threw the whole mess into the slop bucket and started all over again.

People recovered from typhoid all the time. There was no reason to get so rattled. In a minute or two a neighbor would come up and she'd be able to send for a doctor.

Time dragged on. Suddenly there was a loud knock. Natasha was so relieved to think someone might have come to help her that she ran across the room, drew back the latch, and threw open the door. On the landing, holding his cap in one hand and a large package in the other, stood Misha, Grand Duke Alexis's chauffeur.

"Mademoiselle Ladanova." The chauffeur bowed almost imperceptibly and thrust an expensive box of sugar-coated almonds into her hands. "A gift from His Imperial Highness."

Natasha took the box of almonds in a daze; it was a big package, awkward. She shifted it from arm to arm, not quite sure what to do with it.

"His Imperial Highness is very concerned about your aunt," the chauffeur said with quiet gravity. "When I returned to the school he instructed me to drive back here and make sure she was resting comfortably. Is she?"

"Oh, no," Natasha blurted out the truth, too upset for polite lies. "She's terribly sick. You mustn't come in. It's typhoid and it might be contagious."

"Please don't trouble yourself, Mademoiselle. I had typhoid as a child, and His Imperial Highness particularly requested that I have a look at your aunt and report her condition to him, so—if it wouldn't be too much of an intrusion?" With a small, polite bow the chauffeur stepped over the threshold, strode to Aunt Marya's bed, and made a clucking sound of dismay. "Well, it's typhoid all right—but don't despair, Mademoiselle. I've seen much worse cases."

"You're a doctor?"

Misha smiled for the first time, exposing a set of strong white teeth. "I'm from the Caucasus. My mother was a midwife in our village, and I learned a lot from her. Your aunt is sick—no one would deny that—but she'll get better, God willing."

Natasha was so happy to hear that Aunt Marya's case wasn't serious she could have embraced him.

"And now, Mademoiselle," Misha said, "we need to get your good auntie here some help." Abruptly he bundled Aunt

51

Marya in blankets, scooped her up in his arms, and began to carry her toward the door, her long white nightgown trailing behind like a flag.

"But where are you taking her?" Stunned by this sudden turn of events, Natasha ran after him, but the chauffeur was already halfway down the stairs and heading toward the front gate.

"His Imperial Highness instructed me to take her to the Hotel Venezia where she could be treated by his personal doctor," Misha called over one shoulder. "Please watch those steps, Mademoiselle; they're much too steep."

Natasha caught up with him at the curb. "But you can't just take her off like this," she said breathlessly. "When they find out my aunt has typhoid they won't let her into the Venezia, and besides, I don't have enough money to pay such a doctor. Thank you, but you had just better carry her back inside."

"Pardon me, Mademoiselle," Misha said, "but His Imperial Highness specifically said you weren't to worry about the money. Now if you'll just get into the car, we'll get your auntie to somewhere warm and comfortable." He held open the door.

Giving up the fight, Natasha climbed in beside her aunt, feeling confused and relieved at the same time. Perhaps she should have protested more, but Aunt Marya obviously needed more help than she was capable of giving.

For the better part of two weeks Aunt Marya lay in the Hotel Venezia, racked by fever and delirium. Certain her aunt was dying, Natasha never left her side, eating all her meals on trays brought up from the main dining room, sleeping on a small cot she persuaded the management to wedge in between Aunt Marya's bed and a French armoire. Gradually Natasha became conscious that Grand Duke Alexis was hovering in the background, making sure the food she could hardly force herself to swallow was well-prepared, ordering fresh flowers, arranging for three shifts of nurses, and daily visits from his own physician.

One afternoon he actually came to call, bearing a large box of Viennese chocolates, but he stayed so briefly and said so little that Natasha was left with the distinct impression that he was uncomfortable in her presence. Or perhaps he was only wary of falling ill himself. She could hardly blame him for being careful. Typhoid was a disease that eliminated most visitors completely. If her aunt had not been so ill, Natasha might have found this unofficial quarantine galling, but fortunately she was almost too busy helping the nurses give alcohol rubs and change sheets to notice.

Slowly, despite all her fears to the contrary, Aunt Marya's condition began to improve. With her thin arms and fatigue-ringed eyes she looked impossibly frail, and it was obvious it would take months for her to regain her health completely. Still, she was alive! Reading to her from the newspapers or plumping up her pillow, Natasha marveled at how much she loved this woman. She would never take her for granted again; from now on, she promised herself, Aunt Marya would have the best of everything.

Madame Laurier entered Natasha's suite at the Hotel Venezia like an explosion, embracing her impulsively, kissing her on both cheeks. "You lucky girl!" She gave Natasha another hug and then a third.

"Madame?" It was startling to be set on so unexpectedly. Natasha submitted awkwardly, feeling mildly embarrassed.

"What luck, *quelle chance!*"

"Luck, Madame?" Natasha drew back, confused.

Madame Laurier laughed, took off her coat, and tossed it carelessly onto the chair. "Surely you don't pretend to be ignorant of how Grand Duke Alexis feels about you? Oh, he has a bad case; it's written all over his face."

It couldn't be true. Walking over to the Gramophone, Natasha lifted the needle abruptly off the record. The music halted midbar with a scratching sound that put her teeth on edge. "His Imperial Highness has only told me he admires my dancing." Her voice was calm, but in the back of her head she could feel an unwelcome revelation moving forward to center stage where it could no longer be ignored.

She faced the room again, fumbling for the right words, "I hope you're mistaken, Madame, because you see, I admire His Imperial Highness very much. I'm terribly grateful for what he's done for me and my aunt, but he's married, so it would be a sin for him to take any interest in me except as a patron," she stumbled on, conscious she was being overly blunt but not knowing any other way to say it. "Besides, I couldn't . . . that is, I don't care for him—not that way."

"*Tiens*, you Russians are impossible to understand!" Madame Laurier shrugged her shoulders dramatically. "Why, any French girl in your position would give her right arm for such attentions. A young, handsome, wealthy man like Grand

53

Duke Alexis—*mon Dieu*, how often in a woman's life do you think a chance like this comes along?" She paused and looked at Natasha sharply. "Is there someone else?"

"No, Madame."

"You lie badly, my dear," Madame Laurier said gently, "very badly indeed. Well, I suppose that's to your credit. You can't have had much practice at your age. But you should try not to blush so when you tell a falsehood, and you would be much more convincing if you would stare at something besides the toes of your shoes."

Madame Laurier picked up her gloves with studied calm and tapped them lightly against her left wrist. "So there *is* someone else. Ah, well, that puts a different light on the matter." She cleared her throat. "My admiration for you grows, my dear. How could you possibly have had the time to carry on a love affair, much less the cleverness to escape detection? Who is he?"

"Sergei Maximov." Natasha raised her head defiantly. Sergei might not be a member of the Imperial Family, but he was handsome, intelligent, a wonderfully talented dancer, and she had every right to care about him. In a way, it was a relief to have things out in the open. She braced herself for a sharp reprimand, a threat of dismissal, but to her surprise Madame Laurier settled down in the chair and contemplated her with what could only be described as intense relief.

"But Sergei's been gone for *years* dancing with Diaghilev's company. How could you possibly be having a liaison with him?"

"Liaison?"

Madame Laurier laughed and her face relaxed. "You don't even know what the word means do you?"

"No, Madame." What did it matter what she knew or didn't know? She loved Sergei—it was as simple as that.

Madame Laurier stopped laughing and her eyes grew sober. "Natasha," she said quietly, "let me give you some good, sound French advice. Grand Duke Alexis loves you; he's a wealthy, powerful man. You're already the subject of a considerable scandal, and it's now up to you to decide if you want that scandal to be glamorous or a complete disaster." She held up her hand to forestall Natasha's objections. "Yes, I know your aunt was ill, but in the eyes of the public that will make no difference. Simply by accepting these rooms you've compromised yourself beyond any hope. You should be aware that if you reject the Grand Duke and lose his protection you will probably be dismissed instantly from the Maryinsky and will most likely never dance again—at least not in Russia. If, on the other hand, you accept his affections, you will live in the utmost luxury, and there is a good chance you will become as famous as Kschessinskaya or Pavlova. You're an extremely talented young woman; don't be a foolish one."

"Thank you for your advice, Madame," Natasha said with quiet stubbornness. She would refuse the Grand Duke no matter what the consequences, even if it meant she had to give up ballet. He had been wonderfully kind, but she could never bring herself to encourage a man she quite frankly didn't love, a man so far above her socially that any honest relationship between them was impossible.

"Natasha, be practical for heaven's sake." Madame Laurier got to her feet and strode impatiently across the room to the windows where a late blizzard was in the process of burying St. Petersburg. The snow reflected on her face, bringing out all its angular intensity. "Be honest with yourself. If Sergei returned your love, he wouldn't be in Paris; he'd be here with you."

The truth in her words cut. Many times, under more rational circumstances Natasha had told herself the same thing—that she was a fool for loving Sergei. Not once in three years had he written her an affectionate letter or expressed the least desire for her to join him. Yet despite her better judgment, she kept clinging to his memory; her love for him was an old sore, one she'd grown accustomed to through loneliness and habit. Even now, the thought of giving him up was painful, like losing an arm or leg.

"Although I find this difficult to mention," Madame Laurier continued, looking distressed, "there's also your aunt to think of. It's going to take her a long time to get well. Without proper medical attention, she could easily have a serious relapse."

Her words touched a sore spot. "I'd do anything to keep my aunt alive," Natasha said quickly, "anything at all."

The two women stood in silence for a moment, digesting Natasha's words. The implications spread like an echo until the whole room seemed to vibrate with them. Natasha felt something cold move down her spine, as if her whole body were being filled with ice water. How stunningly simple: the heart of the matter wasn't Sergei or the Grand Duke, not her career, not even love or the lack of it. Aunt Marya needed constant medical care, special foods, complete freedom from worry for the forseeable future, and there was only one way she could get it.

Three magnificent white horses harnessed to a fast Russian troika with curled, gilded runners and red leather seats stood stamping and steaming in front of the Hotel Venezia. Grand Duke Alexis, dressed in a splendid sable coat, helped Natasha inside and piled furs around her until all that was visible was her nose. There was something dashing and almost military about him this evening. Oh, he was a handsome man, there was no denying it, broad-shouldered and dark haired, every inch an aristocrat.

Natasha clasped her hands under the furs to keep them from trembling. It was all she could do to prevent herself from bolting out of the sleigh and running back upstairs to Aunt Marya. The night air was so cold it took the breath from her lungs. In Archangel there would have been wolves howling in the taiga on such a night, but here the only sound was the drone of a distant train somewhere on the other side of the Neva.

The Grand Duke took the reins in his heavily gloved hands and expertly guided the horses into the flow of traffic. He seemed in a fine mood, and he obviously knew how to handle the animals, holding them back at corners, letting them have their heads when there was no one in the way. "Have you ever ridden on the river?" His words steamed out of his mouth as the runners sent up a shower of wet snow that peppered the fur and stung Natasha's face.

"No, Your Imperial Highness." She looked away, not wanting him to see the resentment in her eyes, frightened that he might suspect how unwilling she was to be here with him. Her aunt's life might very well depend on her ability to appear amiable, yet hypocrisy of any kind went against her nature. She was a terrible liar. She would have so much rather told him the simple truth: that she liked him, that she even thought he was handsome, that he had been most kind, but that any other sort of relationship between them was out of the question. But the price was too great.

Natasha took a deep breath, settled back, and tried to calm herself. If she was going to sell herself, she could at least make a good job of it. She forced herself to smile at the Grand Duke. He smiled back so kindly it instantly made her feel guilty.

"Would you like to take a ride on the ice?" he steered the

troika around a heavily loaded wagon by a mere flick of the wrist, and smiled at her again, obviously proud of himself.

"Yes." She would do whatever he wished.

"Wonderful. What a game girl you are. My wife would be terrified to death." He steered the troika skillfully over a snowy embankment, out onto the Neva. The ice was ten feet thick, worn to a sheen. The horses lunged into the night, pulling the sleigh along behind as if it were weightless. Soon St. Petersburg was nothing but a white blur on the far side of the river.

Natasha felt her spirits rise. It was a real adventure, dashing through the night like this next to such a good-looking man, and despite her worries she found herself thoroughly enjoying it. There was no use borrowing trouble. Perhaps Madame Laurier had been wrong. The Grand Duke had only asked her to accompany him to inspect some property he owned near the Quai d'Argent, and perhaps he would ask nothing more. It wasn't much of a hope, but she held on to it, trying to convince herself it was reasonable. After all, here they were alone together yet he'd said nothing about love. *Boje moy!* He hadn't even touched her hand.

The cold wind seized her breath and took it away as the sleigh bells jangled crazily, warning other drivers. For what seemed like hours they glided effortlessly, runners cutting through the frost, making a tinkling sound like that of breaking glass. High above them, in a pure black mid-winter sky, the moon was circled by a ring of ice crystals.

Suddenly the Grand Duke pulled in on the reins, bringing the troika to a stop. "Here we are." He pointed to a large house on the Quai d'Argent, built out of pale blue slate. Half a dozen windows gleamed cheerfully, casting carpets of gold light out onto the ice.

"Who lives here?"

The Grand Duke smiled as if he had some secret joke. "Come in and I'll introduce you."

As Natasha walked through the iron gate she saw a garden with hedges and trees trimmed in the French style, leafless now. What a lovely place this would be in the spring, especially with the river to sit beside. The house itself had a delicately carved door, with a brass knocker in the shape of an angel blowing a large trumpet.

"Gabriel," the Grand Duke said, pointing to the angel. "An appropriate symbol for these times, don't you think? After all, he's the one who ushers in the Last Judgment." Instead of knocking, he inserted a little brass key into the latch. "Come in," he said pleasantly.

Natasha stepped over the threshold into the most amazing hallway she had ever seen. Flowers were everywhere, grouped on every possible surface, twined along the stairway, draped over the walls, massed against the windows. Orchids, chrysanthemums, roses, gardenias, lilies, violets, simple wildflowers from the steppes, great orange tropical blossoms she had never seen before. It was impossible to imagine that such things could exist in Petersburg in the dead of winter. They must have cost a fortune.

Red and lilac, umber and spice: the smells and colors of the blossoms overpowered her. For some reason she couldn't articulate she felt lost, as if she had wandered, not into an entry hall but a dark forest. Natasha bit her lower lip to keep from trembling. Why was she being such a fool? After all, it was just a house. A fine house, true, but she had seen fine houses before. Kschessinskaya's mansion on the Kronversky Prospect, for instance, was much larger.

Sensing her discomfort, the Grand Duke took her hand. It was all she could do to keep from flinching at his touch.

"You're frightened?"

"Yes," she said curtly. Another girl would have probably managed something coy and flirtatious, but she was blunt by nature, hopelessly honest. Fortunately he didn't seem to mind.

"Don't be uneasy. There's no need. Come now," he said, "let's look around."

"Won't the people who live here object?"

"Don't worry. They're old friends of mine." He offered her his arm and drew her smoothly forward. "As I recall the drawing room is through this door."

Taking his arm, she let him lead her through the rooms, each finer than the last. Everything was furnished in the most exquisite taste, subtle yet luxurious. Rose-colored silk hung in the drawing room; the sideboards sparkled with crystal and silver. The kitchen was a marvel of modern efficiency with an icebox, great gleaming counters, a gas range. There was a library, a glassed-in conservatory full of more plants, a Finnish sauna with cedar benches. Even the servants' quarters were fine and spacious.

"Now for the upstairs." The Grand Duke guided her up the spiral staircase, past a series of marvelous paintings delicately framed in gold. Boats floated on the bluest water imaginable; red poppies exploded from a field of wheat.

."That's a Renoir," the Grand Duke explained, "and the other's a Matisse."

Like most Russians, Natasha was unfamiliar with the names of French artists, but she found their work stunning. She stood for a long time looking at the colors that seemed to swirl off the canvas. Some of her nervousness dissipated into wonder. How different these paintings were from the flat, stylized icons she had seen at church or the heavy oil portraits that hung on the walls at the Imperial School. After she had had her fill of the paintings, the Grand Duke took her arm and led her to the second floor.

Upstairs there was a bath with hand-painted tiles, and a sitting room done in light green silk. But the best of all was the bedroom that looked out over the garden. The walls were papered in tiny blue forget-me-nots, and the same pattern was repeated in the curtains. More flowers appeared in the thick Oriental carpet, intertwined with birds of every description. The furniture was simple but beautiful: an antique dressing table with a heavy beveled mirror, a canopied bed covered with a spread of embroidered silk, an armchair upholstered in dusky rose satin.

Natasha looked at the fire that burned cheerfully in the white-and-blue tiled Russian stove. "Oh, how lovely," she flinched at the sound of her own voice, embarrassed to have spoken like such a child.

"I'm glad you like it." There was a strange, husky timbre to the Grand Duke's voice. He took the brass latch key out of his vest pocket, and, without a word, opened her hand, placed the key in her palm, and closed her fingers around it. "This is your room, your house," he said simply. "A present from someone who admires you more than you could possibly imagine."

She wanted to protest, but the words stuck in her throat. Drawing her to him, he kissed her gently on the forehead and then passionately on the mouth. Lifting her in his arms, he carried her to the bed and laid her down on the silk spread. The silk was cold beneath her hands, and she was frightened. She thought of her aunt, and of Madame Laurier's warning. She could not afford to offend him.

Feeling her tremble, he drew her closer and kissed her again on the eyelids, the neck, the wrists, whispering to her that she had nothing to be afraid of, pouring out a torrent of

59

love and reassurance. He adored her; he would never hurt her.

He undressed her carefully as if she were a child, petting her until she stopped trembling, and then caressing her until she trembled again. His fingers were skilled and intimate, gliding lightly across her skin as if he already knew every inch of her body. When she was naked in his arms, 'he bent her back over his knees, arching her back, kissing her nipples, drawing them into his mouth until they were hard under his tongue, running his hands through her hair, whispering to her all the while.

She had never imagined that submitting to him would be a pleasure, and so when the pleasure came it took her by surprise. Bit by bit she relaxed under his touch, let her mind glide into the darkness he was building around her. His arms were strong, his body lean and surprisingly muscular. He moved her, pulled her forward like the horses had pulled the sleigh across the ice of the Neva, until she was all skin, until she was plunged into a place where the lightest brush of his finger made her shudder with desire.

She no longer thought.

When he had inflamed her breasts until she couldn't hold still under his hands, he turned to her legs, running his fingers up and down, approaching her thighs and retreating until she wanted to beg him to go on. Her whole body felt like a liquid, like a running stream; she floated on it, borne forward, drifting under his touch, struggling away from him, returning, drawn to the maleness in him that was so different from her own femaleness.

When she was ready, he entered her slowly, bit by bit, thrusting with all his force only at the last. She cried out in pain, and he covered her with kisses, held her until the hurting disappeared, until there was only pleasure again building up under her spine, lifting her up off the bed toward him.

She had never felt such complete physical pleasure. The thought came to her that they were dancing, that he had partnered her in a way she had never been partnered before—that this was the ultimate *pas de deux* of which those of the stage were only faint imitations. Without thinking she understood suddenly that the basis of all dance was sexual, that music and love and all the arts sprung from this and this alone.

He pulled her closer, moving more rapidly, breathing in short gasps. The weight of him pinned her down, pulled her into him until she could feel his ribs pressing against hers, measure the girth of his leg bones. The energy in her spine built and exploded, running to her neck, shaking her entire body. She cried out in pleasure, grasped his shoulders, fell back stricken, and exhausted.

He lay still for a moment, then slowly began to move again, petting her breasts, rocking her back and forth between his thighs. Drawing her into a sitting position between his legs, he stroked her hair, kissed her, breathing in her breath, filling her lungs with his. This time when she cried out, he cried out with her, pulling her so close she couldn't move.

He held her for a long time after that, gently stroking her hair, and then without a word he lay her down on the bed, stretched out beside her, took her in his arms, and fell asleep. For Natasha sleep was a long time coming. The depths of passion she had discovered in herself confused and alarmed her. To her surprise she found that she, who had lately begun to consider all religions pure superstition, had a sense of having sinned against something; worse yet, as she lay in this warm comfortable bed she was becoming increasingly afraid of some kind of punishment she could not define, not even to herself. Ridiculous—yet perhaps not. What if the Grand Duke lost interest in her now, or what if she found herself pregnant with his child?

The blue forget-me-not wallpaper, the heavy walnut posts of the bed gleaming in the firelight, calmed her. After all, he had given her this house. Was this the present of a man who intended to abandon her? He said he loved her; why couldn't she accept that and be at peace? True, she didn't love him in return, but she liked him well enough. He was handsome, generous. He would take care of her, protect her, and probably, if Madame Laurier were right, further her career. Best of all, her aunt would be happy here.

The Grand Duke turned in his sleep and threw one arm over her protectively. Natasha froze, afraid she might wake him. His arm was heavy and unfamiliar on her chest. How strange it was to sleep with a man. She felt a hundred years older than the girl who had climbed into the sleigh a few hours ago. She lay absolutely still, afraid to move a muscle for fear of disturbing the Grand Duke again. Irrationally, she thought of Sergei. An odd mixture of sadness, relief, and defiance stirred in her. Natasha closed her eyes and tried to make her mind a blank, but the sky was beginning to turn a pale, watery gray when she finally fell asleep.

The next morning, in the clear light of day, she realized how foolish she had been to worry so much. At breakfast Alexis was all attention, buttering her toast, pouring her tea, piling up pillows, entertaining her with witty observations that made her laugh despite herself. Servants, who seem to have appeared out of nowhere during the night, discreetly served them and then cleared away the dishes. When the servants finally left the room, the Grand Duke pulled Natasha to him and kissed her lightly on the lips.

"Are you ready for another surprise?" He was playful like a child with a secret.

"Yes," but she wasn't sure. There had been perhaps too many surprises already.

"Yes, my darling Alexis," he prompted.

"Yes, my darling Alexis." It was a litany she would often be asked to repeat in the coming months. The Grand Duke rewarded her with a smile; encircling her waist with his arm, he led her up to the top floor where seven magnificent windows overlooked the Neva.

Natasha stared in amazement at the full-length mirrors mounted along the walls and the long polished barre that spanned the great room from end to end. In one corner stood a grand piano; over it hung an original Degas depicting two ballerinas bending forward to tie the ribbons on their shoes. Everything was perfect, right down to the soft oak floor.

She could see at once that it was as fine a rehearsal room as any in the Imperial School.

5

December, 1916

"Brava!"

"Brava!"

Flowers pelted the heavy blue and gold curtain behind Natasha's head, falling to her feet, piling up on the stage until it seemed she was wading through waves of red, pink, and gold roses. In front of her the audience swayed, doing a ballet of its own, the dark dress jackets of the men counterpointed by the glittering diamonds and explosively brilliant silks of the women.

Natasha was their drug tonight, their river of Lethe. Outside the Maryinsky Theatre reality was as cold and grim as a Siberian winter. A war was raging, the government was toppling, there were shortages, hunger, riots, and strikes, but as long as Natasha danced for them, this audience at least, could forget the unforgettable. For the space of a few hours, they could imagine that it was 1786 and they were watching the first performance of *La Fille Mal Gardée* ever given. They could pretend that the French Revolution had never happened, that all of recent European history was a bad dream, that nobility and monarchy ran on a rising current, that there was no Lenin waiting in the wings to ring down the final curtain.

Selecting a single long-stemmed red rose from one of the bouquets, Natasha kissed it and tossed it in a long arc toward the front rows where the wounded soldiers sat. The red petals fell on the upturned faces like spots of blood; arms flashed in the air as the men strained for the flower; seizing the rose in midflight, a triumphant soldier pressed it to his lips. He smiled through the bandages that swathed his face, radiantly happy as a child, and blew a kiss to Natasha that caused a lump to form in her throat. Quickly she turned away, blinking back tears, bowing gracefully as the audience clapped on and on, calling out her name.

They gave her twelve curtain calls, and would have given

her thirteen or perhaps even twenty had she not signaled to the stage director that she had had enough.

Safe in her private dressing room, Natasha poured herself a glass of warm champagne and settled back into the pillows of the overstuffed couch. A plate of fresh cucumber sandwiches lay on her makeup table next to several pots of theatrical paints, half a dozen eyeliners, a tangle of ribbons, two jars of hairpins, a pile of press clippings, and a tiara of white feathers that had seen better days. It would have been simple enough to tell the maid to clean things up, but Natasha frankly liked the mess, which reminded her that this was her room and no one else's.

Tonight Alexis was with his family, celebrating the birthday of his eldest daughter. The theater was virtually empty—the audience having left long ago—and a great peaceful silence was slowly settling on the building, muffling everything like drifting snow. On evenings like this Natasha often stayed in her dressing room until one or two in the morning, indulging herself in the increasingly rare luxury of being absolutely alone. These were the times when she took stock of her life, and tried to puzzle out what she was doing, for despite the success that should have made her perfectly content, she was often unaccountably restless.

Tonight, however, she was in a good mood, and she thought back over the ballet with satisfaction mixed with fatigue. She had danced well—not as perfectly as she knew was possible, but fluidly and exactly. The role of Lise in *La Fille Mal Gardée* was pleasant, romping and sweet without a hint of the suicidal morbidity that seemed to be the stock-in-trade of so many of the great classic balletic heroines. It had been fun to be her, to dance the light steps of a very young girl in love, but on the other hand, it had been so exhausting. Lise was the kind of part that consumed a dancer from the feet up. At present every muscle in Natasha's body called out for a massage and a hot bath. Obviously the sensible thing to do would be to call for her car and go home, but she was frankly too tired to move.

A knock on the door startled her, and Natasha sat up quickly, wondering who in the world it could be. Probably the janitor. Buttoning the top buttons of her dress, she padded barefoot over to the door, opened it, and stared blankly at the young man who stood in the hall. He was of medium height, dressed in evening clothes that barely concealed the strength of his chest and shoulders, a man with a physical presence so overwhelming he could only be a dancer. He stood with a loose, unassumed grace, almost un-Russian in its ease, but there was a question on his handsome face, and his smile was unsure.

"Natasha?" His voice ran through her like a blade. She must be having an hallucination: a letter from Rome only a few weeks ago . . . a war on . . . travel impossible . . . surely he was thousands of miles away. Bewildered, she stood for what seemed forever, trying to match his face to the face of the boy who had left five years ago. The hair was darker than she remembered; he seemed taller, and yet those eyes—blue and flashing like Siberian ice—were unmistakable. No one else on earth had eyes like that.

"Sergei?" Her voice was dry and tentative, barely a whisper. Natasha groped for words, so rattled by an explosion of contradictory feelings that sense fled right out of her mouth.

Sergei's smile turned into a grin. "*Mon Dieu,* you look as if you've swallowed a canary. I didn't mean to startle you." Taking her hands, he embraced her Russian style, kissing briskly on both cheeks and then half waltzed her back inside the dressing room. "Let me have a look at you, Natasha; it's been too long." He inspected her with friendly amusement, as if they'd only parted an hour or two ago. "What a beautiful woman you've become."

"Nonsense, I look a mess." Natasha closed her mouth, horrified at her own bluntness. She should have said hello, asked him how he was, inquired after Diaghilev, made a bland remark about the war or the time or the weather. Instead, she seemed to be possessed by some demon of tactlessness. Worst of all, when she had said she looked a mess, she'd spoken the truth. Her makeup was only half removed, and there were still bits of powder caked on the backs of her hands. As Sergei swung her in front of the mirror, Natasha became acutely conscious of her bare feet and sweat-streaked hair. Oh, wonderful. She looked like one of those crazy holy men who hung around in rags outside the cathedral begging for kopecks. Alexis must have given her at least a hundred beautiful dresses, but Sergei, as usual, had caught her at her worst.

"You look superb, ravishing," Sergei smiled, and despite herself Natasha smiled back. So his foreign travels had taught him to be gallant. "I saw you dance tonight and you were a vision. I've never seen a better Lise." His praise warmed

Natasha, and she smiled, feeling sixteen all over again. The touch of his hands brought back old memories, ones that were probably better off buried in the past. She thought suddenly how fine it would be to dance with him again. She hadn't really had a decent partner since he left. No, that wasn't fair. She had had superb partners, but she had never felt matched with them the way she had with Sergei.

Sergei looked around the room at the bouquets of yellow roses massed everywhere, tutus hanging from hooks like bunches of giant rainbow-colored chrysanthemums, rows of *pointe* shoes neatly arranged along a shelf that occupied half the wall. "You've done well for yourself." He smiled one of those radiant smiles she remembered all too well. "My congratulations."

"Thank you." She wanted to say something pleasant and intelligent but her mind was a complete blank. Obviously she had to do something besides stare at him as if he'd come back from the dead, or he was going to think she'd turned into a complete idiot. "I heard Diaghilev's been letting you do some choreography."

Sergei shrugged. "Some, but not enough. Still," he smiled again, "one makes do." He sat on the couch and took her hands in his as he filled her in on the details of the company's recent American tour. She realized he was talking to put her at ease and was grateful and a little surprised. The Sergei she remembered hadn't even noticed when other people were uncomfortable, much less done anything to remedy it. Going abroad had obviously done him a world of good.

For a good quarter of an hour Sergei reminisced in an amusing, witty way about the past five years. So much had happened to him since he'd last seen her, he couldn't begin to explain. Diaghilev was amazing; a tyrant and a genius all rolled into one, so afraid of the Atlantic crossing that at the sound of the sirens announcing their arrival in New York he had leapt into a lifeboat, convinced the ship was going down. But one had to forgive him for all his eccentricities because of the dancing he inspired. Sergei was sure Natasha had never seen any thing like it.

As he talked, his fingers brushed her wrist lightly, insistently, in a way that gradually grew more intimate. Lulled by his words Natasha gave her hands over to him without thinking. They were old friends, meeting after a long separation, trying to make contact. Suddenly something like an electric shock ran up her arm, and she pulled away, confused by the inappropriateness of her emotions.

"Would you like some champagne?" she said abruptly. Collecting herself, she assumed an air of hospitality, bottle in one hand, glasses in another.

"Do I alarm you?"

"Only by appearing out of nowhere." The truth was more complex than that, but she struggled to conceal it. The emotion she had just felt was entirely out of place, crazy when she thought about it. Sergei was virtually a stranger. She had a whole life now that he knew nothing about... Alexis... her career—and here she was responding to his touch like a lovesick girl. Natasha felt a little ashamed of her own lack of self control, and more than slightly embarrassed. What exactly was it Sergei did that made her feel this way around him? Possibly there was some scientific explanation. She had once read a piece by Stendhal on the chemistry of mutual attraction; she'd have to look it up again when she got home.

Turning back to the champagne, Natasha poured it carefully, searching her mind for some innocuous subject that might diffuse her nervousness. "How in the world did you get through the German lines?" she said at last.

"I came by way of Siberia."

She imagined the endless train ride, the ice, boredom, and unremitting cold. "Whatever for?"

"To see you." He reached for her hand again, and, startled, she countered him with a champagne glass. "I offend you, don't I?" he said quietly.

"Yes, I mean no, I mean..." She stopped confused and annoyed. If this was his idea of a game she wanted no part of it. Perhaps the west had accustomed him to sudden flirtations, but in Russia the rules were different.

Sergei seemed to read her thoughts. "I'm afraid I've become outrageous." There was a sincerity to him she hadn't noticed before. Surprisingly enough, he seemed almost humble. "Things have happened to me lately that have made me realize life is too short to be spent in boring proprieties." His face was suddenly grave.

"What sort of things?"

"You heard, perhaps, that my mother died?"

"Oh," she had no idea what to say. "I'm so sorry."

"The truth is, I came back to settle her estate. In the course of closing up our house I've had to go through all her personal effects. I don't know if you understand what that's like, but it does something to you that's quite profound." He captured her hand again and held it, lacing his fingers with hers. She knew she should pull away, probably order him out of her dressing room altogether, yet how could she now in the face of such obvious grief? She felt each of his fingers pressing into the palm of her hand, the rims of his nails, the cool circles of his rings.

"So the truth is, you really didn't come back to see me." Natasha's cheeks tingled and her mouth was dry. She groped for innocent words, simple truths.

"No," Sergei said quietly, "I really did come back to see you, but I only discovered it once I was here. You see, you've become a well-known figure, not just in Russia, but in Paris, New York, all sorts of places. I kept hearing your name from the most unexpected people; rumor had it that you'd turned into something of a phenomenon, that you were the most exciting new dancer since Pavlova. Frankly, I didn't believe it, but I was intrigued. I remembered you as very good, but hardly the prodigy people kept describing to me. Still, as I said, I was intrigued, and when my mother's death brought me back to St. Petersburg I said to myself, 'Well, I'll just look her up and see what all the fuss is about.' To tell the truth, the most I'd expected was a pleasant twenty-minute call during which we would exchange mildly boring, completely untruthful summaries of our lives. I knew about you and Grand Duke Alexis, of course—everyone does—and I'd imagined that you'd," he paused and looked at her strangely. "May I be frank?"

"Sergei, I can't recall anything ever stopping you from being frank. Go ahead—stick in the knife."

He smiled wryly. "Well, frankly then, I'd imagined you'd gotten to your present position primarily by sleeping with your Grand Duke." She stiffened and pulled away. "Now don't go flying off the handle, because when I saw you dance I realized I'd been entirely wrong. You're good, no, more than good—spectacular. There were moments watching you dance Lise when I actually had tears in my eyes. You really are as good as Pavlova, maybe even better, and all the while I watched you I kept thinking how wasted you were here and how much I wanted to dance with you again."

He grasped her hands more tightly, his eyes bright with excitement. "Natasha, listen, for a long time now I've been looking for a partner, for someone who can match my skill. I want a dancer worth choreographing for, not just a superb technician—all of Diaghilev's girls can do *fouettés* until you're sick of the sight of them—but a real dancer, one with some *dusha* in her. You have no idea what it's like to be a creative artist forced to work with inferior materials. It's like Michelangelo being asked to paint on china. No, I take that back. You do know; you must. How many times have you gone out on the stage of the Maryinsky knowing you were a hundred times better than your partner? How many times have you whispered to yourself that old adage: 'A dancer is never really considered great unless she's part of a great partnership'?"

He lifted her hands to his lips and kissed them eagerly. "I know this is ridiculously sudden, Natasha, but hear me out, please. I want you to come away with me." He put one finger over her lips. "Don't say no just because I've said all this stupidly and too fast. I swear, I can choreograph pieces for you that will make both of us famous."

"You're crazy." She pulled her hands out of his, so startled she didn't know whether to laugh at the suggestion or order him out of the room.

"Do you realize what we could do together?"

"It's completely out of the question."

"I knew you'd say that—what else could you say. The problem is you don't yet share my vision of what we can become: the greatest choreographer and the greatest dancer in Europe. Imagine the power of such a combination, the magic of it."

"Sergei," she tried to keep her voice level and impersonal, "I'm very flattered, but—"

"I'm not trying to flatter you, damn it. I'm telling you the truth." He caught her hands again and squeezed them. "There's no way I can let you go after seeing you dance Lise tonight. You're destined to be the vehicle through which I express myself: I can sense it as clearly as I've ever sensed anything in my life. We were made to be partners, Natasha. I'm going to pour my genius into you and make you one of the great dancers of all time. This is no time to let that peasant morality of yours get in the way. Forget your Grand Duke. Don't waste another minute in Russia squandering your talent in front of clowns who don't know the difference between you and the scenery. Come away with me and be the artist you were always meant to be."

Natasha stood up too quickly, spilling champagne down the front of her dress. "Sergei, I think you'd better leave."

"You're pretending to be angry, but frankly I don't believe it. You're bored here—it's written all over your face."

"Not in the slightest," she wheeled on him. "How can you come back after five years with all these insane plans? We hardly know each other anymore. How can you say such things?"

"I have a habit of speaking the truth."

"My God, you're impossible. You come in here and tell me you're in mourning for your mother, knowing that I can't throw you out under those circumstances, and then you make physical advances—don't think I didn't notice—and then propose that I give up my entire career, sacrifice what's left of my reputation, and run off with you in the middle of a world war. You must be out of your mind."

"Am I making you angry?"

"You know you are."

"I apologize, then."

"Don't bother." She'd had enough of him. "Just leave."

He stood up, gathering his gloves. "I'd intended to invite you to supper."

"Frankly, Sergei, I'm not sure I could swallow with you anywhere around. Not to mention that I'm not enchanted by the idea of appearing in public with you after what you've had the gall to say to me tonight."

He looked visibly pained at her words, and his face went pale. "Natasha," he said, "this is no way for old friends to part. I'm sorry. I was tactless, unforgivable really." He paced across the dressing room, apparently quite upset. "You have to understand I'm in a very emotional mood, and I was overwhelmed by your dancing." She felt his words softening her, but then Sergei was always able to charm people when he put his mind to it. Was he sincerely sorry, or was this just another ploy of his? Natasha contemplated him uneasily, divided between accepting his apology and insisting that he leave. "Please have supper with me." He was pleading. "If you do, I promise not to say another word about taking you with me." Despite her better judgment, Natasha's anger dissolved. "I'm truly sorry," Sergei said. It was a sincere apology, one of the few Natasha was ever to have from him.

"Sergei!" Anya Belinskaya was a little drunk, her cheeks flushed, wisps of blond hair hanging in strings along the sides of her cheeks. Enfolding Sergei in a bear hug, she cupped her slender white hands to her mouth and yelled across the restaurant like a fishwife: "Look everybody, look who's here." Two drunken officers at a table near the door waved back happily, while three girls from the corps de ballet who couldn't possibly be old enough to remember Sergei applauded and threw bits of crackers and flowers from the centerpiece.

They never should have come to the Theater Restaurant, Natasha thought, but under the circumstances she hadn't wanted to risk a more intimate place, and besides, Sergei had insisted. Now she saw that, as she had feared, they were creating a minor scandal. As they crossed the main dining room, heads turned. Well, let them talk; she had nothing to be ashamed of. In some ways it was amusing to watch everyone gape. Natasha took a deep breath and strode past the tables full of curious faces, slightly intoxicated with defiance. Tonight she would do what she damn well pleased.

"Will His Imperial Highness be joining you, Madame?" Victor, the head waiter, inquired.

"No, not this evening." Victor's face expressed nothing, but she could feel his surprise. "We'll take one of the small tables near the fountain."

"Oh, no," Anya insisted, "you're joining us."

With a sigh Natasha realized she was in for a drunken party instead of a quiet dinner. Still, maybe it was all for the best. For once she blessed Anya's habit of intruding and taking things over. At least there would be no danger of another serious conversation with Sergei this evening.

Anya's table was littered with empty cognac bottles and cigarette ashes, and everyone sitting at it was monumentally drunk. The two officers, splendid in white uniforms and gold braid, nodded unsteadily, declaring loudly over the noise of the gypsy orchestra how delighted they were to meet everyone or anyone, or no one—they had had too much cognac to sort things out and begged to be excused. The girls from the corps de ballet stared at Natasha with befuddled awe; turning pale, they pleaded various degrees of fatigue, and it wasn't until after they left that Natasha realized they had been afraid she might report them to the management of the Maryinsky.

Anya smiled at Natasha in a way that might have almost been interpreted as friendly, and settled down beside Sergei, draping one arm around his shoulder. Drink seemed to have temporarily canceled out envy, jealousy, all the baser emotions.

71

"Well, what have you been up to?" Anya asked, tapping Sergei playfully on the cheek.

"Dancing." Sergei poured a glass of cognac and passed it to Natasha, then filled Anya's glass and his own.

"Dancing, of course. What else is there." Anya pounded on the table for emphasis, downing quick, nervous sips of the cognac. Taking a rationed cigarette out of a small gold case, she leaned coquettishly over the soiled tablecloth. "How about a light?" Sergei's match made a halo around her face, bringing out the fullness of her cheeks. For no reason at all, she exploded suddenly with laughter, choking on the cognac. There was a rowdiness about her this evening that seemed to come out of nowhere, as if it belonged to a different person altogether. Something's gone wrong for her, Natasha thought.

Anya exhaled a long stream of smoke, coughed, and waved it away with her napkin. "We're leaving," she said abruptly. She put her hand on Sergei's arm. "No, don't get up. I don't mean leaving the restaurant. I mean leaving the country." She stubbed out her cigarette in the middle of her plate and looked at the two of them triumphantly. "The government's going to fall so my father is getting us out, the whole family. He's already sold our land and put the money in Swiss banks. Think the Kaiser will take Switzerland? I hope not, or I'll be in royal trouble."

"You're leaving the Imperial Ballet?" Natasha stared at Anya, unable to believe what she had just heard.

"Going to New York."

"When?" Sergei said. His face was pale, somber. Anya took another sip of cognac and laughed.

"Don't look so glum, the two of you. Nobody died you know. We're just leaving. Getting out while the getting's good with all the money we can salvage before the deluge." She pronounced it the French way: *déluge;* putting one finger in the center of a spoon, she sent it whirling in a quicksilver circle. "By this time next year rubles won't be worth the paper they're printed on."

"That's ridiculous," Natasha said. "Look how normal everything is." She gestured vaguely around the restaurant. "You don't have to leave. I admit there's a war on, but. . . ."

Anya leaned forward, face flushed, eyes glazed. "Natasha, you're living in a dream world, just like everyone else. Face reality for once: the Tsar's lost control. Soldiers are deserting by the thousands. The Bolsheviks, the Germans. . . ." She continued with an endless catalogue of potential disasters.

72

"Still," Sergei interrupted, "surely there's plenty of time."

"I read history," Anya said. "I'm not stupid, and neither is Daddy. Do you know how many French aristocrats were caught napping by the Revolution?" She smiled at Natasha, a dangerous, brittle smile that was no longer friendly. "Now you can have it *all*, Natasha—the juicy parts, the big roles. Dance Aurora; dance Odette/Odile; dance Giselle. I will them to you lock, stock, and barrel."

Anya finished her cognac and set the glass down clumsily on the white linen tablecloth. "I figure you've got maybe three or four months of dancing left." She got up abruptly, pulling on her coat. "Good-bye, Sergei."

Holding on to the back of a chair for support, Anya leaned toward him urgently. "You picked a bad time to come back to Russia, a terrible time." She seized Natasha's hand and shook it in a sudden gesture of friendship. "Good-bye Natasha. I know I've been nasty tonight, but I can't help it. I'm always nasty to you, and now I'm drunk and sorry and telling you the truth: get out while you still can."

Sergei settled down on the red silk sofa, picked up a poker and jabbed familiarly at the fire, sending a trail of sparks up into the darkness of the chimney. Anya's warning had cast a pall over the evening that he seemed dedicated to neutralizing. "How's your aunt?" he asked politely.

Natasha kicked off her shoes and leaned back against one of the pillows. "Aunt Marya moved back to Archangel about a year ago. Said she missed the taiga and her old friends, but the fact is she didn't approve of all this." Natasha gestured at the drawing room, taking in the Persian carpets, the gold-framed Impressionist paintings, the priceless Chinese vases full of freshly cut flowers, a bronze statue of a ballerina frozen in the world's most perfect *arabesque*—so obviously an original Degas.

Pouring herself a cup of smoky Chinese tea, she tried to ignore the throbbing at the back of her head. It was past three in the morning and the cognac she had had at the restaurant had made her feel detached from reality, as if she were floating in a world that only existed in the small hours before sunrise. She never should touch alcohol; she knew better. Not that she ever got drunk, but she got irresponsible, stopped caring about what people said or thought or expected of her. It had been irresponsible to let Sergei see her home, and probably even more irresponsible to give in to his desire to see her house, but frankly, at the moment, she didn't care. She was enjoying his company, and no amount of brow furrowing on the part of Misha or strange looks from the servants were going to force her to ask him to leave. This was her house after all; he was her guest, and she would entertain whomsoever she pleased at whatever time she pleased.

Being in a mild state of rebellion cheered Natasha up considerably. She smiled at Sergei, laughing as he entertained her with more stories about the American tour of the Ballets Russes. His supply of gossip seemed endless: Nijinsky was still quarreling with Diaghilev over half a million francs' back salary he claimed was owed him; the food in New York was incredible—sugared ham, a dreadful drink called Coca Cola; and the Ziegfeld follies, now there was a spectacle—great long-legged half-naked women parading about in six-foot feathered headdresses like *Swan Lake* gone berserk. And jazz, definitely the music of the future. He'd like to choreograph an entire ballet to it someday.

Time passed invisibly, like water running through a tiny crack. They talked and talked, and then silence settled in between them. For a long time there was no sound in the room but the crackling of the fire, no movement except for the lozenges of light that quavered over the small rug near the hearth, bringing blue and red deers, and fantastic flowers magically to life.

"Anya was right," Sergei said suddenly. "You should leave."

"Sergei, don't—"

"Don't tell me not to mention it," he interrupted "I want you to come with me, and not just because you dance. For one thing, I worry about your safety. Things could fall apart here any minute. And for another . . . good God, I don't know how to say this without sounding like a bad imitation of Pushkin . . . I wasn't going to tell you until later, Natasha, but tonight I realized . . . that is I saw . . ." He stopped talking, reached forward impulsively and took her hands in his, pulling her closer to him, enfolding her in his arms. Then bending his face over hers, he kissed her until she was breathless and dizzy.

Natasha tried to pull back. Every second she let Sergei touch her she was betraying Alexis, a man who'd been good to her, whom she loved. She had always thought of herself as a faithful woman; she must tell Sergei to stop, to leave now, not to come back. She tried to be angry with him, but the more she attempted to summon up indignation, the more it dissolved under his kisses. His lips worked at hers, hard, insistent, as if he was searching out the very center of her. As he touched the silk bodice of her dress, her nipples hardened shamelessly under his hand.

I want him to stay. I want him to make love to me. The thought was like a revelation, like a bell ringing in her mind blotting out everything else. There was no way she could continue to delude herself that he was seducing her against her will. She wanted him, wanted him as shamelessly and completely as she had ever wanted anything in her life. Putting her hands on either side of his face, Natasha drew Sergei closer, kissing him back eagerly, almost fiercely, letting him feel her desire.

"Sweet Natasha," he murmured. He laid her back on the couch, so gently, as if she were precious, her body friable and light as dust. One by one he undid the buttons of her blouse, unlacing her undergarments, kissing her ears, her lips, the soft inside of her throat, her eyelids, and finally her breasts, her legs, kissing the backs of her knees, the insides of her elbows, until she lay naked in his arms, her body burning, pressed against his, lost, drowning in him, no longer able to consider anything rational, not even what was good for her, not even the price she might have to pay for all this.

She had felt passion before with Alexis, but it was a pale thing, a caged, domestic animal compared to what she now felt for Sergei. By the time he finally came to her, after caressing her for what seemed hours, she had lost all sense of proportion and time. It seemed to her only that they were dancing again as they had so long ago: a choreography of arms and legs, of the secret parts of their bodies—a dance of such grace and beauty that it left her on the verge of tears.

At the final moment something in her leapt toward him, and he lifted it—or seemed to lift it—into an invisible *levé*. When he came, she came with him, plummeting with him into an intimacy so profound it was almost terrifying. The borders of her body and mind broke and blended with his, and for the first time in her life Natasha knew another human being utterly to the depths, and knew that she, too, was known.

When she came back to her senses, they were lying naked in each other's arms. Sergei was stroking her hair, and the fire had burned low in the grate. In the east the sky was powdered with flecks of red light. Suddenly, with sickening

75

clarity, Natasha realized what she had done. Sitting up she pulled on her underblouse and began to lace it frantically.

"We've got to get dressed."

"What?" Sergei leaned on one elbow and watched her with a blank, content look on his face. Obviously he didn't understand.

"It's almost morning. One of the servants could walk in any minute." She blushed to the roots of her hair, thinking of how humiliating it would have been if Misha had happened on them in the middle of . . . of—she couldn't even bring herself to think the words for what they had done—but even as she pushed them out of her mind, she felt desire wash over her again. Sergei must have seen it in her face, because he reached for her.

"Relax, it's the middle of the night. The servants are all asleep." He tilted back her chin, brought his lips to hers, and kissed her until she was breathless.

"No, it's morning. Look. The sun's almost up." Natasha pointed to the sky, which was growing lighter every minute. "I can hear the boys out on the street putting out the lamps."

"Probably only some drunks."

"No, it's the lamplighters. Sergei, please." His kisses were so lovely and sweet. She knew if she let him go on she'd be lost entirely. "You must go, right now. Before someone comes."

"Come with me."

"I can't."

"Why not?"

"Sergei, please, get dressed." She was getting more and more frantic. Were those footsteps outside the door? Natasha pulled on her dress, fumbling with the buttons. Her hands felt cold and stiff, and her throat was dry with panic. Suppose Alexis himself walked into the room. My God, it would be the end of everything. Alexis was a jealous man. His honor was important to him and he wouldn't take betrayal lightly. It would be the end of their relationship, probably the end of her career for that matter. Alexis was perfectly capable of seeing she never danced on the Maryinsky stage again.

Sergei caught her around the waist and pulled her back down on the couch. "I'm not leaving until you say you'll come away with me."

"Sergei, I need some time." His presence was so intoxicating it was like being drunk just to be close to him. Was she actually considering his invitation to come with him to the

76

West? She didn't know anymore. She only knew she *had* to get him dressed and out of the house.

"Time for what? Life is meant to be grabbed on the run; not put in neat little cages."

"I need time to think things over."

"How much time?"

"A few hours."

"You don't need time, Natasha. You know right this minute what you should do."

"Sergei, please, if you care anything for me at all, give me time to think."

Maybe he sensed he was driving her away by insisting, or maybe he finally realized they were in danger of being discovered. Whatever the reason, much to Natasha's relief, Sergei began to put on his shirt and pants. "My dear girl," he said, "it's just that I can't bear to leave you." He tied his tie, buttoned down his collar, put on his coat, and stood for a minute like a man who wasn't sure what to do next. There was a brief, awkward silence during which Natasha distinctly heard someone moving around upstairs. "I'm staying at the Astoria Hotel."

"Good." She was so distraught she hardly heard what he was saying.

"When will you come?"

"This afternoon," hours jumbled in her mind; she grabbed one at random, "around five."

He kissed her again. "I'll be waiting for you." Somehow she saw Sergei to the door, relieved beyond measure that they didn't encounter Misha in the hall. As he turned to leave, she had an almost overwhelming urge to call him back and try to speak the truth. But what was the truth? Was she seriously contemplating leaving Alexis because of a few hours of love making? And what about Sergei—had he seduced her merely to get her to come with him, or had he felt what she'd felt? What parts of this crazy evening had been real, what parts dangerous fantasy?

Upstairs, in her blue forget-me-not bedroom, the linen sheets felt cold enough to burn her skin. Natasha felt stunned and numbed; her mind seemed to have gone on strike. Throwing her wrinkled clothes into a pile at the foot of the bed, she climbed under the thick satin comforter and fell into a heavy, dreamless sleep.

When she woke winter sunlight was streaming through the

windows. For a moment she had a healthy sense of looking forward to a new day, and then the full force of what she and Sergei had done the previous night hit her in the pit of her stomach. Misha *must* have known what was going on in the drawing room. He'd been with Alexis twenty years and was no fool. And if he hadn't suspected something, then chances were one of the other servants had. This might be her house, but every member of the staff had been handpicked by Alexis. It had never occurred to her before that she was constantly watched. Maybe the servants regularly reported back to him on her conduct. No, that was impossible. Alexis would never be so ungallant.

Natasha called for her bath, poured in half a bottle of sweet-smelling oil, and scrubbed every inch of her body. Then she dressed quickly and ate a hurried breakfast of cheese and tea. Alexis could arrive at any minute; he was an early riser, often surprising her while she was still in bed. In fact, it was strange that he hadn't already appeared.

The morning passed with no sign of him. Ordering lunch, Natasha ate alone with increasing nervousness. Where was he? He always phoned or sent a message when he was going to be detained. She tried to read a popular novel but the words swam on the page in front of her eyes. She tried to sew a set of ribbons on a new pair of *pointe* shoes, but the thread tangled in her hands. As the hours ticked by, she became convinced that Alexis was intentionally staying away because he had found out about her and Sergei.

She remembered a hundred little kindnesses Alexis had done her, and felt ashamed of herself for betraying him. She loved Alexis. He was kind, dependable, a wonderful man. Sergei, on the other hand, was completely irresponsible. How could she, even for a moment, have considered running away with him? She was a faithful woman by nature; she'd been drunk last night and done something shameful, something totally foreign to her true self, but she'd never do it again. Never.

Suddenly Natasha was struck by a revelation so intense it made her gasp. She *would* do it again. She threw down her embroidery hoop and stared at the fire, dumbfounded. *She would betray Alexis with Sergei all over again if she had the chance.* My God, what kind of woman was she? She had actually liked the shameful thing she and Sergei had done last night; she actually craved more. No, that was crazy; it couldn't be true. Every bit of common sense told her she should never see Sergei again, that she should order him to stay away from her house, tell her servants to inform him if he called that she was out, unavailable, or otherwise occupied.

Slipping out of the chair, Natasha knelt down on the rug and tried to pray, but her mind was in turmoil. She tried to recall the icon of St. Michael that had hung over the altar in the little church in Archangel where Aunt Marya had taken her as a child, the one in which St. Michael was slaying the dragon. Maybe God would help her slay this dragon of temptation. But instead of seeing the icon, she saw Sergei; she imagined his hands on her body, the pressure of his lips against hers, and this was a terrible thing for her, exhilarating and frightening at the same time.

It was a long afternoon—one of the longest in her life. Around three she finally heard Alexis's car draw up in front of the house. Throwing a heavy cashmere shawl over her shoulders, Natasha ran outside to meet him, wondering what she could possibly say. She had an urge to confess everything at once, yet reason told her to keep quiet. How could she admit that overnight she had fallen in love with another man? My God, it was unthinkable. She must be insane. She grasped at straws; perhaps if she pretended things were still the same between her and Alexis they would be; perhaps if she ignored her feelings for Sergei they would go away. And please, please let Alexis not have found out on his own.

Alexis looked especially handsome in his white uniform and high boots as he strode up the garden path, framed by the long bare branches of the linden trees, but his face was pale and drawn, and he didn't smile when he saw her. For a moment she wanted to turn and run, but she forced herself to keep walking toward him. There was still a chance he hadn't been told.

"Alexis, I was so worried." Natasha embraced him, honestly grateful for the comfort of his presence. For a moment he embraced her in return, and then his whole body stiffened. Natasha's throat went dry with fear.

"Get back inside, you'll catch cold." He drew away, untangled her arms from around his neck, and stared at her strangely. He looked upset, almost as if he'd been crying. His breath had the faint, sick-sweet smell of brandy, and there was a light stubble of whiskers on his cheeks, as if for some reason he had not taken time to shave.

"Alexis, are you, that is I . . ." She stuttered a few words, confused and guilty, trying to reach him, but there seemed to be a barrier between them. Obviously she should confess before he accused her, but she couldn't bring herself to say the words.

"Please have the goodness to go into the house, I need to talk to you in private." Natasha stared at him, bewildered, torn by conflicting emotions. A dozen sentences formed in her mind and she rejected them all.

"Please." Alexis's voice was cold, uninflected, as if he were speaking to a stranger, yet there was a disturbing tremor under his words. Filled with foreboding, she followed him into the house. He crossed the hall slowly, like a man tired nearly to death. Going into the drawing room, he pulled the door closed and stood for a moment with his back to her. The silence between them was heavy, unbearable.

"Misha brought me the news," he said at last.

So he knew. Natasha stared at him, unable to say a word in her own defense.

"Damn it."

"You're angry?" Her voice was so faint she could barely hear it and her knees felt as if they were made of water. She started to sit down on the sofa and then, realizing what had happened the last time she had sat there, she started and moved quickly to one of the chairs by the fire.

"Angry, grieved, upset. The last twenty-four-hours have been pure hell. Oh, I admit I'm relieved we're rid of the scoundrel—it's a blessing really—but he died in such an ugly way: poisoned, shot, shoved under the ice. It's disgusting."

"Sergei's dead?" Natasha had a bewildering sense of having been left behind by the conversation.

"Sergei who?"

"Sergei Maximov."

"What does Sergei Maximov have to do with any of this? I'm talking about Rasputin. His body's just been found, and Prince Felix Yussoupov and my cousin Dimitri are being blamed for his death. Surely you heard the news?"

He didn't know, he actually didn't know about her and Sergei. Natasha nearly died with relief. Rasputin. She had to bite her lips to keep from laughing hysterically. God forgive her for being happy to hear about the death of another human being, even one as evil as the mad monk, but by some miracle she had been reprieved.

"That's why I was so late," Alexis continued. "I had to go out to Tsarskoe Selo to present my condolences to the Tsarina. You know how she favored that madman. And on top of that the streets were virtually impassable—full of hordes of total strangers kissing each other, yelling that Russia has been saved from the Antichrist. You should see the crowd lining up outside the cathedral of Our Lady of Kazan to light thanksgiving candles. It looks like Easter." He stopped and looked at her in concern. "What's wrong? You seem so pale. Forgive me, dearest. I was a beast to shock you with the news, but I assumed you'd heard."

Sergei waited all afternoon for Natasha, but he wasn't particularly surprised when she didn't appear, nor was he surprised when he attempted to call on her over the course of the next week only to be told she was out. It wasn't going to be easy to convince her to leave a situation as good as the one she had, but Sergei had always enjoyed a challenge. He would write her letters, witty, passionate ones; some he'd compose himself and some he'd copy out of one of his favorite books, a little French gem entitled *Love Letters for Every Occasion.* Natasha was destined to dance his ballets, about that he had no doubt, and in time he would have her.

Under ordinary circumstances, of course, there might not have been much chance of persuading her to leave Russia, but from what he'd seen since he'd come back, the deteriorating political situation was about to change all that. Anya Belinskaya had been right: the whole country was poised on the edge of chaos, all of which meant, from Sergei's perspective, that history was quite likely to deliver Natasha on his doorstep some time in the very near future.

Meanwhile he had other things on his mind: the settling of his mother's estate, an invitation to become the assistant choreographer of a new ballet company that a wealthy man named Fouchier was putting together in Paris—not to mention some very pleasant afternoons spent with Anya in activities that gave him considerable food for thought.

81

6

The stage of the Maryinsky Theatre was entirely possessed by girls dressed in white; thin and delicate, they danced on the shore of a black lake in the middle of an enchanted forest, their arms more like the wings of swans than it seemed possible for human arms to be.

First composed by Tchaikovsky as an amusement for his sister's children, *Swan Lake* had been transformed by the great choreographers Marius Petipa and Lev Ivanov into the apotheosis of female suffering. Now Natasha danced it like a woman being destroyed from within. Every fiber of her body quivered, pulling itself apart. Her legs were two wavering lines, her hands broken wings, fluttering uselessly. In the third act she had been superb as Odile—the temptress who lures Prince Siegfried away from his true love. She had moved with passion, performing the thirty-two *fouettés* in her solo so effortlessly that the audience had interrupted half a dozen times with applause, but now, in the fourth act, as the tormented, abandoned Odette, she had reduced the audience to silence. They had all seen *Swan Lake* danced before, but never quite like this. The steps were Petipa and Ivanov's, but the feeling was Natasha's, taken from the depths of her and spread out before them. All the pain and uncertainty she felt was there on display, transformed into art.

Her life had come to a turning point, and she was being torn in half. On one hand there was Alexis whom she loved and respected, and on the other there was Sergei, now in Paris, whom she longed for with an intensity that nearly made her ill. Almost weekly she got letters from him begging her to join him—brilliant, passionate letters that she read avidly and then tore into shreds and burned, terrified that Alexis might happen on one of them.

The Swan Queen hopes that, redeemed by Siegfried's love,

she can return to her true human form, that she can be what she really is—a woman. . . .

But what was a woman? A thing that suffered passively, martyred the way Odette was being martyred? Or was a woman something else, something passionate and explosive? Natasha danced straight into the heart of the contradiction, seeing what Petipa himself must have seen: that Odette was Odile; Odile, Odette. For decades the two roles had always been danced by the same woman, not merely as a theatrical ploy but to display a profound truth: female nature was divided. There was pain in recognizing that division, but more pain in trying to hide it. Like Siegfried, Sergei could bring her body back to her and yet. . . .

And yet in the end Siegfried betrays Odette, and Odette takes her own life.

A tragedy—perhaps even a warning that she should put Sergei out of her mind altogether—but there was another more unconventional interpretation of the ballet: that Odette who was dying was the false woman, that what was being killed was a life that wouldn't have been worth living under any circumstance. Natasha danced both together: the suffering Odette and the triumphant Odile. On a stage filled with artificial smoke and manufactured lighting, her indecision was so real it was almost painful to watch.

That night the audience gave her twenty curtain calls, yelling until they were hoarse, clapping until their hands were numb. Years later people still remembered Natasha Ladanova's final, stunning performance with the Imperial Ballet. As she stood on the stage of the Maryinsky, her arms filled with flowers, listening to the applause and looking out over the sea of enthusiastic faces, Natasha suddenly realized that she had come to a decision: she would leave Alexis and join Sergei in Paris no matter what the consequences.

The next day she began to make plans to leave Russia, only to discover she was a good three months too late. The war was going badly, trains weren't running on schedule, exit visas were virtually unobtainable. Each afternoon for two weeks she trekked from office to office, only to be told the same thing: there were a thousand applicants for every available space. For the first time she realized how out of touch she had been with what was really going on around her, and she went home exhausted, chilled to the bone, tormented by a growing premonition that something truly terrible was about to happen.

Natasha pulled back the edge of the lace curtain and carefully inspected the street below. A crowd of about a hundred people carrying red flags and banners was moving past the Quai d'Argent, hurrying to join the big demonstration on Nevsky Prospect. Behind them the sky glowed with fires from burning police stations, filling the air with an acrid, oily smoke that hung over the buildings like a pall.

XLEB, MIR, SEMLA—Bread, Peace, Land, the signs said.

The two women carrying the "Peace" sign weren't even wearing shawls although the temperature was a good twenty degrees below zero and dropping. Over the heads of the marchers the trolley lines dripped three-foot-long icicles, and with no vehicular traffic to disturb it for almost a week, the snow had piled up knee deep in the street, forcing the marchers to shuffle along at a snail's pace. Still, they didn't seem to mind. The ragged sound of patriotic songs drifted up to her, punctuated by the distant popping of gunfire. "The Marseillaise" she realized suddenly was a frightening song, especially when sung in Russian. When the marchers got to the part about the enemies' "impure blood watering our fields," they seemed to bellow out the words, and a few of them shook their fists.

Natasha pulled back from the window, shaken. The riots had been going on for four days now, and the end seemed nowhere in sight. For weeks the city had been criminally short of supplies Rumors were rife of whole trains of meat spoiling on sidings, of butter and cream sent off to the soap works. Near the beginning of March the bread lines had often been a mile or more long. A few days ago, the munitions workers had gone out on strike in protest, and the next day the industrial hands and mill workers had joined them. The government had promised to keep order, brought in more soldiers, mounted machine guns on the roofs of buildings and belfries of churches, sent cossacks charging into the demonstrations, but things had only gotten worse.

Boje moy! What was happening? Natasha sat down on the sofa and tried to convince herself that things couldn't possibly be as bad as they appeared. In many respects her sympathies were with the workers, who certainly deserved what they were asking for and more. People were starving, there was no getting around it, and if it took riots to make the government see that, then maybe there *should* be riots. No, it wasn't the riots themselves but the rising level of violence that frightened her. Only last night a commandeered car full of soldiers had come careening down the street, yelling insults and shooting at random. Ever since then she had taken care to stay away from the windows except for those moments when her curiosity got the better of her.

"Tea, Madame?" Kolya, the butler, pushed the delicate English tea cart into the drawing room, spread a cloth on the inlaid table by the fireplace, and proceeded to stoke the samovar. Methodically he laid out the plates of sandwiches, cakes, and petit fours. "Will His Imperial Highness be joining you, Madame?"

Natasha caught herself on the verge of hysterical laughter. Oh, yes, of course, Alexis would be joining her: if he made it through the streets without being recognized or having his car snatched out from under him. Outside Kazan cathedral, twenty-five officers had ben summarily shot only that morning. Madame Laurier, who by some miracle had appeared at the front door around noon with a package of important papers, had brought a hastily printed leaflet that described the execution in chilling detail. Natasha looked at the leaflet and then at the package of papers, a bulky bundle clumsily tied with string, the wrapping limp with melted snow. According to Madame Laurier, the documents inside were of inestimable value; she had literally risked her life to deliver them, but so far Natasha had not been able to bring herself to read a single word. Picking up the leaflet that lay on top of the box, she stared again at the crudely lettered headline; OFFICERS SHOT. A shudder went through her. Would His Imperial Highness be joining her this afternoon in the drawing room for tea and petit fours? Certainly, if he lived long enough to get there.

Getting hold of herself, Natasha managed to make some polite, neutral reply to Kolya's question. The tea was strong and bitter, and she drank three cups of it well laced with brandy. Then she settled back as far away from the windows as possible to wait for Alexis.

"Natasha. Natasha wake up." A hand was shaking her. Natasha opened her eyes, wondering where she could be. It took her a moment to realize she had fallen asleep in her own drawing room. "Natasha." Alexis was bending over her; she took one look at him and nearly screamed.

"What happened to your face!" His left cheek was lacerated, flecked with blood, one eye half-swollen shut.

"A cossack and I had a little disagreement, and the fool came at me with his *nagaika*." The *nagaika*, or whip, had caught Alexis at the chin, slicing up one side of his face nearly to his eye. Natasha reached for her handkerchief and tried to wipe away the blood, but Alexis caught hold of her hand. "There's no time for that now. I want you to get out of here." He pulled her to her feet so quickly she almost stumbled over his boots. "You've got to put on your warmest things, but nothing that looks expensive, nothing that would tempt these maniacs to fire on you—and you've got to hurry. I'd say we have an hour, maybe less, before they start blocking off the street."

"Where are we going?"

"I'm sending you out of the country. There's a truck waiting out front. The driver's been bribed—well bribed, believe me. He's taking you out of the city to one of the suburban stations. You're to board the second train—the *second*, remember that, because the first's a troop train. You have a good chance of getting across the Finnish border with no questions asked. I've already bought a steamer ticket for you. Berth 123, on *The Soderhamm* sailing from Helsinki to Stockholm day after tomorrow."

"Alexis, for God's sake, what are you talking about?"

Alexis's eyes were glazed with fatigue, his uniform torn at the throat. He sat down on the edge of the sofa as if he might fall, picked up a cup of cold tea, and gulped it down wearily. "The Tsar's ordered the Duma to dissolve itself and the Duma's refused; soldiers are refusing to fire on the crowds; the Courts of Justice are burning this very minute." He grabbed a sandwich, ate it, and then grabbed another. "This morning a mob sacked the small arms factory and arsenal at Liteyni Bridge, and opened the prison. The whole city's full of criminals and armed hooligans. I want you out of Russia while there's still time."

"But what about you? You're a member of the Imperial Family. If there's a revolution...." She stopped in midsentence, possessed by a sickening image of guillotines and firing squads. "Alexis, please." She clung to him, frightened, all but forgetting that she had been planning to leave him. Sergei or no Sergei, she did love Alexis, and the idea of abandoning him to be slaughtered was terrible. "Please come with me."

"God knows I'd like to, but I can't. I suppose I should give you some noble speech about honor and duty and all that, but all I know is that a lot of people depend on me and if I ran for it, I could never live with myself."

"Then I'm staying with you."

"No, you're not. You're getting on that train."

She tried more protests, but he was adamant. Later she was haunted by the suspicion that if it hadn't been for Sergei, she would have tried harder to persuade Alexis to leave.

"Here's the number of a Swiss bank account," Alexis pulled a scrap of paper out of his pocket, "memorize it." When at last she was bundled into her plainest warmest coat, Alexis produced an ugly, battered scarf from his pocket and tied it over her head, half concealing her face. Then he kissed her for a long, long time. "I love you so much," he said, "I think I'd die if anything happened to you." Tears were streaming down Natasha's face. Alexis wiped them away with the edge of her scarf. "It's only for a little while, my darling." They looked away, not meeting each other's eyes, knowing it was a brave lie but a lie nevertheless.

The watchtower on the firehouse near Nickolai Station sucked up the flames, burning like a huge cross in the sky. On street corners, crowds stood around bonfires, feeding police documents to the flames. Debts were being wiped out, whole pasts erased. The Astoria Hotel was being looted, its great plate glass windows collapsing into the street as frightened women and children from the English Delegation, which had been housed there, stood outside, shivering in the cold.

Natasha lay under the canvas in the back of the truck, looking out cautiously through a torn grommet hole. Beside her was a suitcase that contained a few changes of clothing, the bundle of papers Madame Laurier had given her, and the Degas, which Alexis had cut from its frame and rolled lovingly in a piece of black velvet. Leaning her elbow on the suitcase, Natasha peered through the hole. The effect was odd, as if everything were bordered by a ragged circle. The first thing she noticed was that from almost every window hung red flags made of the most ingenious materials: old shirts, hastily dyed sheets, red stripes ripped from the Imperial flag. The second was that everyone seemed to have guns, even small children.

Her last view of the Maryinsky Theatre was so strange that later she came to believe she must have imagined it: near the Maryinsky was a large prison, full of men who had been shut up since the Russo-Japanese War. As the truck turned onto Theater Street, Natasha saw that the prison was on fire. The flames reflected off the columns of the Maryinsky, dancing over it, doing a ballet of their own on its baroque facade. On the steps of the theater, fifty or so ragged scarecrows stood watching their prison burn, their painfully thin faces suffused with red light.

"Stop right there," a voice said suddenly. A fist pounded on the side of the truck. Natasha looked toward the front and saw that two soldiers were blocking their way. One was only a boy, not more than thirteen or fourteen, and the other a pock-faced man in a tattered fur hat. Both had their guns leveled at the driver. "What have you got in there, Comrade?" the boy demanded harshly. "Food? Gasoline?"

"Old rags." The driver's voice was gruff, and she heard him cough and spit.

"Rags, is it?" Natasha ducked back under the canvas as the pock-faced man stomped around to the back of the truck, his breath steaming in the cold. She crouched in the darkness terrified. The soldier stuck his bayonet into the canvas, missing her head by inches. He thrust again, nicking her leg. She pressed her lips together to keep from screaming. It wasn't a bad cut, she could tell that, but what if he didn't stop? Sooner or later he would run the bayonet through her.

"Does he have any vodka?" the boy yelled.

"If I had vodka, Comrades," the driver yelled, "would I be driving around in this cold freezing my ass off?"

The soldier gave one more stab, far to the left, and then stomped back around to the front of the truck. "I could commandeer this hunk of junk," he threatened.

"Be my guest," the driver said, "do me the favor. Only I suppose I should tell you that the rags are from the hospital. Blankets from cholera patients. I was taking the whole load to the incinerator. Not a great job, believe me. You want them, Comrades, they're yours."

"Cholera! *Chort vozmi*, get the hell out of here!" Someone, presumably one of the soldiers, kicked the side of the truck, and it lurched into motion again. Natasha lay back, shaking with relief.

Three days later, she stumbled into a hotel in Stockholm, dirty, tired, and still seasick. The desk clerk, a friendly man in a small string tie, immediately thrust a Russian newspaper into her hands. Opening it, she read of the abdication of Tsar Nicholas II. Shortly thereafter she received two telegrams: a long one from Diaghilev inviting her to join the Ballets

Russes, and another from Sergei that read simply: Hotel Les Charmettes, 37 Rue du Moulin-Vert.

The entire lobby of the Hotel Les Charmettes was paved with small blue and green tiles, like the floor of a turkish bath. Oversized plants thrust their way up toward the skylight, the brass pots gleaming dully, the leaves waxed, thick-veined, and languorous. Natasha sat in a large green velvet chair, suitcase in front of her, hands in her lap. She saw Sergei before he saw her, coming across the tiled floor, impeccably dressed in a pale brown suit, a newspaper rolled up under one arm.

"Natasha." Smiling, Sergei hurried forward and, to her surprise, reached out and shook her hand. "Welcome to Paris."

Something plummeted inside her. How, after all those letters, could he greet her so coldly? She stood up and faced him, still expecting to be kissed, but he seemed superficial and remote. Incredible as it seemed he was treating her as if they were merely two distant acquaintances.

"I've scheduled a rehearsal for you for tomorrow morning." Sergei informed her breezily.

"A rehearsal?" She thought for a fleeting moment she must not have heard him right.

"Of my new ballet, *Griselda*. A wonderful piece; the French are just crazy about ballet. My dear, you won't believe the enthusiasm; we haven't played to anything less than a full house yet. The Ballet de la Cité is simply cleaning up. Everyone wants to forget the war for an evening. Fouchier is in seventh heaven. Ah, I nearly forgot. You don't know who Fouchier is, do you? Well, who can describe him? He's an aristocrat, a libertine; he likes a pretty face—male or female. He's bailed out Diaghilev half a dozen times and he's the money behind the Ballet de la Cité. Without him we wouldn't have lasted a week. Now about that rehearsal. . . ."

"I think you should cancel it, Sergei."

"What?"

"I'm not sure I'm staying in Paris." Natasha stood and picked up her suitcase.

"But I thought you'd decided, that is I assumed. . . ."

"I assumed something, too." She was hurt and angry and in no mood to hide it. "I assumed there was something between us. I assumed all those letters you wrote meant you wanted me, not just as a dancer but as. . . ." She grew angrier and

89

more embarrassed. "Frankly I didn't come thousands of miles just to perform in *Griselda* or whatever you're calling your latest creation. Find yourself another dancer."

"Natasha, darling. . . ."

"Don't you *darling* me, Sergei Maximov." She knew it sounded childish to rave at him like this, but she couldn't help herself. My God, she had left Alexis in all sorts of danger, and for what? "A handshake isn't my idea of hello."

"Natasha, darling, whatever are you talking about? Have I seemed unaffectionate? You know I adore you. *Cherie*, have mercy; you can't leave. Seeing you again was so overwhelming that—"

"So overwhelming that you couldn't bother to get acquainted before you started telling me my work schedule? So overwhelming that—"

Reaching out, Sergei pulled her to him, and abruptly covered her lips with his. The kiss was intoxicating, dissolving her anger. Natasha resisted for a moment, then relaxed in his arms, feeling his mouth against hers, drowning in the smell of his hair and the taste of his lips. Of course Sergei loved her; how could she have ever doubted it? Within a few seconds her heart completely triumphed over her mind, and by the end of the evening she had forgotten Sergei's initial coldness and was no longer asking herself if it had been wise for her to come to Paris.

Paris in the summer of 1917 was a grim place compared to the Paris of other years. Everything was rationed: butter, gasoline, meat, bread, sugar. Clothing could only be bought on the black market and shoes were impossible to obtain at any price. The war, raging for several years now, had taken a terrible toll. The streets were full of wounded and maimed men and, if it hadn't been for a government ordinance forbidding the wearing of mourning, there would have been thousands of women in black. To make matters worse, the political situation was definitely unstable; inflation was rampant, and sections of the French army, disheartened by steady losses and seeing no end to the war, were in the midst of a major mutiny.

But for Natasha it was a wonderful summer—perhaps the most wonderful of her entire life. She knew, of course, that the war was still going on, she even volunteered to work two nights a week rolling bandages and organizing hospital supplies, but the titanic struggle between Germany and France was like distant thunder. The only two things that were really important to her during those three months were ballet and Sergei. Later she would get to know Paris, falling in love with its boulevards and cafés, but during the months of June, July, and August of that enchanted summer she frequented only two places: the studios of the Ballet de la Cité on the Right Bank and the Hotel Les Charmettes on the Left.

Griselda was a brilliant ballet. Natasha was stunned that Sergei had been able to put together anything so perfect. During the mornings and afternoons Sergei worked with her, teaching her sequences, insisting that every step be danced exactly as he had imagined it. Afterward, excited by an entire day of touching each other in public, they would return to the Hotel Les Charmettes, fall into bed, and make love for hours at a time.

After a while the loving and the dancing seemed to blend into each other. What Sergei gave her in bed, Natasha gave back to him on the stage. *Griselda,* as a result, was not only a success, it was something of a landmark. Even the dance critic of *Le Figaro*, who was notoriously hard to please, spent a page and a half discussing the Ladanova/Maximov partnership, calling it, only partly in jest, the most important thing to happen to ballet since the invention of the *pointe* shoe.

This was happiness: lying next to Sergei, sensing the outline of his body against hers in the dark. Natasha pressed her cheek to his back, feeling his spine, the solidity of his shoulders. After the war was over, they would travel all over Europe together, lie in a hundred different beds in as many cities, and as long as Sergei was beside her every place would be home.

The white curtains at the double windows caught the first morning light, passing from gray to a luminous light blue. Sergei stirred and turned to Natasha still half asleep, his sex hard against her belly. Brushing his blond hair off his forehead, she drank in the beauty of his face. How vulnerable he looked in his sleep. It pleased Natasha to think that no one else ever saw him this way. Leaning forward, she made her hair into a tent around his face, hiding him in the tangles, kissing him quickly.

Sergei woke and reached for her breasts. He kissed them slowly at first, then more quickly, first one then the other. Natasha arched her spine, pressing closer, feeling intoxicated. It seemed to her she could never get enough of him. Time dilated and then stopped altogether. Every one of her senses became more acute: she could smell the fragrance of the chestnut trees five stories below, the subtle undertone of soap on Sergei's skin, the sting of tobacco smoke on his lips; she could literally feel each hair on his body as he lay under her. His hands were whole landscapes; his fingertips, mountain ranges that moved down her belly to the inside of her thighs.

She lowered her face to his, kissed him, and tastes exploded in her mouth: salt, orange peel, lemon, and something dark and bitter like unsweetened chocolate. When at last Sergei entered her, it seemed as if she could feel something more than his body: something impersonal and slightly terrifying that satisfied her completely.

Later she would see how ironic it had been to find such pleasure in a country at war, and it made her wonder if always through history, even during the worst times—even during the barbarian invasions or great plagues—there hadn't been lovers like her and Sergei, living happily in their own world, isolated from the great upheavals that were shaking the rest of mankind.

One memorable afternoon as they stood on the banks of the Seine watching half a dozen ragged women and children fishing, Sergei spoke of his father. "We never had a real conversation," his voice was casual, and he seemed to be looking at the river, but Natasha knew better.

"Did you try?"

Sergei picked up a flat stone, took aim, and sent it skittering across the water in the direction of the Pont Royal. "Oh, yes, I tried—a hundred times. But my father was always so remote, as if he had better things to think about. He was a military man, a general, and I think he wanted me to be one, too. The fact is, I believe I disappointed him."

"Yet you said he encouraged you to study ballet."

"Odd, isn't it?"

"Not so odd, if you ask me."

"Why not?"

"He must have loved you very much."

"I never thought so."

"But he must have, nevertheless."

Sergei looked pleased, almost shy. "It's a pleasant thought," he said.

"You know," Natasha wanted to put an arm around him but she settled for touching the sleeve of his coat. "You keep so much of yourself shut up inside that sometimes I think you're going to pop like a bubble."

Later, back at Les Charmettes, they had had a great porcelain tub brought into their room. Wrapped in each other's arms, they floated together in the bubbles until the tiredness leached out of their fingers and toes. When the water grew tepid, they made love slowly, like great slick fish, then made love a second time on the big bed, and a third time—laughing and silly—in front of the French windows so Natasha could see Paris spread out beneath her.

When it grew dark, they sent down for a light supper, eating it while sitting cross-legged on the bed, wiping their mouths and fingers on the sheets. Afterward, on impulse, Natasha decided to try on Sergei's clothes. It amused them both to see her standing in front of the cheval glass in his shirt and tie, smoking one of his cigarettes, his cane in her hand.

"I see I've gained a younger brother," Sergei laughed as Natasha coughed on the cigarette smoke and came up smiling. Taking off his hat, she sent it spinning into a corner, and threw herself into his arms so hard she nearly knocked the breath out of him.

That evening Sergei read her the poems of Baudelaire from a small blue leather book with smudged pages. His French was precise, his accent nearly perfect. Resting in the crook of his arm, Natasha thought of the future unfolding brilliantly in front of them like Japanese paper flowers dropped in water.

Later she would remember this day as one of the last times they were really happy together.

"Where are you going?" It was a week or so after their conversation by the Seine, early morning, hardly light out, but Sergei was already up and dressed. Natasha sat up in bed and pulled the sheets around her bare shoulders.

"For a walk." Sergei took his hat from the closet and retrieve his favorite pair of Italian gloves from the night table.

"What do you want me to order for breakfast?"

"Whatever you want."

"When will you be back?" She could see that for some reason the question annoyed him, but she had to ask it. For the last three or four days he had taken to leaving for hours at a time without telling her when he might return, insisting that the process of putting together his next ballet was proving more complicated than he had anticipated.

"I'll be gone until this evening." Sergei took a small black notebook from his pocket and consulted it, not meeting her eyes. "*Vot dosada*." He sighed. "A whole afternoon wasted on business. Don't forget you've a rehearsal at one." He gave her a quick kiss, and left, still looking at his notebook.

That morning, Natasha finally faced the fact that something was changing, that little by little a door was closing between them, leaving her on the other side. But why? It simply didn't make sense. Where their love had been she felt a vacuum, as if Sergei were no longer with her most of the time, as if he were slowly stepping out of her life, yet there were no specific instances to point to, nothing he had done that she could seize on as proof. True, he'd been gone a little more than usual lately, but that was hardly reason to get upset. They still worked together constantly.

Yet she *was* upset. Skipping her morning class at the studio, she walked along the Seine for hours, trying to convince herself it was only her imagination. After all, it wasn't as if Sergei had stopped making love to her or suddenly become cold and distant. There were still moments, increasingly infrequent, when everything was easy and pleasant between them, when their bodies and minds fit together like pieces of a puzzle.

Finally she decided that all this fretting was ridiculous. Their relationship was only changing, as all relationships did. Everyone knew that honeymoons didn't go on forever. Grabbing at Sergei would be a fatal mistake; he seemed so skittish, so obviously afraid of being tied down. If she simply relaxed and let him do whatever he needed to do, everything would be fine. There was no use brooding like this; she had to take herself in hand.

In a burst of good resolutions, Natasha went to the studio and set to work. She danced until she was exhausted and covered with sweat, then took a cab back to the hotel, sent for a tub, and took a long, hot bath. By the time Sergei came back, she was in a good mood, full of plans. When she heard his key in the door, she went running to greet him with the suggestion that they take in a concert or play, but one look at his face, and the words froze in her mouth.

"Natasha, we have to face reality." But reality was precisely what Natasha no longer wanted to face. They were sitting in the Tour d'Argent, the most public place they had been together since she arrived in Paris. When Sergei had told her he'd made the reservations, Natasha had briefly been able to convince herself that this dinner was his way of announcing to the world they were a permanent couple. Now she saw he had only taken her here because he knew she wouldn't make a scene in public. The pressed duck choked her; she put down her fork and took a sip of wine, dreading what he might say next. Sergei ate his bread slowly. Even at this moment he looked so damnably handsome, she could have forgiven him anything.

Sergei cleared his throat. "Things have been too intense between us lately," he said abruptly. His words hurt although they were only a confirmation of what she had suspected for days. For a moment she felt speechless and stunned, as if he had physically hurt her. Why was he doing this? Why was he systematically dismantling everything between them? She knew—absolutely knew without a doubt—that he had loved her. Not at first perhaps; at first, she suspected, he had only been trying to get her to stay in Paris to dance *Griselda*, but there had been times during the last three months when he *must* have cared.

"How can love ever be too intense?"

Sergei shook his head and poured himself another glass of wine. "I expected you to say something like that."

"Sergei, please." She was frightened, but somehow she managed to keep her voice level. "Please, explain what's happening."

"I don't think you'd understand."

"Try me, please."

Sergei drank off the wine and wiped his mouth with the edge of his napkin. Anyone who didn't know him would have thought he was completely in control of himself, but Natasha knew better. "All I can say is that you're made for grand emotions, Natasha, and I'm not. Life should be pleasant, light like this champagne." He held his glass to the light so she could see the bubbles. "You take life too seriously, and when I'm with you I also take it too seriously."

"Tell me the truth." She was in a rage now; she wanted to lean across the table and knock the wineglass out of his hand, but she held herself back. "You're tired of me, right? You got what you wanted, you got me to dance in your ballet, and now you're ready to move on."

"That's not true."

"Liar."

"Natasha, don't."

"You're leaving·me, aren't you?"

"I was afraid you'd react this way."

"I'm hurt, upset. What did you expect? That you'd tell me you were leaving and I'd just kiss you on both cheeks and wish you a bon voyage?"

"I just think we need some time apart, to think things over."

"How long? A week? Six months? A lifetime?"

"I think I should move out and you should get your own apartment."

"And then?" She knew she was interrogating him, but she couldn't stop.

"Then I'll go on choreographing ballets for you. Fouchier's promised me a more or less free hand. We can keep working together, just like before."

"Only work together?"

"More perhaps." He looked down at his hands, not meeting her eyes.

"Perhaps?"

"Perhaps."

"Did you ever really love me?"

"Of course I loved you; I love you now for that matter." Reaching across the table, he took her hands, turned them over, and kissed her palms. "You rush at everything, Natasha; you want too much, too soon. You need to relax, give things between us time to sort themselves out."

"I feel as if everything we've ever said to each other was a lie."

"Don't be silly." He chucked her under the chin as if she were a child. "Come on, smile." And because she couldn't refuse him anything—not even now, when he was leaving her—she actually smiled. Later that smile was a bitter memory, a piece of self-violation that made her feel ashamed whenever she thought of it. Sergei relaxed, and picked up his fork. "That's better," he said. "That's my girl."

The next day Natasha began to search for an apartment. She could have left Paris, of course. Diaghilev still wanted her, and after *Griselda* there probably wasn't a company in existence that wouldn't jump at the chance to acquire Natasha Ladanova, but there were two things that kept her in France. First, she hoped—ridiculous as it might seem—that Sergei would change his mind, and second, he really was the best choreographer she had ever worked with. He'd been right: they were a perfect combination, and she was too much of a dancer not to recognize that if she left, she would be sacrificing some of the best roles ever created for her.

She could never bear to look back on that terrible autumn after Sergei left her. It was a time colored by pain and nausea, made worse by the fact that she still saw him every day at the studio. Memories of the bad times they had had together were painful, memories of the good ones unbearable. She found herself counting backward, establishing phantom anniversaries: three weeks ago they had made love in the big porcelain tub; two weeks ago he had still been kissing her as if he meant it; eight days ago they had had that terrible dinner at the Tour d'Argent; a week ago he had moved out. How could so much have happened in so brief a time? How could everything have fallen apart so fast?

In some ways the worst part of it all was that she no longer knew herself. She had never been the kind of person to collapse under adversity or to lie around feeling sorry for herself. The Natasha Ladanova she knew should have been taking long brisk walks, planning a trip to the Riviera to recover under the palm trees, looking up old friends. Instead, she was spending the hours after rehearsals sitting in a hotel room, coming apart.

Among other things, she was sorry now that she had left Alexis. The news from Russia was terrible. In October there was a second revolution and the Bolsheviks seized power. Alexis's letters stopped abruptly, and for the first time Natasha felt the full impact of loneliness and exile.

7

Paris, 1921

Zazie Dupois arrived at the apartment on the Ile St-Louis a little past nine o'clock holding her three-year-old son, Leonce, in one hand and a bag of fresh rolls in the other. Zazie had been one of the pleasant surprises of Paris. Storming into the Ballet de la Cité office one day four years ago, she had seized on Natasha at once as the perfect candidate to replace the roommate she had just thrown out. Zazie's logic had been hard to resist: she had heard Natasha needed an apartment and Zazie had one; Natasha didn't know Paris and Zazie, who had lived most of her adult life on the Left Bank, knew the city inside out; Zazie could cook and one look at Natasha told her, correctly, that Natasha probably lived on milk and crackers. In short, in exchange for a promise to split the rent, do the dishes, and tolerate her smoking, Zazie would take care of Natasha.

In war weary Paris, where housing was almost impossible to find, it had been a bargain too good to turn down. Natasha had moved out of the hotel that very afternoon, lugging her suitcases up the five flights of narrow stairs to a strange apartment composed almost entirely of one huge kitchen that sported a view of the Eiffel Tower (*hopelessly trite*, Zazie had exclaimed) and a large copper-bottomed frying pan that Zazie had lovingly transported to Paris from her mother's restaurant in Lyon.

Although Zazie's knowledge of Paris was invaluable those first few weeks, who was to look out for whom soon became a moot point since Natasha's new roommate immediately announced—almost before the suitcases were unpacked—that she was pregnant by a married lover who had abruptly decided not to leave his wife. In the end it had been Natasha who had taken care of Zazie, found her a new apartment where the concierge wouldn't ask too many questions, arranged for her to give birth at a private lying-in hospital, and made sure Leonce came into the world with a proper supply of diapers, receiving blankets, and small white undershirts. During the course of all this the two women, drawn together at first by nothing more than convenience, were transformed into close friends. In many ways taking care of Zazie had been the medicine that had cured Natasha of the worst of her depression over Sergei—something for which Natasha was still grateful.

"He's getting fat," Natasha said, picking up the squirming Leonce and planting a kiss on her godson's forehead. Leonce laughed and reached for her hair with pudgy baby hands. He was an energetic child who liked nothing better than to crawl under the sofa in pursuit of the cat who was frankly terrified of him.

Zazie collapsed into an armchair, kicked off her ridiculously high-heeled red shoes, and poured herself a glass of mineral water, added a slice of lemon, and then heaped in three tablespoons of sugar. Anyone looking at her comfortably round figure would never have suspected that Zazie, too, had once been a dancer. Several years older than Natasha, she had performed for almost three years with the ballet of the Paris Opera before deciding—much to the distress of her mother—that ballet was too demanding.

After she quit the Opera, Zazie had first studied art and then Medieval Literature at the Sorbonne—neither of which had many practical applications in the real world. But practicality wasn't Zazie's strong point. Having made up her mind to be happy, she was willing to settle for whatever amused her for the moment. She dressed flamboyantly—like a *poule* Natasha teased—combining peasant blouses, short skirts, and endless silver bangles, with outrageous stockings and shoes with heels so high they would have sent most women to the hospital. Her private life was a series of brief, intense love-affairs—all with married men; her real love, she claimed, was Leonce, whom she spoiled shamelessly. At present she worked part-time for *Technique*, a small scientific publishing house on the Left Bank, editing pamphlets on veterinary medicine and agricultural chemistry, a job she seemed to find completely satisfying.

"Hope most of your money's still in Swiss francs," Zazie said, fingering her bracelets, "because I just read the bottom's fallen out of the German mark. They say that in Berlin it's soon going to take a wheelbarrow full of paper just to buy a loaf of bread."

Natasha thought of her slowly diminishing bank account in Lucerne, snugly ensconced in what was probably the safest currency in the world. At least she had no worry on that score. If the Swiss franc went down the drain, all Europe would go with it. It was a pity Alexis hadn't had time to give her more money—as he would have certainly done if he could have foreseen that a second, Bolshevik, revolution would follow on the heels of the March uprising. But then no one in his right mind could have predicted the chaos Russia had gone through since the end of the war. Only last year, with the capture of Odessa, had the Civil War more or less ended, the Reds finally defeating the Whites, and still refugees brought out horror stories of bandit gangs, mass executions, starvation, people simply disappearing never to be heard from again.

There were members of the Russian nobility driving taxicabs on the Champs Elysées these days, countesses working as char women at the Gare du Nord. She was lucky to have gotten out with anything at all, lucky to have enough money to supplement the ridiculously low salaries Fouchier paid his dancers. Her present apartment, crammed with souvenirs from three European tours, was comfortable if not elegant, and the Ile St-Louis—although hardly the Rue Rivoli, had the advantage of being quiet, and near the water. Sometimes in the winter the Seine even reminded her of the Neva, especially if she looked away from Notre Dame.

Natasha settled down beside Zazie, took Leonce on her lap, and began to feed him *petites madeleines*, small shell-shaped sponge cakes that were his particular favorites. "Heard anything from your mother lately?" she asked. The two women had grown to know each other so thoroughly over the last four years that their conversations were like telegraph communications: little was said, much implied. Madame Dupois, widowed since Zazie was a child, was famously ill with all sorts of vague complaints that kept Zazie constantly wondering if she should move back to Lyon to nurse her—despite the fact she and lovely, illegitimate Leonce would have hardly received a warm welcome from the neighbors.

Zazie shook her head. "Not a word. Frankly I think she's stopped writing out of spite because she knows I go crazy when I don't hear from her. The last news I had from my aunts was that the restaurant was flourishing, but you'd never know it from Maman's letters. According to her, she's living from hand to mouth." Zazie took another sip of her lemonade, and ran her fingers briskly through her short curly red hair. Although the color was bright enough to be henna, Natasha knew for a fact that it was natural. "Let's change the subject. I can't think about Maman for more than five minutes in a row without worrying myself to death. What about Alexis? Any news?"

Natasha shrugged. "The same. All I've been able to find out is that he and his family disappeared about the time Kerensky's government fell apart. I keep hearing rumors that they were trying to get out of the country by way of Siberia, but there's no way of knowing for sure. Sometimes, when I'm feeling particularly blue, I go around to the émigré cafés and ask about him, but either no one trusts me enough to say where he is, or he's somehow managed to vanish into thin air." Natasha handed Leonce to his mother, got up abruptly, walked over to her desk, and took out a letter in an elegant, embossed envelope. "Have a look at that."

Zazie inspected the British stamp, then opened the envelope and spread the letter out on the table next to the rolls and water pitcher. Her eyebrows shot up like exclamation points. "*Mon Dieu*, this is from Isadora Duncan!"

Natasha smiled. Zazie's perpetual childlike enthusiasm was one of her better traits. "I didn't think you'd get so excited."

"But I simply *worship* Isadora Duncan. You have no idea. Mother always thought her theories about dancing were simply horrible: Greek postures, flowing robes, bare feet, natural movements. And then there was that scandal about all her lovers, and those two children of hers who died in an automobile accident. I wasn't allowed to even mention the name Isadora Duncan at home, but I thought she was wonderful anyway, so alive—and so brave to insist on dancing just the way she wanted to."

"The Bolsheviks have evidently invited Duncan to come to Moscow to start a school; she wants me to come visit after she's established."

"But why?" Zazie pulled at one of her long silver earrings and looked puzzled. "You don't dance anything alike, and besides, I always heard she hated classical ballet."

Natasha retrieved the letter and put it carefully back in the envelope. "Evidently she heard about the new piece Cocteau's written for me. Also, she claims to have always wanted to talk shop with some of the major Imperial ballerinas, but since the Petrograd Soviet turned Kschessinskaya's house into their headquarters, and Pavlova's left permanently, I'm about the only one left who has a chance of getting in. Alexis aside, my background is officially 'peasant'—something my Aunt Marya wouldn't have been too delighted to hear, but convenient under the circumstances." Aunt Marya had died over two years ago, but Natasha still felt a pinch of grief when she spoke of her.

Zazie gave Leonce a sip of the lemonade, wiped his mouth off with a napkin, and turned him loose. Immediately he headed for the pile of toy soldiers and wooden trucks that Tante Natasha kept in an antique trunk beside the sofa. Soon he was happily conducting baroque military campaigns in which the soldiers were constantly being shot and then suddenly resurrected. Natasha watched him play, wishing her own life offered such simple alternatives.

"You're going, of course." There was a very small edge to Zazie's voice that only a close friend would have detected.

"I'm not sure."

"You know you're a fool don't you?"

Natasha smiled wryly. "Oh, yes, I know."

Zazie sat up abruptly with a clash of bracelets, her red hair sticking out on either side of her head in a way that was almost comic. "Just how long do you intend to let your life come to a stop for that man?" *That man* was Sergei, whom Zazie had actively disliked ever since Natasha had told her about him. As a matter of record, the only time she and Natasha ever really fought was when Sergei's name entered the conversation. That he was a brilliant choreographer, that he had almost single-handedly created Natasha's international reputation, that he was lionized and adored by all Paris made no difference to Zazie. From her point of view, Sergei was a *salaud*, a rat, a *mauvais type*, a bad sort, and all sorts of other French epithets Natasha had never been able to fully translate. "How often do you see him?" Zazie demanded. "Be honest."

"Every day at rehearsals."

"I mean *really* see him."

"Once or twice a month."

"You mean to tell me that once or twice a month Monsieur Sergei Maximov deigns to allow you to cook dinner for him, listen to his problems, and wash the dishes afterward?"

"I'm not unhappy with the arrangement."

"The hell you aren't." When Zazie was mad, she looked fierce, like one of those avenging French angels who had sat knitting beside the guillotine as the heads fell. Her dark eyes narrowed, and she leaned forward in her chair. "That's no way for a woman to live."

"Zazie, let's not start this again."

"You're how old?"

"Twenty-six." There was no use trying to stop Zazie once she got on the subject of Sergei. Natasha took a deep breath and decided to wait it out.

"Twenty-six, beautiful, talented, famous," Zazie waved her hands dramatically as if she could list half a dozen other virtues, "and you're wasting your life on a man who only sees you as a *vehicle* for his own talents, who won't even go to bed with you, who for all you know is probably a homosexual."

"Zazie, for heavens sake. . . ."

"Calm down. It doesn't matter one way or the other if your darling Sergei is a *pédé* or the greatest gift to *les femmes* since Don Juan. The point is, he shows no interest in *you*, yet you go on hanging onto him because of some wonderful weekend or other you had on the Left Bank a million years ago. This isn't love, my dear; it's some kind of mental illness. You need someone else, *un vrai amant* who'll bring you flowers, rub your back at night, tell you how divine you are."

"Like the pharmacist." The pharmacist, Zazie's current lover, was a running joke between the two of them. Married, with six children, he was famous for his habit of bringing Zazie odd gifts, such as thermometers.

"Exactly like the pharmacist," Zazie picked the lemon slice out of her lemonade, sucked on it, and made a face. "You need a regular man, *cherie*. It's the truth. *Je te jure*."

Three nights after that conversation, the audience in the theater of the Comedie des Champs Elysées moved restlessly in their seats as they waited for the curtain to rise on Cocteau's new ballet, *Eurydice in Hell*. Scandal had been in the air for weeks, bruited about the cafés, whispered in the drawing rooms of the wealthy in the Seventh Arrondissement. Those crazy artists who had caused a near riot a few years ago with the avant-garde ballet *Parade* were planning another attack on French culture, a ballet rumored to be so unmentionably shocking that the chief of police had actually been persuaded to post extra men around the theater in case the crowd got out of hand.

Everything on the program pointed to trouble. The sets for *Eurydice* were by Pablo Picasso, a painter who had no respect for anything, especially the human face, which he seemed to delight in turning into ugly, blotched cubes. Most of the music was by Erik Satie, an elderly, irascible man— some called him a genius—who a number of years ago had challenged the director of the Paris Opera to a duel because the director had refused to consider a production of Satie's pseudo-Christian ballet *Uspud*. Satie had once actually been arrested for sending obscene, insulting postcards to dance critics. Now he sat in the front row among those same critics, his arms folded stubbornly across his chest, monocle clenched in his eye, looking neither to the left nor right, a fragile man of fifty-four with a small goatee that gave him a mildly demonic look.

Next to Satie sat Coco Chanel, the famous fashion designer, who it was rumored, had created a series of amazing costumes for tonight's performance, and next to her was Jean Cocteau the poet who had written the scenario. Cocteau, a small, boyish-looking man whose hair stood up like a bottlebrush, was wearing a loud, polka dot tie designed, it seemed, to get on everyone's nerves. Next to him, marvelously dapper in formal evening dress, was Emile Fouchier, the wealthy balletomane who was footing the bill for this evening's extravagance—tens of thousands of francs it was rumored—but then Fouchier, who made a fortune in munitions during the war, could well afford it.

The students in the balcony, who had come well supplied with rotten fruit, craned their necks to get a better look—not so much at Fouchier, whose private debaucheries were so well known as to have become boring, but to catch a glimpse of the last member of the entourage, Sergei Maximov, the young Russian who was competing with Massine for the title of the premier choreographer of Europe.

A major question had plagued the student cafés in the Latin Quarter for a good two years now, argued incessantly over endless cups of coffee, debated in the place of the merits of Spengler's new theory of the decline of the West or Jung's recent revelations about the unconscious. To wit: was Sergei Maximov or was he not the lover of Natasha Ladanova, the former Imperial ballerina who had somehow been persuaded to dance the leading role in tonight's debacle?

Opinions among the students were mixed. Maximov's handsome blond good looks and aristocratic bearing inclined most of them to believe he was Ladanova's lover. On the other hand, those students who were in love with Natasha—and there were a goodly number—pointed out hopefully that

Maximov was associated with Diaghilev and Cocteau—not to mention Fouchier—leaving the possibility that his devotion to women was somewhat less than actively enthusiastic.

The students had a long time to discuss the matter because the performance was for some reason delayed well past nine o'clock. When at last, after a rather banal overture, the curtain finally rose, the audience, most of whom had come to jeer, sat in shocked silence. Where were the bizarre costumes and garish sets they had practically been promised? Was this Cocteau's idea of a joke?

Bathed in soft blue light, the stage was practically bare except for three large mirrors ranged along the back wall. In front of the mirrors Natasha was in the process of executing what appeared at first glance to be an excerpt from *Giselle*. Contrary to all expectations, her tutu was strictly classical, white with a small stiff skirt and tight bodice discreetly studded with seed pearls. Were these Chanel's outrageous costumes? These tights of smooth creamy silk, these small ivory *pointe* shoes? *Mon Dieu*, they might just as well have gone to the Opera.

Natasha moved languidly across the stage to Satie's music, beautiful and remote as an ice sculpture, each step technically correct but curiously enervated, as if she were too tired to put much energy into her performance. The most astute among the critics saw that she was mixing together various classical pieces.

In the front row Fouchier suddenly pulled a large gold pocket watch out of his vest and began to count off the seconds silently, moving his large, rather fleshy lips like a man who was savoring a good dinner. Eleven... twelve... thirteen ... fourteen...

As Fouchier reached fifteen, the first dead swan dropped onto the stage with a wet thud, followed by another and still another. There was a roar of disbelief from the audience. Women screamed angrily and men leapt to their feet, but that was only the beginning. Suddenly, behind Natasha, all the mirrors shattered at once: through the first mirror came a pair of Negro jazz musicians in skin-tight red suits blaring away on saxophones; through the second a group of half-naked acrobats and jugglers; through the third two famous Parisian wrestlers dressed as cubist robots. Almost before the audience could understand what was happening, the robots grabbed Natasha, ripping off her tights and tutu, exposing a flesh-colored leotard on which Picasso had painted voluminous breasts, and fish-shaped crotch. Suddenly the theater was filled with a cacophony of crazy noises: roaring lions, screaming toucans, Morse code tapping out obscene messages, honking horns, explosions, breaking glass.

"DANCE IS DEAD!"

"CLASSICAL BALLET IS DEAD!"

"WE PROCLAIM A REVOLUTION IN DANCE!"

Raymond Radiguet, Cocteau's nineteen-year-old lover, had crawled up on the stage and was bellowing into a loudspeaker. Natasha danced to Radiguet's words, to honking horns, to the jazz. She was a dervish, an acrobat, a ballerina all at the same time.

"BORING ART IS FOR BORING PEOPLE!

Natasha's performance was truly remarkable, but most of the audience was past caring. As Radiguet continued to insult them, the critics stood on their seats and shook their fists at the stage; students heaved fruit and rotten vegetables at the dancers; the Countess of Banville, long a patron of the arts, had public hysterics and had to be carted off to the hospital.

Natasha's last view of the audience before the curtain crashed down was of an outraged, white-faced mob of Frenchmen in evening clothes, storming toward her as if they were about to retake the Bastille.

Natasha leaned up against a lamppost in the pouring rain and laughed so hard tears ran down her cheeks. She'd fled the theater so fast that she didn't have an umbrella, five francs for a cab, or even a *jeton* to call Zazie, and now she was stranded on the Champs Elysées in a thunderstorm wearing a pair of satin *pointe* shoes and a coronet of wet feathers. Thank heavens she'd been able to snatch up her coat on the way out or she would have been reduced to wandering the streets of Paris in a flesh-colored leotard with a fish painted on the crotch. Picasso notwithstanding, the gendarmes would probably have arrested her for indecent exposure.

Gaspodi, the French were impulsive! Who would have ever thought they'd rush the stage like that? Right at the end they'd looked more like a lynch mob than an audience. The memory of Cocteau standing on his seat, waving his arms like a windmill, sent her into another bout of hopeless giggles. Madame Laurier would have had a fit if she'd seen those dead swans plopping down on the stage. Wonderful, impossible, ridiculous Paris! Where else in the world did people care enough about art to riot over it.

"Excuse me, Mademoiselle," a voice said in heavily accented French, "are you quite all right?"

Natasha looked up to find a man, impeccably dressed in an evening jacket and black tie, staring at her with concern. He appeared to be in his late twenties, tall and slender with pale green eyes, light brown hair, and a slightly off-center nose. His small, neatly trimmed, aristocratic mustache reminded her of the ones favored by American fliers during the war.

"I'm fine," she said in English, trying to suppress her laughter, but the look on his face as he took in her toe shoes set her off again.

"Well I'll be darned," he said in a mildly awe-struck voice, "you're Natasha Ladanova, the dancer, aren't you? I saw you in Vienna a few months ago, and in London last fall. I've seen Pavlova perform, but I thought your *Giselle* was better than hers. You're really on your way to the top."

"Thanks, but at the moment I'm more on my way to pneumonia"

"Oh," he said gallantly, "then let me offer you my umbrella."

She moved gratefully under the cover of his umbrella. Usually she was reluctant to take favors from strange men, but the thought of walking all the way back home in *pointe* shoes put a different light on things. "What I really need," she admitted after a short silence, "is a cab. I have to get over to the Ile St.-Louis, and I don't think I can make it in these." Her shoes were two sodden lumps. The dye from the pink ribbons had run down her ankles and was making a puddle at her feet. "The problem is I don't have a franc at present. I wonder Monsieur . . . ?"

"Ward," he supplied. "Trey Ward from Boston and happy to make your acquaintance."

"I wonder Monsieur Ward if I could borrow cab fare?"

"Of course, of course," his face brightened wonderfully at the prospect of helping her, "a lady in distress. Nothing I like better to tell the truth. It'd be my pleasure."

"You're very kind."

"Well, you see," he smiled pleasantly, "rescue's my specialty. Once, on the Orinoco, I flew out a whole village just before a flood hit—men, women, children, and chickens. Nothing to it really. I have my own plane, a real beauty of a JN-4D that I picked up for a song after the war." He hailed a cab and held the door open for her. "Say, would you mind if I rode along with you and saw you safe to your place? Paris can get pretty tough at night."

She told him her address, and he settled down beside her at a respectful distance on the wide leather seat, and gave the driver precise directions. He obviously knew Paris well. Natasha sat back, relieved to have someone else take care of things for once.

As they drove, he told her a few things about himself: his real name was Albert Waltham Ward III, nickname Trey, and his family had been in shipping every since the first of the great whalers set out from New England in the mid-1700s. He had gone to Harvard, taken a degree in biology, flown over France during the war, lost a few friends, and been downed himself twice by the Germans, escaping miraculously with nothing more than a broken nose and a few cuts. When peace came, he'd still been restless so he'd signed on to fly a mail run for a year in South America. Besides flying, his real passion in life was ballet, a subject over which he had an impressive command. When he was fifteen he had seen Nijinsky, and immediately decided he wanted to be a dancer, but his mother had quashed the idea on the grounds that ballet was too effeminate.

"That's a pity," Natasha said, thinking that he was too tall and thin to have made a good dancer anyway. There was something whippetlike about his body that suggested speed rather than endurance. She realized suddenly that he had talked so much to spare her from explaining what she was doing wandering around half naked in the middle of a thunderstorm. His tact was touching, not the kind of thing she usually associated with Americans.

The cab pulled up in front of Natasha's apartment, and Trey smiled and shook her hand vigorously. "It's been a real pleasure to meet you, Miss Ladanova," he said. "If you ever need rescuing again just call. Or if you'd like to see Paris from the air." He gave her his card, neatly embossed: Albert Waltham Ward III, addresses in Boston, London, and Paris. "I think you're the berries," he said, "I really do." Tipping his hat in farewell, he climbed back into the cab and permitted himself to be carried off into the rain.

The berries? As she let herself into her apartment, Natasha wondered what in the world he could have possibly meant. Kicking off her wet *pointe* shoes, she went into the bathroom, turned on the hot water in the tub, and shook in some bubblebath. Then she sat down in front of the mirror and began to unbraid her hair. *The berries?* The two words rolled around in her mind, becoming odder every minute. In less than three weeks the Ballet de la Cité was going on its first American tour. It was time she brushed up on her English.

"Damn Fouchier!" Sergei was storming around Natasha's apartment in a rage, vowing he would go back to Diaghilev, form his own company, do anything rather than work another day under Fouchier's thumb. "*Durak! Merzavets!*" When Sergei cursed he always did so in Russian, which Natasha had to admit was more equipped for serious invective than French.

"For heaven's sake, Sergei, tell me what's wrong."

"*Chort vozmi!*"

Half a bottle of chardonnay and three brandies later she had him calmed down enough to find out what was wrong: it seemed that the whole upcoming American tour of the Ballet de la Cité was going to be a fiasco because Fouchier (*sukin syn*), disturbed by the French reception of *Eurydice*, had announced at the last minute that the entire repertoire was to be strictly classical.

"Eight months I spent creating a new jazz ballet for that *tvar*, and now he puts it on the shelf." Sergei pounded his fist on the table. Since he had stopped dancing to devote himself to choreography, his body had filled out: his arms growing thicker, his face becoming fuller, more Russian. He was as handsome as ever—more so perhaps—but now in addition to good looks he radiated power. Natasha could well believe he might decide to leave Fouchier

Ultimately he quieted down and they went out for dinner, had a Pernod at the Café du Dome, and then strolled along the Seine. By the time they got back to Natasha's apartment on the Ile St-Louis, Sergei seemed calm, but it was only an illusion. He drank steadily and morosely for about an hour, then put on his coat, mumbled an apology, and left abruptly, nearly tripping over the cat on his way out.

After she had seen him off, Natasha poured herself a glass of chilled chardonnay and sat down to think. Zazie's lecture three days before the debut of *Eurydice* had disturbed her more than she liked to admit. Resting her chin against her hands, Natasha stared at the Degas she'd brought from her house on the Quai d'Argent, and tried, not for the first time, to take stock of her life and make sense of the last four years.

It had been obvious in the fall of 1917 that Sergei no longer had any intention of renewing their love affair, but gradually Natasha had become aware that he might be open to a more casual arrangement, something more along the lines of friendship. For her part she had still wanted him in her arms, in her bed, and in her life ("Oh, you fool," Zazie had said, "*quelle bêtise!*"), and so a new sort of connection had developed between them—casual on his part, secretly intense on hers. Natasha had learned her lesson. She no longer inundated Sergei with emotions; she became an excellent actress, skilled at not seeming overly pleased when he appeared, or distressed when he forgot to call. She never mentioned that she loved him or allowed him to suspect the depths of her feelings for him.

It was an unbalanced, crazy way to live, yet most of the time Natasha was more or less content. She and Sergei worked together; they were friends; he came to dinner several times a month, and if their relationship was not exactly as she would have wanted it to be, it still seemed the best life had to offer. Sometimes she did, indeed, think of extracting herself, of following Zazie's advice and finding some other man who would take more interest in her, but each time she was stopped by the realization that other men had no appeal for her—none at all. She thought of Trey Ward, staring at her the other night with such undisguised admiration. There were hundreds of Treys in her world—handsome, intelligent, altogether pleasant men who would have been delighted to get to know her better—but Natasha had learned long ago that it was better to ignore them. When she was with another man she always compared him to Sergei, and found herself dissatisfied and frankly bored.

Natasha dumped the bread crumbs back on the table, finished her wine, and stared out the window until the sky changed from gray to opal. It was a beautiful morning, chill and cold with just the slightest hint of fall in the air. The Seine was smoky, blue, flanked by slow-moving barges. Paris was a beautiful city; she had a fantastic career. So what if things could be better with Sergei. It was always better to enjoy what you had than spend time mooning over what you didn't have. Getting up from the table she set about making herself a good Russian breakfast of hot kasha and strong tea.

"Sergei, Natasha, over here!" Dressed in a full-length red fox cape, Anya Belinskaya stood on the dock, waving her gloved hand frantically at Sergei and Natasha as they walked down the gangplank and stepped onto American soil. Behind her, Fouchier was busy directing the unloading of the scenery, issuing incomprehensible frantic orders in French to a team of burly New York longshoremen. Ignoring Fouchier, the longshoremen threw an expensive mirrored pool from *Giselle* into the back of a truck with an ominous crash, and then went back for a pair of artificial trees swathed in cheesecloth and canvas. The Ballet de la Cité had a six-week engagement at the Metropolitan Opera House—that is, if any of the scenery survived.

Anya hurried around the longshoremen who were struggling with the roof of the cottage from *La Fille Mal Gardée*, her tiny high heels clicking against the concrete. Sweeping forward with the grace that only a superb dancer could manage under such circumstances, she folded Sergei in an embrace and kissed Natasha enthusiastically on both cheeks, Russian style. Natasha smelled the sweet, unfamiliar scent of Anya's perfume, fresh and very American—like hay or clover. The passing years had done nothing but make Anya more beautiful: her blond hair, bobbed stylishly around her ears, gave her a frail, boyish look, and her eyes were still as blue and innocent as they had been the day Natasha first met her. Under the red fox cape she wore a short silk dress, scooped deeply in front, covered with hundreds of tiny black beads that caught the light every time she moved, an effect that was not lost on the longshoremen who had stopped loading the scenery and were frankly staring at Anya, one of them pursing his lips into a silent whistle.

"Welcome." Anya hugged them both again. "*Zdrastvuyte,* my dears. You can't imagine how glad I am to see both of you again." Tears welled up in her eyes. "Our poor, poor country," she said, "whatever are the Bolsheviks making of it. But at least you're here. At least you got out safely, and now you'll dance for these American barbarians."

Natasha had never seen Anya so open, so eager to please. She insisted on hearing every detail of their trip, commiserating over the delays caused at immigration by the clumsy Nansen Passports that had just been issued to all Russian émigrés, who, thanks to the new Soviet government, were now officially stateless. Had they had a good voyage? Been seasick? She was so happy to see them, they just couldn't imagine. Taking Natasha by the arm in a sisterly fashion, Anya led her to a glittering, cream-colored sports car that seemed to take up half a block.

"A Cadillac sport Phaeton," Sergei observed admiringly.

"I drive it myself," Anya motioned for them to climb in. Taking the steering wheel in both hands, she fumbled with something and the motor purred to a start. "The only problem is, I get endless tickets. When my father was alive it distressed him no end paying for them, but now that I'm half an orphan I can drive any way I please." Anya smiled sweetly, as if forgiving them the need to say something consoling about her father. Natasha tried to remember how long ago Count Belinsky had died. Two years? Three? She remembered hearing that he had done well in America, that Anya had come into a great deal of money.

Releasing the hand bke, Anya pulled abruptly out into traffic. She drove with style and audacity, talking all the while, dodging taxicabs and trucks with amazing nonchalance. "You will stay with me, won't you, Natasha dear," Anya said unexpectedly,. "Fouchier's got you booked into the Algonquin on Forty-fourth, which is fine if you want to meet Dorothy Parker, but the rooms are small and there's no view at all. I've got a whole brownstone on Sutton Place that mother and I just rattle around in. Please. *Pojaluysta*." It was clear from her tone of voice that she really wanted Natasha to be her guest. "Sergei can look after himself, but you're bound to be exhausted by the pace here." Anya smiled hopefully at Natasha, offering her friendship shyly, as if she were afraid it might be rejected. How fine that after all these years they could put away the competition that had always separated them. Natasha hastened to accept and Anya beamed with gratitude. It was amazing how much she had changed. For the first time since that year long ago, when Anya had been suspended for six weeks, Natasha felt sorry for her. Anya was obviously lonely since her father's death. It couldn't have been easy: moving to this brash, new country.

New York was the most amazing city Natasha had ever seen. Huge glass and steel towers rose on either side of the streets, glittering against a violet haze. In Times Square great electric signs flashed garishly, advertising products she had never heard of. Each building seemed to exist in a period of history all its own, as if all the architectural styles in the world had been chopped into pieces and reassembled randomly in downtown Manhattan: Pennsylvania Station was an ancient roman temple; banks looked like churches, churches like banks. A bit of Egypt stood next to an imitation Gothic cathedral; gargoyles stared at Greek friezes.

"The problem with this country," Anya observed as they pulled up to a stoplight, "is that you can't get a drink anywhere—not legally at least. My God, have you ever heard of anything so uncivilized as Prohibition? Americans are obsessed with alcohol the way the French are obsessed with sex. It's ridiculous, barbaric, this Volstead Act. For almost a hundred years Delmonico's was one of the best restaurants in the world, and now they can't even cook with wine." Anya grew shy suddenly. "But I'm talking too much, aren't I? It's only that I'm so happy to see you, so excited. It's felt like exile here, like Siberia."

"But surely you've been dancing?" Natasha said.

"Dancing? Where? With whom? The only ballet in America comes in the way you just did: on a foreign tour. Of course there's the Denishawn team—Ruth St. Denis and her husband, Ted Shawn—full of phony Eastern mysticism, and no technique worth talking about. The last time I saw St. Denis she was doing some kind of pseudo-Egyptian thing. Do you think for one minute that anyone who's been through the Imperial School could participate in such a sideshow?"

Natasha thought about describing Cocteau's *Eurydice* to Anya and then decided against it. Obviously Anya was in no mood to hear that in Paris the most important ballet of the season had featured acrobats and jazz musicians.

"A few months ago Fokine actually choreographed a ballet in a speakeasy." There was a hint of weariness in Anya's voice. She pulled over to the curb in front of a large brownstone town-house, stopped the engine, and sat back despondently. "So you see what I've had to deal with. I've thought of going back to Europe of course, even of dancing with Diaghilev, who's asked me enough times, but my mother's been ill and asking her to move again at her age is simply out of the question. So I take lessons, I practice, I keep in shape, but for what?"

"So Fokine did a ballet in a speakeasy," Sergei said, "how interesting." Natasha could feel the wheels spinning in his head—his new jazz ballet, a speakeasy, Fouchier's stubbornness, the possibilities—but Anya was oblivious, lost in a brown study of her own.

"As far as dance is concerned," Anya continued wistfully, "America is a wasteland."

"Say rather an uncultivated field," Sergei suddenly suggested.

"An uncultivated field?"

"The soil only needs to be turned over, the right crops planted. I know I push the metaphor, Anya darling, but with the right financial backing it ought to be possible to start at least one good ballet troupe here." His face flushed with excitement, and he spoke quickly, with conviction. "After all, America's a huge country. You could tour for months without ever crossing the border."

"Founding a ballet troupe of any size would take millions," Anya observed.

Sergei smiled at her, a long sweet smile that Natasha couldn't remember seeing on his face for years. "Yes," he said pensively, "I suppose it would."

During the six weeks that the Ballet de la Cité stayed in New York, Anya's hospitality proved a godsend. Although Anya herself was rarely home, her house in Sutton Place was an island of sanity in this crazy country where ladies wore silver flasks of bootleg gin in their garters, and no one seemed to know the difference between a serious dancer and a movie star. At Sutton Place the samovar was always steaming no matter what hour Natasha came home from a rehearsal or performance. The servants, who moved unobtrusively through the cheerful, sumptuous rooms, were all Russian, some of them having been with the Belinsky family since St. Petersburg. Sutton Place was like a piece of Imperial Russia miraculously preserved from the ravages of history.

Living with Anya's mother was another unexpected pleasure. A delicate, cultured lady who had once been intimate with the Tsar's sister, Countess Belinskaya read avidly in four languages and was a walking expert on everything American. From her Natasha learned of the more cultured side of American life, of the writers, artists, and poets, many of whom had voluntarily exiled themselves abroad to escape what Anya had so accurately called "the wasteland." Countess Belinskaya introduced Natasha to the poems of Ezra Pound, to Carl Sandburg whose *Smoke and Steel* explained the American worship of industry, to the young novelist F. Scott Fitzgerald, who was said to have caught what was now being called the Jazz Age better than any other contemporary writer.

The only thing Natasha regretted during those six weeks was how little she saw of Sergei. Although he appeared regularly at rehearsals, he often left before they were over. She wondered if he was still brooding about his new ballet.

"Pour me some coffee, Mama darling," Anya said, appearing unexpectedly in the conservatory one morning as Natasha and Countess Belinskaya were lingering over breakfast. "I have the most splitting headache ever visited on a human being. I swear they're passing off crankcase oil as Scotch these days." Anya slumped into one of the wicker chairs, rested her chin on her hands, and squinted at the winter sunlight pouring in through the windows. Her lips were pale and there was a small brownish blotch on her cheek that Natasha had never noticed before.

Countess Belinskaya frowned. "I wish you wouldn't indulge yourself so, my dear," she admonished as she picked up the heavy silver pot and poured Anya a cup of bitter black coffee. "I suppose you went up to Harlem again to one of those terrible speakfreelys."

"Speakeasies, Mama," Anya corrected. She took several gulps of coffee and the color came back into her cheeks. "As a matter of fact, Sergei and I dropped by the Cotton Club to hear Ethel Waters. What an experience. I swear to God the woman could make a Russian gypsy *die* with envy the way she sings."

As Anya launched into a description of the evening she'd spent with Sergei in Harlem, Natasha felt a momentary pang of jealousy that was, of course, foolish. Sergei didn't come home exhausted from dancing every evening the way she did, so there was no reason in the world why he shouldn't see some of the famous nightlife of New York, and if Anya wanted to accompany him, well, that was only natural seeing that Anya was the one who knew the city. Still, as comfortable as Sutton Place was and as fond as she had become of the Countess, Natasha found herself wishing she had stayed at the Algonquin.

A week after that breakfast with Anya, the Ballet de la Cité gave its last performance to a crowd that was only moderately enthusiastic. Natasha, who always had trouble dancing her best when the audience didn't appreciate it, was frankly relieved the American tour was over. In three days the entire company was scheduled to sail for France, and she looked forward to returning to her apartment, calling up Zazie, and doing something indulgent—like spending the entire afternoon shopping on the Rue de Rivoli. She was, in short, preparing for a comfortable return when Fouchier took her aside.

"I'm afraid I have some bad news for you, Natasha," Fouchier pursed his thick lips as though he had accidentally tasted a sour wine. "Maximov has quit."

"Quit?" Natasha stood numbly, holding a box of toe shoes, refusing to let Fouchier's words penetrate her mind.

"Left us in the lurch, as the Americans say. I gather he's not going back to Paris."

"You can't be serious."

"Oh, I'm afraid so. He's handed me his resignation—the little *cochon*. But don't worry. There are other choreographers in the world. Massine is growing restless, I hear."

Dropping the box of toe shoes on her dressing table, Natasha pulled on her coat, jammed her new black cloche hat down on her head, and hurried out of the theater.

At the Algonquin she ran up three flights of stairs, ignoring the elevators. The halls were narrow and quiet, carpeted with a thick wool rug that sported red and green lozenges. Sergei's room was at one end, between two immense potted plants. Balling her hand into a fist, Natasha knocked on the door so hard she nearly skinned her knuckles.

"Who's there?" Sergei opened the door dressed in a stiffly starched formal shirt adorned with a pair of dazzling diamond studs. His face was half covered with shaving cream, and he held a razor in one hand. A gray-and-white striped morning jacket with a small white carnation in the lapel hung on the chair beside him, next to a black tie and top hat.

"Fouchier says you're leaving the company," Natasha blurted out the words, not caring how she sounded. The time for pretending cool indifference was over. "Please tell me it's not true."

"Natasha, calm down." He looked surprised and not altogether pleased to see her.

"How can I calm down?" She paced his room from window to bed. "Are you coming back to France with us?"

"No." Sergei wiped the shaving cream off his face with a thick white towel and looked at her helplessly. "I'm staying in America."

"My God, why? You heard Anya. It's a wasteland."

"I have prospects." He shrugged his shoulders uncomfortably the way he always did when he was particularly upset. "I've found some money, enough to start my own company. It's a wonderful opportunity."

"Congratulations." She didn't want to sound bitter like this. What kind of friend was she that she couldn't be happy for him? "Really," she said more softly. "Congratulations, I mean it." She tried to say more, but the words stuck in her throat.

He didn't ask her to join him, so, on top of everything else, they'd obviously not be working together anymore. Sergei would be over five thousand kilometers away, separated from her by the entire Atlantic Ocean. She'd see him every two or three years or so at best. But there was no use thinking about that. She had to get hold of her feelings. Forcing herself to appear calm, she sat down stiffly on the edge of the bed.

"Who's putting up the money?" she asked brightly, attempting a poor parody of a smile.

Sergei hesitated. "A patron."

"He must be very rich."

"I suppose you could say that."

Natasha opened her mouth to ask another question and then, to her embarrassment and dismay, broke into tears. *Gaspodi*, she was making a fool of herself. Angrily she wiped away the tears with the back of her hand, but they kept coming. What a sight she must be, nose red and dripping, bawling in front of him like a baby, but she couldn't seem to stop.

Sergei sat down beside her, pulled a handkerchief out of his back pocket, and put it in her hand. "Natasha, don't." He put his arm around her. "It isn't the end of the world." Too miserable to talk, Natasha hid her face against his chest. "We'll still be friends."

"No, we won't. Not really. For years we've been drifting further and further apart, and now you'll disappear and I'll never see you again."

"Of course you will." Suddenly he lifted her face to his and kissed her. Natasha was so surprised she stopped crying. "I care about you Natasha, very much, but it's always been so hard with you. You always wanted too much of me." He kissed her again. "Damn, I shouldn't be doing this."

"Why not?"

"Not today." He sat back, half pushing her away.

Natasha rose awkwardly to her knees on the soft mattress, put her arms around his neck, and drew him to her. If she didn't say something now she would lose him completely and forever. "Make love to me, Sergei," it wasn't what she'd meant to say at all, but the words came out of their own accord and as soon as she heard them she knew she meant them. "Make love to me now, here."

"You don't know what you're asking."

"Yes, I do." Putting her lips against his she kissed him with all her might. For a moment he resisted her, and then he began to return her kiss, running his hands over bare arms hesitantly.

"You really want me to make love to you?"

"Yes."

Pushing her back down on the bed, he pulled at her stockings, stripping them off her legs, kissing her face and cheeks, running his tongue over her breasts through the thin material of her blouse. Pulling the diamond studs out of his shirt, he threw them on the floor. Quickly, never letting go of her, he stripped off his clothes, and pressed his body to hers, spreading her back against the cold sheets. Twining his legs around hers, he drew her closer and then turned her so that her back was to him. Natasha tried not to ask herself why he was willing to make love to her now after all those years of not touching her. She closed her eyes, willing herself not to think.

Sergei's hands massaged her shoulders—the hands of a dancer, so strong, and sure, and sensual she wanted to cry from the pleasure of his touch. As she lay wrapped in his arms, all the years and the distance between them seemed to dissolve. His body was not quite as she had remembered it. His arms were thicker, his shoulders firm and heavy. No, it was not the body of the boy she had loved but the body of a grown man. The sense that time had touched him and was transforming him moved her deeply.

When at last Natasha came, she had a sense of flowing out to him, of being so vulnerable and open she could feel her skin melting into his. Sergei stopped for a moment, turned her to him, and kissed her. Then he, too, came, violently, his whole body shaking. Afterward he lay on her breast, exhausted and quiet as she stroked his hair.

Natasha closed her eyes and leaned back against the feather pillows, utterly content. For the last four years there had been a knot inside her that nothing had been able to dissolve. Now, for once, she felt completely at peace.

"Natasha." She opened her eyes to find Sergei staring uneasily at the clock on the bedside table. It was 11:35. "I have to go."

"Where."

"It doesn't matter." He got up abruptly and went into the bathroom. She heard the sound of running water. When he emerged he was dressed again, except for his coat.

"But where are you going?" She was bewildered, unable to believe he was actually going to leave so quickly.

Sergei slipped into the morning coat, adjusted the flower in his lapel, and picked up his top hat. "I'd be a coward not to tell you, but I'm not sure how to go about it." Awkwardly he handed her her dress. "You'd better put on your things. I'm due somewhere at noon."

"Where."

"St. Vasily's Cathedral. Anya's waiting for me there."

"What do you mean?" She looked at the morning coat, the flower, the hat, and a chill suddenly went through her.

Sergei sat down on the edge of the bed and took her hand. "I'm sorry. I didn't want to hurt you, but you have to know: Anya and I are getting married. She's putting up the money for the company; she's also pregnant, so it has to be done as soon as possible." His voice trailed off.

Natasha sat stunned, unable to think or move.

There was pain in his face. "I don't love her. It's a marriage of convenience, an opportunity for me to get out of this dead end I've fallen into with Fouchier." He dropped her hand. "My God, don't just sit there staring at me like that; say something."

"I think," she finally managed to say, "that you're the biggest bastard I've ever known."

Three days later Natasha sailed for France with the Ballet de la Cité. Not more than a week after she arrived in Paris, she was sitting in an émigré café on the Left Bank when a heavily bearded man in a shabby overcoat came up to her table and sat down. It was Misha, Alexis's chauffeur. The Grand Duke, Natasha learned, was hiding with his wife and family at Zemlo, one of the smaller country estates. They had no money, almost no food, and if they weren't somehow gotten out of Russia immediately, the Bolsheviks would probably track them down and shoot them.

8

Moscow, 1922

It was a grim February afternoon, some thirty degrees below zero with the thermometer still falling; in Red Square a light flurry of dry snow made the nine golden asymmetrical domes of the Cathedral of St. Basil the Blessed seem as if they were swathed in a veil: Natasha closed her eyes against the sharp edges of the wind and pulled her hands deeper into the cuffs of her coat. At least her coat was warm, unlike those of most of the people who hurried by the Kremlin wall, their heads lowered into the wind. Long, plain, black, and slightly shabby, the coat had been purchased at a secondhand store a week before she left Paris. It was heavier than it should have been—much heavier. Thank heavens none of the customs officers at the border had taken it into his head to heft it, or she would have been sitting in some Soviet prison this afternoon instead of standing in Red Square. Natasha ran her gloved fingers surreptitiously over the thick wool lining. Sewn into it was ten thousand dollars' worth of gold coins and bills—all the money she had in the world.

The money was intended for Alexis but the problem was she had no way to get it to him. For days she had struggled through the fantastic red tape of the new regime, trying to get an internal visa to travel to anywhere near Zemlo, but every step of the way she had met with opposition from uncooperative officials. The Soviet government, she was told, was delighted to have a dancer of *Gaspoja* Ladanova's caliber return to her homeland to visit the famous Miss Isadora Duncan; perhaps Natasha might even consider a guest performance with Ekaterina Geltser, now the chief ballerina in Soviet Russia. But as for allowing her to travel anywhere but between Moscow and St. Petersburg—or rather Petrograd as it was now called—was simply out of the question. She had to understand that they simply couldn't guarantee her safety, and besides, she was told in no uncertain terms, they had more serious things to worry about: bread was rationed, housing impossible to find. Frankly, she should count herself fortunate they had granted her a first-class ration card.

Petrograd itself had been a nightmare; Natasha still couldn't think of it without a shudder. It wasn't just the empty shops, boarded-up windows, bullet-pocked buildings, and ragged people that had bothered her, but the fact that so many of her old friends were either dead, missing, or in exile. Back in Paris she had heard rumors that the new government had proclaimed something called "The Red Terror," but she had discounted the tales of mass exterminations as too fantastic to be true. Who could possibly believe that the Cheka, Lenin's secret police, were systematically eliminating not only the aristocracy but the whole middle class? That torture was used to obtain confessions? That one fine spring morning all of the officers in Sebastopol had been rounded up and summarily executed?

Now, as she tried unsuccessfully to look up old acquaintances, Natasha realized to her dismay that the refugees had indeed been telling the truth. The aristocracy was virtually gone as if it had never existed, almost a whole generation extinct—every man, woman, and child swallowed up, their fine homes divided into shabby apartments, their libraries burned, their cars commandeered for the military. Ballerina Mathilda Kschessinskaya's mansion had been turned into the headquarters of the Petrograd Soviet. Madame Laurier was either dead or in a prison camp, no one knew which.

After a while Natasha had simply stopped asking after people. For the first time she realized what a miracle it was that Alexis and his family had escaped. How had they managed to elude the Cheka? How had they gotten all the way to Zemlo without being recognized and shot? She tried to imagine what it must be like for Alexis to be a hunted man, and the thought made her very nearly frantic. She *had* to get to him before the Bolsheviks did, yet she was stuck hundreds of kilometers away, powerless to do anything but worry.

And worry she did, with a vengeance. Within a week of her arrival in Petrograd, her appetite had disappeared and she found herself starting at small sounds, turning around suddenly in the street for no reason. The idea that Alexis was marked for death by the Cheka kept her awake nights in a way that no amount of vodka could remedy, and in the mornings, when she looked into the mirror to brush her hair, she saw she was growing as grim and washed-out as Petrograd itself.

In Moscow things were a little better. She had known no one here. Even though her hotel was so cold that the water (when there was water) froze in the sink, and bed bugs and rats kept her awake at night, she preferred surroundings with no memories attached to them. Yet she was infected with a feeling of desperate haste. Something had to be done immediately, but what?

Natasha took one last look around Red Square, and then began to stride through the snow. Since she hadn't seen a cab all afternoon, there was a good chance she was going to have to walk all the way to Duncan's school. Still, she was wearing a good pair of solid English boots so it really didn't matter. What mattered was seeing Duncan and asking for her help. The famous dancer was known to be close to Lunacharsky, the Commissar of Education. If she took a liking to Natasha, she might be able to procure her an internal visa, or at least permission to travel somewhere near Zemlo. On the other hand, Duncan was said, in the West at least, to be an ardent Communist, so there was an equally good chance she would not only refuse Natasha's request but turn her over to the Cheka. Natasha started north along the river, feeling the weight of the coins in her coat. It was a big gamble, but she had no other choice.

Isadora Duncan's school was located at 20 Prechistenka Street in a mansion that had once belonged to Alexandra Balashova, a ballerina from the Moscow Ballet who had emigrated to the West. Built originally by a successful vodka distiller, the building was squat, heavy, and, like all buildings in Soviet Russia, badly in need of a coat of fresh paint. The columns flanking the entrance were chipped, and the heavy oak door had been patched hastily with no attempt to match the grain.

After knocking for several minutes to no avail, Natasha turned the knob and let herself in. It was as cold as a tomb inside and her heart sank. If the Soviet government wasn't even giving Duncan heat, what could she expect Duncan to do for her with regard to Alexis? The entrance hall sported a wide white marble staircase and two massive, icy-looking marble benches. Natasha walked toward the stairs thinking that perhaps everyone was on the second floor.

Suddenly, before she could take another step, the huge

mahogany double doors at the top burst open, and a troupe of forty or fifty children dressed in red velvet tunics came pouring down the steps. Set against the grimness of revolutionary Moscow, the children were like a vision of some better world. Laughing, all talking at once, asking a thousand questions, they crowded around Natasha. Behind the children walked a tall woman with short cropped dark red hair, about forty, swathed in a long flowing blue robe of Indian silk.

"You must be Miss Ladanova," the woman said cordially, advancing across the cold tile floor. "I'm Isadora Duncan." She shook Natasha's hand, smiling one of the most honest open smiles Natasha had seen in weeks. "I'm so glad you finally decided to pay me a visit. We should have met long ago in Paris, but fate obviously had other designs. Do you believe in fate, Miss Ladanova? Never mind, no need for you to answer that. Now let me be completely honest with you. I know this is rather abrupt, but I want you to know at the very outset that I dislike ballet. In my opinion it contorts the human body in an unnatural way. I don't see how anyone can breathe in those ridiculously tight costumes, and as for dancing on your toes, you might as well be a giraffe. But on the other hand, I respect your dedication to the art. Welcome to my school."

Natasha stared at her, trying to think of some reasonable reply to such an astounding speech. Her first impulse was to launch into an impassioned defense of ballet, but then she remembered Alexis. It wouldn't do to alienate Duncan in the first five minutes. On impulse she put her arms around two of the children, and drew them to her. "How lovely your students are, Miss Duncan."

Isadora smiled as if she had just been handed a prize, and Natasha knew she had done the right thing. The two little girls rested trustfully next to Natasha, their heads pressed against her waist. They were indeed lovely children, the prettiest and best fed she had seen in weeks. She thought of Alexis's two girls, starving to death perhaps at this very minute, and the brutality of the revolution came home to her again.

"I love children," Duncan was saying. "You must stay a week or two at least and see these two dance. They move like angels." The little girls smiled happily, although it was obvious they didn't understand a word of the strange mixture of English and French their teacher was speaking. Isadora put her hand gently on the head of the youngest and stood silently for a moment as if she had forgotten Natasha was in the room. Then, all at once, she seemed to recollect that she had a guest. "You must be cold and tired, yes?" she said briskly.

"A little."

"Well, alas, I have nothing to offer you but a warm blanket. No tea, no coffee, not even any hot water yet today due to the fuel shortage. But come along. We'll talk about dance and warm ourselves with our enthusiasm."

Dismissing the children, she led Natasha into a room furnished with low couches and blue curtains that covered most of the walls. A handsome young man lounged in one corner drinking vodka from a bottle. As Isadora and Natasha entered the room, he got up abruptly without a word and stalked out. "My friend, the poet Sergei Essenin." Isador offered Natasha a seat on one of the couches and presented her with a large, rather moth-eaten blanket.

"Now," she said in broken Russian, "*Davay pogavorim.*"

For the next six hours Natasha sat talking with Isadora Duncan in a room so cold she ordinarily would have retreated into numb silence after twenty minutes. It was an explosively intimate encounter, one Natasha could only look back on later with amazement. Isadora seemed to have none of the inhibitions of ordinary people. She was by turns enthusiastic, inspiring, maudlin, and ecstatic—jumping from one subject to another as easily as she leapt across the stage. She criticized classical ballet, explained her own rather simple theories of natural movement, shared her vision of a world in which all children would be encouraged to dance spontaneously, asked Natasha for her opinion on the best way to please Russian audiences, confided—for no obvious reason—that she was desperately in love with Essenin, who was a good fifteen years her junior.

Halfway through the conversation, Natasha found herself thinking that perhaps Duncan was crazy. How could anyone reveal so much to a total stranger? Yet at the same time she was so intelligent, so alive, that she made all of grim, cautious Soviet Russia seem like a bad, boring dream.

For almost five hours Natasha tried to decide whether or not she could trust this lovely, impulsive woman with the truth. To mention Alexis would be to take a terrible chance, one that could result in the death of at least four people. Finally she decided she had to wait until she knew Duncan better. A mistake at this point could be fatal. Shuddering,

Natasha drew the thick blanket closer about her shoulders. The Cheka could be anywhere, even in this elegant room with its soft blue hangings. One word in the wrong place, and Alexis—like Madame Laurier—might disappear forever.

For over a week Natasha walked to Duncan's school every morning, returning to her hotel through cold dark streets that chilled her to the bone. Actually, despite the terrible weather, she was glad to have something to do to take her mind off Alexis. Then, too, during those eight or nine days she learned something that influenced her own dancing profoundly: not a technique, Duncan had no technique as such to impart, but rather a new attitude toward the human body itself.

Over infinite cups of tea, Isadora patiently explained her theories, taking Natasha into the studio to illustrate them. One memorable morning they even danced together on the thick carpet, their breaths steaming in the cold air, Natasha in her best pair of toe shoes, Isadora barefoot, hair hanging down her back. Afterward, Isadora pulled Natasha to her and hugged her impulsively.

"You should give up ballet; you could dance so wonderfully if you'd only stop thinking about it."

"But I like to think. When I don't think, I get so sloppy."

Isadora laughed. "But do you have fun?"

"Oh, yes, great fun."

"You're a prisoner of technique." Isadora flopped down on the couch, breathless. "The Imperial School caught you when you were too young to know better and. . . ." She made a twisting motion with her hands.

"But," Natasha said earnestly, "technique is necessary." She fumbled for the right words. "It's what gives form to the dancing, and without form you're likely to end up with a mess." She sat down beside Isadora and pulled one of the blankets over her feet. "Also, and I know this sounds a bit strange, to my mind classical ballet mirrors a universal harmony, a world where everything is in perfect balance—call it God's world if you want to."

"There isn't any such world, or any God either for that matter."

"But even if there isn't, we can create it in art, at least for a few hours at a time, can't we?" Natasha leaned forward, impassioned. "If perfection doesn't exist, then why not *make* it exist."

"Ah, you Russians," Isadora said with a laugh, "so sincere,

so obsessed with the big questions: God, death, perfection. For me dancing is something simple, spontaneous. You think too much."

"No, I don't."

"Yes, you do. In fact, you've been thinking abut something for days. Now," she put up one hand, "I know I'm changing the subject, but don't bother to tell me I've made a mistake, because I never make mistakes about things like this. Something's on your mind; I can see it in your body when you dance. You're worried about something, aren't you?"

A sudden wave of fear made Natasha feel as if she were suffocating. Was she so transparent? If her thoughts really were written all over her face, then she didn't stand a chance—not in Soviet Russia with the Cheka listening at every keyhole. On the other hand, maybe the time had come to tell Duncan the truth. After all, the longer she put it off, the greater the possibility she'd be too late to help Alexis.

"Well, what is it? Come now, we've become too good friends to have secrets from each other." Isadora crossed her arms over her chest and sat back against the cushions. There was curiosity in her eyes, perhaps even sympathy, but could she be trusted? There was no way to know in advance. Natasha took a deep breath. She thought of everything, of Alexis, of the Cheka, of the danger not only to him but to herself, and then quickly, before she could change her mind, she recounted her vain attempts to get an internal visa; rapidly, without pausing, she spoke of Alexis and his family and the real reason she had come to Moscow.

Tears came to Isadora's eyes, and her soft round face grew solemn as she heard Natasha's story. "You poor thing; how perfectly terrible," she said at last. The idea that the Grand Duke had two young daughters with him particularly upset her. How could anyone threaten the lives of children for something as ephemeral as politics? Children were so dear to her—she had lost two of her own. Taking a large, spotlessly clean handkerchief from the pocket of her robe, she wiped her eyes and blew her nose.

Natasha shouldn't get the wrong impression. She, Isadora Duncan, approved of the revolution in very nearly every way; it was a wonderful new start for mankind. Lenin was God as Christ was God, because God is Love, and Christ and Lenin were all Love. Her own *Dance Slav,* in which she personified the suffering people, had moved audiences all over Russia.

126

Nevertheless, the Bolsheviks were human and this time they had obviously made a terrible mistake.

Putting away her handkerchief, Isadora announced she was touched that Natasha had confided in her in such a life-and-death matter, but then that was as it should be. After all, they were both dancers, both dedicated to the same art. It was obvious Alexis and his lovely young daughters would have to be smuggled out of Russia. It was a pity life demanded such subterfuges, but she promised to do what she could.

What Isadora Duncan could do when she set her mind to it turned out to be quite considerable. The next morning, when she came down to the lobby of her hotel, Natasha found a large, brown official envelope waiting for her. Inside was an internal visa, authorized by Lunacharsky himself, granting her permission to travel to Vychegda, a small town located only ten kilometers from Zemlo.

Vychegda consisted of two long rows of dilapidated hovels sitting on either side of a ditch purporting to be a road. It was a place impossible for a stranger to pass through without attracting attention. At the house of the *predsedatel,* or village chairman—the Soviet equivalent of a mayor—crowds of curious, ragged children surrounded Natasha, begging for kopecks and sweets. The Chairman, after examining her passport and asking every possible question about who she was and where she was going, insisted on stoking up an ancient samovar, laying a much-mended cloth across the rough wooden table, and serving her a thin beet borsch in a battered brass bowl that looked as if it had been knocking around since the time of Catherine the Great.

"A school inspector, eh?" The Chairman leaned toward Natasha, his breath reeking of stale cabbage. He was an old man with a tobacco-stained yellow beard and a large bulbous nose.

"Yes. The Party is going to establish schools in all rural areas." The lie about being a school inspector wasn't a great story to hide behind, but since she had a visa signed by the Commissar of Education there was at least an even possibility that no one would bother to check.

The Chairman blew his nose between his fingers and wiped them on his tattered jacket. "My oldest boy can read a bit," he said proudly. "One of the priests taught him."

"Where's the priest now?"

"Oh, we had to shoot him, of course. Counterrevolutionaries

don't last long in Vychegda, Comrade Inspector." Natasha swallowed her fear and forced herself to finish the rest of the borsch, aware the Chairman was watching for a reaction.

"I'll mention your zealousness in my report, Comrade," she said evenly. "Moscow will be pleased."

The Chairman grinned, revealing the fact that he had lost most of his teeth. He looked convinced, but there was no way to tell for sure. Taking a sip of tea, Natasha attempted to change the subject.

It was late afternoon before she could get away, and the weather had turned foul. A bitter wind flecked with snow blew out of the north, making the ten kilometers seem more like twenty. By the time she reached Zemlo, half snow-blinded and so numb she could hardly think, it was almost twilight. As she struggled up over the last hill carrying the heavy parcel she had brought all the way from Moscow, Natasha heared the sound of an axe echoing through the fir trees. A small peasant's hut of unpeeled logs stood in the clearing, its steeply pitched roof extending nearly to the ground. In front, a tall man in a long shabby, sheepskin jacket was chopping wood, sending up a furious spume of chips.

"Good evening," Natasha called out as she struggled through the drifts. As a child in Archangel she had learned that peasants were generally suspicious of strangers and liked to be greeted from a good distance. *"Dobriy vecher."*

The man straightened up, lowered his axe, and stared across the fifty-some meters of snow that separated them. His battered fur hat was pulled low over a weatherbeaten face covered with a ragged beard. A scar ran from his eye to his chin—the kind of scar that could only have been made by a cossack's *nagaika.* "Who's there?" he said suspiciously. The sound of his familiar voice startled Natasha so much she stopped short. My God, it was Alexis. She felt a rush of joy that almost made her drunk. For weeks she had been trying to face the fact that perhaps he was dead, and now here he was, standing in front of her, healthy and in one piece. Dear Alexis. Natasha stood rooted in the snow, not knowing whether to laugh or cry. She wanted to call out to him, but she was so moved the words stuck in her throat.

"Who's out there?" Alexis raised the axe to waist-level, and took a step forward, the fresh snow grating under his boots.

"Alexis, it's me. Natasha." Throwing down her parcel she began to run toward him, her boots slapping as she struggled through the knee-high drifts.

Alexis peered at her through the shadows, wary as a wolf, looking for a moment as if he might turn and run. Suddenly his whole face relaxed, and he broke into a grin. "Tasha!" Throwing his axe down in the snow, he strode toward her. They met under the shadows of the giant fir trees, collided in a passionate embrace that nearly knocked Natasha off her feet. Almost before she knew it, she was in his arms, clasped in a bear hug that took her breath away.

"*Milaya, dushechka,*" his voice shook with emotion, "what a wonder. I never thought I'd see you again."

Taking off her gloves, Natasha touched his face with the warm palms of her hands, ran one finger along the scar. He was dirty, terribly thin with a hunted expression in his eyes, yet somehow he managed to carry the rags he was wearing as if they were his old white and gold uniform. How handsome he was even now. No one would ever mistake him for a peasant—which wasn't, when she thought of it, altogether a good thing.

"You're crying," Alexis said gently. He wiped away her tears with his sleeve and then laughed. "It's just like the day you left. You were crying then, too. I think my youngest daughter Elena, who is crazy about moving pictures, would call this a *rerun.*" Natasha grinned. "That's better," Alexis said. "Cry in this weather and you're likely to freeze solid."

"Alexis I missed you so much." She wanted to tell him of the loneliness of exile, of the hundreds of times she had thought of him and regretted leaving, but there were no words strong enough to encompass the last four years.

"Darling, Natasha," Alexis drew her to him and kissed her gently and then with passion. "My God," he said, drawing back abruptly. "I'll never forgive the Bolsheviks for keeping us apart." He paused for a moment and cleared his throat. "My wife is here, you know, and the two girls." He dropped his arms to his sides. "Things are in such a mess."

The hut Alexis ushered her into was plastered with manure, lit by a single coal oil lamp, closed and smoky with no furniture, not even a bench. A huge clay peasant's stove filled half the room, on one end of which, under a pile of ragged blankets, lay two girls in patched brown smocks. At the other, hotter, end a short woman in a man's overcoat and felt boots was stirring something in an iron pot.

"My dears," Alexis said, "allow me to present Mademoiselle Natalia Yakovlevna Ladanova, formerly of the Imperial

Ballet." Natasha felt a moment of panic as Alexis's wife turned toward her. Surely Anastasia must resent her. She steeled herself for a cold reception, for anger and disdain. Anastasia couldn't possibly enjoy meeting her husband's mistress. She might even order Natasha to leave at once, and it was a long, cold walk back to Vychegda.

"My dear Mademoiselle Ladanova," Anastasia's voice was low and thin, like the voice of a young child. She was undeniably plain, her hair streaked with gray, her hands callused, yet there was no hint of envy or resentment in her soft, slate gray eyes, only a timid sweetness. Extending one hand as if she were still in her drawing room in St. Petersburg, she smiled shyly. "This is an unexpected pleasure."

Natasha relaxed under the warmth of Anastasia's smile, relieved that she wouldn't have to trudge ten kilometers in the dark.

"Elena, Vera, this is Mademoiselle Ladanova, an old friend of your father's." Elena, who must have been all of thirteen, coughed and hid her face behind the blanket, but Vera the older of the two rose to the occasion. Pulling the edge of the cover up around her shoulders, she made a small formal curtsy.

"Good evening, Mademoiselle," she said sweetly in perfect French. "*Enchantée.*"

"You will stay for dinner, won't you." Anastasia poured the contents of the iron pot onto a single, large, unglazed plate, cracked at the edges. A few gray potatoes lay on a pile of equally gray kasha.

"Yes, thank you." Natasha looked at the small pile of potatoes, the hungry girls watching her politely. Then, setting her parcel on the ground, she opened it and began laying the contents out beside the plate: two slightly moldy cheeses, five loaves of black bread, sausages, pickled herring, home-brewed vodka, three packs of tea, cooking oil, two kilos of white rice—all bought in Moscow, with much haggling, for the exorbitant price of three gold coins and a fistful of paper rubles.

"I didn't know there was this much food left in the world," Anastasia said softly. "Bless you." Going over to the other end of the stove, Anastasia put her arms around her daughters and sat quietly for a moment, stroking their hair. Then she got up briskly, picked up a knife, and began to slice off thick chunks of fragrant black bread.

For the next three days Natasha slept, ate, and lived with

Alexis and his family, coming to love them all as if they were her own. Elena was shy but bright; Vera laughing and impulsive; Anastasia infinitely kind; Alexis as witty and irrepressible as ever despite the fact that he had been reduced to living on kasha and potatoes. For three days, drinking hot tea and huddling together for warmth, they talked endlessly as the wind whipped huge drifts up around the cabin, sealing them off from the outside world. By the end of that time Natasha had come to like Anastasia so much she almost regretted ever having gotten involved with Alexis. As long as she and Anastasia had inhabited different worlds, it hadn't seemed to make any difference, but now Natasha could see that Anastasia must have suffered when she discovered that her husband had a young, beautiful mistress. Natasha wondered if finding out about her and Alexis had been as painful for Anastasia as finding out about Anya and Sergei had been. Had Anastasia cried and felt as if her life were over? Had she suffered the way Natasha had suffered? Natasha hoped not and she was especially careful, as the days went by, not to give Anastasia further cause for worry.

The story of the family's escape from Petersburg was little less than miraculous. They had stayed far too long, through almost all of that terrible autumn of 1917 as Kerensky's government fell apart and the Bolsheviks consolidated their power.

"It was my fault," Alexis admitted. "I thought I could do something, bring some semblance of reason to the disaster that was overtaking the country, and then, when I saw I couldn't, I felt honor bound to stay and try anyway." He turned to Natasha, his face as serious as she had ever seen it. "You know," he said, "it's a funny thing about honor—all my life it's been one of my chief concerns, but now I think it's fading from the world, that perhaps in the brutally practical future our country has embarked on no one will even know the meaning of the word. So I'm an antique, a museum piece."

Anastasia put her hand softly on her husband's shoulder. Threading his fingers through hers, Alexis looked at her fondly. "Anastasia wouldn't leave without me," he said, "absolutely refused."

"Of course not," Anastasia smiled sweetly. "Whatever could you have been thinking of. Our place was with you." Natasha felt a pang of jealousy. Would she ever belong to someone so completely that she'd be willing to do as Anastasia had done?

She thought of Sergei, and then quickly put him out of her mind. There was no loyalty there, no possibility of a shared life. Only craziness and pain.

Alexis took a sip of tea and continued in a subdued tone. "We needed democracy, a government that actually responded to the people, but what Lenin gave us that December was the Cheka."

Although they had already gone into hiding in Petrograd, the Cheka had come close to finding them. Members of the Romanov family were of the highest priority, so much so that it had been dangerous for Anastasia or the girls to do the simplest things, like standing in line to buy bread. In late January friends had warned them they were about to be arrested and they had fled at the last minute, using their servants' passports, hiding in boxcars and woodsheds, crouching in freezing water under bridges while Red soldiers stood overhead.

In February, after terrible hardships, they had reached the country estate of Anastasia's parents only to find it burned to the ground and everyone dead but a few old peasants. Then Elena's lungs had become inflamed and they had wasted precious months nursing her in an abandoned boxcar. Night after night, Alexis had gone out under the cover of darkness to steal food from root cellars, leaving Anastasia and the girls to wonder if he would ever come back. They had sat in darkness for hours on pallets of moldy straw, praying for him, singing hymns to keep their spirits up. Somehow they had managed to survive. But always there had been the feeling of being hunted, of knowing that any moment could be their last.

In the summer of 1918 they had finally arrived at Zemlo just in time to hear that the Tsar and his entire family had been murdered. Using their false passports, Anastasia and Alexis had posed as their own servants, but there had been problems from the very beginning. For one thing, they spoke too well, rousing suspicions every time they went into Vychegda. For a few years there had been too much turmoil in the region for anyone to go to the trouble of investigating, but now that the Civil War was over and things had quieted down the Chairman had started to make inquiries. Thanks to the protection of some peasants who had known Alexis as a boy, and because they had lived virtually as hermits, they had managed so far to escape the Cheka. Still, it was obviously only a matter of time before they were found.

"So you see," Alexis said, throwing more logs into the stove, "you came at the right moment." The girls passed around tea laced with some of the precious vodka and tiny slivers of cheese on black bread, and the discussion grew more animated. Elena and Vera laughed, Anastasia's pale face flushed with happiness, and even Alexis seemed to relax. Now that Natasha had arrived they felt they had a chance, slim perhaps, but still a chance. For the first time in months, they discussed the future. What was the best way to travel? What routes were still open? Should they try to disguise themselves as peasants, or use the false passports they had and hope for the best? Sitting around the great stove, they formed and discarded plan after plan for getting out of the country.

The problem was Elena, who had never really recovered her health. She was obviously too ill to travel in any way that might expose her to the cold, but none of them was even willing to consider any strategy that involved leaving Elena behind to join them later. Finally, after a heated debate, it was decided that Natasha should return to Vychegda and bribe the Chairman to issue them travel permits—under assumed names—to go south to Odessa, where they could hire a fishing boat to take them across the Black Sea to Turkey.

"You want what?"

"Four travel permits and four tickets?"

"For whom did you say?"

"My aunt, uncle, and two young nieces."

"Hmm, I see." The Chairman picked a splinter out of the table and began to pick at his teeth with it. His tiny suspicious eyes were stuck in the folds of his cheeks like currants in a loaf of unbaked Easter bread. Natasha tried to keep the disgust out of her face. For three hours they had been having the same conversation, repeated with endless variations. She wanted four tickets, four permits, and the price kept going up.

The Chairman fingered the gold coins that lay on the table. "It's a pity your relatives don't have proper documents, Comrade Inspector."

"I told you, their house was burned by White soldiers. They lost everything."

"A pity all the same." The Chairman smiled at her blandly, and took another swig of vodka from a tin drinking cup. "I should turn this problem over to one of the Comrades on the District Soviet." He looked at her sharply. "You'd have no objection to that, I suppose?"

Natasha struggled to keep her face expressionless. "Of course not, only there's the problem of the little girl, my niece. She's sick."

"And needs to go south at once?"

"Exactly." Reluctantly Natasha took another gold coin out of her pocket and placed it on the table next to the others. "Surely exceptions can be made."

The Chairman looked at the gold with unconcealed greed. "Exceptions can be expensive. There are certain risks involved." He picked at his teeth vigorously. "Very expensive."

"That's all I have," Natasha lied.

"A pity."

Rising to her feet, she swept the gold angrily into her hand. "If this isn't enough, we can wait for the District Soviet to make inquiries. In fact, I'd appreciate it if you'd direct me to the nearest representative of the Cheka. Counterrevolutionaries can appear in the most unlikely places." My God, what if he called her bluff? The Cheka would shoot Alexis and his family on the spot and her, too, probably. Natasha clasped the gold coins tightly in her hand and tried to keep from trembling. "There are irregularities here in Vychegda, Comrade," she said sternly.

The Chairman blanched and dropped his toothpick. "Please calm yourself, Comrade," he pleaded. "Arrangements can be made. The little girl, as you say, is ill. Human compassion, special circumstances. . . ." He stretched out a dirty hand with badly bitten nails, and, without a word, Natasha spilled the gold coins into his palm. "Ah," he grinned, "what a hard bargain you drive." He bit the coins one by one, stowed them in the ragged pocket of his shirt, picked up the tin cup, took a deep swig of vodka, and coughed moistly, wiping his lips with the back of his hand. "You must have peasant blood in your veins, Comrade."

Outside, somewhere deep in the forest, a wolf howled a long, eerie howl. The moon was full, but inside the tiny cabin, sealed against the cold, it was so dark Natasha could hardly see her hand in front of her face. Above her, on the heated platform, Elena, Vera, and Anastasia were all asleep, breathing softly. Natasha and Alexis were sitting on a pile of blankets with their backs against the warm stove taking small sips of hot tea and talking in whispers. They had just ripped the money out of Natasha's coat, counted it, and rewrapped most of the coins and bills in a compact belt of braided rags that Alexis planned to wear tied around his waist during the long trip south, which would begin tomorrow morning at the train station in Vychegda.

For a while they spoke of the journey, the inevitable delays, Elena's health, the problems the family might encounter once they got to Odessa, which was a Red stronghold. Then, abruptly, Alexis fell silent.

"Is something wrong?" Natasha carefully put the tea glass down so none of the precious contents would spill. Firelight fanned through the door of the stove, making Alexis's face appear to waver in the shadows.

"Natasha," Alexis unbuttoned his sheepskin jacket slowly and sat for a moment gazing into the fire, "we've had a good life together, but I think we should face the fact that we may never see each other again."

"Don't say such things."

Alexis shook his head. "I have a feeling—call it a presentiment if you will—that Anastasia, the girls, and I may not get out of Russia."

"That's a morbid thing to say." She passed him the tea glass, and he put it down without drinking from it.

"Believe me, I hope I'm wrong. But just in case I'm right, there's something I want to say to you, that is," he cleared his throat, stopped, began again. "I want you to know that I've always been very fond of you."

"Alexis, are you trying to say that you loved me?"

"I still do, actually."

"Oh," she was touched, and a little guilty at the same time. He'd done so much for her, cared for her more than anyone had, and all the while she'd been obsessed with Sergei. Why couldn't she have given Alexis more of what he'd given her? She thought of Anastasia, asleep just above them. Was Alexis Anastasia's Sergei? Why was it love so rarely matched love?

"I'll miss you, Natasha."

"Don't talk that way. By spring you'll be in Paris. We'll be drinking your health together in the Café du Dome."

"Do they have good wine?" he forced a smile.

"The best Montrachet. And you can meet my friend Zazie and her son, Leonce. You can't imagine how beautiful Paris is when the chestnut trees are in bloom. Spring's the best time."

"Then come here and let me say good-bye until spring." He drew her to him, lifted her face to his, and kissed her softly. Then he held her for a long time, until the fire burned low in the stove and the shadows turned cold. Finally he released her without a word, and they crawled up onto the platform to sleep, Natasha between Vera and Elena, Alexis next to Anastasia.

Many hours later, Natasha woke to the sound of the cabin door splintering. An avalanche of frigid air tumbled into the tiny room, overpowering the heat; harsh white light from a dozen lanterns spilled over the startled sleepers, waking Elena and Vera who sat up blinking and confused. For a moment, all Natasha could see were shadows.

"Citizen Romanov," at the foot of the sleeping platform a short, stocky Red Army officer pointed a drawn pistol squarely at Alexis's head, "you're under arrest." The first thing Natasha felt as she heard those words was a fear so intense she had to put her fist in her mouth to keep from screaming out loud. They were trapped, cornered with no way out. "Get up," the officer barked, "and put your hands where we can see them."

Elena and Vera began to cry. "Hush, hush." Natasha drew the girls to her, trying to quiet them, her fear turning into anger. Barbarians, idiots, breaking in in the middle of the night, terrifying children. Behind the officer stood the Chairman from Vychegda, grinning nastily, flanked by four soldiers, all heavily armed. Cowards, all of them. Afraid to do their dirty deeds in the daylight.

"By whose authority am I under arrest?" Alexis stood up, ignoring the gun.

"On the authority of Comrade Dzerjinsky, head of the Extraordinary Commission for the Suppression of Counter-revolution." The officer enunciated each word coldly and precisely. For the first time Natasha noticed how young he was—twenty at the most. He had the face of an adolescent boy, blotched with acne, fat-cheeked, a face that would have looked innocent, even a little stupid if it hadn't been so full of hate.

"It's the Cheka," Anastasia's voice was barely a whisper but so permeated with terror it made the hairs on Natasha's arms stand up.

Alexis montioned for Anastasia to be silent. "And on what charges do you arrest me?" he demanded.

"Counterrevolution, espionage." The young officer surveyed Alexis with unconcealed hostility. "You're enemies of the people."

"That's ridiculous. My family and I have lived in absolute isolation. We're not spies; we're not enemies of anyone; we've done nothing."

"Shut up." The officer motioned to the soldiers. "Take all the women outside, except Citizeness Ladanova."

"Oh, my God," Anastasia moaned, "you're going to shoot us aren't you, just as you did the Tsar and his poor family. Please don't hurt my girls. They're just children."

Natasha grabbed onto Elena and Vera, holding them against her body. Both girls were trembling with fear. "You can't have them."

"Calm down, Citizeness," the officer said sharply. "We're sending the whole pack to Moscow. You can visit them at the Lubyanka Prison."

Natasha faced him stubbornly. "No."

"Volodya." The officer made a quick motion and a soldier strode up to Natasha, planted the butt of his gun in her stomach, and shoved her over backward. As she lay in a heap on the floor trying to catch her breath, she heard them laughing at her.

"Lots of spirit in that one," the Chairman observed.

Dizzy and a little sick, she struggled to her feet. Elena, Vera, and Anastasia had been herded over to the door. Natasha made a move toward them, but the soldier stopped her again, shoving the butt of his gun against her stomach.

"Want another tumble, *baba*," he grinned.

"Go to hell," Natasha hissed through clenched teeth.

Anastasia stood in the doorway, her arms around her two daughters. Her pale face was flushed, her feet planted stubbornly. "We can't go outside; it's too cold, and my little girl's ill."

"*Chort vozmi*," the officer cursed. "What a stubborn pack." He motioned for one of the soldiers to wrap a blanket around Elena's shoulders. "The girl's plenty warm now, so shut up and don't cause any more trouble."

"Where are you taking us?"

"Like I said, back to Moscow." He looked away uneasily, not meeting Anastasia's eyes. "Don't worry, you'll have a heated compartment to travel in. The little brat will be just fine."

"And my husband?"

"We want to question him for a bit, and then we'll send him along after you."

A look of immense relief crossed Anastasia's face, a relief Natasha didn't share. The man was lying.

"Don't go, Anastasia.'"

"Tell her to shut up," the officer said, "or she's going to get hurt."

"Natasha, please." Anastasia turned to the officer. "I want to say good-bye to my husband." Pushing past the soldiers, she kissed Alexis lightly on the lips, and the two embraced. Then pulling the blanket more tightly around Vera and Elena, she allowed the soldiers to lead them out of the cabin.

The officer shrugged. Sitting down on the edge of the sleeping platform, he took off one felt boot and began to massage his toes. "You aristocrats are nothing but trouble." His feet were bound with dirty rags that gave off a damp, sour odor. "And now, Citizen," he said to Alexis, "we need to know where the money is."

"What money?"

"Yesterday Citizeness Ladanova was scattering gold coins all over Vychegda—gold obviously stolen from the people by the Romanov family—and I have orders to confiscate it." He scratched the sole of his foot, put his boot back on, and yawned.

"He didn't steal it from anyone," Natasha said. "It's my money."

"Be quiet." Alexis turned to the officer. "She's lying; she's totally innocent. Here." He pulled the makeshift money belt out from under his shirt and tossed it onto the sleeping platform. Coins spilled out of the rags: dollars, rubles, Swiss francs. "You'll find all the gold you want there, just let her go." Alexis tore open the belt, spilling the rest of the gold onto the blankets. "If you let my wife, and children, and Mademoiselle Ladanova go, you can have all of this, every bit. I'll lie to Dzerjinsky's men in Moscow, tell them I spent it all on bribes, and there was nothing left. Look at it man; there's a fortune there."

The young officer scooped the gold and bills off the sleeping platform into the pocket of his overcoat. "Good," he said. His thick face flushed. "*Ochen xarasho.*"

"Then you'll let them go?"

"Vladya, Kolya." Two of the soldiers reappeared, guns drawn. "Take Citizen Romanov outside to rejoin his family."

"But are you letting them go?" Alexis persisted.

One of the soldiers nudged Alexis in the middle of the back with his pistol. "*Poshli*," he barked, "get going."

Alexis took three steps toward the door, then turned suddenly. Pushing past the soldiers, he strode over to Natasha, grabbed her hand, and pressed it to his lips. "They're going to shoot us, Natasha, all of us." For the rest of her life Natasha remembered the expression on his face at that instant. "Good-bye my dear. Pray for us. I don't mind much for myself, but the girls are so young."

"Listen," the officer said, "no one's going to be shot without a proper trial, get it." He motioned to the two soldiers. "Take Citizen Romanov outside. And you," he pointed to Natasha, "just shut up and don't make any more trouble."

What would he do next? Shoot her? Torture her to find out everything she knew? Fear prickled up Natasha's spine, and she braced herself against the edge of the sleeping platform. She didn't imagine she would last very long under torture, but at least she didn't know anything worth knowing. Maybe they'd just deport her. She tried to pray, but her mind was a blank. All she could think of was how cold it must be for Elena. Poor child.

"Do you smoke?"

"What?"

"I said do you smoke?" The officer was smiling an oily, ingratiating smile. The question was so odd, so completely out of place, that all she could do was stare at him dumbfounded. Why did he care if she smoked or not?

"No."

"Tough luck. It's a comfort when you're breaking your back at some rotten job or other." He sat down on the edge of the sleeping platform, pulled a pouch of Turkish tobacco from his pocket, and deftly rolled a cigarette. "I hear you're a famous dancer."

Natasha nodded, not trusting herself to speak. "Well, I've never seen fancy dancing myself; I used to work in a foundry and after a hard day all any of the fellows wanted to do was drink themselves blind and fall into the sack with a girl." He inhaled a long draft of smoke, and then exhaled it through his nose. "Say, I suppose I should thank you on behalf of the Soviet State."

"For what?"

"For leading us to Romanov and his brood." Then, at the look of horror on Natasha's face he added, "Don't take it so hard, girl. The Cheka's been watching you ever since you applied for a visa. They knew that sooner or later you'd lead them to your Grand Duke." He patted his coat pocket. "I have your whole file right here, so I know all the dirt about you." He stubbed out his cigarette on the edge of the stove. "I have orders to send you back to Moscow, but before that. . . ."

The rest of his sentence was interrupted by a burst of gunfire. Natasha bolted for the door. It was light outside, the sky purple and bruised-looking. The officer grabbed her from behind roughly and pulled her back inside. "Where the hell do you think you're going?" he said angrily, turning her around, forcing her to face him.

But it was too late. She had already seen the soldiers putting away their pistols—and the four bodies sprawled face down on the fresh snow.

9

Vienna

Natasha stood in front of the Plague Monument, a graceful obelisk of granite angels and stone clouds that swirled upward toward the clear Viennese sky. She sat down on the curb, feeling a little dizzy. Three passing nuns, their white headdresses waltzing in the wind, gave her curious looks, but she ignored them. She didn't need their charity or conversation; what she needed was to be left alone to sort out her thoughts.

She had been to Vienna half a dozen times before but without really seeing it, passing from rehearsal to performance, from the Opera House to her hotel with only a quick turn around the Ring Strasse or an occasional stop at a *Konditorei* for a cup of Turkish coffee and a slice of Sacher torte. But this time was different: for the past six days she had walked obsessively, seeing every street in the city, every famous building, museum, palace, and church until she felt like a demented tourist or an amateur mapmaker.

She had needed to return to a place free of associations and memories, a place without a past where the cut and turned fabric of her life could be put together again into a sensible garment. She had to come to terms with the death of Alexis and his family, pull herself together, not collapse into depression or hysteria. Natasha thought back on Moscow with a shudder, remembering the Cheka's main prison on Lubyanka Square where she had been held for nearly a week in isolation in a cold concrete cell without windows. Through the ventilation ducts had come the screams of those being interrogated, as well as whispered words of encouragement from other prisoners. For the first few days she had done nothing but pray for Alexis and his family, pushing away her own fear, trying not to start in terror every time she heard footsteps in the corridor. Then she realized that to keep her sanity she would have to do something more.

On the third day of her imprisonment she had begun a

rigorous program of exercise. Each morning she climbed off the steel sleeping platform, ate the black bread and wormy kasha that had been slipped under the door during the night, and began to rehearse herself mercilessly as if she were preparing for a major performance. She was stiff at first, awkward, frightened, her body unwieldy. The cell was too small to actually dance in, so she was reduced to running through the basic positions over and over, as if she were once more a beginning student in the Imperial School: *demi-plié*, *grand plié*, *rond de jambe*. By working she was able not to give in to despair.

As it turned out, her fears were groundless; she was never interrogated, never even taken to the main office for routine questioning. Instead, one morning two grim faced guards appeared at her cell and conducted her to the intake room of the prison where, without a word, she was given back her clothing and passport. Evidently she was being released, but why? Had Isadora Duncan interceded on her behalf? Had there been some kind of public outcry about her arrest? Had the Cheka feared an international scandal or simply decided she didn't have any information worth knowing? Taken to the station under military escort, she was placed on a train to Austria, her Soviet visa permanently revoked. She never found out why they decided to release her.

Getting up from the curb in front of the Plague Monument, Natasha began to walk rapidly down the Graben Singer Strasse toward the Cathedral of St. Stephen with its gaudy yellow-and-black tiled roof and lacy spires. She would spend the morning wandering through the fourteenth-century nave and then, in the afternoon, she would take a bus out to Schönbrunn Palace for a stroll through the famous formal gardens. And after that?

As she strode down the wide cobblestone street she felt vertigo again, that sense that the world was dancing around her. A thought came to her mind, but she pushed it away quickly. Still it came back, insistent, like a cat that wanted feeding: *Why was she dizzy so much of the time? Was something wrong with her body?* Natasha took a deep breath and strode forward, putting the vertigo behind her. Ridiculous. She was in good health, a little pale and shaken from her imprisonment, perhaps, but basically sound. It was nerves, nothing more. She flexed her arms and felt the strength in her legs. Give her a stage, and she could dance for hours without stopping. But still. . . .

It had been coming on for some time, but she had noticed it most when she had been in prison: the tenderness of her breasts, the swelling in her abdomen. Her urine had smelled strange, her hair had lost its luster: she had told herself she must see a doctor as soon as she got back to the West, yet for some reason she hadn't. For the six days she had been in Vienna she had done nothing but tramp from monument to monument. Why couldn't she simply make an appointment? It wasn't like her to neglect her health this way, something was stopping her. Perhaps she should head over to 19 Bergstrasse and see Dr. Freud.

Another wave of dizziness came over her and she stopped, grabbing onto a wrought iron lamppost for support. The whole street waltzed in front of her now: cabs, pedestrians, even the shop windows turned in three-quarter time. Frightened, Natasha held on until the vertigo passed. Then she walked slowly up to the Ring Strasse and caught a bus to her pension. St. Stephen's would have to wait until another day.

"Please sit down Frau Ladanova." Herr Dr. Gruber was a short, balding man whose desk was piled with dusty medical books. His office had turned out to be located in the suburbs on the unfashionable side of town. Natasha had had to change buses three times, and with each change a bit of Vienna had disappeared until the bland ugly streets had become like bland streets anywhere, full of the promise of anonymity. Despite the inconvenience, Natasha was relieved. There was no chance that any touring members of the Ballet de la Cité would bring their sprained ankles and shinsplints to Herr Dr. Gruber.

"Thank you, Doctor." She sat down in a chair whose well-worn green plush testified to the fact that Dr. Gruber was a busy if not wealthy man. The chair was enfolding and rather comforting. She crossed her carefully gloved hands in her lap, wondering how many other women had sat in it waiting for the same verdict.

Dr. Gruber cleared his throat in a businesslike fashion and picked up the brown folder that contained her chart. "Your tests have come back, Frau Ladanova, confirming my diagnosis."

"And the results?"

Dr. Gruber smiled. "As we thought."

Natasha tried to keep her voice steady but she could feel herself shaking. "Are you sure?"

"My dear Frau," Dr. Gruber said, "there's not the slightest

doubt. My professional estimate of the situation is that you're about three months along."

"*Gaspodi.*" Involuntarily Natasha's hand went to her abdomen, feeling the swelling she had studiously ignored for so many weeks. Rapidly she counted off the time in her mind: February, January, December. She saw Sergei's room in the Algonquin again, the look on his face when he'd told her he was marrying Anya. What a mess. How could he have done this to her on top of everything else? For a moment she was angry, and then, suddenly, she felt a nostalgia and longing so great it almost made her ill. There was a living child inside her body—Sergei's child—and she wanted it. But that was crazy, out of the question. She couldn't support a child. Tears sprang to her eyes, and she wiped them away feeling confused, bewildered, and trapped.

Dr. Gruber offered her a handkerchief and made a sympathetic sound at the back of his throat that would have been comic if she hadn't been so upset. "Surely, my dear Frau, you must have suspected something of the sort when you failed to have your monthly menses."

"Dancers don't have regular periods," she snapped. What a fool the man was. No, she was being unfair to him. He was a perfectly competent doctor. There was no reason why he should know her body wasn't like the body of other women.

"Ah," Dr. Gruber seemed taken aback, "I didn't know you were a dancer. What sort?"

"Ballet."

"Ah," he looked at her with new respect.

"Herr Doctor."

"Yes?"

She searched for some way to say what had to be said. "Dancing is the only way I have of supporting myself; I can't rejoin my company in this condition and I have no way to take care of a child." She stumbled over the word *child* but plowed ahead. The words cut her. She wanted to beg for help or protection, for some way to go through with the pregnancy. Half a dozen thoughts ran through her mind at once: she could borrow money from Zazie—no, Zazie didn't have any money; she could go back to Paris, but there would be a scandal and she couldn't dance anyway; she could go to a convent where the nuns took in women in her condition, but then they'd probably demand she give the child up for adoption. She could ask Sergei for help, beg him to give her enough money to raise their child, but with Anya in her sixth

144

month and holding the purse strings, the chances of getting a penny out of Sergei were so slim as to be nonexistent. Natasha took a deep breath, and asked the one question she had not wanted to ask. "Do you know of any way . . . that is, can you recommend anyone . . . to help me out of this situation?"

Dr. Gruber's face froze. "You're not married?"

"No."

"And the father?"

"Married to someone else."

"A bad situation. You should have been more careful Fraulein. Girls who play with fire get burned."

Natasha was so angry at the unfairness of his reprimand that it was all she could do to keep from yelling at him that she was suffering over this decision, that she was in pain, that he could have no idea how hard it was for her, but somehow she managed to hold her tongue. Looking down at her hands so he couldn't see the defiance in her eyes, she made her voice soft and pleading. "Please, Doctor," she said, "I'm alone in this city; I don't have anyone else to turn to," words that at least had the virtue of being true.

Dr. Gruber was obviously flattered. His small eyes glittered and he tapped the ends of his fingers together in a staccato. "You're an artist?"

"Yes."

"A dancer."

"Yes."

"Well, my dear Fraulein, let us just say that in Vienna we sometimes make exceptions for artists." He picked up a pen and scribbled something on a sheet of paper. "Here's an address. If anyone asks you where you got it, you don't know—do you understand?" He looked at her sternly. "I could lose my license for giving you this."

Natasha walked up and down in front of the blank gray building for over two hours, holding the crumpled address Dr. Gruber had given her wadded up in her fist. In her purse were five hundred schillings, the last of her Swiss bank account, received by cable from Lucerne yesterday morning. For four hundred, she could have the abortion, leaving her just enough to buy a train ticket back to Paris where she could rejoin the Ballet de la Cité as if nothing had happened. Fouchier had recently written a long, profuse, witty letter begging her to return without delay. The public missed her; there were constant inquiries. Her trip to Russia had made her a romantic figure; the mere mention of her name in connection with a ballet would guarantee a sold-out house. Cocteau asked after her almost daily; Gertrude Stein had expressed a desire to meet her.

Walking up to the big double doors, Natasha looked at the neat brass nameplate. The operation would be clean, safe, harmless—rather like extracting a tooth, a pleasant-voiced lady had told her on the phone. She was to wear low-heeled shoes, bring aspirin, and under no circumstances eat any solid food for at least eighteen hours before her appointment.

So easy, so simple, yet for the past two hours she had been paralyzed by indecision and second thoughts. The more she tried to sort things out, the more uncertain she became. This child growing inside her was all she had left of Sergei, a living bond between them that not even he could break, but why would she want such a bond? How could she possibly care so much about the child of a man who obviously didn't love her? It was so confusing. Had she, in some way she didn't fully understand, transferred her feelings from Sergei to the baby? Or was she still in shock from Alexis's death, operating on the same kind of instinct that made women want to give birth after great wars and natural disasters.

And then there was the moral question—equally confusing. She'd never been a particularly religious person except in times of crisis, but now she discovered compunctions in herself that she'd never suspected. Many people considered abortion murder—certainly the state did since it had made the operation illegal. And the Church? She searched her memory trying to recall the Russian Orthodox position on abortion and came up with a blank. As far as she could remember, it had never been mentioned in her presence, not even during her childhood back in Archangel.

Looked at rationally, of course, the answer was obvious. She should go ahead with the operation. She was young; there would be plenty of time to have other children if she wanted—at a better time in her career.

Natasha strode up the steps and reached for the door knocker. The brass was cold in the palm of her hand. Yes or no? Did she always want to sacrifice everything to her dancing, or were there other things in life that she really wanted, things she had a right to that had nothing to do with ballet? And what about the love she felt for this child, was it any less valid because she couldn't explain it, because it was attached in some irrational way to her feelings for Sergei and her grief over Alexis?

What was it Pascal had said? That the heart had reasons that reason didn't understand.

Natasha thought again of the child that would be a part of her and a part of Sergei. A face floated toward her, imagined, a baby's face with Sergei's blue eyes and her own dark hair, a tiny beautiful face almost real enough to touch. She turned for a moment, feeling that there was someone beside her, but the street was empty with no one in sight; a piece of newspaper blew sideways along the cobblestones, a dog turned the corner. She looked at the knocker again and then into her own heart.

Suddenly she knew beyond a doubt that if she went inside she would regret it for the rest of her life.

The café was almost empty, and Natasha had the whole back corner to herself. In her purse she had a ticket to Paris, good for any day of the week, but for some reason she had been lingering on in Vienna. She put her hand lightly on her abdomen and smiled to herself, content to stay where she was for the time being. Under her dress her stomach was like a lovely round drum, small but growing more visible every day. For the past week her appetite had been voracious. She had eaten chocolate until she was sick of the sight of it, and then bought fruit, two kilos at a time. It seemed she could never get enough apples and pears, oranges and lemons. An odd diet, but the truth was she had never felt better in her life. Now that the dizzy spells had passed, pregnancy seemed to agree with her in a way nothing else ever had.

Ordering a cup of coffee, she unfolded her newspaper and began to translate the Austrian equivalent of German into something more comprehensible. After a while she sighed and sat back in her chair. It was definitely time to leave for Paris. Financially, Austria was in a state of near collapse; the chancellor, Inaz Seipel, who was trying to negotiate a loan through the League of Nations, had once again denounced union with Germany despite strong pressure from the western provinces. The Socialists were agitating for better housing and relief for the unemployed. She inspected the statistics, and took another sip of the bitter, black coffee.

"Miss Ladanova." Natasha looked up from her newspaper to see a tall American in a moss green sweater and tweed jacket beaming down at her. Something about his mustache and slightly off-center nose was familiar, but she couldn't quite place him.

"You don't remember me, do you?" he said cheerfully.

"I'm afraid not."

"I'm Trey Ward. Remember? I rescued you in Paris after that Cocteau ballet where the audience rioted and drove you out into the rain."

"Trey, of course." She shook his hand, glad to see him, glad for that matter to see *anyone* familiar. This morning, for the first time, she had begun to feel lonely and to think how good it would be to get back to Zazie's cigarette smoke and endless gossip. Fouchier, of course, would be another matter. It wasn't going to be pleasant to tell him he'd lost his star dancer for at least a season. The thought of facing Fouchier was one of the main things keeping her in Vienna.

"Would you mind if I joined you?"

"Please do." She could use someone to talk to right now, especially someone who wasn't likely to discuss the fall of the schilling or the Anschluss, and she remembered Trey as a nice, uncomplicated sort who, with a little luck, might even prove entertaining.

"Thanks." Trey took a seat at the tiny table and ordered a cup of coffee and a pastry from one of the white-aproned waitresses. Outside the café, well-dressed Austrians hurried down the Kartner Strasse through the pale spring sunshine. "I suppose you're in Vienna for a performance, Miss Ladanova," he said, smiling at her pleasantly. He had the most amazingly white teeth. She wondered if it had something to do with his being an American. They always seemed so impossibly healthy.

"Call me Natasha, please." He smiled again, as if she'd just handed him a gift. "No, I'm not here for a performance. I'm here for," she paused, not quite sure what to say next. Surely he must notice her condition. "I'm here for personal reasons," she concluded lamely.

"Oh." Trey smiled and immediately changed the subject. She'd forgotten how tactful he was. Putting a spoonful of sugar in his coffee, he tasted it, made a face, and added more. "I'm here for an air race."

"Really?" She settled back in her chair, prepared to be mildly bored. She'd never been particularly interested in planes, but Trey's enthusiasm proved contagious. Evidently the meet was a major occasion. She gathered from his conversation that pilots from all over the world were converging on Vienna.

He finished his coffee and ordered more for both of them, along with a Sacher torte. As Natasha ate, he observed her thoughtfully.

"Say," he said, "I wonder if I could invite you to lunch? That is, if you don't have other plans."

Natasha looked up from the half-demolished Sacher torte, embarrassed. Did she look as ravenous as she felt? It was almost comic the way she ate these days, as if she hadn't had a square meal in weeks. She imagined the baby growing fat and happy inside her. If she didn't slow down, she was going to set some kind of world's record for the most amount of food consumed in the least amount of time. She thought of the hours she had spent in front of mirrors, inspecting her bones, making sure there wasn't an ounce of extra fat on her hips or thighs. She had been one of the lucky ones—a dancer who was naturally slender—but still she had always been careful, skipping rich desserts, passing by cream sauces and butter.

Now she simply ate anything she wanted without thinking twice about it. In some ways, one of the best things about being pregnant was taking a vacation from so many years of discipline. She understood why Zazie had found so much satisfaction in letting herself grow plump and comfortable. To dance, to make ballet your whole life, you had to take on your body as an adversary, struggle with it every minute.

Trey's pale green eyes met hers without a hint that he had noticed anything out of the ordinary about the way she was eating. "I know a nice restaurant near the Schiller Platz—best Schnitzel in Vienna." He called for the bill and paid it, leaving a tip so large the waitress's stolid Viennese face broke into a wreath of smiles. As Natasha stood up to put on her coat, she caught him looking at her strangely. So he had finally noticed.

"The baby's due in September," she said quickly.

"Oh," Trey colored slightly and turned away. "I apologize for staring; it's none of my business really, only I didn't even know you were married."

"I'm not."

"Oh." He was silent for a moment as if processing a startling piece of information. Then he grinned, and shrugged his shoulders. "Well, that's good news, because I'd feel a bit odd taking a married lady out to lunch."

"How about a pregnant one?"

"It's a first on all fronts." They laughed at the pun, and he

149

helped her on with her coat. "Seriously, if you need any kind of help. . . ." Trey was suddenly all concern.

"No, thank you. Everything's taken care of, but it's sweet of you to offer."

The restaurant near the Schiller Platz was pleasant but not so elegant that Natasha felt out of place without a hat and gloves. Once again she realized that Trey had anticipated all problems. The Schnitzel was wonderful, the wine was light and pleasant, dry with an aftertaste of something fragrant.

"If it were late summer," Trey said, "I'd ask you to come out to the country with me for a first-class Heurigen party."

"What's Heurigen?"

"New wine. The villagers serve it in their own courtyards, right under the arbors, and everyone gets royally smashed and polkas till dawn."

"Sounds like fun." The wine had relaxed her and she sat back, feeling better than she had in days. He was a kind man; it was pleasant to be spoiled.

"Too bad there isn't any Heurigen in the spring."

"I'm probably not up to polkaing until dawn anyway." He smiled but said nothing. She was impressed with the way he had avoided mentioning her pregnancy ever since he had understood that she didn't want to talk about it. His green eyes were politely noncommittal. They were strange eyes, pale and quiet—either very deep or very blank, she couldn't tell which. She got the impression he was too rich ever to have had to work much, but he didn't seem unaware of life the way so many of the rich did. She remembered suddenly that he had flown over Germany during the war, lost friends. That probably made the difference.

They had a long, pleasant lunch. Afterward she said goodbye quickly, pleading another engagement.

For the next three days in a row Trey took her to lunch, always meeting her "by chance" in the same café on the Kartner Strasse. As she downed endless helpings of spaetzle, sauerbraten, and Linzertorte, he told her more about himself: he had lost his father when he was eight; at present his mother lived in the family house in Cambridge, Massachusetts, half the year and in London the other half. She was a patron of the arts, always giving money to starving geniuses of one sort or another. As for himself, personally he liked the neatness of cubism, but some of the other, wilder things they were doing in Paris these days left him cold. Cubism was a little like ballet, didn't she agree? The balance of it, the level of abstraction?

She agreed and disagreed and had a thoroughly wonderful time. Trey was one of those rare and disappearing entities: a good conversationalist. Best of all he had unexpected quirks that made it impossible to put him into any neat category: he loved jazz and classical music; German philosophy and detective novels; and most of all, of course, ballet. When she told him about meeting Isadora Duncan in Moscow, he was fascinated. What did Duncan look like? Was she really as temperamental as everyone said? And what was the state of the Imperial Ballet now that it had been taken over by the Bolsheviks? Had she seen Ekaterina Geltser dance?

She could tell he wanted to ask her more about her trip, but when she abruptly changed the subject he followed her without skipping a beat. Sometimes she wondered why Trey spent so much time trying to please her.

At the end of the week, she finally left for Paris.

"Goddamn it!" Fouchier yelled. "How *could* you do this to me!"

"Do this to *you*?" Natasha suppressed an urge to pick up an ashtray and heave it at his head. The insensitive, self-centered creep. *Crétin, durak.* Silently she swore to herself as the little, thickset man paced around the room waving his arms melodramatically.

"I had the whole season built around you."

"Well unbuild it." She looked out the window at the Seine, wishing she'd stayed in Vienna a week or two longer. Already her presence in Paris had created a minor scandal. Damn the dance world for its endless gossip, and Fouchier for acting as if her pregnancy was the end of the world. She'd planned to borrow a little money from him to tide her over until after the baby was born, but as soon as she had walked into his office she'd seen it was out of the question. Fouchier was the type who only threw help your way when you didn't need it. Fill one of his theaters and he'd cable you thousands of francs anywhere in the world, but come to him with a real need, and nothing to give in exchange, and he'd act as if he was down to his last sou.

"The programs are already printed. You're booked to do *Swan Lake* in London in less than three weeks."

"The first pregnant Swan Queen on record."

"Shut up. How can you even dare to joke about such a thing? Look at you; *mon Dieu* you're as fat as a cow. Why in heaven's name didn't you come to me sooner, when we could have done something?"

"Emile, I happen to want this child."

"Good," he said, "have it then; only when you're done with your breeding don't expect to walk back in here and become a prima ballerina again as if nothing's happened. I know dancers; I *know* what happens to them when they get pregnant. You'll be out of shape for months, maybe years." He walked over to his desk, took out a sheaf of papers, and waved them in her face. "Do you realize the expenses I have, the money it takes to run a ballet company? People donate to La Cité because they want to see Natasha Ladanova dance, not some half-trained understudy. Who am I supposed to put in your place. I suppose you never thought of that?"

"It won't be forever."

"That depends." Fouchier's face was suddenly closed and businesslike. "It's been a bad year for us. First Maximov leaves and now you. My personal funds aren't endless you know."

"I'll be back in less than a year."

"I wouldn't count on it."

"What does that mean?"

"It means I can't make you any promises. For the last few seasons you've been one of the best dancers in Europe, but from now on it's anybody's guess what's going to happen to you." He sat down in his overstuffed red plush chair and put one hand dramatically on his forehead. "Take a year off, take two, and then we'll see. If the company's still intact, then I may be able to take you back—if, of course, you can get yourself back into decent shape."

Natasha stalked out of the offices of the Ballet de la Cité so angry at Fouchier she could hardly see straight. She should have known better. The idiot. What did he think dancers were? Machines? A miracle was happening inside her, as beautiful as any ballet ever performed, and he was blind to it. So her career was as good as over was it? She'd show him a thing or two. After the baby was born she'd go straight to Diaghilev.

Outside the sky was leaden and a cold wind was blowing. Natasha took a deep breath and plunged down the front steps two at a time, almost colliding with a tall man hurrying in the opposite direction. The man caught her by the shoulders to steady her; Natasha looked up and found herself staring into the familiar face of Trey Ward.

"What the hell are you doing here?" she said bluntly.

"What a reception," Trey responded. "Maybe I should back down those steps and try it a second time."

"I'm sorry," Natasha said. "I'm angry and it has nothing to do with you. But what *are* you doing here, Trey? You pop up in the most unlikely places."

"Frankly," Trey said with a grin, "I'm pursuing you. I flew in from Vienna this morning and went straight to your apartment. Your concierge said you'd gone over to Rue de Trémouille, so I thought I'd track you down and see if I could talk you into another lunch."

"How about a drink instead?"

"That bad, is it?"

"You don't know the half of it."

He took her to a small café around the corner and they ordered two Pernods. Natasha drank hers down instantly and Trey ordered her another. The sweet licorice felt strange on an empty stomach, but at least it calmed her a little.

"What's the main problem?" Trey asked sympathetically.

"Money." Natasha put her elbows on the table and rested her head on her hands. "I can't work for at least a year, and frankly I'm just about broke. My friend Zazie has invited me to move in with her, but I hate to impose."

Trey looked at her oddly and took another sip of Pernod. Natasha realized suddenly that it might have sounded as if she was asking him for a loan. How embarrassing. Diplomacy definitely wasn't her strong point this morning.

"Natasha," he said after a long, somewhat uncomfortable silence, "I want to ask you something, but I don't know quite how to put it. I thought about doing it in Vienna, but I got cold feet."

"Ask ahead," she said, wondering what could be so important that he'd followed her all the way to Paris to discuss it. She calculated quickly that he must have missed the last two air races. For Trey to do that, whatever it was must be important indeed.

Trey sat back and took a deep breath. "My God," he said, "I didn't think it was going to be this hard to say." He paused and then began again. "Let me see, I think I recall telling you I was shot down twice during the war," Natasha nodded, wondering what all this was leading up to.

"The first time was nothing," Trey took a quick drink of Pernod. "I got off with hardly a scratch. The second time I wasn't so lucky. We crashed in Flanders, on the Allied side of the lines, thank God. I had a copilot, a Jewish kid from the Bronx named Mark Jacobs. He died right in front of me; bled to death from a neck wound and there wasn't a thing on earth I could do about it. I still have nightmares about Mark sometimes."

"Trey, I'm so sorry." What an odd, irrelevant conversation. She wondered whatever could have inspired him suddenly to confide his war experiences to her.

"I was wounded—badly. Took a lot of shell fragments in my legs and back." He drank the rest of his Pernod, set the glass back on the table, and took a deep breath. "When I woke up in the hospital, I knew something was wrong because the nurses wouldn't look me in the eye. Then the doctor came in and broke the news: unlike Mark, I was going to live—only with a catch." She waited for him to go on, but he stopped and lapsed back into a moody silence.

"What kind of catch, Trey?" she prompted.

"Let's get drunk," he said, "very, very drunk or I won't be able to tell you."

"I can't drink very much this early in the morning."

"Okay, then you can watch." He ordered three more Pernods and tossed them down one after the other. His face flushed and his green eyes grew bright. Natasha thought, not for the first time, what a handsome man he was. She wondered what could possibly be bothering him so much that he had to get drunk to tell her about it. He'd always seemed so cheerful, but then you never knew what kind of pain people carted around in them that they never let on to. Trey was obviously more complex than she'd given him credit for.

After he finished his fourth drink, he lined the saucers up in a row and ordered a fifth, drinking half of it and then pushing the glass away. "My dear Natasha," he said, "you are an exceptionally beautiful woman and I am now exceptionally drunk." He smiled. "So drunk that I feel no pain, a state I haven't let myself get into for a number of years. I am drunk enough, in fact, to tell you my secret, the tragedy of Trey Ward, a petty tragedy as great tragedies go—no Lear or Othello but mine own, as the poet says." He leaned forward, his voice thick from the alcohol. "I can't father a child. Nasty trick of fate, yes? Almost funny when you think about it. Albert Waltham Ward, the third—and the last. A comic war injury; hardly heroic. Not the kind you can even speak of in front of a lady unless you're very, very drunk indeed."

It took a moment for the implications of what he was telling her to sink in. She wanted to comfort him, but she couldn't think of a thing to say, so she just sat there until he put his face down on the table and began to sob. "Damn the Krauts," he said angrily, "damn them all to hell."

Zazie's apartment smelled like flowers and yeast. On the table were a basket of fresh rolls, a pot of strong coffee, and a bouquet of daffodils in a glass jar. Natasha thought how everything in Paris tended to look like an Impressionist painting. On the floor Leonce was stretched out on his stomach drawing pictures of fabulous beasts with the colored chalks she had brought him from Vienna.

"Trey is willing to do *what?*" Zazie said. They had been talking for almost half an hour before Natasha had been able to bring herself to mention Trey's offer. Now she wondered if it had been a good idea, especially since Zazie was looking at her as if she'd suddenly exploded a bomb between the table and the sofa.

"He's promised to put a hundred thousand dollars in an irrevocable trust for the child if I agree to marry him."

"*Mon Dieu,*" Zazie said, sitting down suddenly. Her bracelets clinked together with a soft metallic sound, and her great full skirt billowed up around her like a sail. "*Mon Dieu,* I'm speechless."

"He says he wants a family."

"Does he love you?"

"He says he does, but he admits it's too early to tell for sure."

"How do you feel about him?"

Natasha dumped the cat off her lap and brushed the hairs off her plum-colored smock. "I don't know really; I'm confused, I guess—tempted, a little frightened. I like Trey a lot—he's wonderful to talk to and as considerate as any man I've ever met—but there's no way I could honestly say I love him. Frankly, I keep wishing it was Sergei who was asking me to marry him, but even *I've* got enough sense to know that's not about to happen."

"Do me a favor," Zazie said, lighting a cigarette and inhaling quickly, "don't mention Sergei around me. It brings out my black widow spider instincts."

"I'm tired," Natasha leaned back and put her legs up on

the ottoman. "Tired of the whole thing. When Alexis died something changed in me. I don't see things like I used to. I used to imagine Sergei would turn up some day and confess that he couldn't live without me, and we'd get married and travel the world together dancing—maybe even form our own company. I kept expecting that someday we'd live this exciting, exotic life—a sort of endless honeymoon, never even speaking a harsh word to each other. Well, it hasn't happened and as far as I can see it isn't going to. It isn't easy to pack up the grand passion of your life and put it in mothballs, but I think I've finally done it." She spread her hands in a gesture of relinquishment. "I know that may sound melodramatic, but it's true. I have simple desires these days. All I want to do is concentrate on my career and my baby, and Trey's offered me a way to do that. He's a good man. My child needs a father."

"And the sex part?"

"He says I can have lovers if I want them, but I doubt I will."

"A hundred thousand dollars, stability, a marriage of convenience. You're worrying me, *cherie*," Zazie said, blowing a large blue smoke ring. "You're sounding much too practical, much too French."

Three weeks later Natasha married Trey Ward in a civil ceremony with Zazie as a witness. On their wedding night Trey undressed Natasha slowly and held her in his arms for a long time, stroking her swollen abdomen gently. His body was lean and strong but there were scars on his back and along his legs, marks where the army doctors had sewn him back together piece by piece like a badly ripped blanket. Natasha felt his sex resting against her buttocks, limp and shrunken, and thought of the pain he must have undergone, of the suffering and humiliation it must have caused him to lose his manhood.

From that moment on she felt a great tenderness for Trey, as if he were not so much her husband as another child who needed taking care of.

10

London, 1933

Natasha stepped back to admire the pigeons wheeling around Lord Nelson's column, the white undersides of their wings fluttering crisply like scraps of paper against the cold London sky. As an Englishman equipped with umbrella and bowler strode along the other side of the square, hundreds—perhaps thousands—of birds suddenly swirled up around him, taking flight in patterns so complicated you could hardly trace them out if you tried; yet in all the years she'd been watching, Natasha had never seen one bird run into another. Imagine a stage full of dancers trying the same thing: there'd be chaos, broken bones. Natasha smiled to herself as a new cloud of pigeons settled down at her feet to receive the crumbs Winn was tossing onto the pavement. If you didn't know better, you'd think those birds had been choreographed.

Winn threw another handful of crumbs to the greedy pigeons and grinned happily. She was eleven years old, plump and jolly with flaxen blond hair and a direct, honest nature, an outdoors sort of child who loved anything that swam, crawled, galloped, or flew. Mother and daughter stood for another ten or fifteen minutes feeding the birds, a striking pair: the pretty little girl in jodhpurs (so out of place this far from the stables), and the slim woman in the exquisitely cut black crepe suit who stood holding her hand.

The last eleven years had been kind to Natasha. Her hair was still dark without a thread of gray; her face fuller, more peaceful; her eyes softer. But there was nothing soft or lax about her body. Under the delicate crepe was a flat stomach, strong legs, powerful arms. Almost thirty-seven now, she still danced with the power and force of a twenty-year-old, which was a good thing since tastes had changed considerably of late. Baby ballerinas had suddenly become the rage: thirteen-year-olds like Irina Baronova.

Odd how quickly time passed. Natasha watched her daughter happily feeding the pigeons and thought that there was nothing like having a child to make you feel the years rolling by. She remembered how after Winn's birth she had returned to ballet, sweating for months to get her body back into shape. It had been hellishly difficult at times, but despite Fouchier's dire predictions, she had picked up her career. Then, with Trey's money and moral support behind her, she had finally been able to concentrate all her energy on dancing.

Eleven years and it all seemed to have taken place in the blink of an eye. Natasha had imagined a stately progression from youth to middle age, but it was more like climbing on a roller coaster. Life moved so fast that, if you weren't careful, you could miss it altogether.

Winn shook out the last of the crumbs and turned the paper bag inside out. "Mama," she asked bluntly, for Winn was a direct child, perhaps too direct for her own good Natasha sometimes thought, "can we buy more biscuits for the birds or go to Harrod's for tea and take home sacks of cream puffs and eclairs for Sofie?" Sofie was Winn's massive Scottish deerhound whose only known vice was an irresistible urge to chew Natasha's ballet slippers to pieces.

"But Sofie doesn't like cream puffs," Natasha pointed out.

Winn grinned happily. "Yes, Mama, but I do." She was hard to resist, a charmer who could get anything she wanted out of Trey just by asking for it, but Natasha liked to think she herself had more resistance. Children needed discipline, but how did you discipline a beautiful little girl who never did anything worse than get her jodhpurs dirty? When she was Winn's age she had already been working for six years with Madame Rochina, getting up at four in the morning to practice at the barre before she went to school, but Winn was more like Trey. Her needs were direct and practical: love from her parents, a pretty dress, an occasional sweet—she lacked the driving ambition, the inner disquiet that lay at the core of a born dancer. All of which was probably for the best, although Natasha did sometimes wish Winn would show more interest in ballet.

Winn's blue eyes glowed at the thought of Harrod's tea tables piled with petits fours and eclairs. "Please, Mama," she begged. "Take me to Harrod's and I promise not to ask for a single thing for the rest of the week."

"We'll see," Natasha said. Winn's promises were to be relied on; if she said she wouldn't ask for anything else, you could bank on it. Natasha took the paper bag that had held the bread crumbs, folded it neatly, and stuffed it in her purse. "We have to go to Freed's first."

"Harrod's has such lovely cream puffs." Winn sighed, put her hand in Natasha's, and looked up at her with patient endurance. Natasha smiled, amused. Children had such simple greeds. How nice it must be to want something as easy to obtain as cream puffs.

When some fifteen minutes later Natasha and Winn entered Freed's, Mr. Horner, the assistant manager, came over to them right away, his tailcoat flapping behind him like penguin wings, his face a map of cordiality. It was dancers such as Pavlova and Natasha who had made Freed's insignia—a pair of winged ballet slippers—world famous, so on those rare occasions when Natasha entered the shop the young men who actually made the shoes and the old ladies who sewed on the satin covers paused for a moment in their work, and there was a sudden hush as if in the presence of visiting royalty.

Freed of London's, located on St. Martin's Lane right off Trafalgar Square, was as famous in the world of dance as Chanel was in the world of fashion. Ever since 1928 when Frederick Freed had opened his first shop, Freed's had been making the best ballet shoes in the world, elastic, durable, and, most important of all, comfortable. A dancer's feet, especially when she was on *pointe* for any length of time, took incredible punishment. Natasha had learned in her first days at the Imperial School that the best shoes really lasted only about fifteen minutes before they were ready to be thrown out or demoted to rehearsal use. Pavlova had gone through an average of 350 pairs a year, and the Ballets Russes spent 18,000 each season just keeping its dancers shod. Natasha herself never ordered less than three hundred pairs a year, and that, coupled with the fact that she was now one of the most famous ballerinas in Europe, made her in Mr. Horner's eyes a very important customer indeed.

"Ah," Mr. Horner exclaimed, his pale eyes lighting up behind his pince nez, "Mademoiselle Ladanova, Miss Winn, good morning. This is indeed a delightful surprise." Fishing a large red lollypop out from some secret recess behind the counter, he presented it to Winn with a flourish.

Natasha saw Winn happily ensconced on a high stool near the door, and then, after exchanging endless strings of pleasantries with Mr. Horner about the state of the weather, followed him into the shop to talk to Henry, her "maker." The personal "maker" was the secret that had allowed Freed's to produce an absolute custom fit, unrivaled by any other shoemaker in Europe. When a dancer entered the little shop on St. Martin's Lane for the first time, a model was taken of her foot and she was assigned to someone like Henry who would thereafter be personally responsible for making her shoes for the duration of her career. From then on Freed's could ship shoes to her anywhere in the world.

Natasha spent a fruitful fifteen minutes with Henry going over the small problem she had recently been having with her heels. If she could come in next week, he suggested, they could take a new model of her foot, and he would make her up several dozen pairs of shoes in time for her upcoming performance in the new Vic-Wells production of *Coppélia*.

Natasha thanked Henry for his time, and promised to return the following Wednesday for the fitting. She had just walked into the front part of the shop to take leave of Mr. Horner when she heard a familiar voice calling her name.

"Natasha, Natasha Ladanova." Anya Maximova was standing near the counter, a pair of slippers in one hand and a fur muff in the other. Or was it Anya? At first Natasha wasn't sure. This woman seemed so much older. The voice was Anya's, but could that be Anya's face? Natasha remembered a round-faced madonna, this woman was gaunt, her cheekbones sharp, her skin sallow and unhealthy-looking. Even the woman's hair, piled around her head in the same smooth coronet that Anya had always worn, looked lifeless. Her green wool suit was obviously expensive but a bit outdated, the skirt too short, the jacket lacking shoulder pads, but worst of all it hung on her as if it had been made for someone else.

It was Anya all right, Natasha was sure of that now, but the change was shocking. Her first thought was that Anya must have been terribly ill, but how could that be? Only a few days ago she had read in *Le Monde* that Sergei's company was giving a series of performances in Paris at the Theatre Champs Elysées with Madame Maximova dancing three of the principal roles, but how could a woman as thin as Anya have danced anything? There was no strength in those lungs, no energy in that body.

"*Preevyet*," Anya called out casually, as if it had been twelve days instead of twelve years since they had last seen each other. Dropping the slippers back on the counter, she strolled over to Natasha, enfolded her in a bony embrace, and

160

kissed her Russian style on both cheeks. Natasha got a strong whiff of French perfume, mouthwash, and something else underneath. Anya stepped back and tucked a wisp of hair into her braids, a gesture so familiar it was almost painful. "*Kak dela?*" she said pleasantly. "How goes it with you?" She waved her fur muff around the room as if taking it all in. "What luck to run into you, darling. Sergei and I just came over on the Channel ferry yesterday to see about our bill. We seem to owe Freed's some terribly intimidating sum and *Gaspodin* Horner has absolutely refused to ship us more shoes until we pay up."

"How's the Ballet de la Cité doing?" Natasha asked, too stunned to think of anything else to say. Sergei, failing to establish a company in America, even with all of Anya's money behind him, had bought out Fouchier some time in the early twenties. For over twelve years Natasha had studiously avoided meeting him and Anya—a feat that had been relatively simple to accomplish since she moved around a great deal and his troupe, no longer based in Paris, was usually on tour. The world of ballet was small, however, and she had known that ultimately she would see the two of them again. Still, it was shocking, like a cold bath or a sudden fall.

"The Cité's falling apart," Anya said, tucking another stray wisp back into her braids. "Didn't you hear? After I lost most of my money in the stockmarket crash, we had to go out and beat the bushes for patrons. A German Jewish couple named Blumburg took us over for a few years, but when this Hitler thing heated up they got nervous and decided to move to Brazil. So here we are, on Freed's doorstep, out of *valyuta*. Can dancers dance barefoot, I ask you? We have a chance to go to Berlin for the entire summer—visas and everything. Goebbels's a real balletomane, declared the whole company honorary Aryans, can you imagine? But Mr. Horner says *nyet* on the shoes."

"How much do you need?" Natasha asked.

"Who knows, darling." Anya shrugged a totally Russian shrug. "Five hundred pounds I think. I keep telling Mr. Horner I'm going to have to pawn that pearl necklace Mama gave me on my wedding day, but the English are so unsentimental when it comes to money—worse than the French when you get right down to it." Anya patted down her fur muff as if it were a live animal, took a rather battered-looking Russian cigarette from her purse, and lit it with a small silver lighter: "I followed your career in the papers: Les

161

Ballets Suédois, Diaghilev, the Camargo Society, Vic-Wells Ballet—you've made quite a name for yourself and married a rich man to boot, but then you always were the luckiest of us all." She inhaled the smoke through glossy red lips, letting it spill back slowly into the air. Was there a tiny trace of jealousy in her voice, or was that just Natasha's imagination? Natasha remembered how there had been a period of her life—especially right after Winn was born—when, despite Trey's kindness, she had brooded endlessly about what she had missed out on, whole days when it had seemed to her that Anya was living the life she, Natasha, should have lived.

Anya's hands went nervously back to her hair; her cigarette made an arc of smoke, then another. She was like a bird, like one of those pigeons out in Trafalgar Square endlessly flapping her wings, only without the bird's poise and power. "I heard you had a child, a daughter." She coughed delicately dabbing her lips with her cuff, her eyes bright and restless.

"That's her over there." Natasha pointed to Winn who was calmly finishing off the last of the lollypop. "Winn, come over here a moment, dear." Winn reluctantly climbed down from the stool, lollypop clutched in one hand. "This is Madame Maximova, an old friend."

Winn surveyed Anya with the uneasy expression of an honest child who knew that some extra effort of politeness was about to be required of her. "How do you do, Madame?" she said cautiously.

Anya took another drag on her cigarette. "A sweet-looking girl," she said to Natasha.

"Thank you."

"A dancer?"

"No."

"A pity. But then she doesn't really have the body for it, does she? Breasts already, and all that. How old is she?"

"Eleven."

"Breasts at eleven. No, it's obviously out of the question."

"That isn't a very nice thing to say," Winn observed bluntly.

"What?" Anya stared at the little girl as if not quite able to believe she'd actually spoken.

"I said that it's not nice to say things about people's breasts, especially when they can't help it. I know I'm not going to be a dancer like Mama, but it isn't very polite of you to talk about it in front of me like I'm deaf or something. How would you like it if I made fun of *your* breasts?"

"Winn," Natasha interrupted quickly, "that's quite enough."

She turned to Anya. "I'm sorry. I'm afraid my daughter isn't very big on the conventional social graces."

"Children," Anya waved her hand airily, "who can ever predict what they'li say next? The child is obviously distressed that she lacks your talent, *cherie*."

"Excuse me," Winn said with an ominously stubborn look on her face that Natasha recognized all too well.

"Winn, go over there and sit down and we'll discuss this later." Pressing her lips together, Winn strode back to the stool and sat down, arms folded across her chest, a perfect miniature of outrage.

Throwing her cigarette to the floor, Anya put it out neatly with the toe of her shoe. Then she dredged up her purse and began fumbling around, bringing up pencils and scraps of paper. Opening a red morocco wallet, she brought out a picture. "This in my son, Mihail. Very talented." There was obvious pride in her voice. Natasha peered at the small dog-eared photograph and was greeted with the sight of a gangling blond boy in tights and a short tunic posed in a stiff *arabesque* against a black velvet curtain. "It was taken at the Teatro Colón in Buenos Aires last year," Anya explained. "The Blumburgs persuaded us to tour South America."

The photo was out of focus, but it was clear Mihail favored Sergei. Natasha looked quickly at Winn. The resemblance between the two children was so strong she wondered if Anya noticed it. But if Anya noticed anything, she kept it to herself.

That evening when Natasha returned from rehearsal, she found Trey propped up in bed reading H. G. Wells's new best-seller *The Shape of Things to Come*. Science fiction had been his passion for the last three or four years, and he sometimes devoured half a dozen books a week, preferring those that described flights to other planets. He often joked that as soon as possible he was going to trade in one of his planes for a rocket ship.

"Hello sweetheart," he said. Pouring a cup of coffee from the thermos he always kept on the night table, Trey handed it to her as she kicked off her shoes and plumped down on the bed beside him. Their bedroom was a sanctuary with rose-colored wallpaper, pink silk curtains, and a great canopied bed that purportedly had once belonged to one of Edward VII's mistresses. Tropical plants blossomed on the tables, sat in rows on special shelves along the windows, or hung from the ceiling, filling the air with the scent of jasmine and wild ginger. Long ago Trey's mother, bless her soul, had insisted on installing in the Belgravia house that most American of luxuries: central heating, an act for which Natasha daily gave thanks. After hours of shivering in underheated studios, there was nothing more pleasant than coming home, throwing her leg warmers into a hamper and slipping into a thin silk robe.

Trey put an arm around Natasha, drew her to him, and kissed her lightly on the cheek. "Have a good day?"

"Not bad. You'll never guess whom I ran into at Freed's: Anya Maximova." As Trey sat back against the pillow with his hands behind his head, she described the meeting with Anya in detail, glad to get it off her chest. Trey was sympathetic, amused by Anya's comments about Winn's breasts.

"Sounds like she has the tact of a hippopotamus."

"Less." Natasha giggled.

"Winn's no slouch in that area, either. It must have been quite an encounter."

"*The Charge of the Light Brigade* right there in the middle of Freed's. If I hadn't ordered Winn back to her stool, Anya would have gotten the surprise of her life."

They joked, talked, and drank coffee for about an hour more and then, without a word, Natasha reached over, took a bottle of warm oil from the night table, and began to rub Trey's chest and shoulders. Six years ago, in the summer of 1927, he had gone to the famous Balmont Clinic in St. Moritz for a series of glandular injections by the pioneer of modern hormone therapy, Dr. Dietrich Schwartz. At first the results had been disappointing, but slowly changes had begun to take place in Trey's body. At the end of two years he and Natasha had finally, after a number of unsuccessful attempts, been able to consummate their marriage.

Natasha ran her hands over Trey's bare chest, feeling the contours of his muscles, the hard ridge of his breastbone. His flesh was warm and firm under the palm of her hand, taut like rubber. He was slender as a greyhound, well-proportioned, with a flat stomach, tight hips, strong, lean legs. Spreading the warm oil over his thighs, she kneaded them until he sighed slightly and relaxed. Tentatively she slipped her fingers between his legs. For a long time she caressed him delicately, with feathery lightness. Then, bending down, she began to kiss him, moving her tongue in small, quick circles.

Trey stirred and took a deep breath. About one time in ten when she touched him like this, he would get excited and pull her to him. At first it had seemed strange, almost embarrassing, to manipulate him this way, but over the years she had gotten used to it. His orgasms, when he had them, were so quick she could barely feel them, but she had gotten used to that, too.

Afterward, Trey was perfectly willing to caress her for as long as she wanted, but often it was enough just to be held, to go to sleep in his arms. Exhausted by constant rehearsals she needed very little these days. It was almost as if Trey's lack of real desire had built up a corresponding lack in her, as if there was nothing to pull her into the mystery of sex, none of the sting of passion, no masculine energy for her to push against, fight, and finally succumb to. Frankly, if Trey hadn't wanted another child so much, she would have been quite happy not making love at all.

Tonight as she massaged him, she knew at once that it wasn't going to work. No matter how she kissed or touched there wasn't the slightest flutter of energy. After about a quarter of an hour, she gave up and they fell asleep.

A week later Natasha was sitting in the conservatory sewing ribbons onto the *pointe* shoes that Freed's had just sent over by special messenger when the phone rang.

"Hello, Natasha, this is Sergei."

"Sergei who?" It couldn't be his voice, not after all these years. It had to be some other Sergei, some other. . . . Natasha's mind rocked back and forth, admitting and denying the obvious.

"Sergei Maximov. Listen, I was wondering if we could have lunch together some time." Natasha stood up, dumping the *pointe* shoes on the floor. Through the open doorway she could see Winn kneeling on the living room rug, playing with a puzzle. A hundred times over the past twelve years she had rehearsed the things she would say when she finally spoke to Sergei again, and now she couldn't think of a single one of them.

"Natasha, are you still there?"

Natasha took a deep breath, sat down in the chair, and looked at the tiny black holes in the ivory mouthpiece of the receiver. "*Preevyet,* Sergei," she said finally, "it's been a long, long time." Her hands were shaking and she felt like breaking into hysterical laughter. What a ridiculous reaction. She'd gotten over him completely years ago, but the sound of his voice had give her such a start. It was like seeing, or rather hearing, a ghost.

"I hear the Royal Horse Guards Hotel has managed to entice a real, live French chef across the Channel. How about it, Natasha? You know what they say: hell is where the mechanics are French, the lovers American, and the cooks English. Surely you could use a vacation from steak and kidney pie." His voice was light and pleasant, as if they'd just parted on friendly terms a day or two ago.

"I don't know, that is. . . ." Natasha thought about Trey and Winn and immediately felt guilty. What was wrong with her? It wasn't as if Sergei had called her up and asked her to commit adultery. Besides, it might be interesting to see him after all these years. On impulse she accepted his invitation, and then hung up feeling happy and apprehensive in equal proportions.

The restaurant of the Royal Horse Guards Hotel was almost empty at this hour since it was too late for lunch and too early for tea. Only one other couple occupied the huge dining room, a pair of American businessmen who seemed completely absorbed in their cigars.

"Anya drinks," Sergei said bluntly. "She's ruining her liver, not eating enough. How long she can go on dancing in this state is anyone's guess." He sighed and leaned his elbows on the table causing the wine in the tall stemmed crystal to tremble. "I'm worried about her, *konyechna*, but it's an impossible situation."

In front of Natasha the white linen-covered tables spread in endless rectangles like a giant chessboard. Her food sat untouched on the table: a salmon with head and eyes still intact nestled on a bed of crisp lettuce, three new potatoes in a sauce of unsalted butter, a lemon cut into the shape of a fan. Natasha was in the state of mind that made eating impossible: elated, confused, so overwhelmed by her own emotions that the idea of putting a piece of salmon in her mouth was ludicrous.

The force of her own feelings after twelve years surprised and alarmed her. She had imagined, when she accepted Sergei's invitation, that seeing him would be like seeing an old friend, that, if anything, she would still feel a little resentment. No doubt they would reminisce about the past, grow a little nostalgic, and part with insincere plans to have lunch together again some time. But it wasn't working out

166

like that at all. This was ridiculous. People were supposed to fall out of love after twelve years. How could she still care so much about Sergei, especially considering what he'd done to her the last time they met? What was wrong with her? Here she was an intelligent woman with a wonderful career, married, with an almost grown daughter and Sergei could still make her feel as if she were sixteen, shy, and awkward as a colt.

Time had passed. Why couldn't she get that through her head? If she had any doubt that they weren't back in St. Petersburg, all she had to do was look at Sergei. He was heavier, his hair thinner, his blue eyes lighter as if the years had bleached the color from them. Oh, he was still strikingly handsome, make no mistake about it. But he no longer looked like an innocent angel on an icon. He looked like a real man with real problems—and yet here she was in love with some fantasy out of the past, probably on the verge of making a fool of herself again.

When she got home this evening she was going to get down every book on psychology she possessed and figure out what was going on. Probably it all had to do with her unconscious; maybe Sergei was imprinted there like a thumb print on a piece of white paper, or maybe the whole problem was that she'd never really had a father. Freud's theories were so popular that surely one of them could explain it.

"She drank the whole time we were in Paris. Very nearly missed a performance," Sergei was saying. Well, the least she could do was listen to him, and the news about Anya was truly terrible. There had been times when she'd wished disaster on Anya for stealing Sergei away from her. But apparently, like everything else except her obsession with Sergei, the desire for revenge had a limited life span.

"Can't anything be done?"

Sergei shook his head and hunched his shoulders forward as if embracing some invisible despair. "I've tried everything from hiding the vodka and locking her in her room to putting her in a private sanatorium in Switzerland. Nothing works. She is, as you'll remember, immensely persuasive, able to wheedle liquor out of the most unlikely people even when I see to it that she doesn't have a sou to her name. I've found her concealing it in perfume atomizers, teapots; in fact, the first hint I had that something was seriously wrong was when I discovered vodka in one of Mihail's baby bottles."

"Why does she do it?"

Sergei shook his head. "Who knows? She's what the English call a 'dipsomaniac'—which means, I gather, that she has an incurable craving for alcohol. Her father, Count Belinsky, evidently had the same problem and I understand it runs in families. Did her mother ever mention it to you, by the way?" Natasha remembered Countess Belinskaya dressed in her pearl choker and black lace pouring tea from a silver samovar in the drawing room at Sutton Place.

"No, she never did."

"It was the family secret," Sergei took a sip of wine and put the glass back down on the table, "but frankly I have another theory."

"What's that?"

He leaned forward, "I think she drinks because of me."

"What do you mean?"

He grinned ironically. "Come on, Natasha, can't you imagine? You knew me well enough—*you* know what I'm like. My work is everything to me. What I'm trying to do is create something out of nothing and, like all artists, I'm never sure if I'm going to be able to carry it off. I have this vision in my mind of angels dancing, *angels*," he made an expansive motion with his hands. "But every time I try to choreograph that vision into a ballet I suffer the pangs of hell knowing reality is never going to match up to what I can see in my mind's eye."

"But you're one of the most successful choreographers in Europe."

"Wrong. I'm a famous failure. All great artists are. And I've paid a perilous price even for that. I don't see much of my family. My son, Mihail, for example, I suppose I love him as much as anyone on earth, but if I see him alone once a month it's a minor miracle. And then there's Anya. She's always needed companionship, and I'm not the man to give it to her. There're a few things I've had to face about myself over the last few years, and one of them is that I've no talent for intimacy. Work is the beginning and end of my world. There isn't a human relationship on earth I wouldn't trade for a perfect ballet. I suppose that makes me a cold son of a bitch at heart, but I can't help it, and Anya can't face it, so she drinks."

Underneath all the bravado, Natasha could feel his pain. His soul, his Russian *dusha*, was like a box, she thought, studded with nails, wrapped in barbed wire, containing something beautiful and vulnerable that he was never willing to

168

reveal. She wanted to reach out to him, to comfort him, but she knew comfort was something he couldn't accept, that pity was the thing he dreaded most. "That's a pretty grim picture to paint of yourself," she said in as neutral a voice as she could muster.

"But an honest one."

"Why don't you give it all up for a season, take some time off to be with Anya and your son?"

"Because I don't want to give it up, damn it. I'm thirty-seven years old, nearly thirty-eight, and I can feel my life running through my fingers. I don't have a day or a minute I can waste. And besides, it wouldn't work. Anya hates my creativity, envies the hell out of it because all she's ever been is a superb technician and she knows it. Not like you. You always had passion, but she only had the execution—the ability to imitate. Anya Belinskaya, the perfect monkey. I was a fool to marry her."

He saw he had upset her, and his tone changed instantly. "Forgive me. I shouldn't be so cruel about Anya, but I'm bitter I suppose. What I was trying to say, in my own tactless way, was that I should have married you." Natasha pulled back, and Sergei grabbed for her arm, closing his fingers tightly over her wrist. "Wait, listen. I mean it. I never cared about anyone but you—that is, as much as I'm capable of caring—and if I'd married you, you'd have understood my work. You'd have understood my obsession because you have that same obsession yourself."

She shouldn't listen to another word of this. She should get up, leave at once, and go home to Trey. So *that's* why he'd called her. Because his wife didn't understand him, because he was in London, lonely, and wanted an affair. How classic, how very predictable.

Sergei bent his head suddenly, kissing her hands, turning over her palms. "I had to see you again, Natasha." His words were like sandpaper, wearing her down. As his lips pressed against her skin, she felt a sexual attraction to him so strong it was frightening.

"You have a wife, remember." She was shaking, trembling all over. She wanted to withdraw her hands, but she couldn't.

"Anya and I haven't slept together for at least five years. She doesn't want sex. She wants to make a meal of me."

Natasha pulled both her hands out of his, picked up her coat, threw it over her shoulders. It was a struggle not to look back at him as she left the restaurant, but somehow she managed it.

A few days later she was combing Sofie on the living room rug when Roberts appeared in the doorway with an armful of pink rosebuds so huge it gave him the slightly ridiculous air of being a walking flower garden. "Excuse me, Madam," Roberts announced with true sangfroid, "but these just arrived for you."

Natasha got to her feet, brushed the dog hairs off her skirt, and inspected the card that dangled from a tiny silver ribbon attached to one of the stems.

> *To My Darling Natasha,*
the card read:

> *In memory of the night we first danced together.*
> *Love,*
> *Sergei*

Natasha grinned, pleased in spite of herself. No one had given her anything like this for a good sixteen years, not since she was living with Alexis. So Sergei had remembered that she'd worn pink rosebuds the night they danced *The Buccaneer*. For a few moments she stood, smelling the flowers, remembering her debut on the stage of the Maryinsky, how frightened she had been, how Sergei had kissed her for luck. She looked around the lavishly furnished living room, at Sofie stretched out on the Oriental rug, at the Degas that hung in the place of honor over the grand piano, and the thought came to her that she was living in a museum.

In each of the tall wooden cases that lined the exhibition hall, fine Florentine goblets caught the afternoon light; spiraled and delicate, with stems as thin as a breath, they sparkled in reds, aquas, rusty golds, like dancers waiting to perform. In front of the goblets, a row of Victorian paperweights lay on strips of green felt, clearest crystal bursting with tiny flowers, glass ribbons, miniature animals no bigger than a pebble.

Winn laughed with delight, running from one case to another, discovering a bottle shaped like a bear, a string of beads taken from some ancient Egyptian tomb that looked like a row of soap bubbles. Winn loved glass, and the Victoria and Albert Museum had one of the finest collections in the world.

Natasha strolled behind Winn at a leisurely rate, not looking at anything in particular, simply allowing herself to be soothed by the colors and shapes. With Trey off on a flight to Scotland, there were few better things to do on a rainy afternoon in London than go to the Victoria and Albert. Passing in front of a large mirror, she caught sight of herself, dressed in light blue chiffon, her dark hair caught up off her neck with a blue ribbon, slender legs ending in a pair of wet galoshes. The sight of the galoshes made Natasha smile. Such ridiculous boots; someone with a sense of humor should choreograph a ballet especially for galoshes. Too bad Cocteau had abandoned dance for film.

"*Preevyet*, Natasha." Sergei was standing behind her, dressed *à l'anglaise* in a dove gray three-piece suit, umbrella perched jauntily on one arm. "Imagine running into you here, *milaya*," he said and grinned wickedly. "By chance, of course. Ah, the fickle ways of fate. For two days you don't take my phone calls, and then we're thrust together at random thanks to a mutual love of Victorian paperweights."

"Sergei, you're impossible!"

"True."

"You followed us, didn't you?"

"I stand convicted, my dear Madam, of the crime of slinking behind you on the tube like some character out of the great English Sherlock Holmes series." Sergei gave a mock bow. "Impose your penalty—draw, even quarter me if you wish, but please don't stand me up against the wall and shoot me like the Bolsheviks would like to do because the bullets would simply ruin one of Savile Row's finest suits."

"Aren't you ever serious?" She should be angry that he'd followed her, especially since she'd made it plain she didn't want to see him, but instead she found herself ridiculously glad, as if a cloud had suddenly lifted off the day. Still, he was being outrageous. Natasha glanced nervously over at the other side of the room where Winn stood enraptured in front of a display of small crystal dishes. One look at Sergei, and Winn would have a million unanswerable questions.

"Is that your daughter?"

"Yes."

"Robust girl, very Russian-looking."

It was odd to stand there, knowing Winn was his child, yet not see the slightest suspicion in his face. Natasha experienced a small twinge of pain as if something had twisted inside her. The pleasure she felt at seeing Sergei disappeared. "What do you want?" He sensed her change of mood and sobered instantly.

"I want to see you alone."

"Why?"

"To talk."

"About what?"

"About us."

"Sergei, there *isn't* any us, not anymore."

"Then just see me and we'll talk about whatever you like." He was pleading now, sincere in a way that touched and confused her. "I'll tell you about all the ballets I plan to choreograph for you—the ones that will make Markova green with envy. Please." The words were innocent enough, but there was something in his eyes so passionate and seductive that for a moment she wanted nothing more than to let him take her in his arms. She must be crazy, out of her mind. The thought that she was on the edge of doing something so irresponsible chilled her back to reality.

"Sergei, we had something once and now it's over. Why don't we just leave it at that."

"You don't want to see me?"

"No."

"I don't believe you."

Out of the corner of her eye Natasha caught sight of Winn coming toward them. The last thing she wanted was for Winn to meet Sergei. "I have to go," she turned awkwardly and hurried over to her daughter.

"Mama, come see the glass elephants."

"Very pretty." She hardly knew what she was saying. She could still feel Sergei standing behind her, watching them. With great effort, she managed to produce a smile. "We need to go home now, *solnyshko*."

"But why Mama? We only just got here?"

Natasha thought of Winn's uncompromising honesty and wondered for a moment if it would be any use to lie. Perhaps she should just introduce Sergei as her former lover and get it over with. But that was ridiculous. The child was only eleven years old and she couldn't possibly suspect anything. Choosing her words carefully, Natasha forced herself to keep her voice light and casual. "We have to go now, *koshechka*, because we have some very serious *Winnie-the-Pooh* to finish reading before I have to go to rehearsal." Although Winn

172

could read perfectly well herself and had been doing so for years, hearing Natasha declaim the part of Eyore in a thick Russian accent always sent her into gales of laughter.

Winn smiled so innocently it was almost painful. "That would be great, Mama." Taking Winn by the hand, Natasha led her quickly out the opposite door.

Three days later Natasha stood in the wings of the Sadler's Wells Theatre watching Stanislas Idzikowsky and Alicia Markova rehearsing a sequence from Les Rendezvous. The piece had no serious message, but still it was well worth watching. Over the years Natasha had learned that, like herself, the best dancers had secrets that could not be taught, only observed. Markova, for example, possessed a speed and elegance that were simply dazzling. Natasha had been watching her off and on for a good eight years—ever since the two of them were with Diaghilev—and she still hadn't figured out precisely how Markova did it.

"Excuse me, Miss Ladanova." Fiona Storey, the costume mistress, was gesturing frantically. "There's a phone call for you. Man says it's an emergency."

Natasha ran so fast she nearly broke her neck on the overturned flats littering the backstage area. Her first thought was that something had happened to Winn—a riding accident— or that one of Trey's crazy experimental planes had crashed at last. Grabbing the phone out of Fiona's hand, she put the receiver to her ear.

"Hello," she said breathlessly. "Hello."

"Natasha? This is Sergei. Wait, don't hang up." Something in his voice made her pause. "I'm in trouble."

"What sort of trouble?" He sounded honestly upset.

"Anya's been drinking again—worse than ever." There was nothing jaunty or arrogant in his voice, only pain and confusion. As she stood clutching the impersonal black telephone, he recited into her ear a terrible litany of hidden bottles and fights, of a cigarette that had nearly set a chair on fire, of Anya waking in the middle of the night crying out that invisible things were crawling on her, of an ugly scene in a restaurant where she had thrown a plate of hot soup. "She's convinced I'm having an affair with you."

"But that's ridiculous."

"She's left me. Gone back to France and taken the boy with her. I begged her to try the sanatorium again, but she spat in

173

my face, said I was just trying to get rid of her. I swear to
God the woman reads minds."

"Sergei, you haven't *done* anything." But he was too upset
to listen, blaming himself, blaming Anya, all the Russian
melodrama pouring out of his soul.

"You know what I think God is?" He was almost yelling
now; she imagined him pacing the hotel room the way he had
years ago when he was furious at Fouchier. "God's not
Tolstoy's supreme Good and Reason. He's a demon who plays
with us for the fun of it, a monster with a perverse sense of
humor."

"Sergei, sober up. You sound like something out of
Dostoyevski." She wanted to be there, to shake some sense
into him. It was frightening to hear him going on this way.

"The Bible claims the Kingdom of God's inside us. Well, I
look inside, I look at my life, and what do I see? A desert full
of disappointments. And do you know what I hear? I hear
God laughing, the bastard."

"Sergei, stop it!"

"So I throw this life back in his face. I tell him His
Kingdom is for fools and idiots."

"Sergei, give me your address." It took her five more
minutes, but she finally got him to tell her he was staying at
the St. George.

Sergei's suite at the St. George was an odd combination of
elegance and chaos. The furniture, of the massive Teutonic
variety favored by exclusive hotels half a century ago, was
upholstered in a pretty floral pattern, the walls painted a
shade of blue so cheerful it was positively un-English. Through
the wide double windows Natasha could see a bit of the
Thames, a brown curve of water, neat and precise as an
architect's drawing, but inside pandemonium reigned. Expensive leather suitcases stamped with the Belinsky crest lay
everywhere, spilling their contents on the rug, presenting
formidable barricades in front of windows and doors. Discarded
cones of fish and chips littered the parquet tables; delicate
Florentine wastebaskets overflowed with sardine tins and
empty bottles.

Sergei was sitting in the middle of the unmade bed,
clutching a red-labeled bottle that Natasha instantly recognized as Stolichnaya, the strongest Russian vodka money
could buy. Unshaven, dressed in a white shirt and a pair of
badly creased pants, he looked ill and tired. It occurred to

her that he had never let her see him this way before; for the first time she was aware of the age in his face, as if a mask had suddenly fallen away to reveal all the mortality, the fragility he had kept so carefully hidden.

"*Zdrastvuyte*, Tasha." Sergei took a long swig of the vodka and then put the bottle down on the bed table with drunken care. "Welcome to the madhouse. Most of the inmates are on vacation right now, but if you just wait around they'll probably be back." Retrieving the bottle, he took another drink of Stolichnaya.

"Sergei, stop that."

"What a greeting from an old friend. Not even hello. Just 'Sergei, stop that.' Haven't you heard?" He waved his arm in a gesture of mock grandeur. "Vodka is the ultimate solution to all the world's pain. Ask Anya. Ask *any* Russian. A nation of dipsomaniacs marching forward under the banner of Marxism-Leninism. So I give you a toast. *Za smerty; za jizen*—to death and life, in that order."

Natasha took off her hat and threw her coat on one of the suitcases. She felt sorry for him, but she knew from past experience that sympathy was the one thing he could never tolerate. "Sergei," she said briskly, "are you aware that you're scaring the hell out of me?"

"I am?" He put the bottle down, clumsily this time, tipping over and spilling some. "I'm sorry." He dabbed apologetically at the vodka with the corner of a pillowcase. "I was just indulging in our national sport: despair."

Natasha cleared one of Anya's slips from a chair and sat down, wondering what to do next. It was always hard to tell how Sergei was really feeling. On the one hand, he might simply be putting on a grand self-destructive show for an invisible audience, an act she'd seen him perform more times than she cared to count. But, on the other hand, there was always the possibility that this time his despair was real. She'd read somewhere once that when people threatened suicide you should always take them seriously, but could Sergei's veiled hints be considered threats? She paused for a moment, choosing her words carefully. "I came over here," she said at last, "because I was afraid you might hurt yourself."

"Not a bad idea. Care for a game of Russian roulette? I think there's a gun around here somewhere, but no bullets, alas. Perhaps room service would provide them if we came up with a big enough tip."

"Sergei!" She didn't know whether to laugh or cry. He had

to be the most brilliant, impossible, erratic man on the face of the earth.

"I'm sorry. I'm being a bastard. It's my one real talent." He swung his legs over the edge of the bed, and straightened his tie. The effect was remarkable. "You're good to me Natasha," he said soberly, "better than I deserve. I haven't given you much have I? Except pain and lots of it. Come here and sit beside me and let me be sincere for once."

She got up and went over to the bed, wanting to say something bright and witty, but not finding the words. Sergei took her hands in his and pulled her down beside him. There was a long silence, delicate as an eggshell. Finally, Sergei broke it. "Do you know what I want?" he said simply. "I want to forget the present as if it never happened. I want twelve years back." He paused. "I want you, Natasha."

His words left a vacuum behind them that seemed to swallow up every sound in the room. Natasha looked at his blunt strong fingers intertwined with hers. A dozen different emotions washed over her, leaving her inarticulate. She felt, rather than thought, of her life with Trey, of how his lovemaking had been an anesthetic, numbing her over the years, putting the woman part of her to sleep, and, as she thought of the waste, desire blossomed in her again, desire so intense it was like something burning under her skin, and she realized that no matter how crazy it seemed, no matter what the consequences, she was going to let Sergei make love to her.

He lifted her fingers to his lips and kissed them lightly. "Do *you* want me?" Natasha nodded, not trusting herself to speak. Leaning forward, Sergei put his hands on either side of her head and tilted her mouth to his.

That afternoon something physical in Natasha thawed, and she knew that no matter what happened in the future she would never again be completely happy with Trey. Sergei undressed her slowly, taking off each piece of her clothing, kissing her over and over again, running his fingers under the back of her slip, around the edges of her breasts. Every touch brought a flood of memories: that first night on the red silk sofa in her house in St. Petersburg; the little hotel room in Paris with the double windows; the great porcelain tub where they had floated naked in each other's arms; the evening she had dressed up in his clothes.

As he caught her to him, rubbing his hips over hers, kissing her eyelids and neck, it seemed to her their present bent and touched their past—that they were twenty again, that they had never hurt each other or been enemies, that there was no pain or betrayal, no revolution, no years at all, only this single, seamless afternoon.

He excited her again and again, until she lost all sense of where she was and what she was doing. After a time the memories stopped and her mind became a perfect blank, a metronome to her body. After what seemed hours, Sergei suddenly drew her so close his nails bit into her flesh. He was a force moving through her rather than touching her, and when he finished she lay in his arms at peace.

Later she would go back to that spring in London and count off the days on her fingers, unable to believe there had only been thirteen of them—thirteen days, a rosary of disillusionment, strung out in a long row like the glass beads in the Victoria and Albert Museum, each one a little less polished than the last. Most often she remembered the first five days when she had come to Sergei's room every afternoon after rehearsal, feeling so intensely alive it seemed to her she might burst with happiness. After so many years of waiting, her appetite for lovemaking was endless, her pleasure in even the smallest things intense beyond description. Sergei had only to drag the tip of his finger over her wrist for her to feel a silly fluttering inside, and she spent hours lying beside him in perfect contentment. But when they tried to talk, things began to go wrong with a speed that was alarming.

"What are you going to do about Anya?" she'd asked him on the afternoon of the sixth day.

Sergei had looked at her strangely. "What do you mean?"

"Are you going to tell her about us?"

"Why bother?"

"But. . . ." She stumbled to a stop, confused.

Sergei surveyed her with a slightly distant look, like a man considering the purchase of a new car. "You worry too much." He settled one of the pillows behind his head and leaned back comfortably. "What do you think of Frederick Ashton?"

"What?"

"Frederick Ashton, that new choreographer over at Vic-Wells. Do you think he's as good as I am or just a flash in the pan?"

Natasha was stunned. How could he possibly have changed the subject when she had been trying to talk to him about something so important? Perhaps he hadn't understood.

*   *   *

"I worry about Winn," Natasha said. "She's so sharp; sometimes I'm sure she suspects something, and she's not the type to keep a secret." They were sitting at a small table in Sergei's room, eating hot buttered scones and drinking their tea Russian style, without milk. It was the afternoon of the eighth day. Sergei selected another scone and buttered it methodically. Whatever pain he had felt about Anya seemed to have disappeared without a trace. He looked healthy, self-satisfied, almost maddeningly content.

Natasha put down her teacup. "Sergei," she said quietly, "did you hear what I said? I'm worried Winn suspects there's something going on. You have no idea how bluntly honest the child is. And I'm worried that, even if she doesn't know about us yet, my leaving Trey may have a terrible effect on her in the future. She's often felt left out of my life because I'm a dancer and she isn't, and I'm not sure now she'd respond to such a dramatic change. She might see it as total abandonment."

"She'll survive."

"What?"

"You know I've been thinking of doing a ballet of Huysmans's *Against the Grain*. *Là-Bas* would be more exciting, of course, but given the censorship situation I imagine that's out of the question."

"Sergei, I was talking about my daughter."

He picked up the white china teapot. "More?" Without waiting for an answer, he refilled her cup.

"Mama, what are you doing?"

"Nothing dearest." Natasha crumpled the note she had been writing, and forced herself to smile at Winn. Her life suddenly seemed crowded, complicated beyond belief. There was not enough time for Winn, for Trey, for her work. She had to lie constantly and, worst of all, remember her lies later. Not an easy task, especially when Winn was around to keep track. Recently she had begun to think that having a lover was rather like being required to commit all of *War and Peace* to memory—exhausting beyond belief. It might have been easier if she'd been able to talk the problem over with Sergei, but every time she brought up the subject of feelings he looked at her as if she were speaking a foreign language.

Winn curled up next to her, and Natasha stroked her hair, thinking guiltily that she had neglected Winn lately. Winn knew, of course, that things had been different in the past few weeks; she *must* know, but she hadn't said a thing—which, as far as Natasha was concerned, was a bad sign. If Winn was suddenly displaying tact, she must be confused, perhaps even frightened.

Natasha winced at the thought that her involvement with Sergei might be harming her daughter. How did other people manage to live two lives at the same time? Possibly the problem was that, like Winn, she simply had no talent for deception.

"You don't mean it."

"Of course I mean it." Natasha sighed and tried again. Madame Tussaud's had to be the oddest place in London to have a discussion of this nature, but she'd wanted to pick somewhere neutral where they'd be unlikely to run into anyone they knew—and a hotel room, under the circumstances, was definitely out of the question. So here they stood, sandwiched in between Edward VII and Queen Victoria. "It just isn't working out."

"What do you mean it's not working out?" Sergei peered at her anxiously through the velvety gloom. His crisp white suit caught the blue lights in a way that was ghostly and vaguely disturbing. For almost two weeks they had been sleeping together every afternoon, and each day he had seemed less real to her. With Trey she had gotten used to a certain kind of intimacy, an easy flow of feelings, an unspoken sense of understanding, but the more she saw of Sergei the more she felt she was running up against a stone wall. Only his body was there. The inner part of him was closed off as securely as if he'd had it committed to the Tower of London: he talked to her about the new company he wanted to form; the ballets he would choreograph for her; about anything and everything but himself. After less than two weeks she was beginning to dread getting into bed with him the way she dreaded opening nights.

"There's Anya to think of." The least she could do was give him a decent excuse, and a wife was one of the best. Besides, having virtually lived with Sergei for the past thirteen days she was beginning to see Anya's side of things.

"I told you I'd divorce her." But he'd told her no such thing. Perhaps he'd assumed she'd know, that she could read his mind—anyway, it didn't matter anymore. Sergei moved out of the light so she couldn't see his face, but she could feel the anger and amazement in his voice. Well, why shouldn't he be amazed? For years she'd been his doormat. This whole conversation must come as something of a shock to him. He stood there, a white shadow, demanding she explain herself.

Natasha looked at her watch and saw she had only half an hour until she was due at the theater. "Sergei," she said as gently as possible, "I made a terrible mistake. Look, I don't know any diplomatic way to say this, so I'll be blunt: I don't love you. I thought I still did, but I don't—at least not enough to hurt Winn and Trey."

"What about all the time we spend in bed; I suppose you're going to tell me you don't like that either?"

"On the contrary, I like it far too much."

"Natasha, you can't do this to me."

"So it's *you* I'm doing it to?"

"Of course," he sounded honestly surprised.

"Sergei, that's just the problem. You see everything in terms of yourself. When I was younger I didn't understand. I thought you were St. Michael on a white charger, the most perfect man in the world. I thought you knew everything there was to know. But I'm not sixteen anymore." She suddenly felt very tired. "You don't understand, do you?"

"No."

"You're incapable of love and intimacy. You're like the world's most perfect thinking machine: you create marvelous ballets, give a great performance, but in the end there's no *dusha.*"

"You're crazy."

"I don't think so." She felt pain, bittersweet sadness, but no regrets. Perhaps the regrets would come later.

Leaning forward in the darkness, Natasha kissed Sergei lightly on the cheek. Then she turned and walked quickly past the wax statues, out of Madame Tussaud's museum into the clear spring sunlight of Marylebone Road.

Book II

TATIANA

11

Cambridge, Massachusetts, 1951

Tatiana Ward sat at her desk wrapped in a flannel robe, drinking a cup of instant coffee, and thumbing through the latest issue of *Balance*, a magazine published twice a month by a group of Harvard undergraduates that purported to cover dance in all its forms from "an original and unbiased perspective"—although Tatiana, who was a personal friend of the editor, knew for a fact that at least half the articles were pilfered directly from the *New York Times*. This issue, for example, contained a recycled piece of Balanchine's recent adaptation of *La Valse*; a quasi-scholarly analysis of Maximov's new ballet *Quetzal*, in which the young critic tried—and failed, in Tatiana's opinion—to make a connection between color and movement; and a rave review of *Dance*, the new Fred Lewis musical that had just opened in Boston.

Tatiana quickly skimmed the review of *Dance* and decided she'd like to see it. Tap dancing wasn't exactly her style, of course, but in this particular case a new young performer named Michael Macks was evidently proving extraordinary. She ran over the description of Macks's dancing again: "*stunning . . . impeccable timing . . . a marvelous combination of rhythms and counterrhythms*." Too bad tickets were fifteen dollars apiece.

Suppressing a small pang of regret, Tatiana closed the magazine and looked out the window at the Radcliffe Quad. At four o'clock in the morning it was still dark: blue drifts covered the bicycles in the racks in front of Cabot Hall; tree limbs swayed under cottony white mounds; the sidewalks in front of the dorms were mere tracks leading toward an icy expanse of street. Inside the room, thanks to the ancient cast-iron radiator that joggled and spat puffs of steam, it was almost too hot to breathe, as evidenced by Tatiana's roommate, Ruth White, who lay sideways across her bed, all the covers kicked into a tangle on the floor, snoring peacefully, the pink tips of her curlers arranged neatly around her skull like a set of radio antennae.

Tatiana grinned and took another sip of coffee. Ruth's side of the room looked as if it had recently been struck by a major earthquake or looted by a pack of drunken Visigoths. A cheap print of Van Gogh's *Starry Night* hung crookedly over her bed; three or four rare Leadbelly records shared the floor with a pile of pamphlets from the Harvard chapter of the Save the Rosenbergs Committee, decaying banana peels, crumpled cigarette packs, and a tumble of botany books. Ruth's battered paratrooper bicycle, which she was convinced half the thieves in Cambridge had their eyes on, had been rolled into the elevator, dragged up to the room, and locked to a spindly floor lamp. All of which just went to prove you couldn't judge a roommate by how much junk she left around for you to trip over.

Tatiana took another sip of the bitter coffee and contemplated her own side of the room, thinking—as she often did—how much ballet had influenced the way she regarded space. She might not know what she was majoring in, or what she was going to do with the rest of her life, but thanks to thirteen years of ballet lessons, she would certainly never have any trouble finding a matching pair of socks. Since home was only a few blocks away, she had gotten into the habit of going there when she wanted something, thus her closet was nearly empty, her books few and carefully arranged, her dresser drawers as neat as a cubist painting. Covered with a brilliant red satin quilt—a gift from her sister, Winn, who had picked it up for next to nothing in Hong Kong on her honeymoon— Tatiana's bed glowed warmly in the dim light. On the wall behind it was her most precious possession: a small Degas depicting two dancers bending over to tie their shoes—one of the few things her mother had managed to bring out of Russia when she fled the Bolshevik Revolution. A little less than a month ago, on the occasion of Tatiana's eighteenth birthday, her mother had given the painting to her along with another photograph of her father, framed in heavy antique silver.

The photograph, which now sat on Tatiana's desk next to her portable typewriter, showed Trey Ward as he had looked a good sixteen years ago: a tall, handsome blond man standing in front of a sleek single-engine plane, waving at the invisible camera. Tatiana tried for a moment to conjure up an image of the real man and failed. She'd been only two when he died of hepatitis in India while accompanying her mother on a world tour, and although there were endless snapshots of him holding her, she had no memory of him at all. Not, she thought ruefully, that she hadn't looked for substitutes.

Tatiana sighed slightly and made her regular early morning attempt to face the fact that she was by nature too impulsive for her own good. Take the last six months for example: one day she was a Democrat, the next (after meeting Ruth) an ardent anarchist, then suddenly indifferent to politics. And then there were the Harvard boys, God help her, classes and classes full of them: handsome, lean, with quick minds and even quicker hands. It was only January and she'd already fallen in love half a dozen times, only to find herself wondering after a week or two what she'd ever seen in the poor sucker.

Her mother had been amused, called it all an excess of Russian *dusha*, but Tatiana sometimes worried about her own lack of common sense. She was always plunging into projects, giving away her favorite things, probably the only student in the recorded history of Radcliffe to have declared six different majors before the second semester of her freshman year.

Drinking the last of the coffee, Tatiana rinsed out the cup with some mineral water, dried it, and put it on the windowsill. Then she hurried to her dresser and pulled on a pair of tights, leg warmers, and a bright turquoise leotard cut low at the neck. Over these she quickly donned a man's wool shirt, bulky green sweater, wool socks, blue jeans, rubber boots, and then—swearing softly to herself—a long violet-and-gray plaid skirt: another gift from Winn, so beautifully cut it seemed to swirl around her in a cloud.

Winn was always trying to persuade her to dress in a more feminine fashion, having informed Tatiana bluntly that she was getting too old to run around in boys' clothes, but Tatiana herself favored the Hepburn look—sloppy sweaters, slouch hats, baggy pants—in which, by some miracle, she always managed to appear spectacular. Although only of medium height, she had the long-limbed, leggy grace of a fashion model, complete with auburn hair that often made strangers compare her to America's most famous covergirl, Suzy Parker. In actual fact, Tatiana looked like a younger version of her mother: the same rose petal skin, the same touch of Tartar around the cheekbones—but the truth was Tatiana was even more beautiful, by far the most beautiful of all the Ward girls of her generation. Her eyes were blue, not a normal blue but a deep, shimmering, aquatic violet like the blues in the antique Victorian paperweight her mother kept on her desk. They were eyes that startled and seduced without meaning to, and they were forever getting Tatiana in trouble, attracting men in whom she had no interest and for whom she had no time, causing her professors to suddenly lose their train of thought, provoking invitations to lunch and dinner that, had she accepted half of them, would have made her too fat to dance anything but the Mother Ginger in *The Nutcracker*.

Tatiana fumbled with the snaps on the skirt, fulminating silently about the ridiculous Radcliffe rule that made it illegal for the girls to appear in public wearing pants. It was perfectly idiotic when you thought about it, especially in the dead of winter. Students at Radcliffe regularly got frostbite in completely unmentionable places.

Closing the last snap on the skirt, she settled it down over her jeans, feeling as if she had just climbed into a laundry bag. Sometimes she was tempted to move out of the dorm and go back home, but on the other hand she liked living with Ruth, and it was probably healthier, too—psychologically speaking. After all, here she was without a father, an absolutely classic example of the disruption of the whole Oedipal system. Or was it? Darn. She should have read those psychology books more closely, taken a few notes. Then she wouldn't have gotten a C on the hour exam, plus she'd have some idea whether she faced a life of sanity or weekly sessions on some rich shrink's leather couch.

Well, in any event, it didn't really matter. Tatiana wrapped her muffler around her neck thinking, not for the first time, that no matter what her professor in Psych 10 would have said, she and her mother were too close sometimes for their own good. It wasn't easy being the daughter of one of the world's most famous ballerinas: not if you wanted to dance yourself, or at least thought you did. Sometimes Tatiana envied Winn her ability to take life as it came. Her sister was forever doing normal things like shopping for clothes and organizing fundraising drives for the Red Cross. Oh, there were moments when Tatiana suspected Winn felt left out— even a touch jealous—but if she was tormented by any grandiose ambitions to go on the stage herself, she never let on. For all her earnestness, Winn was a dilettante; she had even managed to go off to Paris and play at being an artist for a few months before she met Drew and got engaged. Amazing when you thought about it. Playing at dance was something Tatiana couldn't have done even if someone had been crazy enough to pay her to try.

Turning out the light, Tatiana picked up the green book bag that contained her *pointe* shoes and tiptoed out of the room, leaving Ruth snoring quietly.

"How does she do it?" Colin Wilson whispered to Tatiana as the two of them stood next to each other at the barre. Colin was the only male in the early morning class, a dedicated dancer who had made the ten thousand mile trek from Melbourne, Australia, to Boston solely for the purpose of studying at the Ladanova School of Classical Ballet. It was six o'clock and the students, exhausted and sweat-soaked, were watching Natasha demonstrate a complicated sequence of steps. Dressed in a sea green leotard, she seemed to float across the studio without touching the floor, spine erect, arms supple, a vague smile on her lips as she passed from one dappled patch of lamplight to another.

"I swear," Colin observed in his thick Aussie accent, "your mum has wheels instead of toes."

Tatiana contemplated Natasha with mixed feelings of pride and despair. She didn't mind so much getting up at four in the morning to take lessons, but when she saw her mother at the age of fifty-six glide across the studio with the grace of a woman half her age, every gesture perfect and full of feeling, she felt as if she had two left feet, the balance of a rhinoceros, and no talent worth talking about.

Natasha suddenly executed a stunning *grand jeté*, landing as lightly as a feather, and Tatiana mentally threw her hands up in the air. *Who* could compete with that? Natasha stopped and Tatiana came back to her senses. This was getting out of hand. She was being too hard on herself. She was good; everyone said so. Last summer in San Francisco, Christensen had practically begged her to stay on and dance with the company, and when she'd auditioned for the School of American Ballet in November she'd been admitted to the upcoming summer session without question. Balanchine himself had even taken her aside and reminisced about the years he and her mother had spent with Diaghilev. But, come to think of it, was that a good sign or a bad one? Balanchine had been as friendly as Santa Claus, but one of the problems of being Natasha Ladanova's daughter was that you never knew if you had real talent or if people were just attracted to you because of her.

Actually, Tatiana only worried this way when she was standing at the barre. Once she actually started dancing it was different. The next hour passed in a blur as she imitated the sequence again and again until her legs ached and her breath caught in her chest.

A few blocks away in a large colonial house on Salem Street, Winn Compton opened the door of the hall closet and inspected her linens, each piece of which was embroidered with her initials. Winn had the neatest closets in Cambridge, or at least she liked to think she did. In this one, for example, the sheets were arranged by size, color, and age: oldest on top (ready to be demoted to the rag basket in the basement as soon as they started showing holes that couldn't be mended), double sheets marked with safety pins in the upper-left-hand corners, pillowcases resting on a small ivory and sandalwood rack of their own that Winn had picked up in Kowloon for a song. Sometimes, when Winn was feeling a little down, which wasn't all that often, she would go through the house closet by closet, opening each door, filling herself with a sense of peace and order.

Perhaps it was silly to derive so much satisfaction from merely being a good housewife. Heaven knew there were more exciting careers, but Winn had seen firsthand what they did to you, and as far as she was concerned they weren't worth the price. Ballet, for example, had practically eaten her mother alive, and her sister, too, for that matter. Poor Tatiana was a freshman in college and should be doing all sorts of exciting things the way Winn had in her freshman year at Wellesley: dating handsome young men; going to dances; getting herself invited up to Dartmouth for the Winter Carnival and down to Columbia for the big football games. But instead she was virtually a prisoner, waking up every morning at some truly horrible hour to take lessons, and running back to mother's in the afternoons after class to practice some more.

Sometimes, when Winn was taking stock of her conscience, she had to admit to herself that, although she loved Tats, she resented her just a little for getting so much of Mama's attention, but Winn wouldn't have traded places with her on a bet. No, she was happy taking care of Drew and the house. They had a good marriage, traveled a lot, and if she wanted excitement there was always the *Sybelle*, Drew's boat (not quite big enough to be called a yacht), which she had learned to sail by herself last summer, a yar little craft, quick and light as a bobber that took her skimming across the bay, pulling the breath right out of her body and taking the skin off her hands. She loved the neatness of that boat, the precisely coiled lines, the sheer whiteness of the sails, the scrubbed deck and polished brass. Yes, with Drew and the *Sybelle* she was perfectly happy.

Well, not quite perfectly happy to be honest. Winn reached into the hall closet and counted the first shelf of sheets, although she knew how many of them there were by heart. She had been married to Drew for nearly three years now and still, despite their best efforts, they hadn't managed to have any children. She stood for a moment, then suddenly leaned forward and put her face down on top of the pile of sheets, feeling the smooth cool surface of the linen. The sheets smelled of lavender and sunshine because she always had Mary, the maid, hang them outside to dry.

Closing her eyes Winn thought about the spare room that would make such a perfect nursery, about the embroidered baby clothes she had bought secretly in Lucerne last spring, hidden in the bottom drawer where Drew wouldn't see them. A wave of nostalgia swept over her—a desire to do something silly like climb into the closet, shut the door behind her, and let the darkness swallow up her disappointment.

That, however, was ridiculous. Winn stood and gave herself a shake, like a dog shedding water. No doubt plenty of women had to live with the fact that they couldn't have children. There was no use brooding about what life didn't give you; the trick was to go on as if you didn't care and hope that in time you really wouldn't. If she felt so strongly about children then she should probably do something useful like work for the PTA—you didn't have to be a parent to do that—or raise funds for the March of Dimes.

Putting her personal pain back in some internal closet of her own design, Winn selected two double sheets from the pile in front of her, walked resolutely into the bedroom, and began to make the bed the way Drew liked it: loose on the sides with the bottom corners tucked in firmly.

"Hang on to your millinery ladies!" Dan exploded into the restaurant, dragging half the snow in Cambridge with him. "I've just engineered the coup of the century!" The Wursthouse was nearly empty, but even so heads turned as Dan threw himself into the wooden booth. Ruth's coffee sloshed onto Tatiana's pastrami sandwich and both girls shrieked in protest.

"Dan!" Tatiana made an attempt to save her sandwich and failed.

"You klutz!" Ruth tried to dam the stream of coffee pouring into her lap.

Dan grinned and turned up the collar of his Brooks Brothers jacket rakishly. A junior at Harvard, he was a short, pudgy boy with large, nearsighted brown eyes that made him look like a chipmunk—a deceptive similarity since Dan was a major wheeler-dealer, having his finger in every dramatic pie, so to speak, that the university offered. In the past three years, besides editing *Balance*, he had almost single-handedly produced three musical revues, overseen all the annual Adams House Christmas plays, and developed a reputation for being the éminence grise behind the Hasty Pudding shows. A boy of endless talent and a ridiculously optimistic disposition, Dan's only apparent problems were sliding grades in chemistry (his major, which he openly loathed) and an ongoing war (conducted primarily by mail) with his parents in Cleveland who were determined that he would be a stockbroker.

Tatiana looked at her ruined sandwich and then at Dan's Adams House tie, its tip dangling into a jar of hot German mustard. He was a snappy dresser—English tweeds, silk mufflers imported from France. Tatiana didn't know another boy at Harvard who had a better sense of color, but really! Being around him was like being around a big clumsy dog. She mopped at the coffee with her napkin while Ruth lit into Dan in Yiddish.

"*Putz.*" Ruth's white blouse was stained with a galaxy of indelible brown spots. Not that she actually minded—you could probably spill sulfuric acid on Ruth's clothes without her really caring—but it was the principle of the thing. "You just wrecked my mother's hope of her only daughter catching a rich Harvard husband."

"I offer myself in his place." Dan made a slashing motion across his throat. "A sacrifice on the field of your fair virginity."

Ruth sneered in a friendly sort of way and lit a cigarette. Tatiana happened to know for a fact that Ruth was indeed a virgin, but it wasn't the sort of thing she liked to have bantered about in public, especially since she had spent the better part of the previous semester perfecting her New York anarchist Bohemian image. "I wouldn't *have* you, Danny boy," Ruth blew a chain of smoke rings one after the other, "not on a platter surrounded by wild rice. Even though you are a Class-A turkey."

"Seriously," Dan said. "I have news."

"What kind of news?" Tatiana gave up on the coffee, having learned from experience that when Dan was excited about something nine times out of ten she would be, too.

"I have wheeled, dealed, wangled, insinuated, manipulated, trafficked. . . ."

"A human thesaurus," Ruth blew some smoke in Tatiana's direction, "do you hear this, Tats? We're in the presence of Roget made flesh."

"Oh, for heaven's sake don't interrupt him," Tatiana protested, "or he'll use it as an excuse to take forever."

"In short," Dan continued, unperturbed, "I've gotten us three tickets for *Dance*."

"The new Fred Lewis musical?" Tatiana couldn't believe it. *Dance*, indeed. Everyone knew the show had been sold out for weeks. It wasn't every day Boston got a Broadway smash with the original cast. Only last week the paper had reported that scalpers were getting forty dollars a ticket. "Where are we sitting? Last row balcony underneath the seats?"

"Front row balcony, and we'll be able to see just fine. You'll be able to count every tooth in Michael Macks's head."

"Who's Michael Macks?" Ruth inquired with forced indifference, trying very hard to appear unimpressed.

"Ruthie, Ruthie, you amaze me. Michael Macks is an almost unheard of phenomenon: a white man with rhythm. I'd say there's a good chance he's going to turn out to be *the* tap dancing sensation of the decade—possibly the Fred Astaire of the fifties—and he's absolutely ravishing, blond as a Greek god." Dan reached for Tatiana's sandwich and began to munch sanguinely on the damp bread. "Now, having cleared that up, let me inform you ladies I have once again perfected a plan."

Ruth and Tatiana both groaned. Dan's last plan, which had involved the three of them getting themselves locked into the Peabody Museum after closing hours, had been nothing but trouble. Instead of being interesting as Dan had promised, it had proved excruciatingly boring. They had looked at the dinosaur bones until they were blue in the face, fallen asleep on a ratty leather couch in front of the passenger pigeon display, hungry and annoyed with one another, and just missed being caught by the janitor in the morning.

"No, really," Dan protested, "listen. After tonight's show a big cast party is going to be held—free drinks, all the shrimp you can eat."

"I don't drink," Tatiana said.

"And I," Ruth said, "don't eat shrimp. Poor little things. Curled up like fetuses. Slaughtered in their prime."

"Shut up you two," Dan said. "I have the address and we're going. I personally don't intend to sacrifice my chance to meet Fred Lewis in person—not to *mention* Michael Macks."

"Are you crazy," Tatiana pushed the rest of her ruined sandwich toward Dan, and put her elbows on the table. "At a party like that they're bound to have bouncers. Big burly types from Southie who'll take one look at us, know we're under age, and throw us out on our ears."

"Glad you mentioned it." Dan pulled a piece of paper out of his pocket. "I've reviewed the age barrier problem from all angles. Now here's what we have to do. You," he pointed to Tatiana, "have to throw away those frumpy clothes and get yourself something fashionable for once: a black dress maybe, very sexy, very understated, and then a pair of high heels— and I mean *really* high ones, the French kind you can hardly walk in, with little straps across the instep."

"But I hate heels. The last time I wore a really high pair I sprained my ankle and couldn't dance for a month."

"It doesn't matter. We're going for image here. Impractical shoes make a woman look more mature. What I have in mind for you is a cross between Suzy Parker and Marlene Dietrich. Don't worry about your hair and makeup because I'll do that for you. Just concentrate on the dress. I'd try Filene's basement for starters. As for Ruth," Dan looked at Ruth with a flicker of despair, "this is going to be a challenge."

"Thanks a lot."

"Something tailored maybe, suggestion of career woman. Glasses to hide your cherubic face."

"I never thought of myself as particularly cherubic," Ruth protested.

"And I," Tatiana said, "in case you haven't noticed, bear absolutely no resemblance to Dietrich—especially where it counts."

"Never fear, dears," Dan polished off the last of the pastrami with a flourish. "I know your inner souls. Just put yourselves in my hands."

The Mediterranean lay calm and unruffled under a bright hot sun. Overhead the sky was studded with small lacy clouds

192

frozen in midcourse between Africa and France. Far out on the horizon, just barely visible, a yacht glided endlessly forward, forever staying in the same spot. In front of this static, painted backdrop Michael Macks was a tornado of motion, resplendent in tails and top hat, tearing up the stage, tapping himself and the audience into a frenzy.

Tatiana leaned forward to get a better view as Macks, planting the tip of his cane on the floor, danced around it as if it were a living partner. If there was any plot to all this she had somehow missed it, but watching this frenetic display of energy, she no longer cared. Clicking his heels together, drumming the boards of the stage, Macks leapt, turned, and tapped, never missing a beat, his legs moving so fast it looked as if he had at least six of them. When the routine was over and he left the stage, Tatiana suddenly felt let down. The rest of the first act of *Dance* was silly and perfunctory, and if it hadn't been for Ruth jabbing her in the side from time to time she would probably have fallen asleep.

Outside of Macks, the best part of the show was the intermission when she, Ruth, and Dan strolled nonchalantly through the lobby contemplating themselves in the gold-framed mirrors, making desperate attempts not to break into fits of hysterical laughter. This time Dan had outdone himself. Stuffed into a sleeveless black wool sheath, Ruth peered out from behind a pair of enormous horn-rimmed glasses. Somehow, in the elation of getting ready, Dan had persuaded her to let him cut her hair. Now, after hours of desperate brushing it still curled up all over her head poodle-fashion, looking—Tatiana thought with another helpless giggle—like nothing so much as a pot scraper. Dan himself, his boyish face concealed behind a fake mustache, was elegant in a baggy raw silk suit and a polka dot bow tie that made him look a little like Edward R. Murrow on a bad day.

As for Tatiana, she hardly recognized herself. Her luxuriant auburn hair had been coiled in a simple French roll, tiny tendrils brushed forward to curl coquettishly at her temples. Declaring her face already a work of art, Dan had used a minimum of makeup: a touch of rouge to accent her cheekbones, a soft rose lipstick that followed the natural lines of her lips, a brownish-toned mascara that turned her eyes into violet-blue pools behind a curtain of silky lashes. Her dress—bought for $10.95 in Filene's famous bargain basement—was a real find. It was a designer original made of black crepe that clung to her bodice and hips, flaring slightly at her thighs in a way that was simultaneously modest and provocative. At the last minute, from the depths of an Adams House costume trunk, Dan had pulled out the perfect finishing touch: a pair of elbow-length kid gloves, so soft they clung to Tatiana's bare arms like a second skin.

The effect was so stunning that when Tatiana looked in the mirror she felt she was in disguise. The beautiful, sophisticated woman in black who stared back at her from the depths of the glass couldn't possibly be eighteen-year-old Tatiana Ward. Surely in a moment the illusion Dan had so carefully created would collapse and she would see herself as she really looked: dressed in the familiar moss green sweater with the hole in the elbow, hair pulled carelessly into a ponytail, feet thrust into a pair of high-topped black gym shoes with dangling laces.

The odd thing was that everyone else seemed to take her appearance entirely for granted, even Dan who went into his approving eyebrow wiggling, Groucho Marx routine every time she glanced in his direction. And that was only the beginning. As the three of them strolled the length of the lobby, Tatiana suddenly became aware that for the first time in her life the eyes of nearly every man in the place were following her eagerly. Sober Bostonians stared at her furtively over their wives' shoulders looking hungry and humble, and she felt in return pride, confusion, amusement, and a tiny fleck of contempt that they could so easily be taken in by such a silly charade. It was intoxicating in a way, but unnerving, and by the end of intermission Tatiana found herself hiding in the Ladies' Room wishing she hadn't agreed to try to crash the cast party.

"I don't think we've met." An elderly man in a gray suit bent over her, his small eyes bright and somehow malicious. His face, familiar from the endless pictures in *Time*, was a shock up close: pale and foreign-looking, skin pitted, lips thick and moist as if he'd just bitten into a peach. Topping off everything was that part of him the *New Yorker* liked best to caricature: his famous button nose, a pink dab at the center of his face so out of proportion to everything else that it gave the impression of having been put on hastily as an afterthought.

Tatiana looked up, recognized him instantly, and nearly choked on a canape. It was Fred Lewis, the most famous producer on Broadway, and he was actually talking to *her*. Good heavens, what should she say? The dry bread stuck to the roof of her mouth; she tried to say something but no words came out, only a small gasping sound that made her go scarlet with embarrassment.

Lewis looked at her with amused indulgence, obviously pleased to have been the cause of such a reaction. "Can I get you a drink?" Tatiana nodded, feeling like a perfect fool. What in the world was wrong with her? She should be used to famous people. Markova had changed her diapers; Nijinskaya had given her her first teddy bear; she'd been dandled on the lap of Serge Lifar. Her own mother was probably the most well-known dancer since Pavlova. Lewis came back with a glass of water and she drank it down in a gulp.

"You should go easy on that stuff," Lewis admonished. "Doesn't do to get sober too early in the evening, if you know what I mean." He winked, and she smiled back knowingly even though she had no idea what he was talking about. "You know," Lewis inspected the clinging lines of her dress appreciatively, "you're a very pretty young lady."

"Thank you," Tatiana managed to say.

"What's your name?" He poured a glass of champagne and casually handed it to her.

"Tatiana Ward."

"Never been in a musical have you?"

"No, not exactly, that is. . . ."

"Well," Lewis went on smoothly without waiting for her to answer. "I've got a good eye, and I can tell you something Miss Tatiana Ward: you've got the body of a born dancer." Tatiana started to say something, but he raised his hand impatiently. "Now don't tell me you can't dance—I already know that—what I'm saying is that with a little help, some lessons, a few changes in the right places, you could be on Broadway." He pulled a small square of white pasteboard from his pocket, uncapped a gold fountain pen, scribbled something, and thrust it into her hand. "Here, come by my hotel tomorrow, and we'll talk it over."

Turning his back, Fred Lewis ambled into the crowd surrounding the punch bowl and was immediately taken over by a tall blonde in a white fox stole. Tatiana looked at the card in her hand, not knowing whether to laugh or cry. Thirteen years of ballet lessons, 40,000 *pliés*, a broken ankle, pulled ligaments, up at four in the morning every day since she was five, and Mr. Fred Lewis had taken one look at her and thought that maybe, just *maybe*, with a few lessons he could turn her into a second-rate tap dancer. Tatiana read the card, grinned, then giggled outright.

"You know," a voice said behind her, "you should watch it with that guy." Tatiana turned to find a man of about twenty-eight standing on the other side of the buffet holding a glass of champagne in one hand and a toothpick loaded with bacon and water chestnuts in the other. He was handsome in an outdoorsy sort of way: blond hair, powerful arms, a barrel chest, thick blunt fingers, and a pair of intelligent blue eyes that were smiling at her with amused condescension. Although he was wearing a dinner jacket and black tie, he looked the type who'd be much more at home in a wool hunting shirt. Tatiana wondered briefly if he was an athlete—but then, he was too light for football, too short for basketball, and somehow he didn't look like the kind of man who would care to pass his time waiting to get up to bat.

"Lewis is the original dirty old man." He ate the bacon and water chestnuts off the toothpick, threw it carelessly down on the white linen tablecloth next to an ice swan full of chicken liver paté, and looked Tatiana up and down. "Of course, you look as if you know the score, but just in case you don't, I think I should tell you he's got a casting couch."

"A what?"

"You know. A couch where he tries out all the girls before he puts them in his shows." Tatiana was sincerely shocked and her face must have showed it because his manner changed abruptly. "Listen, I didn't mean to offend you."

"You didn't, not in the slightest," she said stiffly. After all, she was modern. She'd read *The Kinsey Report*. How dare he make it sound as if she was some kind of little prude. Tatiana's ears tingled and she realized angrily that she was blushing. "Thanks for the warning," she said, disliking him intensely, "but I can take care of myself." She turned and walked away, annoyed to realize as she did so that he was still smiling.

"Great coup, Tats," Dan observed stuffing another shrimp into his mouth. His mustache had slipped alarmingly, he'd lost his bow tie, and if Tatiana's suspicions were right he was well on his way to being drunk. Dan Groucho Marxed a few times, chomped on the shrimp, and grinned at her archly. "How *do* you do it?"

"Do what?"

"I mean here I stand, an aspiring thespian of the first order, every drop of my corn-fed Cleveland blood throbbing at the thought of meeting real Broadway luminaries, and I'm ignored," He mugged helplessness. "No, let's not say ignored, let's say nonexistent, invisible, as attractive as the bubonic plague, whereas you—equipped only with the slinkiest little black dress this side of the Charles River—have lured into your lovely feminine snare not only Fred Lewis but Michael Macks as well."

"What do you mean Michael Macks?"

"That guy you were gabbing with next to the ice swan."

"*That* was Michael Macks?"

"You bet it was."

"But he looked so different on stage."

"It's the makeup," Dan observed, cramming another shrimp in his mouth. "Besides, you could hardly expect him to come to a cast party in his tap shoes."

Tatiana was suddenly overcome with a sense of having been terribly rude. "You can't imagine how I spoke to him."

"Don't worry about it. He probably just thinks you're a would-be dancer with an axe to grind. That kind of thing happens to famous people all the time."

"But I wouldn't want him to think I was rude to him just because he was famous," Tatiana was horrified.

"Great," Dan said with a grin. "Then go over and apologize. Reassure the guy that you hate him for himself alone."

Tatiana took a deep breath, walked over to the buffet table, and tapped Michael Macks on the shoulder. "Excuse me." He turned, saw her, and an unexpected smile lit up his face. "I'm afraid I was extremely rude to you and I just wanted to say...that is..." She fumbled for the right words. Darn it, how could someone good enough at English language to get into Radcliffe suddenly start sounding as if she had the vocabulary of a Laplander. "You're a really wonderful dancer." What a non sequitur. He probably thought she was out of her mind.

"Thanks." His eyes were mildly amused, but then who could blame him. She must sound ridiculous.

"And what I wanted to ask you, if you don't mind, is have you ever had any training in ballet?"

"What makes you think that?"

"Well, there's a way you leap—you know, in the middle of that long routine you do on the beach—it's got a lightness to it, a kind of lift, if you know what I mean, that you usually only see in serious dancers." Oh, no, now she'd implied that the kind of dancing he did wasn't serious. She should give up, locate her coat, and get out of there before she made a complete fool of herself.

But if Michael Macks noticed the slip he chose gallantly to ignore it. "How do you happen to know so much about ballet?" He set his drink down on the table, and looked at her with cool seriousness, as if she'd taken him by surprise.

"I'm a dancer."

"You're kidding."

"No, really. I've danced with the San Francisco Ballet for two summers and this May I'm going to the School of American Ballet to study under Balanchine."

"A serious dancer in *that* get-up?" He suddenly broke into a grin. "Do you mind my asking how old you are?"

"Eighteen."

"Oh, no. Eighteen. A ballet dancer." He began to laugh a jolly, explosive laugh. "Oh, no."

"What's wrong with that?" It made her feel a little huffy to be laughed at.

"I'm sorry," Macks gasped between laughs. "I'm truly sorry but it's just my luck. You see, I stood around looking at you for the better part of an hour thinking you were one of the best looking women I'd seen in a long time, and now I find out you're a dancer. Fate has it in for me tonight."

"What's wrong with being a dancer?" Tatiana asked, feeling distinctly miffed.

"I've sworn them off as prospective girlfriends."

"Why?"

"Well, it's a long story. Let's just say that I've come to that advanced age when a man is in the market for a wife. Both my parents were dancers and it didn't work out too well, so I'm trying to do things differently. But it doesn't really matter because you're far too young for me anyway."

"I am *not*," Tatiana said hotly, annoyed at the idea of being treated like a child.

"Yes, you are. In fact," he took the champagne glass out of her hand, "you shouldn't even be drinking this stuff. You go driving home and have a wreck, and we'll be in hot water."

"I wasn't drinking it. I was just holding it so I didn't look out of place."

Michael grinned and handed the glass back to her. "That's the most sensible remark I've heard all evening. You're right. Anyone around here who isn't drinking like a fish, or at least pretending to, would definitely look out of place."

* * *

198

"Well," Dan said with a tinge of envy in his voice as they embarked on the long MTA ride back to Harvard Square, "you and Michael Macks certainly hit it off. What *did* you talk about all that time?"

"Nothing much," Tatiana leaned her head wearily against the battered leather cushion. Outside the window the Charles River was a black strip of motionless water bordered by a trickle of headlights. It was well past midnight; Tatiana did some rapid calculations and realized she was going to get two hours' sleep at most before her morning lesson.

"What do you mean 'nothing much.'" Dan persisted. "You stood around talking to him for hours. Surely he said *something* worth remembering."

"Actually we talked about Marius Petipa." Dan's face went so blank it was almost funny, but he'd spent too many semesters at Harvard to admit he didn't recognize the name. "You know," Tatiana grinned, taking pleasure in grinding in the salt a little. "the great French choreographer who did the *Grand pas de Wilis* in *Giselle*. And then he told me all about an ice fishing trip he's planning to take in New Hampshire."

"Sounds terribly boring," Ruth yawned.

"He knows an amazing amount about ballet," Tatiana observed.

"Probably just an excuse to stand there looking down your cleavage," Dan suggested. "It's your basic horny intellectual ploy. I know the type, being one myself. He'll probably call you tomorrow and ask you out."

"I doubt it. He said I wasn't his type." Tatiana suddenly realized she would have loved Michael Macks to call her.

But he didn't, of course. A few weeks later she came down to the bell desk in Cabot Hall to find in her mailbox a glossy postcard from New Hampshire informing her the fishing was great. After that she heard nothing from Michael Macks and by the end of the spring semester, with four exams to take, three twenty-page papers to write, and a chem lab to finish, Tatiana had almost managed to forget anyone by that name existed.

12

New York

At Eighty-third and Broadway molten sunlight glared off the second-story windowpanes of the School of American Ballet, turning them into a row of blinding golden squares that dazzled pedestrians and made bus drivers shade their eyes for a moment as they passed by. Founded in 1933 by George Balanchine and Lincoln Kirstein, the school had become in the last two decades quite simply the most famous professional dance academy in the world, training over ninety percent of the dancers in the New York City Ballet, sending its graduates to every major company in Europe and America. Like Harvard or Oxford, the SAB marked its students for life. No one leapt higher, moved more lightly, seemed more at ease than a dancer trained under Balanchine's supervision. And no students in the world put more effort into making ballet appear effortless.

Inside the school on this particular July morning, the three studios were already like ovens. In Class C, the advanced class, thirty-three students gasped for air as their sweating fingers slipped off the barre and perspiration trickled down the backs of their legs. In the long mirrors their misery was multiplied; seen from the right angle, it stretched to infinity. *Pliés, tendus, frappés*—under the critical eye of teacher Felia Doubrovska all thirty-three students launched obediently into the warm-up exercises even though it was already over a hundred degrees and getting hotter. Yesterday a girl from West Virginia had fainted right in the middle of the adagio movements, fallen to the floor with a thump that had startled everyone into nervous laughter. Then she'd gotten up, of course, and gone on with the class. Madame Doubrovska had offered to send for a doctor, but the girl had refused all help, even broken into tears when it was suggested she take the rest of the day off. The SAB had 413 students enrolled this year from among whom Mr. Balanchine would select at most five or six to apprentice with the New York City Ballet. With odds like that you couldn't risk a reputation for weakness or fragility.

Tatiana took a deep breath and tried to focus on part of the light blue wall in front of her, imagining it was a cool stream somewhere high in the mountains. Years ago her mother had taught her the trick of putting her mind somewhere else—of not feeling her body when it was in pain. Tatiana had been raised on stories of dancers who went on despite all odds: performing with sprained ankles, dislocated shoulders, broken legs, and now that training stood her in good stead. While the other students suffered in the heat, she removed herself from it, projecting an illusion of cool detachment that Madame Doubrovska noted with approval.

"Veddy gud," Doubrovska said in her thick Russian accent. Covered with heavy makeup, Doubrovska's face had a worn air, as if she had suffered all possible sufferings. For a moment Tatiana contemplated the unfairness of ballet: great dancers aged at different rates. Some were through at thirty-five, some could go on well into their sixties. Doubrovska was perhaps the finest teacher Tatiana had ever had—outside of her own mother, of course—but her body had begun to give out on her. Those famous legs that had once danced for Nijinskaya and Balanchine had lost much of their power and elasticity. How many years did Tatiana herself have before the same thing happened to her? Better not to think of it. Better to look at the wall and imagine cold blue water.

Doubrovska touched Tatiana lightly on the shoulders to indicate she should lower them slightly. Tatiana responded obediently and received another smile of approval. "Gud," Doubrovska observed, "veddy gud indeed."

After class, as the students jostled one another in the dressing room, taking off their identical white skirts, pink tights, and pink *pointe* shoes and putting on their street clothes, Tatiana could feel the tension still humming away under the conversations about diets and podiatrists. The girls were friendly, lending one another combs and hairpins, making plans to have lunch together, but beneath it all there was an anxious sense of everyone watching everyone else. Throwing her gear into her book bag, Tatiana escaped as quickly as she could, feeling simultaneously insecure and elated. On the one hand she loved the SAB better than any place she'd ever been. On the other, she wasn't sure if she was up to it.

It was Saturday, which meant she had the rest of the afternoon free for a change. Striding down the street, she tried to ignore the heat that glittered off the asphalt, surrounding the cars and pedestrians in visible waves. Posters urging her to buy Defense Bonds were plastered on all the newsstands, and the headlines shouted about battles in Korea: victories, disasters, whole cities evacuated.

Tatiana mopped at her forehead and scanned one of the stories. Strange how out of touch you could get from the real world. Here the United States was at war and all she could think about was that she'd been ordered to lose at least fifteen pounds. Mr. Balanchine, she'd been told in no uncertain terms, liked his dancers pared to the bone. Tatiana sighed, remembering the old daguerreotypes in her mother's bedroom: bevies of Maryinsky ballerinas in their old-fashioned tutus, round and plump with small protruding stomachs. Too bad fashions had changed.

The Mildred T. Walker Club in the West Seventies was a kind of combination residence hotel and convent for young women, a singularly ugly place with expiring potted palms in the lobby, chipped wooden furniture that appeared to have been purchased at a giant rummage sale, and rooms equipped with windows that seemed specifically designed to exclude as much air and light as possible. The rules at the Walker were draconian: no smoking, no drinking, no cooking in the rooms, no pets, beds to be made every morning, room to be swept every other day, lights out at ten. But the most amusing, to Tatiana at least, were those that had to do with men. She could see the reason for rule #25 (no men permitted above the first floor), but what about rule #26, which read in part: "Young ladies receiving gentlemen callers in the lobby will remember that three feet are to be kept on the floor at all times." Sometimes, as she stood brushing her teeth in the communal bathroom, Tatiana found herself wondering if the late Miss Walker had had a fetish about virginity or simply been a contortionist with a sense of humor.

When she returned to the Walker after class this particular afternoon, she found Beth, one of her three roommates, sprawled out on the right-hand bunk painting her toenails a screaming shade of red while she listened to the blaring radio. Anyone looking at Beth would have known immediately that she wasn't a dancer. Short and plump, of Hungarian descent, Beth already had the easy maternal look of a mother of six (which, she had confided to Tatiana only yesterday, was precisely the number of children she intunded to have).

Beth, who was studying to be a secretary so she could support herself until she got married, obviously had no intention of ever going on a diet.

"Guess who called while yah were out?" Beth said, in the purest Bronx, frowning slightly as she applied a second coat of polish to her big toe. She leaned back a little to admire her handiwork.

"My mother?"

"Nah, not on the phone, dummy. In person."

Tatiana tried to think of someone living in New York who might have taken the time to pay her a visit and failed utterly. Her friends from Harvard were scattered all over by now: Ruth on a botanical expedition; Dan out in Hollywood working for an uncle who had something to do with the movies. Winn and Drew were in the south of France, and only two days ago Tatiana had gotten a letter from her mother saying that she'd be spending the rest of the summer in eastern Canada working with the newly formed National Ballet.

"I give up," she said, plopping down on the bunk across from Beth. "Who was it?"

Beth blew on her toenails and grinned happily. "A man— and boy was he sumpthin'. I gotta good look at him in the lobby. Say, yah sure know how to pick 'em."

"A man?" Tatiana was sincerely puzzled. Winn and Drew had some banker friends in the city, but she could hardly imagine any of *them* dropping by the Walker to pay their respects. "What did he say his name was."

"Didn't say honey."

"Well, what did he look like?"

Beth paused, nail polish brush in midair, took a few chomps on her Juicy Fruit gum, and appeared lost in thought. "Well, he was kinda tall, but not too tall if yah know what I mean—blond hair—don't remember what color his eyes were, but he had on this real nifty white suit, expensive like. Big chest. Coulda been a wrestler. Know any wrestlers?" Tatiana shook her head. "Well then, he's a mystery man, honey, but yah won't have to wait long because he said he was comin' back around three."

Tatiana glanced at her watch and saw that it was nearly half past one. "What did this guy say he wanted?"

Beth screwed the nailbrush carefully back into the bottle, and pushed her permanently waved black hair off her damp forehead with one plump hand. "Hey kiddo," she smiled knowingly, "wise up will yah?"

Half an hour later Tatiana stood in front of the overstuffed communal closet, her wet hair wrapped in a towel, trying to figure out what to wear. If this was some friend of her mother's or Winn's, she should look minimally presentable, but it was so hot that frankly she'd prefer to throw on a pair of shorts and a halter. Finally she compromised with another of Winn's presents: a full-skirted dress of frothy light green eyelet lace with a low scoop neck and no sleeves to speak of.

When the hall buzzer rang at a quarter after three, she climbed into the Walker's rickety elevator and descended to the lobby, wondering once again as the brass cage rattled from floor to floor who in the world was waiting for her. The elevator lunged to a stop, and the main doors opened with a crash. There, standing in the lobby next to a perished potted palm, was Michael Macks dressed in a crisp white suit that made him look like a visitor from some cooler, more pleasant planet.

"Welcome to the wicked metropolis of New York," Michael said with a grin. "I've come by to see if I could corrupt you by taking you over to Lonnie's for a bowl of cold borsch."

"Cold *anything* sounds good," Tatiana said, "but I'm afraid I've already been corrupted. I've been here nearly two weeks you know."

"But the Boston hasn't rubbed off yet," Michael countered. "I know the symptoms. Hard work, early rising: you ballet types are Puritans in tutus. Seriously, how about coming to Lonnie's with me. I know we don't know each other very well, but actually I'm quite harmless."

"How did you know I was in town?"

"You let it drop that you were coming to the SAB this summer, and I've got a great memory for facts when they're combined with pretty faces. Frankly, it's pretty boring here after the end of May. All the good-looking girls go away to play summer stock. Still trying to decide if I can be trusted? Let me persuade you." Tossing his hat onto the potted palm, he suddenly broke into a soft shoe:

> Let me show you Manhattan
> From bottom to top
> Every horse in Central Park
> Every Irish cop.

Michael clicked his heels and whirled to a stop nearly knocking over a large brass ashtray full of sand. "How do you like it?

Wrote it myself when I was about seventeen for a musical I called *Fifth Avenue Follies*. Want to hear the chorus?"

"Are you always this silly? I don't remember you being this silly in Boston."

"In Boston," Michael grinned retrieving his hat, "I was on my good behavior, but the truth is silliness is my profession. I dance silly dances in silly musicals and love every minute of it. As a matter of fact, if you won't come to Lonnie's with me, I threaten to dance around the lobby of this place until you give in."

"The lady behind the desk would never survive it."

"Then take pity on the old bat and come have a drink with the fastest set of feet this side of the Hudson."

Tatiana grinned back at him. "How could I refuse the famous Michael Macks."

"Oh, you can't," Michael said, "none of the girls can. One click of the heels and they melt like butter. It's Fred Astaire's secret, you know. I stole it from him."

Lonnie's Restaurant on West Forty-third was so synonymous with Broadway that it was almost impossible to mention one without the other. Large and noisy, table-crammed, so full of cigarette smoke you could hardly see your hand before your face, it had been for over forty years *the* place for actors, directors, producers, lyricists, and critics to mingle, gossip, make deals, and, above all, eat. Tonight was no exception. Tatiana looked up at the caricatures that hung on every available inch of wall space—Ethel Merman, Fred Lewis, Irving Berlin—and then out over the crowded tables at the flesh and blood celebrities: Yul Brynner, who only an hour ago had been playing the King of Siam at the St. James, was quietly consuming a plate of potato pancakes; Mary Martin, who had just come in from her umpteenth appearance in *South Pacific*, was putting away a huge wedge of strawberry pie; and was that playwright Anita Loos over by the bar or just a plausible imitation?

"Having a good time?" Michael asked pleasantly, pouring her another cup of coffee. He'd just finished his nightly performance in *Dance*, but, as usual, instead of looking exhausted he seemed to be bursting with energy. His hair was rumpled, his tie on a little crooked, his coat thrown carelessly over the back of the chair. In front of him sat a big mug of dark German beer, capped with a cool head of foam. Lonnie's, he'd explained two nights ago, was his home away from home.

"The best time of my life." Tatiana smiled happily and

sipped Lonnie's thick fragrant coffee as she looked around for more celebrities. The best time of her life was an understatement. For the past week, under the guise of corrupting her as rapidly as possible, Michael had been taking her everywhere: to the Village to eat spaghetti at Rocco's; to the Sun Sing Theater in Chinatown; to a backstage birthday party for Fred Lewis—complete with painted sets of Cannes, a plaster fountain spouting pink champagne, and Freddy Martin's orchestra stolen from the Astor Roof for the occasion.

Tatiana looked at Michael who was matter-of-factly drinking his beer and felt a combination of pride and confusion. He was so good-looking it was ridiculous; even his eyes, which she hadn't really noticed much at first, had turned out to be something special, changing color according to what he wore. And his sense of humor was boundless. She'd probably laughed more the last seven days than in the rest of her life put together. How often did you meet a man who was better looking than Leslie Howard, funnier than Mickey Rooney, and could dance like Fred Astaire?

Oh, Michael was a real find all right, but the question was: what did he see in *her?* Ever since he'd appeared in the lobby of the Walker—ostensibly to welcome her to New York—he'd kept reappearing, so persistently that even the hatchet-faced woman who ran the reception desk was beginning to give her knowing smiles. Tatiana took a deep breath and tried to summon up all her experience with men, which admittedly wasn't all that extensive. Was Michael interested in her romantically or was she just some kind of temporary whim? He was so . . . she looked in frustration for the right word . . . so darn *friendly*. All the Harvard boys she had ever gone out with would have been pulling their King Kong act by now: grabbing at her in dark doorways, trying to cop a feel, at least trying to kiss her—but Michael hadn't so much as laid a finger on her. All he'd done was treat her to some wonderful times, tease her mercilessly about being far too young for him, and then take her home at daybreak to the Walker to endure the amused glances of Beth, Nan, and Suzy who were certain she was having an affair.

Affair? Fat chance. He thought she was nothing but a kid. Tatiana drank her coffee with such intense concentration she hardly tasted it. Well, so what. She was having a great time seeing New York. After years of getting up at four o'clock every morning for lessons, it was about time she kicked up her heels a little. If she had a brain in her head, she'd be happy Michael's interest in her was probably only temporary. All this nightlife was wearing her out to the point where she could barely stumble up the stairs at SAB, much less dance twelve classes a week.

Tatiana automatically took another sip of coffee, locked in that frustrated state where reason fails utterly to convince. Her head felt like a beehive.

"Say," Michael's voice broke into her thoughts. "Was there a canary in that cup? Because if there was, I think you just swallowed it. A penny for your thoughts. Or considering the way you look maybe I should up my offer."

"I was just thinking about how much I'd like some cream in this stuff," Tatiana lied, nonplussed to be caught. "But the SAB has me on a diet."

"Ah, ballet." Michael grinned. "The province of the skinny, the flat-chested, the bottomless wonders of the world. Have you ever thought you might be too much woman to fit the skeletal standards of Mr. Balanchine?"

"Sometimes you talk like you don't particularly like ballet, and other times you sound like an expert."

"I admit," Michael observed, "that I have a vendetta—probably because I never had what it took to be the next Nijinsky." For a moment he was serious—it was odd to see him that way, like an actor suddenly stripped of his makeup. Then, all at once he was finishing up his beer, grinning at her like a man incapable of being anything but completely entertaining. "Feel like taking in some cool jazz, born recently out of bebop?"

"Sure." She had no idea what he was talking about, but it didn't matter. She'd go anywhere he wanted.

"Finish off that coffee and we'll head for the Village. There's a place down there—the Black Cat Café—where I used to work as a waiter before the war. Best cool jazz in town. We'll have a great time if I can possibly persuade the bouncer you're a perfectly legal eighteen. Maybe if we agree to just let you drink Shirley Temples, Jake won't give us the boot."

Tatiana smiled gamely, wishing he wouldn't tease her so about her age. If only she were ten years older, then maybe. . . . The thought spiraled on, completing itself in all sorts of ridiculous ways, none of them satisfactory.

Two days later Tatiana and Michael stood in the lobby of the City Center waiting in line for tickets. The Center, home to the New York City Ballet, was a Moorish fantasy of gaudy green and blue tiles, pink marble Corinthian columns, tiny carved fleurs-de-lis. Tonight, according to the posters, Jerome Robbins's *The Cage* was premiering along with *Pas de Trois*, and *Bourrée Fantasque*. Tomorrow there would be a completely new program: *The Duel, Capriccio Brillante, Orpheus, Cake Walk;* and on Sunday evening two of Tatiana's favorite ballets: *Prodigal Son* and *The Firebird*. Tatiana smiled, running her tongue over her lips, tasting the names as if she were in the presence of a fantastic smorgasbord.

"What shall it be, Tats?" Michael asked.

Tatiana quickly chose *The Cage*. After all, how could you go wrong with choreography by Robbins and music by Stravinsky? Especially when Nora Kaye was dancing the principal role.

"Two tickets for tonight, please," Michael pushed the money underneath the glass and received two strips of colored pasteboard in return.

"Mihail," The voice was Russian, authoritative. Tatiana turned to see none other than George Balanchine, founder and artistic director of the New York City Ballet, striding across the lobby. "Mihail Maximov."

"Oh, no," Michael said in a low voice, looking around like a man in search of sanctuary.

"What's wrong?"

"My cover's about to be blown again."

"*What* are you talking about?"

To Tatiana's utter amazement, Balanchine headed straight for Michael, grasped his hand, and began to shake it cordially. "How's your dear mother?"

"Fine, Mr. Balanchine."

"Married again, I hear—to a wealthy Italian no less." Balanchine positively glowed with good humor. "Anya always did have a way of looking out for herself." He smoothed back his thin gray hair and looked at Michael pleasantly. "I saw *Quetzal* the other day. Your father's in top form. Tell him for me that instead of competing for audiences we should do something together for a change." He seemed to notice Tatiana for the first time. "Hello, Miss Ward."

"Hello, Mr. Balanchine." Tatiana's tongue nearly stuck to the roof of her mouth. Talking to Balanchine was like talking to God. No matter how hard she tried, she never got used to it.

"Classes going well, yes?"

"Yes, Mr. Balanchine."

"Talented girl," he observed to Michael. "Her mother all over again. But you know all about that, of course, yes? *Dosvydanya* then." Balanchine nodded in a courtly, old-world manner and walked quickly into the theater, leaving behind him a silence thick enough to cut with a knife.

"Natasha Ladanova."

"Sergei Maximov."

"I don't believe it."

"Neither do I."

Tatiana and Michael were sitting in the Automat, half hysterical with amusement, eating cardboard lemon meringue pie and drinking milk straight from the bottles.

"Our secrets are out."

"Exposed."

"You're not only a dancer, but the daughter of a dancer. I'm cursed, positively cursed."

"Why didn't you tell me?"

"Why didn't you tell *me*?"

"You changed your name."

"So did you."

"No, I didn't. My father was a Ward. Girls always take their father's names."

"The only place you can make a buck with a Russian name these days is selling atomic secrets or swinging from a trapeze in the circus."

"Mihail Maximov to Michael Macks. Not very inventive if you ask me. Why didn't you change your name to something really different," Tatiana said, giggling, "like Harry Silvertoes?"

"I wanted to keep the initials."

"Why?"

"I had a lot of monogrammed towels."

Tatiana nearly choked on her milk. "You're ridiculous."

"And you're the picture of sophistication, especially with pie crumbs on your chin."

"Say," Tatiana said, "do you suppose our parents ever danced together?" They spent the next half hour comparing notes and decided it was very likely.

"Want another cup of coffee?"

"No thanks," Tatiana was curled up on the Danish modern couch in Michael's living room. For the last three nights they had taken to coming to his apartment in the Village to wait out the time before the Walker opened in the morning.

Tatiana settled back comfortably on a large green corduroy pillow and amused herself by playing Sherlock Holmes. Interesting how much you could tell about a man once you saw the place he lived. One whole wall of this apartment, for example, was dedicated to pictures of Fred Astaire, whom Michael had met in person when he was thirteen and whom he quite frankly idolized. The others sported travel souvenirs from the era when he'd toured the world with his father's company: a blanket from Brazil; a hat from the Australian Outback; a German drinking mug. There were no curtains on the windows because Michael was in love with light and air; no rugs on the floor because he often practice his dancing— minus tap shoes—in the small hours of the morning.

Tatiana ate a single potato chip and inspected a framed photograph of Michael's mother, taken when she was sixteen or so. In the picture the future Mrs. Maximov posed stiffly in an elaborate velvet dress: a small round-faced blonde with braids wound around her head Russian style. There were no pictures of Michael's father anywhere because, as Michael had explained in some detail, the two of them didn't get along.

Licking the salt off her fingers, Tatiana finished off the last of her coffee as Michael got up to fiddle with the automatic record changer on his Columbia 360, a new invention that was inclined to be temperamental. The machine faltered for a moment; then a disk fell smoothly onto the turntable and the wail of a jazz saxophone filled the silence.

"Tats," Michael said settling back down next to her on the couch, "I've been thinking."

"About what?"

"About how beautiful you are." For a moment he seemed serious, then he grinned, spoiling the effect. "Not many woman look good with their mouth full of potato chips."

"Michael!" Why did he have to tease her all the time? Tatiana turned away, hurt.

Michael took a slow sip of Scotch and continued on, oblivious. "Too bad you're just a kid—hardly dry behind the ears. You're undersize, off-limits, and worst of all, you're a dancer. If you were a fish, I'd have to throw you back. . . ."

"Michael, stop it." She suddenly felt on the edge of a completely childish tantrum. It was cruel of him to keep reminding her that she was so young, as if it were her fault.

What was she supposed to do? Find a magic pill to give her wrinkles and gray hair? Tatiana got to her feet, spilling potato chips all over the couch. Snatching her purse off the coffee table she started toward the door.

"Where are you going?" Michael's puzzled voice pursued her.

"Out. I've had it."

"Tats, what's wrong? Did I do something?"

"Yes." She stared furiously at the wooden floor, not trusting herself to look up. Tears stung her eyes. He was right—she was immature. An older woman would have probably thought of some cutting comeback, but here she was once again about to make a total fool of herself.

"What did I do?" Michael persisted.

"It's not what you do; it's what you *don't* do."

"What's that?"

"You don't take me seriously, damn it!" she yelled, actually stamping her foot. "You never, *never* take me seriously." To her horror Michael threw back his head and started laughing.

"Stop it. Stop laughing at me. I may only be eighteen, but I happen to be a *person*."

"Oh, Tats," Michael made a heroic effort to control his laughter and succeeded. "You've got it all wrong." He reached out, took her arm, pulled her down onto the couch beside him, and looked at her soberly. "You don't really know do you?"

"Know what?"

Instead of answering Michael simply leaned forward, wrapped his arms around her, and kissed her. His lips were warm and hard, exploring hers gently at first, then with an insistence that moved her. Kissing Michael was nothing like kissing the boys at Harvard. Tatiana relaxed, letting her body mold to his, letting him lead her forward into the kiss. Her whole body suddenly felt weightless and insubstantial. Behind them the jazz saxophone went on endlessly. When the record was over, Michael released her reluctantly and sat back. "I should take you home, Tats," he said abruptly.

"Why?" She was confused, and disappointed. She wanted to go on kissing him.

"Because," Michael said, touching his lips lightly to her forehead. "I take you much *too* seriously."

13

July 5, 1951
New York, New York

Dearest Mama,

I hope things are cooler up there in Toronto than they are down here. Yesterday I walked by Lord & Taylor's windows and noticed they'd engineered a fake snowstorm to advertise their winter furs—bleached cornflakes, glass icicles—all of which should give you some idea of how desperate we New Yorkers are for a break in the weather.

My classes at SAB are wonderful despite the fact that it's hot enough in the studios to fry eggs on the mirrors. Doubrovska's a genius of a teacher, just like you promised—full of stories of St. Petersburg and the old Imperial School, which, of course, make me feel right at home.

My best news is that I've met the most WONDERFUL man! His name is Michael Macks and he's a dancer, too—only not our kind. He's actually famous, does tap dancing in Broadway musicals, and is ever so funny and witty and handsome. He's been taking me out for a couple of weeks now and we've seen simply everything in Manhattan from the Metropolitan Museum to Ethel Merman. By the way, an interesting coincidence: I found out, quite by accident, that Michael (real name Mihail) is the son of none other than Sergei Maximov, founder of the Manhattan Ballet! Can you believe it? Sometimes I'm convinced the world of dance only has about three hundred people in it, total. Michael bet me five bucks that you and his dad must have danced together some time back in Russia in the dark ages, but I said I doubted it because you'd never even mentioned working with Maximov.

So do I win my bet or lose? Let me know by return
mail, and don't worry about me because (1) Doubrovska
told me straight out that I'm her number one student
this summer, and (2) I'm having the time of my life.
                        Love and kisses,
                              Tatiana

Natasha reread Tatiana's letter three times, trying to convince herself she'd misunderstood it. Then she abruptly went
into the bathroom and filled the old-fashioned claw-footed
Canadian tub with steaming hot water. What she felt was
quite simply panic, as if her life, which had been going
on a level course for years, had suddenly veered like a
dancer who makes a bad turn and plunges through an open
trap door.

Submerging herself beneath the mounds of spice-scented
bubbles, she tried, with limited success, to stop worrying.
She should have expected that when Tatiana went to New
York she would meet Sergei's son. The world of dance was
impossibly small. Two people involved in it would inevitably
come in contact with each other.

So what was wrong with her? Why did she feel as if life had
played a cruel joke on her personally? *Boje moy!* Tatiana
probably wasn't even seriously interested in this Michael
Macks. Chances were she was just temporarily dazzled, that
the whole thing was nothing more than a summer romance
that would be past history by September. Two young people
interested in dance meet, have a few good times, and go their
separate ways. What could be more natural? Tatiana had had
half a dozen boyfriends over the course of the last year, so
why should this one be any different?

Still, suppose. . . .

She wouldn't suppose. Turning on the faucet, Natasha
added more hot water to the tub until the skin on her legs
turned beet red. *Sergei's son with Tatiana.* The thought
continued to be painful, like a hatpin piercing her forehead.
Closing her eyes, Natasha lay back against the rubber pillow
the hotel had so hospitably provided and forced herself to
remember things she had spent the last nineteen years trying
to forget.

It was amazingly difficult. She gave up, sat back, and tried
again. Fragments of the past floated randomly through her
mind: London before the war, Trey in his leather flight jacket,
the old house in Belgravia. The year 1933 was like a fish,

slippery and hard to hold on to, swimming away from her every time she tried to touch it. Natasha took a deep breath and forced herself into a more scientific frame of mind. If she were willing to make the effort there were obviously exact dates to orient oneself by. Tatiana, for example, had been born December 26, Boxing Day in England, when all the doctors were on vacation and the hospitals understaffed. That meant she must have been conceived on... Natasha counted the months on her fingers... around the end of March. Surely she and Sergei had parted company well before that—the last of February or the first week in March at the very latest. And then she'd gotten her period. She remembered it distinctly now, seeing the signs and feeling relieved that history hadn't repeated itself.

Well, of course it hadn't! Natasha picked up a washcloth and scrubbed herself vigorously as if washing off the last bits of suspicion. You simply didn't get accidentally pregnant twice by the same man. That was the stuff melodramas were made of. Winn and Tatiana both Sergei's daughters? Ridiculous. Why, the odds must be a million to one.

But Trey was incapable of fathering a child. I knew that at the time and so did he, yet we both chose to ignore.... Rubbish. How could she even think such a thing? Of *course* Trey was Tatiana's father. For a moment she felt guilty, as if she'd violated his memory: good, kind Trey who'd hardly ever spoken a harsh word to her in his life. He'd had all those treatments in Switzerland, and although he might never, poor dear, have been much of a lover, certainly he'd had the *capacity* to get her pregnant during the last four or five years of their marriage. And besides, Tatiana was obviously a Ward. People were always commenting on how much she looked like Trey's Aunt Faith—same hair, same bone structure, even the same way of nibbling on her little finger when she was mulling over something important.

But Tatiana's eyes were Sergei's.

That was probably the stupidest thought she'd had in twenty years! Natasha got up out of the tub, reached for a towel, and began to dry herself with hard, quick strokes. Tatiana's eyes were her own; she was *not* Sergei's daughter.

The temples of Siam loomed ominously against a blood red sunset. Feathery and massive at the same time, they seemed to be on fire, as if each individual stone were a fragment of some distant spiritual conflagration. Framing the temples were the pillars of the imperial palace: red, gold, pagan, exotic, and above all sensual—a proper setting, Natasha thought, for a love story that wasn't quite a love story and a courtship that never quite came off.

It was interesting how much the sets for Rogers and Hammerstein's *The King and I* reminded her of the scenery back in the Maryinsky so many years ago. For economic and asthetic reasons most serious ballets now took place in front of colored backdrops with no props to speak of. All the pomp, the spectacle, the wonderfully intricate world of theatrical illusion seemed to have been relegated to popular entertainments like Broadway musicals. Natasha remembered the night she had danced with Sergei in *The Buccaneer:* the revolving stage with oriental gardens, real boats suspended in midair, tons of sand strewn around plaster palm trees. Kschessinskaya would have felt right at home in Hammerstein's fake Siam—although dancing in hoopskirts with Yul Brynner might have been a bit unsettling for her.

"Having fun, Mama?" Tatiana whispered.

Natasha smiled and nodded. It had been good of Michael to get them tickets on such short notice, especially since *The King and I,* which had only opened in March, was playing to standing room only crowds. Natasha thought back to the lunch the three of them had had together a few hours ago. Tatiana had been so proud, so eager for her to like Michael. Not that it was difficult. He was a good boy—a man really, but she couldn't help thinking of him as a boy—polite, amusing, considerate and so totally unlike his father she secretly suspected he had taken a vow to resemble Sergei as little as possible. All of which, of course, presented a very serious problem.

On the stage a miniature ballet entitled *The Small House of Uncle Thomas* was now in progress—nicely choreographed by Jerome Robbins with some marvelous special effects; especially during Eliza's's crossing of the river. Ordinarily Natasha would have watched it with interest, but instead she found herself looking down at her hands, folding and unfolding her program, and worrying a mile a minute. She had cut her Canadian trip short for only one reason: to come down to New York and advise Tatiana (diplomatically of course!) not to become deeply involved with Michael. She'd imagined a lunch with just the two of them, during the course of which she would ask a few subtle, motherly questions, scent out how serious this relationship was, and gently point out to Tatiana the obvious reasons why it was a bad idea.

A good plan, but, as it turned out, a completely unworkable one. Natasha glanced over at Tatiana, who was absorbed in the show, her lips parted slightly, her eyes sparkling with pleasure. Who could have thought she could have changed so much in less than two months? When she left Boston Tatiana had been a girl: shy, a little unsure of herself, given to working too hard and wearing frumpy clothes. Now, dressed in a thin shift of butter-colored linen, her hair arranged in a French roll, she was so obviously a woman, and even more obviously a woman in love, that the idea of giving her advice was almost ludicrous.

What was Natasha supposed to say? *Excuse me, dear, but I've rushed here to tell you that about nineteen years ago I cheated on my husband, had an affair with your suitor's father and there is just the slightest chance—only the slightest, mind you—that he's your half-brother?*

Ridiculous. Absolutely out of the question. How, when there was so much doubt in her own mind, could she even bring up the subject with Tatiana? And what other objections could she possibly make to Michael?

A little while ago on stage, Yul Brynner had been singing something about a puzzlement. Natasha couldn't have agreed more.

Tatiana took a sip of her daiquiri and smiled tolerantly. "Are you trying to tell me Michael's father screwed around, Mama? I already know that. My God, Maximov's *famous* for his divorces and marriages. A new young thing every four years or so, right? Ballerinas all—and some younger than Michael"

"His mother was Anya Belinskaya. We were at the Imperial School together. A beautiful girl, but. . . ."

"But she turned out to be an alcoholic."

"You know?"

"Michael's told me everything. How his mother abandoned him when he was six; how she used to get drunk and throw things at his father. The whole mess." It was Natasha's second day in New York and she and Tatiana were lunching at the Talan, a Russian restaurant on West Fifty-seventh Street that had always been their private refuge during museums and shopping trips. The conversation was going as Natasha had known it would: badly. Not that Tatiana was annoyed—far from it. She was being so reasonable, so pleasant about what

216

she must only see as Natasha trying to interfere in her life that it was mildly awe-inspiring. Natasha tried to imagine how she would have felt if Aunt Marya, say, had told her not to get involved with Sergei. She suspected she wouldn't have had a tenth of Tatiana's patience.

"Michael and I don't have secrets from each other."

"I'm sure you don't but still...." Natasha paused, groping for words. "There's your career to consider," she continued lamely, "not to mention your education."

Tatiana didn't buy it, not for a minute. "Mama," her voice was full of affectionate exasperation, "what *are* you talking about? New York's the center of the *world* as far as ballet's concerned. If I decide to stay on in September I can do more with my career here in a month than I can do in Boston in a year." She reached across the table and grasped Natasha's hand with sudden tenderness. "I know all about that time you were stuck in Vienna and couldn't find a job. I know how you feel about dancers being able to do something besides dance. Well, don't worry. I've already talked to one of the deans at Barnard and she's agreed to let me enter in the fall if I decide not to go back to Radcliffe; so if I break a leg or flop entirely I'll still have more than my ass to fall back on."

"You're much too young to be so seriously involved with a man. Not that I don't like Michael. He's charming, handsome; I can see why...."

Tatiana grinned and threw up her hands in mock surrender. "Mama, give me a break. Too young? Just for the record, how old were you when you first fell in love?"

Natasha smiled despite herself. "Sixteen."

"Postively ancient of you, Mama. Who was it?"

"A Grand Duke," Natasha quickly lied.

"Did you do it?"

"What?"

"You know, do it—make love with the Grand Duke?"

"Uh, well, yes actually." My God, this younger generation was frank. Natasha felt herself blushing.

"What was it like?"

"Tatiana, if you think I'm going to sit here and tell you about my sex life, think again."

"I was just curious," Tatiana said and grinned shyly, "because you see, Mama, Michael and I haven't done it yet, and I wanted to know what was coming."

"I'm sure there are books on the subject." Natasha said it so primly she was suddenly amused with herself.

"All of which make the whole thing sound like minor surgery." Tatiana sighed and took another sip of her daiquiri. "I don't need a chart of polliwogs ganging up on an egg. I need to know what it's like when you really *love* someone."

"You really love him then?" Natasha felt a sudden chill.

"More than you can imagine," Tatiana said seriously. She suddenly put down her glass and smiled warmly. "But if you're afraid of prematurely becoming a grandmother, Mama, you can relax. At the rate Michael and I are going. I'll be old and gray before we ever get to third base."

"Third base?"

"An American expression, Mama. Taken from baseball."

"Ah, yes, baseball," Natasha said blankly. Things between Tatiana and Michael were even more serious than she'd imagined. The thought was cold and square like one of the ice cubes in her drink, and it chilled her to the bone.

"I'd like to speak to Sergei Maximov, please." Natasha stood at the back of the restaurant in a phone booth so small it felt like a cage. Foolish doodles were scrawled on the wooden panels, as if a group of demented children had been let loose with pens. The air in the booth was stuffy but she had closed the door—not because she was actually afraid of being overheard, but because she wanted to contain herself, to hold in her emotions any way she could.

"Who shall I say is calling?"

"Natasha Ladanova." There was a respectful flurry on the other end of the line. Over the years Natasha had sent the Manhattan Ballet a good half dozen of their best dancers, but she had never once contacted them in person. "Just a moment, Miss Ladanova." The receiver briefly fell silent, then clicked into life.

"Hello."

"Hello, Sergei?"

"No, this is Mr. Maximov's secretary. Just a moment please." More waiting. Natasha looked at the telephone. The tiny round fingerholes in the dial were like so many eyes staring back at her. She was tempted to hang up, forget the whole thing. She might be making a terrible mistake meddling in Tatiana's life. If Tatiana found out she'd probably never forgive her.

"Hello, Miss Ladanova?"

"Yes?"

"I'm connecting you with Mr. Maximov now."

The phone spit and crackled as if an electrical storm were trapped in the wires. More buzzing.

"Hello, Natasha?" It was Sergei's voice, unmistakable after all these years. Natasha opened her mouth to say something, but no words came out. She felt suddenly overcome with nostalgia. "Hello, are you there?"

"Yes," she managed to say, "I'm here."

"What's up?" His voice was brisk, businesslike. She realized she'd expected something else—a warm greeting, perhaps, or at least some indication that he was aware it had been almost nineteen years since they last spoke, but his tone was impersonal, a little abrupt. Natasha tried unsuccessfully not to feel hurt. After all, she was the one who had left him. Sergei'd been bitter no doubt, and it wasn't in his nature to forgive.

"I need to talk to you about something."

"I'm pretty pressed for time right now. Can we make it quick?"

"It's about our children." There was a long silence during which she could almost hear him digesting the word *our*.

"If it's about my son, Mihail," he said at last, "I think you should know I'm not responsible for what he does. Frankly we don't have much contact."

"Are you aware that he's involved with Tatiana?"

"Who?"

"Tatiana, my youngest daughter."

"Like father like son, eh?" Sergei was amused now. "Well, I hope for his sake that she's easier to get along with than you were."

"It isn't funny. I want you to persuade your son to stop seeing her."

"Afraid he'll knock her up?"

"You know Sergei you used to be witty, but living in America has made you crude." She was beginning to get angry.

"And you've obviously turned into one of those prissy ex–prima donnas who. . . ."

"Sergei, I didn't call you up after all these years just to be insulted."

"What the hell *did* you call me up for then, Natasha?"

"I just told you. I want you to ask Michael to stop seeing Tatiana."

"Mihail lives his own life."

"You don't understand."

"Listen, Natasha, I'm a busy man. I don't really have time for one of your marathon conversations about young love or whatever, so—"

"Sergei, shut up for once and listen. There's a chance Tatiana may be your daughter."

"*What?*"

"You heard me."

"How much of a chance?"

"Small, minuscule, practically nonexistent, but a chance nonetheless." There was a long silence on the other side of the line.

"I'll see what I can do," Sergei said at last.

"Thank you." The line went dead. Natasha stood for a moment holding the receiver to her ear, unable to move. She felt angry, confused, bitter, moved almost to tears. Three minutes talking to Sergei, and she was shaking all over like a sixteen-year-old who'd been stood up for a date. She'd never call him again, not twenty years from now, not ever. Going back to her table, Natasha lit a cigarette. Smoking was a habit she had taken up to comfort herself after Trey died. Usually it soothed her nerves, but this time there was no pleasure in it.

Carmen LaGuerra was Sergei Maximov's most recent obsession. Only seventeen years old, Carmen was a thin, high-breasted ballerina, as graceful when she moved as a reed blowing in the wind. Having come straight from Mexico City, she spoke only a few words of English, but to Sergei's mind that was no detriment. On stage, Carmen, with her flowing black hair and tiny feet, was an angel; in bed, she was passionate and greedy as a child. Over the years Sergei had taken to speaking very little to either his dancers or his mistresses, so Carmen's inability to nag him about either his choreography or their relationship was a definite plus. Using her as a vehicle, he had, during the last nine months, created a wonderful cycle of ballets based on Aztec myths, including *Quetzal*, which all the critics were calling his masterpiece. To tell the truth, Sergei was so happy with Carmen he had recently been considering making her his fourth wife—a fact that did not escape Michael as he stood in the wings of the Sarner Theater watching his father rehearse with her.

Sergei, who no longer actually could be said to dance, moved beside Carmen, demonstrating the steps, touching her again and again to correct her. He was still a good-looking man: lean, gray-haired, the type who combined strong legs

220

and powerful arms with a kind of European charm that seventeen-year-olds probably found fascinating. And you had to hand it to him: he was a genius as a choreographer. Without saying a word to Carmen, who wouldn't have understood him anyway, he somehow managed, during the five or ten minutes Michael stood watching, to infuse her with the role he was creating, forcing it on her by some sort of secret osmosis.

Still, there was something about the whole rehearsal that made Michael uneasy, even angry. On the surface his father was simply working Carmen through a new ballet, but underneath something else was going on; a sensual electricity was being created between the man and woman that made Michael feel as if he shouldn't be watching, as if somehow he'd opened his father's bedroom door by mistake.

The rehearsal lasted another ten minutes, and then Sergei brought it to a stop. Signaling to the pianist to stop playing, he patted Carmen familiarly on the bottom, dismissing her.

"Mihail, *preevyet*," Sergei mopped his forehead with a pocket handkerchief and clapped Michael on the shoulder with what was obviously supposed to be an expression of fatherly camaraderie. "I'm glad you could make it." Michael managed a friendly smile in return, wishing as he always did that he could feel some closeness to his father. There always seemed to be a gap between the two of them, as if they were acting out the roles of father and son and rather badly at that. When Michael was a boy there had been a brief spate of years when Sergei was convinced he was going to make a career of ballet. Sergei had pushed and pushed, and Michael had resisted with mute obstinacy, but despite all that, there had been a tenuous connection between them. For the last twelve years, ever since his parents' divorce, that connection had vanished as if it had never existed. Michael had sided with his mother—something Sergei could never forgive him for; leaving ballet altogether, he had changed his name, made a career for himself dancing on the Broadway stage, and in general become everything his father disliked and disapproved of. Even now, he could feel that unspoken disapproval radiating off his father, as Sergei stood smiling an empty, charming smile.

"Can you come into my office for a minute?" Sergei asked pleasantly.

"Sure, Dad."

Although he knew it was unfair, Michael had never much

liked his father's offices. There was something about them that always reminded him of trophy galleries. He disliked the rows of signed photographs on the wall from the likes of Diaghilev, Fouchier, and Pavlova; the citations from the Ministries of Culture of such places as Budapest and Buenos Aires; most of all he disliked the snapshot of himself that Sergei kept in a silver frame on his desk: eleven-year-old Mihail Maximov, the boy wonder, poised in front of a black velvet curtain in a white tunic and black tights, a perpetual reminder to Michael of the career he had, from his father's point of view at least, made the fatal mistake of abandoning.

Usually on the rare occasions when Michael visited his father, they spent an uneasy quarter of an hour or so discussing safely neutral topics, but this particular morning Sergei went straight to the electric coffee urn and began fussing about, measuring out spoonfuls of preground coffee and pouring in water.

"Cream?"

"Please."

Sergei produced two traditional Russian tea glasses encased in miniature cages of silver filagree. As long as Michael could remember, his father had hated paper cups, or even cheap china ones for that matter. His love for beautiful things was one of his more endearing traits.

"Sugar?"

"No thanks."

Sergei filled the glasses, handed Michael a small cream bottle, and sat down at his desk. An uncomfortable silence ensued.

"How's your mother doing?" Sergei asked at last.

"Fine." It was a ritual question between them. Sergei always asked, and Michael always said just that one word: *fine*. If his mother had been sick or in trouble or, God forbid, on her deathbed, he still would have said *fine*, having decided a good ten years ago that his days as a go-between were over.

"How do you like your new stepfather, Signor what's-his-name who makes the fast cars?"

"Signor Marconetti? I've only met him once—last summer in Naples—but he seems like a nice enough sort. Got through the war with most of his auto plant intact, I gather. Was even a bit of a hero: fought with the Partisans against Mussolini."

"Um."

Michael could tell his father wasn't listening. Nothing new

there. He couldn't begin to count the number of one-sided conversations he'd had over the years. You could be pouring out your heart to Sergei Maximov and discover that all the while he'd been dreaming up a new ballet. When he was younger it had made Michael furious that his father so rarely seemed to hear anything he said, but over the years Michael had begun to feel pity more than anger. It must be lonely, cutting yourself off from human contact like that all the time. On the occasion of their divorce, his father's last wife, an English ballerina named Lydia Winters, had informed the press that she was leaving Sergei Maximov because he never cried. The papers had made Lydia's judgment sound perfectly idiotic at the time, but Michael, for one, had understood.

"And how are you doing?" Sergei said suddenly. For some reason it had the feeling of a loaded question.

"Okay."

"*Dance* still packing in the tourists?"

"You could say that." Why was it, Michael thought, that he could be amusing and witty with everyone but his own father? Here he was replying in monosyllables like a sullen teenager. He should make an effort, be more cordial. "Actually, Fred Lewis has had some feelers from Hollywood. You can read about it in the trades if you want. Galaxy's optioned the rights to *Dance*, but, of course, whether or not a film'll get made is anyone's guess."

"Interesting." Sergei said it in a way that indicated he was not the least bit interested. Michael suppressed a feeling of annoyance. If he'd had any sense, he would have remembered his father hated Hollywood. In the mid-thirties, shortly after the Ballet de la Cité folded, Sergei had been invited to America by Busby Berkeley to choreograph a film called *Follies of 1935*, a job that had entailed, among other things, getting two full grown male elephants to dance a Viennese waltz. Sergei, who was in the process of trying to form the Manhattan Ballet, had needed money desperately, so he'd taken on the job, elephants and all, but it wasn't something he enjoyed being reminded of.

"I understand," Sergei said abruptly, "that you're seeing a lot of Natasha Ladanova's youngest daughter."

"How do you know that?" Michael was astounded. He could never remember his father taking the slightest interest in whom he saw or didn't see.

"Let's say I have my sources." Sergei smiled pleasantly, took a sip of coffee, and cleared his throat. "The fact is," he went on, still smiling, "it isn't really all that good an idea you know, Mihail."

"Why not?"

"Just between us men, there may be a little problem there."

"What do you mean 'a problem'? Tatiana's a great girl. Beautiful. Intelligent. A fine dancer." Michael got to his feet. "This isn't Gretchen Schmidt all over again, is it Dad?" Gretchen Schmidt was a young German ballerina who had performed for the Manhattan Ballet under the stage name of Irina Preboda during the late thirties. Michael, who at the age of sixteen had made his debut with her in his father's ballet *La Chinoise*, had developed a terrible crush on Gretchen, only to discover, after he had made a complete fool of himself, that she was sleeping with his father.

"Not exactly."

"What do you mean 'not exactly'? Shit, Dad, isn't there a dancer in New York you haven't taken to bed? Anyway, I don't believe it of Tats. You couldn't possibly have had an affair with her. She's too innocent to have been around the likes of you."

"Calm down, Mihail. I didn't have an affair with your girlfriend."

"I'm sorry." Michael sat down, abashed. "I'm sorry I flew off the handle like that."

"By the way, how *do* things stand between you two?"

"What do you mean?"

"Have you slept with her yet?"

"What the hell kind of question is that? I mean, did you invite me over here to ask me how Tatiana Ward was in bed?" Michael felt himself getting angry again. "For your information, I haven't slept with her. Not everyone sees women the way you do."

"Interesting how the sons of libertines always reveal a Victorian streak." Sergei sat back and clasped his hands behind his head thoughtfully. "My dear, Mihail, I really think you should read a few French novels: LaClos, Flaubert, de Maupassant—open yourself to some of the great pleasures of life."

"I don't need a reading list, Dad."

"I'd say if this Tatiana is anything like her mother, you're missing something."

"Her mother? What does her mother have to do with this?"

"Everything, I'm afraid." Sergei smiled urbanely. "You see,

224

some years ago Natasha Ladanova and I had—how shall I put this?—a brief encounter. We'd been lovers before that, back in Paris during the first world war—but this was more in the nature of old friends having a reunion, the result of which might just possibly have been Natasha's youngest daughter."

"Are you trying to tell me that Tatiana's my sister?"

"Possibly."

"What the hell do you mean 'possibly'? Is she or isn't she?"

"These things are always uncertain. Nevertheless you can see how it might be a good idea for you to stop seeing the girl. Given your hopelessly faithful nature, it all might lead to that ultimate of human catastrophes: marriage—something I myself have dabbled in far too often. And then there would be the children to consider, possible genetic damage and all that."

"You *think* Tatiana may be your daughter, and on the basis of that you want me to stop seeing her?" Michael was so angry he could barely speak. "If I went around avoiding all the daughters of women you'd slept with, I'd have to become a monk."

"Mihail, I've attempted to be pleasant, but enough is enough. I forbid you to see this girl."

"And if I refuse?"

"I hate to threaten you, but things could be unpleasant. Legal action perhaps, if you attempt to marry her."

"Let me tell you something, Father. When I walked into this office, I had no intention of marrying Tatiana Ward..."

"I'm glad to hear it."

"... but the more I hear you talk, the more I realize what a prize she is. I saw you and mother; I had enough of watching stupid, trivial, dishonest relationships to last me a lifetime. If you'd paid more attention to your own marriage you wouldn't have to worry about mine. There's no threat you can make that would convince me to give up Tatiana."

"If you marry her, I warn you...."

"Warn me of what? That you'll disinherit me—you with a ballet company that barely scrapes along from year to year? Don't play the outraged Victorian father; it doesn't suit you."

"You're stubborn, ungrateful, and irresponsible, and you always have been." Sergei's face was red; the veins in his neck bulged dangerously. He made a move toward Michael as if to strike him, then thought better of it. "Marry that girl and it's the last straw."

"Oh, it is, is it? Let me tell you something, Dad. If Tatiana will have me, I'm going to make her my wife."

Father and son faced each other, mirror images of anger and obstinacy. For a moment there was real violence in the air; then Sergei suddenly went blank and cold. It was a chilling performance, as if a stranger had stepped into his skin. "Well, if that's the way you feel about it," he said smoothly. "I suppose you'd better leave." He nodded at Michael, like an acquaintance nodding across a crowded train station: polite and immeasurably distant. "When you see your mother again, Mihail, give her my regards."

Tatiana watched the Staten Island Ferry churning through the grayish-pink water. It was early morning and still hot—the kind of morning that came after a sleepless night when the whole city seemed like a giant balloon full of hot air struggling to rise from its concrete foundations. A warm breeze blew off the bay, and Tatiana's full white skirt billowed around her knees. She turned back to Michael and shook her head sadly. "I'm not sure marriage would be a good idea, Michael, not now at least."

She saw the disappointment in his face and wanted to do something to soothe it, but she knew if she did anything but tell him no, she would quickly be telling him yes. It was painful to turn down the man you loved, especially when rejecting him might mean you would lose him altogether. Tatiana swallowed her regrets and pressed her lips together to keep herself from taking it all back. Ever since that lunch with her mother, she had been trying to take a long, hard look at what she was doing with her life, and she had come reluctantly to the conclusion that Natasha might be right: as much as Tatiana hated to admit it, she might really be too young to get so seriously involved. The problem was that it was hard to tell in advance. Maybe if she married Michael she could go on dancing, but on the other hand. . . . She had a fleeting picture of herself down on her knees scrubbing the kitchen floor with a baby crying somewhere in the background. Not a very romantic image, but then it paid to be realistic *before* you got married, not afterward when it was too late.

"Why not?" Michael stopped as if at a loss for words. "Is it because we're—" He stopped abruptly.

"Because we're what?"

"Is it because you don't love me?"

"Of course I love you, Michael," she made a motion toward him, then checked herself, "but. . . ." She wouldn't share the image of the kitchen floor and the baby, that would be cruel, but somehow she had to make him understand she was afraid of wasting herself. It was common knowledge at the School of American Ballet that when girls got married, they almost never went on to dance with the Company.

"But why, then?"

"I've got my career to think of." She knew she sounded stiff and cold but she had to tell him the truth. "I've been crazy about you ever since I met you—you know that—but I know if I gave up my dancing, I'd never be happy. I'd make both of us miserable."

"Tats, I'm not asking you to give up your dancing. If all I wanted was someone to cook my meals and sort my socks. I'd hire a maid." Michael looked relieved for some reason, as if he'd been expecting something far worse. "Listen, I'm making plenty of money from *Dance*, and there's a lot more in the works. I don't mean to get crass and materialistic, but we won't have to starve in a garret or even move into my apartment. We can afford to live somewhere really nice—the East Sixties maybe. As for housework and all that, you won't have to lift a finger, and if it's the idea of children that's bothering you—well, frankly I'd love to have a child with you—but it can wait as long as necessary."

Tatiana felt as if a great weight had been lifted off her shoulders. Suddenly the morning was clear and beautiful, Michael was perfect, and the world seemed all right again. The wind blew through the thin cotton of her dress and she felt for a moment like a kite, tugging at the ground, eager to be off. "I can hardly believe it," she smiled at Michael, thinking how foolish she had been to doubt him. He was so special, so dear to her: of course he would realize she needed more than a home and family to keep her happy.

"Hardly believe what?"

"That you really understand. Men aren't supposed to be that way. They're supposed to want to boss you around—you know, sort of like Simon Legree."

Michael grinned. "Actually I *had* thought of offering you a life of drudgery, but I didn't think you'd go for it." They both laughed and the tension broke. "Seriously, Tats," Michael slipped his arm around her waist, "I know how important your dancing is to you and I promise you I'll do everything in my power to help you get to the top." He bent over and kissed her behind the ear. "We'll be a new kind of couple."

"A new kind of couple." She repeated the words, savoring them. "I like that."

"I don't want the kind of marriage my parents had." For an instant Michael thought bitterly of his mother drunkenly yelling at his father that he'd wrecked her life. "I don't know how to say this without sounding like the Preamble to the Constitution, but I want us to have a relationship based on equality and mutual respect."

"Life, liberty, and the pursuit of happiness." Her tone was light but he could hear that, underneath the joking, she meant it.

"Something like that." He pulled her to him. "Well," he said, trying to keep his voice steady, "how about it? Do you say *yes*, or do I go down and sign up for the Foreign Legion?"

"Yes." Tatiana slipped her arm through his with a kind of childlike trust that made him feel suddenly protective. She was an amazing girl, so strong and yet so vulnerable. He would see to it she had a happy life, and—Michael added to himself as an afterthought—he would keep his father away from her; as far away as possible.

So it happened, that, in the fall of 1951, on a cool day in early October, Tatiana and Michael were married at Harvard in Memorial Church with Michael's parents conspicuously absent. Anya, too ill to make the long trip from Italy, sent masses of flowers and twelve place settings of antique silver as a wedding present. Sergei didn't even reply to the invitation.

The fan on the ceiling purred quietly above Tatiana's head, the green wooden blades a blur against the whitewashed stucco. From the rafters a small gecko hung upside down eating the last of the mosquitoes. The weather was damp and warm like the inside of a greenhouse. Along the veranda flaming magenta jasmine blossomed in clay pots, and through the screened windows in front of the big double bed Michael and Tatiana could have seen Tortola and St. Thomas if they had only looked. Two of the most beautiful islands in the Caribbean loomed up across a dazzling expanse of clear blue water like giant green lilies floating in God's own private pool. Behind them the trade winds were blowing half a dozen small white clouds toward the mainland.

But Tatiana and Michael, lost in each other, saw none of

this. The islands were famous for water skiing, swimming, fishing, hiking, tennis, sailing, but for all Tatiana and Michael knew about it they might as well have stayed in New York. Three days already, and they hadn't even gotten out of bed long enough to get suntans.

"Happy, Tats?" Michael smiled lazily at Tatiana and she smiled back. They were so foggy with lovemaking she had begun to suspect that her I.Q. went down ten points every time they did it. Michael yawned, kissed her shoulder, and began working his way up to her neck. Tatiana sighed. Small shudders passed through her, like tiny waves lapping their way down her backbone to her knees.

"Not again," she giggled, making a mock attempt to push him away.

"And why not, my dear Mrs. Macks?"

"Because."

"Because why?"

"Because I think we might die—you know, from excess."

"Death where is thy sting?" Michael grinned. He grabbed for one of her breasts and began to run his finger softly around the nipple. "Is it there? Hmm, no, I think not. Perhaps *there*?"

"Michael!"

"Or there, or maybe even *there*."

Excited, Tatiana put her lips to Michael's mouth and wrapped her legs around him, drawing him closer. His body was heavy and warm, enveloping in a way that made her totally secure. Slowly he began to massage her neck and shoulders. Releasing her flesh to him, she let it flow under his hands. Images came to her. She closed her eyes and imagined, for no particular reason, she was dancing on the ocean that lay outside their window; for a moment she was lighter than water, lighter than the sunlight itself, borne up above the dolphins and whales, as quick and weightless as the wind. Then Michael put his mouth to her breasts, teasing the nipples lightly with his tongue, and she was back with him again, anchored solidly to the earth.

With part of her mind Tatiana realized once again how amazing it was. In every book she had ever read lovemaking had been described as a loss of self. D. H. Lawrence had depicted sex as something dark, primal, and consuming. Flaubert had warned her that passion would be destructive, perhaps even insane. Even Hemingway, her favorite author, had led her to expect she would disappear into Michael in some mysterious way, that the force of his masculinity would overwhelm and temporarily annihilate her.

But it hadn't been like that at all. Instead of losing herself in Michael, Tatiana had, to her surprise, found herself in him, not just once but again and again. Each time they made love, she flew for a moment into her own private space, then returned, bringing back some piece of herself she hadn't had before; each time she emerged with the sense of knowing both herself and him more thoroughly.

Now, as she and Michael made love, Tatiana once again found herself wondering why no one had ever written the truth? Why hadn't any of the greatest authors ever said straight out that lovemaking could be kind? That sex could be long and sweet and slow as winter molasses? That bed wasn't always a battlefield where men and women struggled in the dead of night for power and dominance? Why, in all her years of looking in books, hadn't she ever read about a happy marriage?

Michael smiled and pulled her closer until his eyelashes brushed her cheek. Tatiana lay back looking at the ceiling, feeling the curve of his shoulders against her chest, the weight and strength of his legs. They were like the fan, she thought, their bodies turning together in this bed and never stopping.

Tatiana sighed happily. Overhead the wooden blades of the real fan cut the light into quick moving lozenges that fled across the white stucco walls like the silhouettes of dancers. She thought fleetingly of New York and how fine it would be to return to classes at the School of American Ballet knowing that when she came home in the evenings Michael would be waiting for her.

"Tatiana."

"Yes, Madame." Tatiana stood at the barre, it was only early November but already the weather had turned cold and damp. At the School of American Ballet it was once again officially "flu season"—that time of year when dancers collapsed in mid-rehearsal, or suddenly called in sick at the last minute.

"We're short a girl in *Billy the Kid*. Think you might be able to fill in for us tonight?"

"Oh, yes, Madame. Thank you, Madame." Tatiana felt elated, then confused. Dancers from the school were almost never asked to substitute in Company productions. This must be an emergency. Still, what a wonderful chance to show Mr. B. what she could do in front of a real audience.

Felia Doubrovska smiled and nodded at Tatiana in approval as she tucked a long salmon-colored chiffon scarf into the belt of her skirt. It was Doubrovska's habit to give classes with something vapory trailing out behind her. "Perhaps you should run downtown and get a costume fitting," Doubrovska observed casually. "Rehearsal starts in three hours."

Forty minutes later Tatiana was standing on a wooden stool in a large, high-ceilinged loft while three women with pins in their mouths knelt at her feet, furiously tacking and hemming. With a few deft strokes a costume was being created out of yards of light blue calico. Long-skirted, tight-waisted, the dress was perfectly designed to show off her body yet allowed her complete freedom of movement. Working under the famous costume designer Barbara Karinska, the anonymous fitters of the New York City Ballet were some of the best in the world. Few of the great French couturiers could hold a candle to them, and their speed was legendary. Tatiana shifted from one foot to the other, too excited to appreciate the near miracle taking place around her. In a few hours she'd actually be dancing on the City Center stage—a very small role, true, but a role nevertheless. The thought made her elated and nervous by turns. What if she missed a step and fell over her own feet? What if she came on at the wrong time? What if she just froze at the first sight of the audience?

"Try to keep it clean, dear," one of the fitters said as she bit off the end of a thread and inspected Tatiana's costume with obvious satisfaction.

"And hang it up afterward please," suggested a small redhead as she scrambled for another button.

"Mr. Balanchine spends thousands of dollars a year to make you girls in the Company look good on stage," the third woman chimed in.

"'You girls in the Company'" The truth slowly dawned on her. "You mean," Tatiana was incredulous, "that I'm being apprenticed to the *Company*, just like that, with no one even telling me?"

The three women laughed, and one of them tapped Tatiana on the knee to indicate she should step down off the stool.

"She looks so surprised."

"Like she swallowed a fish."

"Apprenticed to the Company and she didn't even know it."

Giving a yelp of delight, Tatiana jumped down from the

stool and bolted from the room, barefoot, her hair flying out behind her like one of Madame Doubrovska's scarves.

Squash balls ricocheted off the pristine walls of the indoor courts with small explosions, as if the members of the New Amsterdam Athletic Club were discreetly popping corn. Men in white shorts and tennis shirts lounged at tables drinking Cokes and beer, their rackets sheltered neatly beside them under canvas covers from L. L. Bean. Women were not permitted in the Amsterdam, but Tatiana was in no mood to take that into account. If she'd had any sense she probably would have called the club instead of barging in this way, but she wanted to tell Michael the news of her apprenticeship in person and see the expression on his face. Checking her watch, she headed down the hall. She only had an hour and a half before she was supposed to report to the City Center.

A scant five minutes later, Tatiana found herself in the ridiculous position of being escorted back out the front door by an amused attendant who kept looking at her and shaking his head.

"Your husband ain't here, lady."

"Please, have another look."

"Seem to me you done enough lookin' for the both of us."

Tatiana took a ten-dollar bill out of her purse and slipped it into his hand. "It's important."

The man folded the money and put it into the pocket of his uniform. "Well, if it mean so much to you, I guess I could give the place the once over again. What you say his name was?"

"Macks. Michael Macks."

A few minutes later Michael appeared in street clothes, his hair still wet from the shower. When he saw Tatiana he grinned and gave her a hug and a warm, quick kiss.

"Hey, Tats, I hear you raided the place."

"I had to find you. I've got great news."

"Me, too." Michael pulled a piece of paper out of his pocket and brandished it triumphantly. "Get a load of this. Lewis dumped it on me this afternoon, right out of the blue."

Tatiana took the paper out of Michael's hands and saw that it was a telegram from a producer named Arnold Glass confirming the fact that Glass was exercising his option to Fred Lewis's musical, *Dance.* Foreboding crept over her. She handed the telegram back to Michael slowly, hunting for the right words. She had a question to ask, only she wasn't sure if she wanted to know the answer. She thought of the stage of the City Center empty and waiting for her, of her new costume hanging neatly on a hook in the dressing room.

"What does it mean?" Her voice was feathery, almost without substance, but Michael didn't seem to notice. Kissing her happily, he broke into a soft shoe around a fire hydrant. "It means Tats, my beloved," he said, taking her in his arms and dancing her across the sidewalk, "that number one, we're rich; number two, we're lucky; and number three, we're on our way to Hollywood."

"Wait, Michael, wait." She pulled him to a stop. "I've got something to tell *you*." She thought about how she had imagined this being a pleasant surprise and she wanted to cry with disappointment. "I've been taken into the Company."

"Into the Company?" He repeated her words as if he didn't understand them, or perhaps, she thought with fleeting bitterness, as if he didn't want to understand them.

"I'm dancing in *Billy the Kid* tonight."

"Tats, that's wonderful." His voice lacked enthusiasm.

"So?"

"So what?"

"So what are we going to do?"

"About what?"

"About the fact that you're going to Hollywood while I appear to be staying in New York."

"You can't be serious."

"What do you mean I *'can't be serious'*?"

"But Tats, it's only a little part in the corps de ballet; you don't mean to tell me you'd stay in New York for that."

"*'Only a little part!'* Michael this is my big chance. Do you know how many dancers would cheerfully strangle their own grandmothers for a chance to dance with the New York City Ballet? Sure it's a little part, but it's a beginning. I can't just walk out on it."

"Tats, Arnold Glass wants me to *star* in *Dance*. You know how much I've wanted to get into movies, well, now I've got an opportunity. You can't expect me to throw that away just because Balanchine or someone finally noticed you exist."

"Who's asking you to throw it away. *Go* to Hollywood if you want, only just don't expect me to come along with you." She heard the anger in her voice, but she couldn't stop. How could she be fighting with Michael this way, Michael whom she loved.

"You don't mean that."

233

"You're right, I don't." She looked at him miserably. "I'm sorry I flew off the handle like that, Michael, but what are we going to do?"

"I don't know." He crumpled the telegram and stuffed it back in his pocket. "It's an impossible choice."

"Maybe you could go out to the coast and I could go on living in our apartment here, and we could fly out to Chicago or somewhere on weekends to visit each other."

"Tats, you're my wife. Married people don't live three thousand miles apart—not if they want to stay married. Besides, look at your schedule. You don't even *have* weekends free."

"You're right," she agreed unhappily.

"I suppose I could wire Glass and tell him I'm not coming."

"Michael you've wanted to be in the movies since you were twelve years old and fell in love with Fred Astaire. How do you think I'd feel knowing I'd made you give that up?"

"About as rotten as I'd feel if I made you give up your dancing." They stood for a moment in the rain looking silently at each other as they realized the magnitude of what they were up against. "Come on, sweetheart." Michael said at last, putting his arm around her. "Let's have some dinner and try to think this out."

That night Tatiana danced for the first time as part of the New York City Ballet, but what should have been a triumph for her was spoiled by the knowledge that neither she nor Michael could think of any way out of the dilemma caused by Arnold Glass's telegram.

A week later, Tatiana took an early morning flight to Boston to talk to her mother. She could have done it on the phone, of course, but things were too serious for that. Michael and she were in a state that could best be described as an amalgam of misery and paralysis. They'd talked, talked, and talked some more, until both of them were thoroughly exhausted, and still there seemed no way to evade the obvious conclusion that Michael's life lay on the West coast while Tatiana's lay in New York. Although she knew it was childish, Tatiana longed for Natasha's comfort and support. Mama was so level-headed. Surely, she could help put this difficult situation into perspective.

"You're asking for my honest opinion?" Natasha said. They were walking across Harvard Yard, both wearing heavy tweed coats and boots. Tatiana looked at Natasha's red cheeks and quick black eyes and thought, not for the first time, that the two of them looked more like sisters than mother and daughter. The idea revived her slightly. Surely if her mother had survived life so well, she could, too.

"Yes, Mama, your honest opinion."

"First tell me frankly how you feel about Michael."

"I love him . . . more than I've ever loved anyone except you and Winn. It may sound crazy, but I don't even think I'm *capable* of loving anyone but Michael. Can you understand that?"

Natasha nodded. "You'd be surprised how well." They took a few more steps through the snow. Winter had come to Harvard Yard. In front of Sever Hall the maple trees were bare, and wet leaves littered the bicycle racks. A light Cambridge mist hung over everything, swathing the bicycles, softening the angles of Widner Library, casting a veil over Memorial Church. Tatiana tried not to look at the church because it reminded her too painfully of her wedding day. How could things have gotten into such a tangle in so short a time.

"Tats," Natasha said at last. "I have to know what you're more afraid of: losing Michael or losing your career?"

"I don't know. Both I suppose. I don't want to be with anyone but Michael, and I don't want to do anything but dance. It's like one of those trick questions they ask in freshman philosophy classes: 'If you were in a shipwreck and there was only room in the lifeboat for your mother or your wife, which one would you take?' How can you make a decision like that?"

"You honestly don't know whether Michael or your dancing comes first?"

"Honestly."

"Well then, here's my advice for what it's worth. I once loved someone and it didn't work out. I wasn't lucky enough to be married to him or to have him really love me in return—in fact, he was bad for me, even cruel. I suppose you might say I made something of a fool of myself over him. After we parted company I . . . more or less gave up on love, or at least on passion. I tell you this honestly so you'll understand. It was then that I decided I'd make my career my life, and I have, and I must admit I've gotten a lot of satisfaction out of it, but the price was stiff. I loved your father, of course, but it was never the same. He was a good, kind man, and he supported my dancing completely, but

235

there was always part of me that remained empty—as if I'd thrown away something precious."

Natasha scraped some snow into the palm of her glove and stood silently for a moment, lost in thought. "You're an extremely talented dancer," she said at last, "and if you wanted to, I know you could go straight to the top. In fact, my first impulse as your teacher is to tell you to do just that. But on the other hand, as your mother, I have to confess to you that I've been lonely. I've had regrets. Maybe it's noble to sacrifice your personal life to your art; maybe it's the most foolish idea ever conceived. I suppose what I'm trying to tell you is that in the end you have to ask yourself what you're willing to give up."

"Mama, I don't want to give *anything* up."

"Tats, you can't have everything."

"Why not?"

"I don't know. I only know you can't."

Tatiana shook her head miserably. "The more I think about it, the more I realize I can't let Michael go out there by himself, but at the same time I know if I go with him I'll feel as if I don't have a life of my own." She kicked at the snow angrily, feeling silly, futile, and trapped. "Why is the world full of such impossible choices?"

Natasha put her arm around Tatiana's shoulders. "I don't know that, darling, but I can tell you one thing: whatever you decide to do, I'll stand behind you."

Two days later Tatiana came home from a performance to find Michael sitting at the dining room table surrounded by three huge bouquets of roses looking more cheerful than he'd looked in weeks.

"I've figured it out, Tats." He pulled her down on his lap and gave her a kiss. "My God, I can't believe how blind we were. The solution was right there in front of us all the time and we were too dumb to see it. Listen, I've arranged with Glass to delay the start of the movie until the season is over. As it turned out, he had another project in the works anyway and didn't mind. The idea is that you take a leave of absence from the Company and come out to California with me for six months—eight at the most. We make the film, then we come back to New York."

"But what if the film takes longer than six months to make?" Tatiana wanted to believe Michael had found a solution, yet part of her couldn't. "What if it takes years?"

"It won't. Glass promised he'd have the whole thing set up and ready to go. In fact, he estimates it'll be more like five months total."

"Since I've been watching the City Ballet, I've seen maybe fifteen dancers take leaves of absence, Michael, and only one ever returned for another season."

"Six months, Tats. That's all I'm asking. Surely our marriage is worth that." He kissed her lightly on the lips. "Please say yes." And because she was tired, discouraged, and could think of no other reasonable alternative, Tatiana agreed to go to Hollywood for six months.

14
Malibu, 1954

The Pacific was as still and gray as a grease puddle. It was cold out on the redwood deck, one of those damp California winter mornings that you only got by the ocean when the air was full of equal parts salt, smog, and sand, but Tatiana didn't care. Ensconced in a black canvas butterfly chair under a cashmere lap robe, she was absorbed in writing her mother a letter. Or perhaps it would be fairer to say she was absorbed in *trying* to write her mother a letter since she had been going at the task for over two hours now without the slightest success.

Dearest Mama, the latest fragment began, *I'm sorry I haven't written sooner but, as you know, having a new baby on your hands is a full-time job. Alysa is a perfect treasure: healthy, fat, and hungry all the time. I'm sending another batch of snapshots along to you so you can see how much she's grown in the past couple of weeks....*

Seizing her pen, Tatiana furiously crossed out the whole page, then sat back and took another sip of rum and Coke. What kind of letter was that to write to your mother? Not that everything she'd said hadn't been true. Alysa *was* a beautiful baby, make no mistake, dark-eyed and dark-haired, so much like her grandmother it was downright uncanny, but outside of that the whole letter rang false. It was cold, stiff, and worst of all a lie. Well, not exactly a lie; just that everything important had been left out.

Tatiana gulped down more of the rum and waited impatiently for the warm burst of contentment to hit her in the pit of her stomach. Out on the beach a light wind had begun to kick up the sand and make small whitecaps. If this kept up the surfers would soon be out, arriving in their wooden station wagons to spend the day darting through the waves like healthy young seals. Too bad she wasn't more like them—all body and no brains. Balanchine had always said dancers should be as mindless as flowers.

Unwadding one of the crumpled sheets of paper at random, Tatiana read it over with mixed feelings of frustration and despair: *Dearest Mama,* this one began, *Guess what! Arnold Glass has finally given Michael a film of his own to choreograph! It's called* Rebel Yell—*sort of a rock and roll version of* Gone with the Wind, *if you can imagine such a thing—and it stars none other than Bobby Fender, that sexy kid from Tulsa all the teenagers are just crazy about!*

Anytime you ended three sentences in a row with an exclamation point it was a sure sign you were faking. Mama wasn't stupid. Send her a letter like that, and she'd be out here on the next plane. Tatiana put her chin on her hands and looked despondently out at the ocean. The problem was there was a real letter in her mind that kept intercepting the phony ones, a letter so desperately unhappy Tatiana didn't dare think about it, much less write it.

Dearest Mama, went the unwritten letter,

> *Help. I have a beautiful, healthy, one-month-old baby girl whom I love as much as I've ever loved anyone in my life, but I'm terribly depressed. I don't feel like myself at all, and I don't know what's wrong. My body feels as if it's made out of lead; my life doesn't make any sense and the thing that scares me most is that I'm angry at Michael all the time. I don't suppose I have to tell you the problem is I'm not dancing. We've been over all that a hundred times.*
>
> *There are some decent teachers out here—Eugene Loring, Gower Champion, Albertina Rasch—but no professional ballet company worth speaking of, unless you want to count San Francisco, which is too far away to do me any good. So here I am, going nuts because I can't perform. As you know, Michael and I were originally only going to stay in California for six months, but it's been over two years now and there's no end in sight. Rationally I know this isn't Michael's fault. He didn't arrange for the first film to take forever, and I certainly had as much to do with getting pregnant with Alysa as he did. But even though I know all this, I still feel as if he welshed on his part of the bargain. Ever since Alysa's birth I've been haunted by the idea that I should leave him, come back to New York, and dance with the City*

Ballet again, but I love him so. How can you love a man and think about leaving him at the same time? Does all this sound completely crazy to you? Have you ever felt anything like it?

All the books tell me I'm just experiencing the classic symptoms of post-partum depression, but as far as I'm concerned that's about as much help as trying to cure cancer by giving it a fancy name. Right now it's nine in the morning and I'm drinking rum and that isn't like me at all. Help me, Mama. I'm really scared.

Tatiana put down her pen and sat for a moment watching the gray sea heave against the gray horizon. Then, getting up abruptly, she gathered the wadded balls of paper and threw them over the railing. The wind caught the unfinished letters, strewing them over the beach like white carnations. If she couldn't write her mother the truth, she wouldn't write anything at all.

It was time to stop brooding and do something practical. Tossing the rest of the rum and Coke after the letters, Tatiana went inside, located a phone book, and turned to the yellow pages. There were so many doctors in Los Angeles—urologists, internists, dermatologists—how in the world did you pick someone to look you over and give you a second opinion? A name at the top of the second column caught her eye: Dr. Vernon DeWitt, a general practitioner with a fancy address in Beverly Hills. She vaguely remembered reading something about him in the newspapers a few weeks ago. He was the doctor who had treated Judy Garland or someone equally famous for exhaustion. Perfect. If she wasn't exhausted then no one was. Picking up the phone, Tatiana impulsively dialed Dr. DeWitt's office and made an appointment.

"Have you ever heard of benzedrine, Mrs. Macks?" Dr. DeWitt asked.

"No." Tatiana tried to take a deep breath, but the air stuck in her lungs. On the surface she was the picture of serenity: dressed in a pale yellow linen sheath, ankles crossed demurely, hands planted neatly in her lap. Her lipstick was on straight, her hair curled attractively, her nylons smooth and unflawed, but under all this exterior order she was in a state of mental anguish so profound it was all she could do to keep from breaking into childish tears.

"Benzedrine's a member of a new family of drugs that's had

240

quite amazing results in cases of mental depression. You might call it one of the wonders of our time." Dr. DeWitt smiled in a way that was obviously intended to be totally reassuring. Everything about his office was bland and soothing, from the nondescript prints on the wall to the oatmeal-colored rug on the floor. Most soothing of all was Dr. DeWitt himself, a lean gray-eyed man who looked more like a small town country doctor than one of the most popular physicians in Beverly Hills.

"I've never heard of this . . . what did you call it?"

"Benzedrine." Dr. DeWitt took a gold fountain pen out of his pocket and unscrewed the cap. "I'm going to give you a prescription to tide you over until you feel better."

"What will it do to me?"

"Perhaps the simplest way to put it, without getting technical, is to say that it will make you feel good. You should have more energy, feel more alert, and you should be virtually incapable of worrying. There are a few minor side effects, however, insomnia for instance." Dr. DeWitt reached for another prescription blank, "so I'm also going to give you some mild tranquilizers in case getting to sleep becomes a problem."

"Thank you."

"This is only a temporary measure, you understand."

"Thank you, Doctor. I understand."

Tatiana had both prescriptions filled in the ultramodern drugstore on the corner across from Dr. DeWitt's office. In one bottle the pills were white and powdery like aspirin; in the other, red and shiny like jelly beans. Stuffing the bottles in her purse, Tatiana drove home, poured herself a stiff rum and Coke, and took three of the white tablets. Then she called the Palms Academy on the phone and registered for their most advanced class in classical ballet.

The Palms Academy on Agua Dulce Avenue was a glass tower of concrete and steel as delicate and insubstantial as an *arabesque*. For almost forty years the Palms had been *the* place in town to study dance, whether it be ballet, tap, acrobatic, Spanish, Gypsy, oriental, ballroom, modern, or some combination of all eight. It was to the Palms that the young Theda Bara had come in 1918 to learn the sinuous gyrations that had made her film *Salome* a public scandal. Here, Shirley Temple had put on her first pair of tap shoes and Betty Grable had learned to kick her million-dollar legs.

Vivien Leigh had studied the fundamentals of ballet at the Palms and Agnes de Mille, who choreographed both *Oklahoma* and *Carousel*, had once been on its staff.

Inside, the studios were painted in the kinds of bright, gorgeous colors that you'd only find in Southern California: poppy orange, pacific blue, sunshine yellow. In Studio C, where Tatiana stood at the barre warming up with the eight other members of the Advanced ballet class, the walls had been graced with a flamingo pink so intense it made her dizzy just to look at them. Closing her eyes, Tatiana concentrated on her body, which was badly out of shape: loose muscles in the legs, flabby abdomen, breasts that felt like overinflated balloons. After months of being almost totally on the shelf, it was a wonder she could even bend her knees. Still, it didn't matter. Energy was coursing through her, moving up her backbone and down her arms like a warm massage.

Dr. DeWitt was a genius. The pills he had prescribed had changed everything almost overnight. Tatiana did a quick series of *pliés*, silently blessing modern science. Who would have ever thought that half a dozen small white tablets taken on a regular basis could have such an effect? In only a few weeks they had made her feel like her old self again. For a moment she was intensely glad to be alive in the fifties, when suffering was outdated.

Opening her eyes, Tatiana permitted herself to look around. On all sides were beautiful women, dressed in tight, shiny rainbow-colored leotards: healthy suntanned blondes, redheads with milk white complexions, Mexican girls with full, round breasts and manes of glossy black hair. No skinny, flat-chested Balanchine types here. Compared to the New York City Ballet with its tradition of baggy warm-up clothes, skipped meals, and endless rehearsals, the Palms looked like a little piece of paradise. How in the world did Hollywood manage to attract so many gorgeous, healthy human beings?

Tatiana contemplated her fellow students with pleasure. Before it had always bothered her to be in a class with such a low level of professional commitment, but now she saw that she had judged everyone too harshly. Such perfectly formed bodies: strong legs, straight spines, high arches. What a pity none of them could really dance. Still, they were a delight to look at.

One of the girls smiled timidly at her and Tatiana smiled back. A whole host of good resolutions ran through her mind:

she'd make the best of Los Angeles instead of fighting it all the time; she'd be a better wife to Michael, a better mother to Alysa. Now she felt so much better she understood that if you were really a dancer you didn't need a company, or an audience, or a theater, or reviewers. You didn't even need Balanchine. You could be like a whirling dervish, dancing for yourself alone.

Tatiana began a series of adagio movements, humming to herself under her breath. After class maybe she'd go see Michael on the set of *Rebel Yell*. They were filming a ballroom scene this week, one of those big spectacular Hollywood numbers with two hundred extras and so many kleig lights you could practically fry eggs on the scenery.

In the ballroom of the Southern mansion it was 1862; belles in hoopskirts and long white gloves waltzed under crystal chandeliers with handsome officers dressed dashingly in Confederate gray. The Civil War was on, the South was winning, and everything was an illusion: the jewels (paste), the dancers (dress extras), even the ballroom itself, which was, in actuality, a part of a leftover set crammed into a large cinderblock soundstage on the back lot of Galaxy Productions.

Still, the dance was lovely to behold: perfectly choreographed it combined fluid movement with complex patterns. Overhead, the camera, mounted on a large mobile crane, dipped and swooped in time to the music, catching every nuance.

"Whatda you think, Tats?" Michael whispered worriedly.

"It's great," Tatiana whispered back enthusiastically. "You've outdone yourself." Hard to remember that only a few weeks ago she had been so angry with him she could hardly carry on a conversation without threatening to leave. She realized now she'd been so busy brooding about her own career that she hadn't taken the time to enjoy what Michael was doing. It was fun really—all the lights and costumes—like Halloween 365 days a year.

Michael frowned. "It's a disaster waiting to happen." For weeks now he'd been brooding about making changes in the script, but Arnold Glass was having none of it and at Galaxy, Arnold ran the show.

"No, it's great, really it is." Tatiana smiled and settled back in her chair. She wished Michael would try to be more optimistic about *Rebel Yell*. Now that she'd hired a nurse for Alysa and was coming regularly to the set every afternoon to bring him his lunch, she understood firsthand the intense pressure he was under. Still, she couldn't help but think he was being too critical of his own work. The choreography was inspired; anybody could see that.

Reaching into her purse, Tatiana took out one of the white tablets and slipped it into her mouth. A mild flavor of geraniums spread over her tongue. How many of these things had she had since this morning? Four? Five? She tried to count and gave up. Why bother? She was definitely taking them more frequently than Dr. DeWitt had prescribed, but it didn't seem to be doing any harm—on the contrary.

As the music flowed on from bar to bar, the whole history of waltzing ran through her head from Gardel to Nijinskaya. Her mind was so fluid these days, running on and on like an endless river, and her body was in great shape. Yesterday she'd signed up for two more classes at the Palms, and she was tempted to add a fourth. She didn't seem to need any rest anymore, or food either for that matter. The only inconveniences were that her mouth was dry, she'd lost weight, and she still wasn't sleeping well—but all that was a small price to pay for feeling so good.

Michael continued frowning and went back to tapping his fingers nervously on the arm of his chair. He'd made a big splash in the film version of *Dance*, even came to the attention of important people, such as Gene Kelly, but choreography was something else again. For months he'd pleaded with Arnold Glass to give him a film of his own to work on, and for months Glass had run him around in circles. Only when Michael's second picture grossed nine million at the box office—a million more than *Show Boat*—had Glass finally given in and handed him the script for *Rebel Yell*. No wonder he felt as if his whole career was riding on it.

Out on the set Bobby Fender was about to make his big entrance. Tatiana leaned forward to get a better view. So far she hadn't seen Fender in the flesh, although like thousands of other Americans she'd watched him on the Ed Sullivan show six months ago, the cameras coyly confined to the upper half of his body. She remembered a handsome, sultry face; a husky voice; and a body that moved in time to the music in a way that suggested interesting things were going on just out of sight. Fender, according to all the fan magazines, was supposed to be even *more* outrageous than Elvis.

The waltz built to a crescendo. Fender was coming down the formal staircase now, bouncing from step to step dressed as a Confederate lieutenant—sword at his side, hat in one hand, singing at the top of his lungs—but something was terribly wrong. His voice twanged; his movements were ludicrous.

Michael was right. What idiot had written this script? Fender went on, but things only got worse. It was obvious he should be in blue jeans playing the part of a truck driver, not prancing around like Fred Astaire. Making one more attempt to negotiate the stairs, Fender slipped, tripped over his sword, and fell the rest of the way, cursing at the top of his lungs.

"Cut!" Michael yelled.

Tatiana giggled and then put her hand over her mouth, horrified to have laughed out loud.

"Take a break everybody." Michael got to his feet. "Go ahead and laugh, Tats," he said. "It obviously stinks. For weeks I've been telling him we've got a rock and roll star on our hands, but that son of a bitch, Glass, is deaf. Do you realize what's going to happen to my career if I shoot this thing the way it's written? The audience will laugh *Rebel Yell* out of the theaters; the reviewers will shred it; and I'll probably end up over at Warners directing *Bwana Devil Meets the Beast from 20,000 Fathoms*.

"It can't be that bad."

"For weeks I've been telling Glass it was all wrong. For *weeks*." Michael picked up the paper bag full of sandwiches and turned his back on the set disgustedly. "Come on, let's have some lunch while I try to figure out how to keep this from being the biggest box office disaster since *Greed*."

"I've made a decision, Tats," Michael threw three lumps of sugar in his coffee and stirred it with the handle of his spoon. They were sitting in the Galaxy commissary eating oversalted potato salad, cole slaw, and the roast beef sandwiches Tatiana had brought from home. Or rather Michael was eating; Tatiana was only going through the motions, keeping him company. "Damn it, I've known ever since Glass first handed me *Rebel Yell* that the Confederate angle was all wrong for Fender, but it's taken me until now to get the guts to do something about it."

"Which is what, exactly?"

"Reshoot the whole damn thing."

"You're kidding."

"Tats, I could write a better script with half my brain tied behind my back."

"But Glass has already approved the script you have. If you change one line, he'll annihilate you."

"Let him. Fifteen minutes ago I finally came to the interesting conclusion that I'd rather be dead than direct the biggest turkey of 1954. To hell with Glass's fancy sets. I'm going to film Fender live." It wasn't a new idea—Michael had been talking about it for weeks—but as he leaned forward his face was flushed with enthusiasm. "I'm going to use the world, Tats—theaters, city streets, back alleys—the places where Fender really belongs."

"But no one's ever made a musical that way before."

"No one's ever made a rock and roll film before either. It's a whole new ball game."

"What about the sound? You'll have traffic, wind, God knows what."

"We'll post-dub it."

"Michael, you're a genius."

He grinned. "Now *that's* the kind of thing a man likes to hear from his wife. I was afraid you'd be upset."

"Why ?"

"Because it means a lot of extra work and I haven't been around much as it is, not to mention that you haven't been in such great shape yourself. I worry about you, Tats. I may not say much, but I worry."

Tatiana smiled and brushed a stray wisp of hair out of her eyes. "I'm fine and so is Alysa. Don't give us a second thought. While you're out on the streets trying to film Fender, we'll be . . ." she tried to think of what she and Alysa could possibly do day after day, ". . . we'll be down at the beach getting suntans," she concluded brightly.

Michael added some mustard to his roast beef sandwich, ate it quickly, then reached for another. "I'll probably get fired when Glass sees the rough cut," he observed as he peeled off the wax paper.

"Good, then we can move back to New York and I can support us on a dancer's salary." Before she would have said this with bitterness, but now she no longer seemed capable of caring about anything. Vaguely, somewhere in the back of her mind, she realized this wasn't altogether a good thing, but she was too relieved to consider doing anything about it.

"How much is that?"

"About two hundred and thirty dollars."

"A week?"

"A month."

Michael paused in midbite. "Does this mean I'll have to give up roast beef?"

"It'll be peanut butter and jelly all the way," Tatiana smiled, thinking how long it had been since she and Michael had had one of these verbal Ping-Pong matches. Once again she silently thanked Dr. DeWitt for bringing her out of her depression.

"Speaking of the East Coast," Michael said, washing down the bread and beef with a swallow of coffee, "when does Ruth's plane get in?"

"This afternoon at two-forty-five. Dan's volunteered to drive me and Alysa out to the airport to pick her up."

"I wish Dan was producing *Rebel Yell* instead of *Glass*," Michael mused, commandeering the last sandwich. "At least Dan's got some brains."

"Dan's never produced a film in his life."

Michael grinned. "In the case of *Rebel Yell* that might be a real plus."

Concrete, glass, smog, exhaust; concrete, smog, glass: Dan and Tatiana were waiting at the airport for Ruth's plane to arrive from Boston. The main terminal shuddered as still another metal giant taxied down the runway, its propellers beating the air into waves thick enough to see. Of all the grim spots on the face of the planet, this had to be one of the grimmest, but nothing about it touched Tatiana. She was wrapped in a cocoon of good feeling, as perfectly at ease as if she were walking on the beach or sitting in her own living room.

Windows shook and metal ashtrays trembled—Tatiana put her fingers in her ears to blot out the roar of the planes, and then changed her mind and transferred them to Alysa's. In honor of her first meeting with Ruth, Alysa was dressed all in pink: pink cap, pink ruffled dress, tiny pink booties embroidered with rosebuds. Her skin was flawless as milk, her eyelashes so long and thick they looked like fringe. Today she was precisely three months and one day old.

"Ruth's plane. . . ." Dan continued to speak but the rest of his words were drowned out by another take-off. In the last two years since he had come out to Hollywood to work for his uncle Warren at MGM, Dan had gone from Brooks Brothers suits to white sports jackets that made him look a little like

Montgomery Clift. In the past, Dan's transformation had made Tatiana uneasy, but now she found it amusing.

Dan cupped his hands to his mouth. "Ruth's plane should be landing any minute," he yelled encouragingly.

"Great," Tatiana yelled back. She shifted Alysa to her other arm, feeling the noise pulling at her like a thousand electric wires. Under the warm baby body, her own hands were cold and shaking. How odd, especially since she didn't feel particularly nervous. The next time she saw Dr. DeWitt, she'd have to ask him if this was one of the side effects of the medication.

They waited fifteen more minutes, then half an hour. Alysa woke, fussed for food, and Tatiana fed her from a bottle, and went to the Ladies' Room to change her diapers. At 5:15—a full two and a half hours late—Ruth's plane finally arrived, and the passengers began straggling off, looking more like refugees than people who had paid several hundred dollars to be whisked across the continent.

"Hello, Hello." Ruth fairly bounded into the terminal dressed in a gray skirt, mustard yellow tights, and a green wool coat that appeared to have been designed for an expedition to the North Pole. Grabbing Tatiana and Dan, she gave them both quick bear hugs. "Good God, Tats," she exclaimed, stepping back for a better look, "what's Hollywood done to you? You look like a remake of *The Bride of Frankenstein*."

"I'm fine," Tatiana said, "couldn't be better." She held Alysa up for inspection. "Get a load of this." Lifted into the air, Alysa smiled with pleasure and stretched out her chubby baby arms. Ruth melted instantly.

"Ooh what tiny fingers; she's adorable."

"Amazing how otherwise perfectly reasonable adults suffer brain damage in the presence of small children," Dan observed with a grin.

"Shut up, you hard-hearted creep. You're looking at the future president of the Radcliffe class of seventy-six." Ruth handed Dan her suitcase and ignored him when he pretended to fall to the floor under its weight. "Seriously, Tats," she persisted, "what's wrong? You look rotten. Is Michael secretly beating you with rubber hoses or something?"

"Wait a minute," Tatiana put up her hand in mock defense, "is this a reunion or an inquisiton?"

"Both. Dan, you moron, why haven't you been taking care of her?"

"Things have changed since Harvard, Ruthie. Our Tats is a

married woman these days." Dan tried to Groucho Marx his eyebrows at the two of them but it didn't quite come off. "I have no intention of being shot by a jealous husband, and besides I've been busy."

"You call that an excuse?"

"It's true," Tatiana said. "Dan's almost managed to produce three films only. . . ."

"Only they fell through at the last minute." Dan grinned weakly. "You don't know what it's like out here, Ruthie. Between television and Joe McCarthy it's a war zone. Utter panic. Look at MGM: a little while ago they were making as many as eleven musicals a year—blockbusters like *Singin' in the Rain*—now they're three million in debt and heads are rolling all over the place. It's like when sound came in during the twenties only worse. The studios are trying any gimmick they can grab—3D, cinerama—but the little black box just keeps siphoning off the audience."

Ruth put her hands on her hips and shook her head. "What is it out here, the sunshine or something? Have you gone blind? Take a look at Tats, Dan, and tell me what you see."

"She looks great to me."

"Great? She's lost maybe ten pounds. What do you and Michael have in your heads? Rocks?"

"I'm fine," Tatiana protested. "I've never felt better."

"No kidding?"

"No kidding."

"Well, okay," Ruth said dubiously, "if you want to go around looking like a human toothpick I guess that's your business. As long as you're happy."

"I'm happy."

"Really happy?"

Tatiana laughed a light, free laugh that shattered through the air like glass. "Happier than you can imagine."

"Well, good," Ruth said, "because I'm going to need all the moral support I can get. I hear Professor Arnold is a cross between Stalin, Hitler, and a venus fly trap."

"Who's Professor Arnold?" Dan asked.

"Head of the Botany Department at UCLA."

"Ruth has an interview with him at ten tomorrow morning." Tatiana observed, "and she's obviously scared out of her pants."

"Who wouldn't be." Ruth moaned. "The man has published eleven books, authored about three thousand papers, and won a Nobel prize. It's rumored he has a nasty temper, chlorophyll in his body instead of blood, and thinks women graduate students are an infestation worse than aphids."

"Don't fret Ruthie; we're with you all the way."

"Hemlock," Ruth moaned melodramatically, clutching at Tatiana, "give me hemlock. Or, better yet," she said, brightening considerably, "hand over that beautiful baby."

15

The spring of 1954 was crystalline, so clearly focused and brilliantly colored that later Tatiana felt she had spent the entire three months looking through a magnifying glass. After years of believing that California had no seasons to speak of, she was aware for the first time of a host of subtle transitions as the arid hills around Los Angeles passed from winter greens to summer browns. In Malibu new birds appeared on the beach, unfamiliar flowers bloomed overnight along the freeways, and the sky lost its moist grays and became light and dry as a biscuit.

Everything that had been so hard before suddenly became easy. It was a period when she said yes to everyone: to Michael when he came home late from reshooting *Rebel Yell* and wanted to go out to dinner; to Alysa, who needed endless cuddling and attention; to Ruth, who had enrolled in graduate school at UCLA and needed someone to complain to; to the new friends who suddenly appeared out of nowhere. Before it had seemed ridiculously hard to meet interesting people, but now suddenly they were everywhere: popping up at the Palms, at Galaxy, even on the beach at Malibu— brilliant, articulate people who seemed to come in couples with names you could repeat as one unit: Laurina-and-Ted, Margot-and-Mark, Vince-and-Vanessa. In the small hours of the morning, when Michael was working and Alysa was safely bedded down in the care of Mrs. Lowrey, Tatiana would impulsively climb into her car and speed over the empty freeways with the top down, drinking in the warm night air. At Vanessa's house she could always count on finding a group of people sitting on the floor around the redwood burl coffee table drinking cheap red wine and having fierce discussions as the latest jazz tinkled away in the background. Vanessa—a full blown blonde from Arizona who always wore squaw dresses and heavy Hopi jewelry—would greet her with a friendly nod and pour her a drink. Tatiana would sit until dawn letting the voices flow over her. Later, as the sky was just beginning to turn pink, she would drive back across the deserted overpasses to Malibu, take a few tranquilizers, and sleep soundly until noon.

You could find anyone at these midnight discussions—itinerant poets, out-of-work musicians, auto mechanics—but most people were involved in the film industry and as she listened to them talk Tatiana became aware for the first time that Hollywood was seething with politics. Writers and actors were being blacklisted right and left, contracts canceled, the industry virtually paralyzed. On the screen it was business as usual— *Brigadoon, A Star Is Born, Guys and Dolls*—while behind the scenes the fear was thick enough to taste.

But the harder Tatiana tried to figure out the reason people tolerated this fear, the more difficult it became. Obviously the man responsible for all this was mad, but no one, not even those who complained the loudest, seemed willing to say so publicly. After a few weeks of trying to get Vince or Vanessa or Margot to explain this to her, she gave up. At another time or place she might have signed petitions, even made public protests against such obvious injustice, but her mood was too detached for her to stay involved in anything. Ideas hit her mind, exploded briefly, then seemed to disappear without a trace. She, who had once cared so much, now cared very little about what happened from one day to the next.

Sometimes she worried that nothing seemed important enough to get upset about, but on the whole everything was light, pleasant, and exactly as it should be.

"Well," Michael said one morning over coffee, "look at this, will you."

"At what?"

He spread the *Los Angeles Times* out on the kitchen table. "The New York City Ballet's coming to town. Shall we get tickets, Tats?"

Tatiana paused with her butter knife lifted over the toast. An odd feeling swept over her—half nostalgia, half something she couldn't quite put her finger on.

"Who's dancing?"

"Tanaquil Leclercq, Patricia Wilde, Maria Tallchief, Nicholas Magallanes, Jacques d'Amboise, André Eglevsky—the usual crew—and some newcomer called Blanche Bender."

"Blanche Bender, you're kidding." She jerked the paper out of his hand, read it, and turned pale.

"What's wrong?"

"I knew Blanche back at the SAB. She was in the class just below me, and here she is dancing in *Pas de Trois* with Tallchief and Eglevsky." Tatiana put the newspaper back down on the table and stared at the toast, the uneaten eggs, the bacon growing cold on her plate. Then she mentally gave herself a shake and picked up the butter knife again. What in the world was she being so morose about? It would be great to see Balanchine's new ballets. She impulsively resolved to go backstage before the performance and say *merde* to everyone, maybe even take them a *merde* present—something silly like a dozen fly swatters or a can of Ajax wrapped in red velvet. *Merde* presents weren't exactly a tradition with the City Ballet, but sometimes dancers exchanged them on special occasions—the more inappropriate and outrageous the gift, the more luck it was supposed to bring.

After Michael left for the studio, Tatiana got out a pad and pencil and began to list some possibilities.

"Tatiana, darling."

"Tatiana, where have you been keeping yourself?"

"Hi, Tats, how's tricks."

The dressing room of the Los Angeles Greek Theater was littered with soft drink bottles, cigarette butts, false eyelashes, and open jars of makeup. As Tatiana made her way past the tables with the *merde* present clutched in her arms, she was greeted, embraced, kissed, welcomed back into the fold of the City Ballet like a prodigal daughter.

"What's in the package?"

"Yeah, Tats, what *merde* do you have for us."

Tatiana grinned and undid the silver and gold ribbons to reveal a tin of chocolate-coated peanuts. There was a sudden silence as the dancers of the corps all stared at her in horror. Good. They thought she'd brought them a real present, an act that, on opening night, was supposed to guarantee disaster.

'Well, don't just stand there. Have some."

Pauline, one of the younger dancers, gamely took the tin and unscrewed the lid. With a whoosh, a huge green snake popped out and bounced across the room, sending everyone into shrieks of relief.

"*Merde* everybody." For a moment, as she laughed with these old friends, Tatiana imagined she really *had* returned to

253

the Company, and then she saw Blanche Bender—small boned and regal—standing in front of the mirror the way a real dancer should stand: toes turned out, pelvis tucked in. Tatiana felt a wave of envy and was instantly ashamed. How could she begrudge Blanche her success?

"*Merde*, Blanche," she called cheerfully.

Blanche, who had always been one of the shyest students at the SAB, blushed with pleasure at being singled out.

Later, as she sat beside Michael in the audience watching *Pas de Trois*, Tatiana clapped until her hands were raw and stinging. During intermission she went to the Ladies' Room, opened one of her bottles, and gulped a whole handful of pills. As she lifted her head from the sink, Tatiana saw her face in the mirror: slack, pale, her eyes full of pain and envy. It was a moment of sudden, stark revelation. She contemplated her own image with growing disgust. What the hell was she doing to herself? If she looked this bad now, how would she look in ten years? Blanche Bender was doing something with her life where she, Tatiana, was merely gulping down pills to numb herself to the fact that she was rotting here.

Tatiana held on to the edge of the sink and forced herself to look into her own eyes. By some miracle she'd been allowed to see herself as she really was, and she didn't want to forget it. Pulling the pills out of her purse, she went into one of the booths and flushed them down the toilet. Then she put her finger down the back of her throat and vomited up the dose she had just taken. Watching Blanche Bender perform had reminded her of who she really was: not some blowzy, pill-popping Hollywood housewife who dabbled in ballet, but a serious dancer who intended to have more to remember when she was old than one season with the New York City Ballet.

"I'm leaving."

"Tats, you can't."

"It's no use, Michael." Tatiana piled another dress into her suitcase, put her winter coat on top of it, and forced down the lid. "I'm going back to New York, and there's no point trying to talk me out of it."

"What about Alysa." Michael stared at her bewildered, probably not really believing she really meant it this time.

"I can't take her with me, but I'll send for her as soon as I get a place."

"Tats, please. Let's talk this over."

"We've already talked, Our agreement was for six months, remember? Well, the six months are long up." Tatiana picked up another bag and began stuffing her shoes in randomly. "Michael, God knows I'd like to stay with you, but I can't. I've tried and tried to get used to it out here, but it's destroying me. I even tried to drug myself so I wouldn't feel the pain, but it just doesn't work. I *miss* dancing. I miss it so much it's poisoning everything else for me." She was on the verge of tears, but she held back, knowing that if she cried she might weaken. "If you want to be with me so damn much, then you're more than welcome to come along."

"Tats, you know I can't. I'm in the middle of *Rebel Yell*, But maybe afterward. . . ."

"Afterward you'll be in the middle of something else." She raised one hand to forestall his objection. "I know you, Michael. I know what these films mean to you. We just have to face the fact that your work means more to you than I do, and that my work means more to me than you for that matter. Not very romantic, but it's the truth." She looked around the familiar bedroom—at her books in a heap by the door, her blouses draped over the chairs. Her whole life felt uprooted and in pieces. "I suppose sooner or later we'll have to get divorced."

Michael grabbed her by the shoulders. "Tats, don't talk that way. Please. It reminds me too damn much of my parents."

"What else can I say?"

"Say you'll give me a chance to keep my part of the bargain. Okay, I know I've screwed things up; I know I've kept you here a lot longer than was reasonable, but just give me one month to wrap up *Rebel Yell* and I swear to you I'll move back to New York."

"One month?"

"I swear it."

"I want to believe you, but I've heard all this before, Michael." Wearily Tatiana sat down on the edge of the bed. "I just don't know."

"Please."

"I suppose I could see if I could arrange an audition with Balanchine while he's out here. Then I'd know one way or the other if there's any chance of him taking me back into the Company. If he says yes, though, I'm going."

"But you'll wait a month?"

Tatiana shrugged and tried to smile. She had a sense of

simultaneously having won and having been defeated. "One month, Michael, but not a day more." She wanted him to come with her more than she was capable of expressing, but she knew that this time if he stayed in Hollywood she wouldn't be staying with him.

A week later, at eight in the morning, Balanchine watched Tatiana dance on the stage of the Greek Theater. After the audition he told her she would be welcome to rejoin the Company.

"Welcome back, Tats," Ada Wilzer gave Tatiana a big hug, nearly spilling her drink in the process. Ada, a regular member of the NYCB corps was a small, lean woman with bright red hair and a long slender nose that gave her a birdlike appearance. "I heard Balanchine's taking you back into the fold. Fabulous." It was four in the afternoon and the farewell reception for the dancers of the New York City Ballet was in full swing. Tatiana stood over the swimming pool on a nonskid portable dance floor, drinking champagne so sweet it almost made her ill. Overhead the purple-and-yellow striped canopy of the rented tent fluttered like a butterfly stuck on a pin. The famous Santa Ana winds were blowing in off the desert, cleaning out the smog, bringing in air so hot it rasped in her lungs. Too bad she wasn't in the pool instead of walking on top of it, Tatiana thought. Her throat had been a little sore for a few days and when she woke up this morning she had a slight headache—nothing serious enough to keep her away from the party, but still bothersome.

Blanche Bender, who had been standing shyly on the sidelines, suddenly spoke up. "We all missed you, you know." Blanche blushed slightly, obviously sincere. It seemed inconceivable to Tatiana that anyone could have missed her, but evidently they had. For the last ten minutes, ever since she arrived at the reception, one dancer after another had come over to welcome her back. Tatiana was taken with a sudden fit of coughing. Covering her mouth quickly with the back of her hand, she murmured an apology.

"Gee," Blanche observed, "that sounds nasty."

"Just a summer cold," Tatiana coughed again. "Sorry. It's been coming for days."

"That's the trouble with all this California sunshine," Ada quipped. "Now what you need is a good dose of Manhattan winter to get you back to the peak of health. Slush, sleet, the sweet sound of steam heat clanging like a freight train beneath your bed at night."

They spent another three or four minutes trading weather jokes and then Blanche and Ada wandered off in search of fresh ice for their drinks. Tatiana took another sip of champagne, reached up, and began to massage her neck. Darn it, she ached all over and her throat was definitely swollen, not to mention some odd shooting pains in her legs and lower back. What a time to come down with something—and the worst of was Alysa would probably catch it, too, all of which would make leaving for New York even more traumatic than it already was. Well, it didn't matter. She had her plane ticket and she was going and that was that. If Alysa got sick, she'd just wrap her up and take her along, and as for Michael. . . . Darn it, she'd absolutely promised herself she wouldn't think about Michael this afternoon. So what if *Rebel Yell* wasn't any closer to being finished than it had been a week ago. When the month was up, it was up.

Taking another sip of her drink, she turned her attention to the crowd milling around the buffet table. You had to hand it to the people who were giving this reception: they really knew how to pack in the celebrities. Over at the oyster bar alone she could see Gene Kelly, Mr. Balanchine, and Cyd Charisse talking earnestly. Well, it wasn't all that surprising when you thought about it. The New York City Ballet's tour was probably the biggest cultural event to hit Los Angeles in the last ten years. Forty-one new ballets never seen before on the West Coast had been performed to standing-room-only crowds. The film community had gone wild, leotards were all the rage, and actresses who had never danced a step in their lives were feverishly signing up for classes at the Palms. There was talk of initiating a permanent series of operas and ballet performances at the Greek Theater, even of forming a resident company.

There was something faintly ironic about the fact that professional ballet was coming to Los Angeles just as she was leaving. Tatiana fished a champagne-soaked strawberry out of the bottom of her glass and ate it slowly, rolling the idea of a resident company over in her mind. Around her everything seemed to slow down gradually, like a record spinning to a stop. Her arms felt suddenly heavy and her tongue tingled unpleasantly. The heat must be getting to her—that and the champagne. She didn't usually drink so much, but it had numbed her sore throat. Another case of the cure being worse than the disease. Oh, well, at least she'd have plenty of time to sober up before she had to drive home.

Tatiana drifted over to the buffet and tried to concentrate on the food, which she had to admit was spectacular: whole pheasants, wild rice, corn on the cob rolled in something that looked like tarragon, silver platters of tiny sandwiches. Blanche was on the other side of the terrace talking to Pauline. After she had something to eat, Tatiana would go over and join them. It was great to be here, really—like Christmas and Thanksgiving all rolled into one. That was one of the best things about the Company: it was essentially a huge, extended family. No use sulking in a corner and missing out on all the fun just because she had a headache. Except that... well, when she thought about it, she wasn't so much *sulking* as feeling off balance.

Tatiana took a step forward and the ground trembled under her. Trying to walk produced an odd sensation, like dancing on a steeply slanted stage. Her legs and arms were leaden and it felt as if someone were driving needles through the back of her neck. In front of her, the palm trees in the yard began to do a kind of hula, multiplying and dividing before her eyes. It took her a minute to realize she must be seeing double.

Good lord, she was having a real, honest to God heatstroke. Tatiana tried to remember what you were supposed to do in a case like this: Sit down? Put your head between your knees? She looked around weakly for a chair, but there were none in sight. Inside the house there'd be some of course, but she suddenly felt too dizzy to take another step.

"Are you okay?"

"What?" Interrupted in her train of thought, she looked up to find the white-coated boy behind the buffet staring at her worriedly. He was young and blond: probably a surfer or a would-be actor when he wasn't slicing roast beef at some fancy party. "I'm fine," she said weakly, and as she uttered the words everything suddenly turned into glue; her body leaned forward of its own accord, and she felt herself falling an inch at a time into sticky nothingness.

"It's the heat," she mumbled at the startled boy. The last thing she remembered before she blacked out was reaching for the table to steady herself and missing it completely.

* * *

The telephone was ringing. Natasha fumbled for it and nearly knocked over a lamp. *Boje moy!* Who could be calling at this hour? It must be nearly three A.M.

"Preevyet," woke Natasha out of a dead sleep and who knew what language she was liable to speak into the receiver—Russian, French, English—long ago all three had blended together in her dreams. "Hello." She switched on a light and sat up against the pillows.

"Mother, this is Michael."

"Michael." Instantly Natasha was totally awake. "What's wrong? Is Alysa sick?"

"No, it's Tats. She's in the hospital. She was at a party, and she just sort of keeled over." He was holding something back; she could hear it in his voice. A fine cold prickle of fear ran down her spine. Natasha pulled the covers up over her shoulders and drew the phone closer.

"Do they know what's wrong with her?"

"They aren't absolutely sure yet, but they took a spinal tap and. . . ."

"And what?"

"There are a lot of lymphocytes in her spinal fluid."

"Michael, what does that mean—translate for God's sake. What do they think she has?"

"Their best guess right now is that it's . . . polio."

"Polio." Natasha clutched the receiver, wishing Michael would tell her this was all some kind of terrible joke. In 1954 there was no word more dreaded than polio. During last summer's epidemic over 30,000 cases had been reported in the United States alone. You didn't have to work for the March of Dimes to know that thousands of victims had been crippled for life. How could Tatiana have polio—Tatiana, whose whole life had been movement and dance? It was unthinkable—the kind of situation that made Natasha want to pound her fists on the night table and rail at the universe. Instead she took a deep breath and tried, for Michael's sake, to keep the fear out of her voice. "How bad is it, Michael?"

There was a long silence that told her more than any words. "She's at Cedars of Lebanon," Michael said at last, "a good hospital, private room, the best doctors money can buy. Right now she's having some trouble breathing so they've put her in a iron lung." This was a nightmare. Surely she was dreaming. Surely she would wake up and find out none of this was true. "But until she regains consciousness no one can really tell if there's been any. . . ." he paused, fumbling for the right words. "I don't mean to frighten you, Mother, but I think you should get out here as fast as you can."

"Of course," Natasha said, "Yes, of course. I'll take the next plane." After she hung up, she sat staring at the phone trying to accept that somewhere at that very minute Tatiana was lying in a huge machine that was doing her breathing for her. For some reason she was suddenly haunted by an image of Tatiana as a little girl of five or six running across the Boston Common, her burnished auburn pigtails flying in the wind. She remembered Tatiana's chubby baby legs pounding on the gravel path, her laughter, even the little blue dress she had had on that day—a favorite one, trimmed in white lace that her Aunt Faith had sewn for her. That was the afternoon Natasha had seen that Tatiana was born to be a dancer—everything in her body had proclaimed it. Natasha thought again of Tatiana's legs. Then turning away from the light, she buried her head in the pillows and wept for her daughter, herself, and all those unreasonable, unfair parts of life that hurt so much and made so little sense.

After a while Natasha sat up again, dried her eyes, and picked up the phone to call Winn and Drew and tell them the news.

"Before you go in to see your daughter, Mrs. Ward, I think it would be best if you prepared yourself for a rather difficult situation." Dr. Kean adjusted his glasses and cleared his throat. He was a short, balding man of about fifty who projected an air of busy, straightforward efficiency that was somehow reassuring. "At the moment, as you know, we have her in a tank respirator."

Natasha reached for Michael's hand and tried to imagine how Tatiana would look, but the image absolutely refused to materialize in her mind. "You mean she's in an iron lung."

"Exactly," Dr. Kean said briskly. "Sometimes when relatives first see the patient in this condition the shock is considerable. What you should understand is that she is actually doing quite well—holding her own as we like to say—so there's no need for any sort of excessive emotional reaction. Not, of course, that you'd be inclined to hysteria, Mrs. Ward, but frankly we've had problems on occasion."

"Is this iron lung . . ." Natasha's voice quavered but she went on, determined to know the worst, ". . . a permanent arrangement?"

"It's hard to say at this stage. Now if you'll excuse me. . . ."

He turned to leave but Natasha stopped him, laying her hand lightly on his arm.

"Doctor, I need to know more about what's wrong with her."

"She's in the acute stage of poliomyelitis, Mrs. Ward; it's as simple as that." She could tell he was impatient to be off. No doubt he had other patients to attend to, but she *had* to understand what was happening to Tatiana.

"What causes it? How did she get it? Is she going to be crippled for life? I have to know the truth, Doctor. Don't spare me."

Dr. Kean looked at his watch. "Mrs. Ward, I'd like to oblige you but I really don't have time for a lecture on infantile paralysis right now. I'm due in surgery in fifteen minutes."

"Please."

Dr. Kean sighed, then shrugged. "Well, let me see if I can make it short and sweet. Poliomyelitis, commonly known as polio, is caused by a virus that attacks the nerve cells controlling muscle movement. The muscles themselves are unharmed by the disease, but are rendered incapable of response. Are you following me?"

"Yes," Natasha nodded, trying to take it all in.

"Good. Now the most important thing for you to know is that the acute paralytic stage usually lasts from about forty-eight hours to a week. After that, there can be steady improvement for anywhere from two months to a year or longer." He looked at his watch.

"Are you telling me there's a chance the paralysis might disappear completely?" Natasha had a sudden sense of having been thrown a lifeline. The shift from despair to hope was so abrupt it made her dizzy.

Dr. Kean lifted a hand in warning. "I don't want to raise any false expectations, Mrs. Ward. No one can predict in advance what the outcome will be. Everything depends on whether the nerve cells have been killed outright or merely damaged. Unfortunately, as I've already indicated, there's no way of knowing the extent of damage until weeks, maybe months, after the onset of the paralysis." He cleared his throat again. "Your attitude can be an enormous help to your daughter. Sometimes the patient gets very apprehensive when she realizes her limbs are unresponsive. If she should regain consciousness while you're with her, I suggest you try to be as encouraging as possible. Now I really must go and start scrubbing for surgery."

"Yes, of course, thank you." He had told her point blank that if she wanted to do Tatiana any good she was going to have to swallow her own fear. Natasha thought of all the things she had been terrified of in her life: mobs, Bolshevik soldiers with guns, loneliness—they were nothing compared to what Tatiana was going through. At that moment she came to a crucial decision: she would never again allow herself to imagine Tatiana doing anything but recovering completely. The paralysis was going to be temporary; the disease was only going to be an unpleasant interlude; Tatiana would not only walk again, she'd dance. She'd believe this and she'd make Tatiana believe it.

Armed with this resolve, Natasha was able to take the mask the nurse handed her, walk into the hospital room, and not flinch when she saw Tatiana lying in the metal cylinder with only her head protruding, Tatiana's hair was plastered to her forehead with sweat. Natasha brushed it aside and leaned over.

"You're going to get better," she said in a loud, clear voice. No matter that Tatiana couldn't hear her. Sitting down on a metal folding chair, Natasha took off her coat and put her purse on the floor. For the next ten minutes, until her visiting time was up, she talked to Tatiana, reassuring her that everything would be all right.

Tatiana distinctly remembered having been at a party for the City Ballet. Mr. Balanchine had been there, and Blanche Bender, and a lot of other people, too. But where was she now? With great effort she opened her eyes but everything was out of focus. It was odd to wake up to nothing but a blur, to see the world as if you were under water with big spots of color swimming around you like fish—odd and a little frightening.

Slowly the spots of color shrank and began to take on definite shapes. There was a whirring sound, a strange medicinal odor, an odd feeling of pressure on her chest. Tatiana could see now that the colored spots were Mama and Michael bending over her, only something was wrong. They both looked so worried. She tried to speak but the words stuck in her throat. Everything hurt: her head, her neck, even the soles of her feet. For a moment she fought to reach out to Michael, but she couldn't life her arms. Giving up the struggle, Tatiana fell gratefully back into a place where the pain couldn't find her.

"She opened her eyes! I swear to God, she knew me."
"What was she saying?"
"I think," Michael's voice broke in midsentence and he had to start again. "I think she was trying to tell us she was okay."

From that hour forward, although they realized it was illogical, Natasha and Michael felt more confident Tatiana was going to recover. Never mind that she was still unconscious and having trouble breathing; she had come around once, so it was only a matter of time before she woke up completely. They told each other she was strong, young, and in good physical shape—all of which Dr. Kean confirmed. In fact, he informed them, there were already signs that Tatiana's case was indeed not as serious as he had at first thought, although once again only time would tell.

That afternoon Natasha went to the hospital bookstore and bought herself three Agatha Christie mysteries; Michael called his service, told them where he could be reached, then went for a walk, returning with two cups of coffee, some stale sandwiches, and a copy of the *Los Angeles Times*. Amazingly enough the world hadn't ground to a halt in the last two days: there was a locust plague in Morocco, the temple of Mithras was still being excavated in London, Arnold Palmer had won the Amateur Championship of the U. S. Golf Association, and Haile Selassie was visiting Bonn. There was even an item about Bobby Fender. It seemed the singer had been so badly mobbed by fans at his last concert in Tulsa that he was asking for police protection. Natasha was a little disillusioned to learn from Michael that it was probably all a publicity stunt. Now that Tatiana was on the mend, she had enough energy left over to enjoy the idea of a world where young girls threw themselves at the feet of handsome young singers in exotic-sounding places like Tulsa, Oklahoma.

The next day Tatiana recovered consciousness fully and the paralysis that had attacked most of her body began to abate. Seventy-two hours later, with Natasha and Michael by her side, she was taken out of the iron lung and transferred to a private room so filled with flowers that one of the nurses jokingly remarked that it looked like a wholesale florist's shop. After they had settled her in her new bed, Michael and Natasha spent a good quarter of an hour reading her her mail. Tatiana, who was badly frightened at the prospect of not being able to move, seemed comforted a little by the flowers and the notes. It quickly became obvious that not only had her friends and teachers at the Palms remembered her, but almost every dancer in the New York City Ballet, from the humblest member of the corps to Mr. Balanchine himself, had sent her a card or a bouquet.

At that same moment on the other side of town, Arnold Glass, head of Galaxy Studios, was thinking—or perhaps it would be more accurate to say he was not so much thinking as silently raving. He was furious. No, beyond furious: he was virtually homicidal.

Glass sat down at his mahogany desk and clenched his hands together to keep himself from doing something stupid, like heaving the intercom through the window. He had just seen the rough cut of *Rebel Yell* and it was . . . words couldn't describe what that piece of *dreck* was. Glass jerked open a drawer, pulled out a bottle of Alka-Seltzer, and shook a tablet into a monogrammed Manhattan glass. Adding some water, he gulped the fizzing mixture, cursing silently.

Michael Macks had screwed him royally. Not more than ten minutes ago he had been treated to the sight of Bobby Fender *schlepping* around in a workshirt like some bum. Bobby Fender—to whom Glass had personally paid $100,000 of his own hard earned money—on the streets of LA singing to a bunch of hysterical bobby-soxers, for Christ's sake. Not only had Macks changed the original script, he hadn't even *used* it—unless you wanted to count one lousy dream sequence that was supposed to have been the climax of the original film. Where were the Civil War scenes, the Rhett Butler bits, the love interest? The whole thing was a disaster from start to finish. As if television wasn't enough of a problem these days, now some snot-nosed amateur had gone and shot a musical like it was one of those goddamn Italian movies where greasy-haired guys in T-shirts went around sucking up spaghetti and stealing bicycles.

Well, Macks had a contract with Galaxy, a good tight one with no loopholes, and he could just get his ass back in here and fix this mess for free or Glass would chop the whole film up into mandolin picks, take a tax write-off on it, and sue Macks for criminal negligence. No film had ever been released from Galaxy without his personal stamp of approval and no film ever would be. If Macks refused to cooperate his career would be over, finished, kaput. Glass would personally see to it that he was blacklisted from every studio in Hollywood.

The only problem was blacklisting was too good for Macks. There had to be something else. A nasty thought occurred to Glass. *Rebel Yell* was a total loss, so why not just release it the way it was, not change a frame of the goddamn thing? Once people saw it, Macks would be laughed out of Hollywood. His career would be wrecked, his credibility permanently destroyed, and with a little luck Fender might even sue him.

Pushing the button on the intercom, Glass leaned back and contemplated his own genius. This was a great plan, one of the best he'd ever come up with in twenty years in the business, and the beauty of it was that it was all perfectly legal. Of course it would take some time to get it in gear, a couple of months to set up distribution. They might as well pull the old trick of opening simultaneously in as many theaters as possible before the word got out. Arnold Glass smiled and downed what was left of his Alka-Seltzer in one gulp. By pulling a few fast moves, Galaxy might even turn a profit. Nice, very nice indeed. The movie industry always reminded him of a battlefield where only the strong survived. Macks didn't know it, but Glass had him in the scope and was just itching to pull the trigger.

Five weeks later Tatiana sat in a wheelchair in her hospital room reading a magazine and trying not to feel sorry for herself. By all accounts she was lucky, although as far as she was concerned the word *luck* had a sour ring to it. Dr. Kean had recently left, proclaiming for perhaps the fourth time that week he was delighted with her progress. The paralysis that had attacked her entire body was disappearing bit by bit. From the waist up she was more or less back to normal, and if she strapped her legs into braces she could even walk a little—if you could call careening around the room grabbing for handholds walking. This particular morning Dr. Kean had made a special point of comparing her to his other patients, telling her that her rate of recovery was practically a miracle— all of which was obviously designed to convince her to be grateful. But then it was easy for Dr. Kean to counsel things like gratitude and forbearance; he wasn't the one in the wheelchair.

"Hi, Tats." The door opened suddenly and Michael entered the room, sport coat slung over one shoulder, dressed in a new pair of tan slacks. He looked especially good today, healthy and suntanned. Of course he should look good, after all, he could go to the beach whenever he wanted, drive a car, walk down the street. Tatiana felt a pang of jealousy and was ashamed of herself. "You need anything?" Michael asked pleasantly, settling down on the edge of the bed.

"A glass of water."

Michael lifted the heavy metal pitcher she was still too weak to lift for herself and poured some water into a paper cup. The water was sweet, smelling of chlorine. Tatiana drank slowly, feeling the coldness slide down the back of her throat. "Shouldn't you be back at the studio?" She knew it wasn't the most diplomatic thing to say, but frankly she wanted to be alone. Whenever she was with Michael lately, she suspected him of pitying her, and pity made her angry. She saw it so often—in the eyes of the doctors and nurses, in the faces of the other patients. Everyone in the whole damn hospital seemed to know she'd been a dancer. Probably she should have been grateful her case was causing so much interest. She probably got better attention for it. What was wrong with her anyway? You always read stories about how disabled people showed such saintly qualities as patience and charity, but when Tatiana looked into herself these days all she could see was resentment and depression.

"I'm not going back to work on *Rebel Yell* until you're on your feet again," Michael took the paper cup, mashed it, and lobbed it into the wastebasket by the door.

"On my feet. That's a good one." She knew she sounded bitter but she simply couldn't help it.

"Tats, Dr. Kean says there's every possibility—"

"Michael, don't *baby* me! I'm stuck in this chair, right? For life maybe. So let's just accept it."

Michael picked up both her hands and kissed them carefully, backs and palms. His blue sweater made his eyes look like a piece of summer sky, and there was such passion in them. Wasted passion. She didn't want him to touch her any more . . . maybe never touch her again for that matter. Her body looked all right for the present but soon, in a few months, the muscles in her legs would start wasting away. The public health bulletin she had made Mama bring her from the hospital library had been quite explicit on that point. She wasn't about to allow Michael to witness her decay. She still loved him, but her body had turned into something alien, something she could barely tolerate thinking about.

"Tats," Michael bent closer and she pulled back a little, not

266

wanting to hurt him but unable to bear another human face so near her own. "I want to say something to you, only I'm not very good with words and I don't know how to begin." Michael stopped and toyed for a moment with her fingers. "What I'm trying to tell you is that I love you."

"I know that, Michael." For a moment the bitterness peeled away and she felt affection for him again. Then the suspicion crossed her mind that, once again, it was only pity making him say this to her. She tried to push the thought aside, but it settled to her stomach, bitter and heavy like an undigested pill.

"My father sacrificed my mother to his work," Michael was saying earnestly. "His career always came first: before her happiness, before mine, before anything. The last few years I've been getting more and more like him, and that scares me Tats."

"Michael. . . ." All of this was too late, wasted. He should have said it years ago before Alysa was born. He should have thought about her when it would have done some good.

"No," he put a finger gently over her lips, "let me give it to you straight. I neglected you; I neglected Alysa. And for what? A couple of films? A chance to try to make Bobby Fender learn his right foot from his left? Well, from this day on I want you to know your happiness is my first priority. To hell with Glass, to hell with all of Hollywood for that matter. As far as I'm concerned, you come first and everything else is just icing on the cake. I mean it. If you still want to move back to Manhattan, we'll leave as soon as you get well enough to travel." Michael bent forward and kissed her. There were tears in his eyes. Tatiana wanted to cry, too, but she felt dry and empty inside. Move back to Manhattan. Why? There was nothing for her there anymore, nothing for her anywhere for that matter.

After Michael left she picked up her magazine with relief and went back to her reading. She was supposed to be using her walker this afternoon, but the sight of the other patients in the corridor depressed her. There had been a time in the recent past, so the books told her, when polio patients had been put in plaster casts or strapped to wooden frames for months to prevent misalignment and help heal the spinal cord, but ever since the Australian nurse, Sister Kenny, had revolutionized physical therapy, hospitals were emphasizing movement. Probably, Tatiana thought, she should be grateful she hadn't been crucified on an immobilization frame; probably she should be delighted that Dr. Kean had ordered her to use the walker. But it was hard to be delighted about anything, especially when you still dreamed every night of *fouettés* and *grand jetés*.

A week later Tatiana was discharged from the hospital. It was a fine, sunny afternoon and Natasha and Michael tried to make pleasant conversation as they drove back to Malibu, but Tatiana, wrapped in a pink blanket from head to foot, sat silent in the front seat, replying only in monosyllables.

"Home again," Michael observed with forced cheer as they pulled into the driveway. Opening the door, he lifted Tatiana in his arms, and started to carry her toward the house.

"Put me down."

"What?"

"I said put me down. Please. I want to walk into the house on my own—not be carried in like a bag of laundry."

"Tats, are you sure. . . ."

"Yes, I'm sure."

Michael started to say something and obviously thought better of it. Natasha, who had been bringing up the rear, quickly handed Tatiana the two metal crutches with extra padding on the tops. Jamming them under her arms, Tatiana began to limp across the porch. Michael and Natasha exchanged worried looks as they stepped aside. Reaching out with one arm, Tatiana pushed open the door and swung herself over the threshold. For a moment everything seemed all right, then suddenly she fell with a crash. Michael and Natasha ran into the house to find her on the floor with the tip of one crutch tangled in the wheel of Alysa's tricycle.

"Are you okay."

"Oh, just great, Michael. Just great. The cripple comes home, you see, in a thud of glory." Tatiana tried to get up again, lost her grip, and fell, banging her arm on the coffee table. "Damn it. Damn everything." Picking up one of the metal crutches, she heaved it as hard as she could across the room. A goldfish bowl crashed to the floor, splattering pink rocks across the carpet. Tatiana surveyed the broken glass and her face suddenly turned pale. "I'm sorry," she said, looking at them, helplessly, "that was really out of line. I apologize to both of you. I just don't know what got into me."

"Tatiana." Natasha walked into the spare bedroom and shut the door behind her. "I need to talk to you."

"I'm too tired, Mama."

"I can appreciate that, but I'm leaving for Boston tomorrow, and before I go, I want to tell you something." Natasha lit a cigarette, inhaled deeply, and flicked the match into an ashtray. "To be honest, you're acting like a spoiled brat."

"Mama. . . ."

"Just be quiet and listen. God knows it's hard enough for me to say this to you after all you've been through, but you and I've always told each other the truth, and this is no time to stop. You're being unfair to Michael—not to mention me. Oh, I know, you've got plenty to feel sorry for yourself about. Life's given you a rotten deal, right? But life gives plenty of people rotten deals. The question is: Do you have the guts to get through this, or are you just going to sit around for the next forty years playing the helpless invalid."

"Mama, I don't have any choice *but* to sit around."

"Nonsense." Natasha stubbed out her cigarette with a firm, stabbing motion. "Every physical therapist we've talked to has told you there's a good chance you can do something to improve your condition. Furthermore, I haven't spent half my life teaching ballet without learning something about the human body. You and I both know that muscles waste away when they aren't used. Well, you aren't using your muscles, Tats. You're letting your legs atrophy, and once that happens you really will be an invalid."

"Just what do you propose I do, Mama?"

Natasha pointed her index finger at Tatiana's legs. "Get out of those braces to begin with."

"You can't be serious. What do you expect me to do? Crawl around the house?"

"Yes, if you have to. Crawl, and then walk, and then run, and then dance, damn it."

"Mama, how can you say that!"

"I can say it because I believe—no, make that *I know*—it's possible." She moved closer to Tatiana and put her arm around her shoulder. "Tats, I wish to God you could have been spared this, but I know you can beat it. I love you and Michael loves you. Don't turn your back on us and retreat into a shell. Fight this thing."

That night, in the privacy of the spare bedroom, Tatiana spent a long time looking into herself, not much liking what she found. Natasha was right: for the past few weeks she had been slowly sliding into a pit of self-pity and despair. She'd been impatient with Michael for no reason, neglected Alysa, been proud and remote when anyone tried to help her. The change in her personality alarmed and frightened her. What was she planning to become? An irritable invalid? The kind of person who made everyone else's life hell? She imagined herself at forty or fifty stomping around on her crutches, nagging, complaining, boring people to death with stories of how she'd once been a dancer.

It was an ugly image and it brought tears to her eyes, but Tatiana pushed on relentlessly. She began to see there was a perverse part of her that liked being ill, that fed on pity and attention; another part, terrified of independence, that welcomed the idea of being taken care of for the rest of her life.

An hour passed, then another. The room grew cool, filled with ocean sounds. Around midnight, Tatiana came to a decision: she had to start taking responsibility for her own life. She had to take whatever strengths she had and hope that maybe with the grace of God, or whatever ruled this crazy universe, somehow she'd be able to overcome her own weaknesses—not just the physical ones, but the inner ones only she could see.

The starting place was obvious.

Unbuckling her braces, she let them slide to the floor. Then swinging her legs over the edge of the bed, she tried to take a few steps unsupported. She fell forward almost at once, banging her chin on the dresser. It was a frightening experience. She'd known her legs were weak, but the braces had been giving her an illusion of support. Why was she doing this to herself? Wouldn't it be better to stop, get back in bed, go to sleep, and give it another try in the morning when she was rested?

No. That was out of the question. It wouldn't make any sense to stop now, not when she'd just started. Wiping the tears out of her eyes, Tatiana tried grimly to get up, but her legs were unresponsive, limp, and rubbery. She tried again with the same results. The upper part of her body worked perfectly but the lower part couldn't support her weight long enough for her to do more than a kind of push-up.

Tatiana rolled over on her back and rested for a minute, taking a few deep breaths. She felt like a turtle: helpless, ridiculous. The fear came again and a perverse voice inside her whispered: she would never walk . . . it was crazy to try . . . she should crawl back into bed and forget the whole thing.

Nonsense. She wasn't going to give up. Every situation had

some kind of solution if you could only see it. Pulling herself into a sitting position, she examined her legs. When she had been dancing every day they had been smooth and muscular, but now they were thin and brittle-looking, the calves partially shrunken, the skin around her ankles laced with veins and slightly bluish. There was no use trying to kid herself that with a few hours of practice she'd be able to walk on those toothpicks.

Tatiana sighed deeply and leaned back against the dresser. Much as she hated to admit it, she obviously wasn't going to be able to do this by herself. Okay, if that was the case, then it was time to face reality and get some *real* help. Only what kind of help? She thought of June Riley, the physical therapist at Cedars who had worked with her for the last few weeks: a nice girl, sweet, but too tolerant. Tatiana could see now that part of her problem was June hadn't pushed her hard enough. No one had for that matter—not even Dr. Kean. She'd been the hospital pet—the poor dancer stricken in her prime. She'd lapped up the pity, feeling sorry for herself, never realizing how insidious it was to be coddled. Thank God Mama had the guts to give it to her straight.

Dragging herself back over to her braces, Tatiana strapped them on and pulled herself to her feet, using the edge of the bed for leverage. Shoving her crutches under her arms, she hobbled to the window and looked out at the beach. The surf was a silver swirl crashing against the sand. Such power in nature, in every living thing for that matter. The trick was to harness that energy somehow—to grab it and make it your own.

Clutching at the windowsill, Tatiana stared for a moment at the full moon. A bat flew skittering across the silhouette of the house next door, quick and light like a scrap of black paper. She watched it for a moment, envying it its freedom of movement. Then carefully, as if she were laying blocks in a row, she began to make plans: she would spend as much time as possible out of her braces; she would drag herself out to the beach somehow and swim every day; she would read everything about polio ever written; she would hire the best physical therapist money could buy—even if she had to borrow from Mama; she would never sit when she could stand; never stand when she could walk. As for Michael, she would try her best to stop taking her frustrations out on him.

It was a long list of resolutions, and it took her quite a while to complete it. When she was done, Tatiana took one last look out the window, then turned and made her way back to the bed. She'd been lost in the dark for a long time— maybe even before she got sick—but she was going to get out even if she had to crawl on her hands and knees. Tatiana smiled to herself, feeling a little silly and melodramatic, but at the same time perfectly serious. In the morning she would tell Michael of her new plans, she would call Dr. Kean and set up an appointment; she would. . . . Her mind spiraled into a labyrinth of lists. The last thing she heard before she fell asleep was the steady crashing of the surf.

16

In Dr. Kean's office two antique wooden mallards floated serenely on the bookshelf next to a silver-framed photograph of Dr. Kean himself holding up a record-size large mouth bass. Tatiana settled down in a chair upholstered in shiny green leather and bright brass tacks, and entertained herself by reading his diplomas. An impressive lot: Harvard, Johns Hopkins.

"So you want me to recommend another physical therapist?" Dr. Kean pulled a small black notebook out of the pocket of a wrinkled linen suit that seemed to have seen better days. Remnants of lunch were on his tie as if advertising that he was too busy a man to be bothered with such conventional things as napkins. He began to fan through the pages of the notebook, paused and peered over his glasses. "I take it Nurse Riley hasn't been meeting your needs for some reason."

"June's good but she's too nice." Tatiana smoothed down her white slacks, slightly baggy over the braces but at least they made her look more or less normal. Too bad long skirts weren't in style. In the past week she had discovered that the less public attention she attracted the better off she was. Polio was the kind of disease that seemed to act like a magnet for pity. She understood now why Roosevelt had never allowed himself to be photographed in his brace: not just because he had a Presidential image to maintain but because no doubt *he* hadn't wanted to see himself as a cripple.

"June's too nice?"

"Frankly, Dr. Kean, Nurse Riley doesn't make me toe the line. When I complain that my joints ache, she lets me take the rest of the hour off. When I fall, she's there picking me up before I know it. I'm a dancer you know—or at least I was a dancer." Tatiana paused for a moment, feeling a stab of pain as she spoke of her career in the past tense. "My mother was

273

my principal teacher and she was absolutely ruthless when it came to physical discipline. When I was only five years old, I took a bad spill trying to show off—and my mother ordered me to get up and go on dancing. I cried . . . I screamed . . . I beat my fists on the floor and had a perfect tantrum, and all she did was stand there calmly telling me to go on. As a result of her absolute refusal to let me slack off, I got so I could dance through things that would stop other girls cold. I learned you have to push your body to the limit if you want to get anywhere with it; I learned the value of a teacher who won't give in to you, the satisfaction you get when someone forces you to do your best. Now, I'm not saying June Riley isn't a good physical therapist. I imagine for some people she's perfect. But she's all wrong for me." Tatiana grinned. "The problem is, Dr. Kean, I'm lazy. Give me an inch and I'll take a mile. I realized a few days ago that June just doesn't have the backbone to cope with me. What I need if I'm going to start walking again is someone who treats me more like a marine drill sergeant."

Dr. Kean surveyed his address book. "The best physical therapist I know is a woman named Kate Hanlon. She studied under Sister Kenny in Minneapolis and she has more experience with the rehabilitation of polio victims than anyone else on the West Coast. The problem is not many patients like her."

"I don't *want* to like her, Doctor."

Dr. Kean nodded. "In that case I'll give you her phone number." He cleared his throat. "I'd like to add that I think this is an excellent decision on your part." Tatiana opened her mouth to say something, but he interrupted. "Now don't worry. I'm not going to offer you any pity, or any compliments either. Frankly, Mrs. Macks, I originally thought you were a spoiled prima donna. I've seen grown men who can only move their thumbs and index fingers. I worked on six-year-olds who are going to be confined to respirators for the rest of their lives. The whole time you've been my patient, I've felt you had no idea how very damn lucky you were to escape with so little damage. My God, Mrs. Macks, you can sit up, you can swallow; put a few simple attachments on your car and you can drive to the store and buy a loaf of bread You have a husband who loves you, a healthy daughter—in heaven's name, what more could you want?"

"I want to *dance* again."

"You're tough," Dr. Kean nodded appreciatively, "very

tough. Odd that I never suspected it. Well, good. Here's Kate Hanlon's phone number." He passed Tatiana a small scrap of paper. As she pulled herself to her feet, he rose with her and shook her hand. "I'm glad I proved to be such a poor diagnostician of character. Kate Hanlon is a real battle-ax. I wish you the very best of luck with her."

"Are you Mrs. Macks?"

"Yes," Tatiana looked at the pixielike woman standing on the porch and wondered what she was selling. Magazine subscriptions probably—or maybe she was collecting for some charity. The woman was dressed in a crisp yellow cotton shirtwaist that clashed outrageously with the brightest mop of carrot red hair Tatiana had ever seen in her life. A new neighbor, probably. That was one of the problems with Malibu: people moved in and out so often you really never got to know them. "Can I help you?"

"The question is, can I help you?"

"I beg your pardon?"

"I'm Kate Hanlon."

"But that's impossible. I mean. . . ." Tatiana blushed to the roots of her hair, realizing she had very nearly said that she was expecting someone larger.

"I suppose," Kate Hanlon said briskly, "you were expecting me to resemble one of those dedicated spinsters who seem to haunt the upper echelons of physical therapy—you know the type: brawny, plain, dedicated but a bit dowdy, with large biceps and a faint brown mustache over the upper lip. Never mind. Let's have a look at those legs." She reached for Tatiana bathrobe and pulled it back with a proprietary air, exposing a double set of bright stainless steel braces. "Hmm," she muttered disapprovingly.

Surely this woman wasn't planning to give her a medical examination on the front steps. Tatiana looked at Kate Hanlon with a mixture of confusion and amusement. How very different this woman was from what Dr. Kean had led her to expect. Battle-ax? Hardly. If you took Audrey Hepburn and dunked her head in henna, you'd have Kate Hanlon. She looked as if a strong breeze would blow her flat on her face.

"How old are you?" Kate said, dropping the edge of Tatiana's robe.

"Twenty-one."

"Young, healthy as a cow I'd wager. No other complications."

"Complications?"

"Allergies, diabetes, anything like that?"

"No."

"Happily married?"

Tatiana thought guiltily of Michael who was still sleeping alone. "More or less."

"Good. Then I'll have you walking in three months."

"What did you say?"

"I said I'd have you walking in three months. Why? Don't you believe me?"

"But Dr. Kean said—"

"Pay no attention to what doctors say. That, Mrs. Macks, is rule number one. And try not to look so shocked. Sister Kenny used to do that—shock people I mean. I remember once when they brought her a little girl on a stretcher who couldn't move anything but her left toe and Sister said "I'll have her sewing in six months" and by golly she did. Positive attitude, that's the key."

"Positive attitude?"

"You aren't sick; remember that. Your muscles are just lazy."

"Lazy, Nurse Hanlon?" Tatiana knew she sounded like a parrot, but all this was happening so fast it was making her head swim.

"Yes, lazy, and don't call me 'nurse.' It only emphasizes the idea of sickness. We'll have no nurses here...no uniforms...no sickroom . . . no doctors if we can help it."

"What shall I call you then?"

"Call me Kate and I'll call you—let me see your first name is Russian isn't it—something odd."

"Tatiana."

"Too much of a mouthful. Imagine me yelling: 'Tatiana straighten that leg!' By the time I get it out you'll have fallen on your face."

"My friends call me Tats."

"Good, I'll call you Tats then. Only remember, please, I'm *not* your friend. I'm your goad, your conscience, your trainer and before this is over you're going to hate my guts. Got that?"

"I think so."

"Good. Then how about inviting me in."

"Oh, yes, of course. Please." Tatiana stepped aside and Kate Hanlon plunged into the house with so much energy the carpet seemed to crackle.

"Where's the room?" she demanded tossing her purse on

the couch. Spotting Alysa in the playpen, she went over and chucked her under the chin. "Cute child."

"Thank you."

Alysa beamed up at the strange lady and stretched out her hand to offer her a rubber duck. Kate took the duck, held it for a moment, then returned it to Alysa. "Pray she never gets polio; and pray they discover a vaccine soon. Have you ever seen a child her age in a respirator? No, I don't imagine you have. Well, pray you don't. Are you religious, by the way?"

"Not really."

"Pity, it helps sometimes, but to tell the truth neither am I." Kate planted her hands on her hips and shook her head. "If there really were a God, I imagine he'd organize the universe a good deal better. I know I would. Now where's the room?"

"What room?"

"The room we're going to work in."

"I thought, that is. . . ." Tatiana stumbled awkwardly. There was something about this little woman that was completely overpowering. Not that she spoke loudly, but there was such authority in her voice you felt as if you should salute her each time she asked a question. Well, Tatiana had wanted a drill sergeant hadn't she? And from the evidence of the last five minutes it looked as if she had gotten precisely that. "Can't we work here in the living room?"

"Impossible. This is going to be between you and me, Tats. Not between you and me and your husband, or your friends, or your mother, or brother, or anyone else."

"Well, I suppose we could work in the spare bedroom."

"Does it have a bathroom attached? With a tub?"

"Yes."

"Good, take me to it."

Tatiana was beginning to feel mildly annoyed. Didn't this woman ever say please? And what in the world did she need with a tub? She clumped down the hall on her crutches with Kate following, glad the spare bedroom had just been cleaned.

"Hurry up a bit."

This was too much. Really. Tatiana stopped and pivoted around to face her. "I'm walking as fast as I can under the circumstances."

"Nonsense. Swing those things in rhythm. You're going to be off them soon, but as long as you're dependent on them you might as well do a good job of it. Come on now: one two,

277

one two." Snarling inwardly, Tatiana did as she was told and to her chagrin found she did indeed move along much faster.

The room, when they entered it, was close and cool, light filtering through bamboo blinds, the carpet dark green and soft under her feet. Tatiana sat down on the edge of the bed as Kate strode back and forth like an auctioneer appraising the furniture for an estate sale.

"Paint it blue," she said at last.

"Paint what blue?"

"The room."

Tatiana looked at her, not comprehending. "Why?"

Kate unbuttoned the top button of her shirtwaist and rolled up her sleeves. "Frankly, Tats, we'd get along much better in the next few weeks if you just did what I told you, but since this is our first day together I'll explain. Blue is a positive color. It's soothing. Your muscles are in spasm at present and our first job is going to be to relax them. You can't get blood to tissues that are wound up like corkscrews."

"Are you telling me the color of the room is going to help bring blood to my muscles?"

"Precisely."

"That's the weirdest thing I've ever heard."

"Sister Kenny put her therapy trainees in blue uniforms, she painted every room in her treatment center in Minneapolis blue. Now, are you going to paint this room or aren't you?"

"I'll paint it," Tatiana said meekly.

"Good, and while you're at it throw away this mattress. I want you sleeping on a board with no more than two to three inches of padding. You might try buying a gym mat of the sort used for tumbling."

"Anything else?"

"Remove all furniture but the bed, take down those blinds so you can get some sunshine in this cave, and oh, yes, have your husband rip up this wall-to-wall carpet." Kate stabbed at the nap with the toe of her shoes. "It's too soft; it'll throw you off stride every time you try to walk on it."

Tatiana fought to keep her composure. "Is there anything more you'd like me to do?" She wondered how Michael was going to react when she told him she was going to start sleeping on a gym mat.

"Yes, you can go into the bathroom and start filling the tub with the hottest water you have while I go out to my car and bring in the salt. And while you're at it, put on your bathing suit."

*   *   *

Fifteen minutes later Tatiana was lying in a tub of nearly scalding saltwater while Kate gently moved her legs back and forth. Although the water had seemed so hot at first that she'd barely been able to get in, she had to admit it was relaxing simply to float in the buoyant solution. Kate worked silently doing various things that seemed to make no sense but which didn't hurt either. Tatiana wondered fleetingly if this red-headed dynamo knew what she was doing, but that, she recognized instantly, was a doubt, and doubt had been absolutely forbidden. Positive attitude. Tatiana inspected her legs, white and thin—two albino eels under the oily surface. Was it her imagination, or was the bluish, pallid skin turning a healthy pink?

"Time to get out," Kate announced suddenly. She bundled Tatiana in a towel and handed her the crutches. In the bedroom a narrow folding table had been set up between the bed and the dresser. Lightly padded and upholstered with brown leather, it looked like the kind of thing Tatiana had gotten massages on during her stint with the New York City Ballet. Kate, who proved to be amazingly strong, helped Tatiana slide backward onto the table so that her legs dangled over the edge.

Kate brushed the damp hair out of her eyes, and grabbed the upper part of Tatiana's right leg. Her hands were firm and warm as if they radiated an energy all their own. Tatiana had a momentary sense of electricity flowing from Kate's fingers to her wasted muscles. Probably her imagination, of course, but still the laying on of hands was something recorded in all religious traditions. Maybe there really *were* some people whose touch could heal.

"This is your quadriceps," Kate said in a no-nonsense voice. "It's the muscle that straightens your knee. Now I want you to imagine yourself straightening your leg."

"I'd like to oblige you," Tatiana said, "but as you can see my legs are as limp as noodles." She tried to make a joke of it, but there was a catch in her voice. What wouldn't she give to be able to straighten her leg.

"I didn't say *do* it. I said *imagine* doing it. Concentrate on the muscle." Kate began to massage her leg. "Think *my leg is going to straighten.*"

"My leg is going to straighten," Tatiana said obediently. Kate put her hand under Tatiana's heel and lifted her foot, straightening the unresponsive leg.

279

"Good, now do it again."

Tatiana obliged.

"And again."

For over an hour they repeated this exercise, first with one leg, then the other. By three o'clock Tatiana was exhausted and discouraged. What use was it to go on bending and unbending? Her legs were dead. She might as well face the fact that she was wasting Kate's time. Swallowing a lump in her throat, she tried to push away the disappointment. She'd imagined somehow that the therapy would be magic. She'd dreamed of herself walking and dancing, of running down the steps to meet Michael instead of clumping along on her crutches. She saw now she'd been a fool to hope.

"Well," Tatiana said as bravely as possible as Kate rolled down her sleeves and retrieved her sweater from the back of a chair, "I guess that's that."

Kate put her hands on her hips. "What are you talking about," she said sharply.

"Nothing's happening."

"You mean to sit there and tell me you expected something to happen right away?"

"Well, uh, yes, that is. . . ."

"Get this straight: physical therapy takes time, guts, dedication. Do you have it or don't you?"

"Well. . . ."

"If you can't stand the heat get out of the kitchen."

"Wait a minute." Tatiana was angry. What right did this woman have to talk to her like this? She was paying Kate Hanlon to be a physical therapist, not a miniature Hitler.

"Besides you're dead wrong. Something did happen."

"What?" Tatiana was so suprised her anger disappeared. "What are you talking about?"

"Your leg, didn't you feel it?"

"Feel what?"

"The impulse in your right quadriceps, the kind of flicker a horse would make getting a fly off its back. It means the nerve cells aren't dead."

"Oh, my God." Tatiana didn't know whether to laugh with joy or cry with relief. "That means I might be able to walk again."

"Of course. I told you so an hour and a half ago. Now when your husband comes home I want him to start repeating these exercises with you. A thousand repetitions minimum, each leg; at least two hours of rest, then another thousand."

"Two thousand repetitions?" Michael had been thinking about going back to the studio to finish up *Rebel Yell*.

"Four thousand, actually. Two thousand each leg—and remember that's the absolute *minimum*. Do you understand?"

Tatiana nodded. "It's like ballet."

"Like what?"

"Like ballet. You do the same thing over and over again—maybe a million *pliés*, two million. No one keeps count. You train your muscles, repeating and repeating the same exercises until it would drive any normal person crazy, and then one day, all at once, the muscles get the message and you're no longer practicing, you're dancing."

"Well," Kate shoved her arms into her sweater and began to button it with alarming efficiency, "I never heard it put that way before, but it sounds like you get the picture. I'll be back tomorrow morning at nine. Have the room painted by then."

Tatiana grinned and gave a mock salute. "Aye, aye, sir."

Kate allowed a small ghost of a smile to play over her face, the first Tatiana had seen. "That's the attitude," she said. "That's the reaction I like to see."

"One question," Tatiana got up, reached for her crutches, and accompanied Kate to the door. "Did you learn all of this from Sister Kenny or are you just improvising as you go along?"

"I do what works," Kate observed briskly. "Sister always said the most important thing was to keep your eyes open and use the brain God gave you. Leaving God out of it, I think she had a point."

That evening, after the first thousand repetitions, Michael drove to a hardware store, and bought two gallons of baby blue paint and a hammer for taking up carpet tacks. Until four in the morning Tatiana sat in the spare bedroom drinking beer, keeping him company as he painted the walls and most of himself in the process. As he worked they laughed, talked, and made jokes about Kate.

"I think we should give her a nickname," Michael suggested. His eyes were bleary from fatigue and the blue paint on the end of his nose gave him a clownish air.

Tatiana grinned. "What sort of nickname?"

Michael paused, brush in the air, blue paint dripping down

his arm. "How about the 'Blue Shrew'—you know, like Kate in *The Taming of the Shrew*."

"The Blue Shrew?" Tatiana giggled. "Great, only she better never hear of it or we'll both be in trouble."

"She'd assign us eight thousand repetitions."

"Or half a million." Tatiana laughed and took another sip of her beer, thinking this was like old times. They'd joked together so little in the past few years. Michael climbed down from the ladder, moved it across the room, and began to slap his brush against the last wall with good-natured weariness. This paint job wasn't going to win any prizes, but at least it was getting done.

Tatiana drank her beer thoughtfully, watching Michael as he leaned forward precariously to get his brush behind the woodwork that ran just below the ceiling. She was touched by his willingness to help her. Such a good-looking man this husband of hers: broad-shouldered, handsome even in a pair of torn blue jeans and a paint-splattered sweatshirt. For the first time in months she felt a faint impulse of physical attraction toward him—what Kate would have no doubt called a flicker.

The room was like a rectangle made out of the Pacific: blue walls, blue woodwork, a blue spread covering the bed. Outside, beyond the window, more blue: a cobalt sky streaked with glaucous clouds, the ocean a vast expanse of cerulean, aquamarine, and turquoise. As Kate unwrapped the hot packs from her left leg, Tatiana settled down to enjoy the view. Everything was soothing, almost ethereal: the heat from the woolen packs, the classical music streaming from the record player. Kate's touch was light and gentle, almost caressing. Amazing when you considered that *gentle* was the last adjective in the world anyone would ascribe to Kate herself.

"Straighten your leg," Kate traced the muscle path with one finger, drawing an invisible map on Tatiana's skin. Tatiana obediently shut her eyes and concentrated on her knees. A flood of memories blossomed in her mind: kneeling to play jacks when she was a little girl, kicking a ball, bending in a long slow *plié* in her mother's studio in Cambridge. Her leg seemed to quiver and all sorts of impulses and flickers coursed through it, but there was no obvious movement. Still, just the sense of being alive below the waist was a major improvement. In the last six weeks Kate might not have worked miracles, but at least Tatiana was allowing herself to hope.

"You're not trying hard enough," Kate said suddenly.

"Sorry," Tatiana murmured, not feeling sorry at all. Kate wasn't being fair. Tatiana *was* trying, but how could anyone give their full attention to this, hour after hour, day after day?

"Listen," Kate dropped Tatiana's leg abruptly, "either you put some guts into this or you can get yourself another physical therapist."

"What?" Tatiana was dumbfounded.

"You heard me." Kate grabbed her sweater, always a sign she was preparing to leave, but that was impossible: the session was supposed to go on another forty-five minutes. Tatiana was angry, then frightened. Kate couldn't mean it; she couldn't really be planning to desert her, not at this stage.

"Kate, please, I'll try harder."

"I don't want promises—I want action." Kate paced across the room, looked out at the ocean without appearing to see it, and paced back. Her face was only a shade lighter than her hair, and her eyes flashed with anger. "You think your legs are the problem, don't you?"

"Why, uh, yes." Of course the problem was her legs; what else could it be?"

"Well, you're dead wrong. The problem's not your legs, or your nerves, or your muscles, or anything else to do with your body; the problem's willpower."

"Willpower?" Tatiana felt hurt, accused, underestimated. She's been doing thousands of repetitions a day, trying with all her might to do the impossible, and now Kate was throwing it all up in her face, telling her it wasn't enough.

"You don't have enough willpower to stuff a gnat's nose." Kate unfolded her arms across her chest. "I know what I'm talking about. I was an army nurse during the war. Normandy mainly. I saw young healthy men with minor injuries turn up their toes and die; I saw others who were so cut up it made you sick to look at them, bounce back. As far as I could see the only real difference was that some of those soldiers had the will to live and some didn't. The problem with you is that you don't have the *will* to walk."

"I do."

"No, you don't."

"How do you know?" Tatiana was livid with outrage. "How can you imagine what it's like to be in my position? I was a dancer, can you understand that? Dancing was my life. And now, because of a piece of random bad luck, because of a stupid damnable virus that no one has ever seen, I'm trapped in my body." She knew she was losing control, but she couldn't help it. All the pain and frustration of the past few months was boiling over. "You've got a lot of nerve, Kate, to stand there on two good legs and tell me I'm not trying. What do you know about willpower? What do you know about being crippled?"

"Straighten your left leg."

"You go straight to hell."

"I said straighten your left leg."

Angrily Tatiana gave the command to her muscle and her left leg suddenly jerked forward "It moved," she said in a small awed voice.

"Do it again." Kate pulled off her sweater and threw it on the bed. "Do it now while you still remember how."

Tatiana, to her own amazement, was able to oblige. Her left leg moved again, not to a fully straight position, but a good two or three inches. "I can do it!" She was crying now with joy and triumph; it was like an opening night, like dancing the most complicated ballet of her life.

Kate embraced her triumphantly. "You've been on the edge of this for days, Tats."

Tatiana looked up feeling foolish because she was crying, wonderful because she had moved her leg, and amazed that Kate was actually hugging her. "You were trying to make me mad, weren't you?"

"Of course. I knew that getting you really angry was the only way I could force you to move that leg.

"Thanks."

"Don't thank me." Kate pointed briskly at Tatiana's right leg. "Now straighten that one." Tatiana tried but nothing happened. "I suggest," Kate said, "that we quit while we're ahead. Up your repetitions to three thousand each leg."

For the next month Tatiana watched with amazement and growing hope as slowly movement returned to her lower limbs. At first she was only able to make the most feeble motions, but Kate was relentlessly positive: pulling out a tape measure each day to record muscle growth; giving her extra cold and hot packs to improve circulation and tone; cajoling, commanding, and pushing until Tatiana didn't know whether to love her for her dedication or hate her for being a monomaniac.

One morning, for example, shortly after Tatiana had actually been able to straighten both legs for the first time, Kate arrived at the session carrying two small discs of iron attached to black leather straps.

"What are those?" Tatiana leaned forward curiously.

"Weights."

"What are you going to do with them?"

"Tie them to your ankles." Kate knelt down and began to do just that.

"You're kidding. One day I manage to straighten my legs and the next you want to put *weights* on them."

"Resistance builds muscles the way adversity builds character."

"Is that your philosophy of life?"

"You bet. Now straighten those legs."

Tatiana tried, but with the addition of the weights it was a lot harder. Cursing silently, Tatiana pushed against the iron. But Kate, as usual, knew exactly what she was doing. After a few weeks of working with the weights, Tatiana's legs were strong enough for her to stand unsupported for several seconds at a time, and by the end of the three months, with Michael on one side and Kate on the other, she was taking her first awkward, shuffling steps.

A few days later, Michael left one morning for the Galaxy lot to resume work on *Rebel Yell*. He'd been back to the studio several times since Tatiana had fallen ill, but only briefly, to take care of minor details. Glass had generously given him a six-month vacation, and since the actual filming was finished and only the editing remained, there seemed no real hurry, especially since Glass hadn't put any pressure on him to complete the project.

Two hours later, Tatiana was startled by the sound of a car door slamming. Looking out the window, she saw Michael's red Thunderbird in the driveway. Why was he home so early? One look at his face as he entered the front door told her that whatever the reason, it wasn't good.

"Damn Glass!" Michael threw his coat on the kitchen table, jerked open the refrigerator, and pulled out a beer.

"What's wrong?"

"What's wrong is that Glass is releasing *Rebel Yell* in rough cut."

"You've got to be kidding."

"I wish I were." Michael opened the beer and chugged down about half of it. Tatiana couldn't remember ever having seen him so angry before. "It's sabotage that's what it is, deliberate sabotage. You should have seen the smile on Glass's face when he told me he'd already started setting up the distribution."

Tatiana still couldn't believe it. "But you haven't even finished post-dubbing all the sound yet."

"Right. And I haven't finished the final edit. I explained to Glass that the thing was only about eighty percent done, but what he said in essence was 'too bad, I'm releasing it anyway.'"

"Michael he can't do this to you."

"Oh, yes, he can. I've called three entertainment lawyers in the last hour and they all give me the same story: Glass is perfectly within his legal rights." Michael drank the rest of the beer, threw the bottle in the wastebasket, and sat down at the kitchen table across from Tatiana. "What I just don't understand is *why* he would want to wreck one of his own films."

"Maybe because you didn't use his script."

"His script stank, Tats."

"I know that. You know that. But does Glass know that?"

"You're probably right; he's probably under the illusion that that piece of trash he approved was the greatest thing since *Gone with the Wind*." Michael got up, went over to the refrigerator and pulled out another beer. "You realize what this means, don't you? I'm going to be box office poison. No other producer will be willing to touch me with a ten-foot pole. If this had been my tenth movie or even my second, maybe they'd give me another chance. But mess up your first job and it's good-bye Hollywood."

"You can still act, can't you."

Michael shook his head. "You don't get it, Tats. Once *Rebel Yell* comes out I'll be lucky to get an offer to co-star with Lassie."

"So you're moving back east," Kate was on her hands and knees, chalking a set of footsteps on the floor.

"My husband's been offered a part in a new musical." Tatiana stood by the window, thinking that soon she would be able to walk through the sand. If anyone had told her a year ago that a ten-minute stroll along the edge of the water would someday seem like paradise, she never would have believed them. One of the good things she'd gotten out of all this was an appreciation for the little things in life.

"I never go to musicals myself," Kate observed, rising from

the floor and brushing the chalk dust off her hands, "a waste of time if you ask me. Of course, your husband gets paid for it, which is a different matter."

"You know, Kate, I have no idea what you do for fun."

"This is my fun," Kate said. "Now try to put your feet in these chalk marks." Tatiana made a tottering attempt, plunked her foot into the first step and missed the second altogether. "No, not like that. If you put your foot outside the lines, you'll be working the wrong muscles."

"You know, Kate," Tatiana said as she made a second, more successful attempt, "I've always been curious about something."

"Curiosity killed the cat. Now walk and try to keep an even gait."

"Actually, I've been wondering if you're married."

"My, we're getting personal today, aren't we. What's it to you whether I'm married or not?"

Tatiana carefully lifted one leg and looked down at the chalk marks, her brow furrowed in concentration. "It's just that I always found it really hard to have a career and keep my marriage in good shape at the same time. I always seemed to be juggling the two, taking away from one to give to the other, and you work so hard. I was wondering how you did it—that is, if you had a husband."

"Well, if it will satisfy your curiosity I'm not married, never have been, and never care to be. For the record I live with my widowed sister and her daughter. Like Katharine Hepburn said, you have to make some choices in life."

"Katharine Hepburn?"

"The only actress in this town who ever says anything sensible. Now quit smearing those footsteps or I'm going to have to get down and draw them all over again. By the way, it's time you bought a bicycle."

"A bicycle! I can hardly walk yet."

Kate snorted audibly. "That's the trouble with you; you never think ahead. It's time you got some rhythm back in your body—unless of course, you want to spend the rest of your life lumbering around like Quasimodo."

"You know," Tatiana said with sudden nostalgia, "I'm going to miss you when we leave California." Looking at Kate in her starched pink skirt and blouse, standing ramrod straight by the exercise table, Tatiana suddenly realized that in many ways she had come to admire this cantankerous, demanding woman: not love her—it would be hard for a saint to love

Kate—but she had come to admire Kate's dedication, her bulldoglike determination.

"Stuff and nonsense," Kate said sharply. "You don't need me anymore. You just need to get some strength in your legs."

"I want to thank you."

"For what?"

Tatiana looked at her in amazement. "Why for helping me walk again, of course."

"It's my job," Kate turned away abruptly, knelt and began to renew the chalk lines. Did her mouth quiver a little just before she ducked her head; was she touched, or did Tatiana only imagine she was?

A week later the enigmatic little woman with the bright red hair put on her sweater, picked up her purse for the last time, and walked out of Tatiana's life as briskly as she had walked in, leaving behind a series of neatly printed orders that included swimming, running every day *no matter what the weather* (underlined twice in red ink), and a program of knee bends and leg lifts that would have tried the stamina of an Olympic athlete.

Alysa dozed in her crib sucking her thumb as Michael and Tatiana packed up the last of the books. It was a clear, warm December day in Malibu, the kind that almost made Tatiana regret leaving California. It was going to be strange to trade in the sand and poppies for sleet and snowplows.

Tatiana straightened up, wiped the sweat off her forehead, and attacked a pile of encyclopedias. She could stand unsupported now for as long as twenty minutes at a time, walk out to get the mail, even push Alysa's baby carriage a hundred yards or so before she had to sit down. She and Michael were getting along better—although making love was something she still couldn't face—and life, although it could hardly be called great, had returned to some semblance of normalcy. Still, although she hated to entertain the thought, there was no doubt that since Kate left, her recovery had been slowing down. Tatiana stood for a moment looking down at the empty box, lost in a new chain of not particularly optimistic thoughts, the kind that would have sent Kate into a ten-minute lecture on positive attitudes.

Out on the beach half a dozen surfers in baggy trunks plunged into the waves, yelling happily at each other as the surf caught them and rolled them head over heels. How pleasant to live the way they did, without ambition, probably without even a thought in your head. Or maybe that was just a romantic illusion. No doubt everyone had problems—even surfers.

Tatiana took a deep breath and went back to her packing. Thinking about what was going to happen if her legs didn't show any more improvement was definitely a mistake. It would be months before she knew for sure and meanwhile, well, meanwhile she might just as well get on with her life. Actually, as far as moving back east went, there wasn't really any choice to be made, not now, not since Michael had had that blow-up with Glass over *Rebel Yell*.

So they were moving—an act that gave you a new perspective on your life. Things you hadn't seen in years suddenly reappeared, making you wonder why you'd ever bought them in the first place. Tying up the box of encyclopedias, Tatiana labeled it and started in on another. Where in the world had they managed to get so many books? Maybe the little monsters reproduced in the dark of night like mice. How in heaven's name were they going to get all these boxes into the new apartment on Ninety-third and Central Park West? It was a good thing Charlie Harris, Michael's agent, had gotten him a fat part in the new Fred Lewis musical, or Michael would have had to lug everything into the elevator himself with her and Alysa standing by cheering him on. Tatiana took a sip of cold coffee and looked wearily at what remained to be packed. At this rate they'd probably make it to New York some time late in 1963.

"Tats, Michael, anyone home?" Ruth was standing on the deck, tapping on the glass excitedly. Michael pushed aside the sliding doors and let her in. "My God," Ruth said breathlessly, and she bounded into the room, "I've been trying to call you for hours. Have you heard the news?"

Michael looked at Tatiana. Their television was crated up, the radios packed away, the phone disconnected, and the newspaper had been cancelled days ago. "What news?" Tatiana put down her coffee cup not knowing whether to expect something good or some complete disaster like a Russian sneak attack. Disasters seemed to have been a mainstay this season.

"Galaxy's released *Rebel Yell*."

"We know," Michael said. "It's no news to us, and frankly Ruth we'd rather not hear about it." He grinned wanly. "As a matter of fact, that's why we're leaving town."

"Don't want to hear about it, huh?" Ruth looked around the room. "Where's your TV?"

"In that big cardboard box. Why?"

"Get it out and turn it on.

"Why."

"Because Michael, my dear, there's a riot going on in downtown Los Angeles this very minute."

"A riot?"

Ruth went for the box and began to pull it apart. "Thousands—and I mean *thousands*—of rabid teenagers are fighting to get tickets to see Bobby Fender." Ruth ripped the last of the excelsior off the television set and dragged it into the center of the room. "Where's an electrical outlet? Come on Michael—don't just stand there. You've just directed the smash hit of 1954. Help me get this thing working. You won't *believe* the film clips of Hollywood and Vine they're showing on the news. It looks like the French Revolution."

17

The mirrors behind the barre reflected the lemon yellow walls of Studio B, transforming them into a line of brilliantly sunlit rectangles striding off toward a glossy infinity. Despite the whir of the huge central ventilators, the air at the Palms had a taste of spring to it this morning: slightly moist and warm with a hint of the first summer smog lingering just under the surface.

Tatiana took a deep breath and sank slowly into a *grand plié* along with some twenty other students. Around her she could hear sighs and grunts as her classmates attempted to rise back with some semblance of grace. The girl in front of her—a blonde in a sea green leotard—had invented a new position for her feet, and was bobbing up, blissfully unaware of the fact that her performance left anything to be desired. Tatiana brushed the sweat off her forehead, thinking that one of the advantages of being in a beginner's class was the unbelievable innocence of the other students. It had taken her a few days to get used to the casual, pleasant way most of them mutilated the traditional postures of ballet, but after that she had found their lack of precision relaxing. After all, if you were trying to stumble your way back to competence on a pair of unpredictable legs, the best way to do it was in front of an audience who didn't know fifth position from third.

For the next five minutes Tatiana did one slow *plié* after another and then joined the rest of the class in a series of elementary *battements*. It might not have looked like much to anyone who knew the slightest thing about professional dancing, but to Tatiana every bend of her knees, every solid sweep away from the ground was a major triumph. Only a month ago her legs had still been trembling like Jell-O every time she tried to do anything more complicated than a box waltz. It was only in the past few weeks, really, that she had become, once again, in a very small way, a dancer.

Unfortunately her endurance still left a lot to be desired. The class only lasted thirty minutes, but after twenty minutes Tatiana, as usual, was forced to sit down on the floor. The teacher and the other students—all of whom were aware of her problem—looked at her sympathetically, but she tried not to absorb any more of their pity than she could help. Too bad Kate wasn't here to bark at her. Tatiana put her head on her elbows and stared at the rosin-coated floor feeling almost faint with exhaustion. Her whole body ached and she was sweating so that her leotard clung unpleasantly.

The music soon came to an end, replaced by a wave of chatter as the students gathered up their possessions and drifted out the door. Only Tatiana stayed behind. For another ten minutes or so she sat, gathering her strength. Then, pulling herself to her feet, she spent another quarter of an hour at the barre stretching: grabbing her left foot with her left hand and trying to lift it above her head in a graceful arc; propping one ankle on the top bar and leaning over her leg, pulling the tendons until they throbbed. Tatiana closed her eyes for a moment and imagined her muscles, still tied in knots like tangled ribbons, and then, as Kate had taught her to do, she imagined herself untangling those ribbons one by one.

Dan's apartment was located on the ground floor of a white, pseudo-Spanish building that came complete with a tiled fountain, three scrawny palm trees, an enclosed court-yard, and a swimming pool. It was around this pool two weeks later, on a particularly warm afternoon in late May, that the three of them—Dan, Michael, and Tatiana—sat drinking cold beers, eating potato chips, and reading film scripts. The scripts, in black-and-brown paper binders, lay everywhere: piled up beside the canvas deck chairs, scattered on the ground, balanced precariously on the card table Dan had dragged out of his apartment for the occasion. Only four months ago, a few days after *Rebel Yell* was released, Dan and Michael had formed D&M, Inc., an independent production company that at present consisted of a small office on Sunset Boulevard, two telephones, and a part-time secretary. But the way scripts had come pouring in you would have thought they were MGM.

Well, that wasn't surprising really. Tatiana tossed the script she was reading aside and picked up another, thinking how desperate everyone sounded these days. All the big studios were hedging their bets by doing adaptations of successful novels and plays instead of looking for original material, taking such best-sellers as *The Caine Mutiny* or *From Here to Eternity* and simply translating them into film form, or picking up such frothy Broadway hits as *The Moon Is Blue*, stories that had a guaranteed audience and more sex in them than television could touch. And when you came down to musicals, the outlook for original material was even worse. Except for a handful of directors, no one was even willing to *look* at a musical that hadn't already made a name for itself in New York. All of which meant that the moment Dan and Michael had put out the word they were looking for original musicals, they had been hit by an avalanche of projects, and so many phone calls from agents and writers they had had to temporarily flee the office on Sunset Boulevard just to get time to read the scripts that had already come in.

Tatiana took another handful of potato chips and ate them slowly. Over the past few months she had read scripts set everywhere, in every conceivable time period: from expensive costume dramas that took place in the court of Marie Antoinette to gritty bits of social realism that involved striking mill workers—wonderful, witty, intelligent pieces that made her feel as if half the talent in America must be going to waste—but the problem was that none of them were quite right for D&M's first film. Dropping the script on the ground, Tatiana picked up another folder with the unpromising title *Song of Love*.

"I can't believe it." Dan located the metal bottle opener, uncapped another beer, and sat back in his deck chair disconsolately. "Here we are, with enough scripts to sink the *Queen Mary*, and we still can't find a story."

"Don't worry," Michael mumbled, engrossed in what he was reading.

"The man says don't worry. Great. Why didn't I think of that." Dan took a swig of beer and grinned. "After all, the only thing at stake here is everything we own in the world, both our professional reputations, and a bank loan approximately half the size of the national debt. Not to mention our investors, who, should they become dissatisfied, will probably make the little homosexual cannibals in *Suddenly Last Summer* look like a pack of boy scouts."

"You're exaggerating." Tatiana smiled at Dan. He was at his most endearing this afternoon, packed into a pair of plaid swimming trunks, his sunglasses sliding down his nose, a pair of rubber sandals on his feet. Somehow it was hard to take Dan's worry seriously when he looked like an overstuffed teddy bear on vacation.

"Of course I'm exaggerating," Dan continued, helping himself to the chips. "That's my great charm. What use is a producer who doesn't exaggerate? The truth, as Oscar Wilde once observed, is for people who have no imaginations." Dan sighed melodramatically. "You know what I dream about nights? I dream that we managed to break Bobby Fender away from Galaxy. I dream of a simple film—called *Sock Hop* or something equally neanderthal—Fender surrounded by rosy-cheeked little nymphomaniacs dancing their charming behinds off, a nice cheap hunk of Americana with no story worth mentioning that would make us millions."

"Fender had a two picture contract with Glass," Michael observed. "Besides, Bobby's promised that if D&M gets off the ground he'll do his next film with us."

"In my dark moods," Dan said, then stopped to take a long chug of beer, "I imagine us a year from now: you crawling on your belly to Fred Lewis begging him to forgive you for backing out of that part he gave you in his new musical; Tats and Alysa reduced to selling pencils on the street, and me in debtors' prison."

"There isn't any debtors' prison, Dan."

"Don't blind me with facts."

"Say," Tatiana interrupted, "if you two are through with the doom and gloom, I think I'm on to something here." She held up the script she'd been reading. "We want something low budget right? Something with a fat part for Michael that's got a lot of dance numbers, some good original songs, and a plot that won't fall apart like wet Kleenex. Well, this may be it. It's called *Song of Love*." Michael and Dan both groaned. "Wait a minute, the title can always be changed. The point is that it's got this great romance between a vaudeville dancer and an opera singer."

"Opera." Michael said it with a moan. "You have to be kidding. Do you know what most people in America do when they hear opera, Tats? They put their hands over their ears or else call the cops and report that a murder is going on. Now if the heroine was a jazz singer along the lines of Billie Holiday maybe you'd have something."

"But this is a movie about class differences; make her a jazz singer and you wreck the whole thing."

294

"How about a ballet dancer?" Dan got up so fast he nearly knocked over his chair.

"What did you say?" Michael stared at him blankly.

"I said how about the heroine being a ballet dancer."

"He's making another joke," Tatiana said, "he's talking about us Michael. The tap dancer and the ballerina, get it? Not in very good taste if you ask me—especially under the circumstances."

"Right," Dan paced over to the edge of the pool and paced back again. "Exactly. You hit it on the head. I *am* talking about you and Michael, but I'm not making a joke. Good grief, I can't believe we haven't seen this before. It's the perfect story: two dancers from different worlds."

"You're serious?"

"You *bet* I'm serious."

"Hmm," Michael took the script from Tatiana and flipped through it quickly, getting more and more excited. "I see what you mean. Plenty of chance for dance numbers, and lots of comic potential if he tries to teach her some tap—not to mention if she tries to entice him into a few *pliés*. Of course we'd have to get this fellow... what's his name?"

"It's a woman and her name is Karlyle, Agnes Karlyle," Tatiana supplied.

"We'd have to get this Agnes Karlyle to do some rewriting. Take out the opera bits and put in ballet instead. Yeah, it might just work."

"The best part is Tats could play the dancer," Dan observed offhandedly, "which would save us the expense of hiring some fancy actress who doesn't know an *arabesque* from an albatross."

"Dan," Tatiana said, feeling a bit more than mildly annoyed, "give me a break. I can take jokes about a lot of things, but dancing isn't one of them."

"Really, Dan," Michael said, "have the sense to shut up."

"Give me one good reason why we shouldn't consider Tats for the part."

"Well, in the first place," Tatiana said, "I hardly thought I'd need to point out to you that, to be blunt, my legs don't work right."

"I thought you were taking classes at the Palms again."

"Sure, Dan, I'm taking classes—sort of the way a great artist who'd lost movement in his hands might take up finger painting as occupational therapy. Oh, sure, I can do all the positions again, even get up on *pointe*, only there's still one little catch: I can only dance maybe ten, fifteen minutes at a time before my knees turn to jelly and I end up on the floor. That aside, say by some miracle, like Michael takes me to Lourdes or something, suppose I *could* dance; the fact would remain I can't act. I've never acted in my life unless you want to count that musical you dragged me into my freshman year, during the course of which, as you may recall, I forgot half my lines and nearly fell off the stage. So, as near as I can figure it, I'm out on two counts: no legs, no talent. Unpleasant but true, and I'd appreciate it if you wouldn't throw it up in my face since I'm still understandably sensitive."

"You don't have to act, Tats." Dan pushed his sunglasses up on his nose and paced back over to the pool, waving his arms enthusiastically. "Films aren't like plays. There's no reaching for the balcony. All you have to do is get in front of the camera and be yourself, plus which my cinematic sixth sense tells me you're going to look so spectacular on camera that if you had the mind of a gerbil and the forensic talent of a department store manikin, the average American male would still cheerfully plunk down a buck-fifty just to see you walk across a room. Listen, I've actually been thinking about this for a long time, but I never saw the right moment to mention it to you until now. But you'd be great, Tats. Take my word for it. You've got the kind of face that was made to be seen in CinemaScope."

Tatiana sighed and took another handful of potato chips. Ever since they were at Harvard together, Dan had been given to these sudden enthusiasms and she knew how hard it was, once he got an idea in his head, to bring him back to reason. "The legs, Dan, you keep forgetting the legs."

"That's the beauty of it. It doesn't matter that you're only good for fifteen minutes."

"Dan," Michael said abruptly, "that's enough. Get off her back."

"No wait." Tatiana waved her hand. "Let him go on. What do you mean it doesn't matter?"

"Film's put together in pieces," Dan explained pushing his glasses back on his forehead. "I know you know that, but you both don't seem to get what it means. Suppose Tats here starts dancing, then falls flat on her face. No problem. You just use the shot up to the point she falls, then cut the rest. Okay, so she's only good for fifteen minutes at a go. Tell me, will you, how many shots last over fifteen minutes—last over three minutes for that matter?"

"Dan, if you don't shut up I'm going to throw you in the

pool. Tats has had enough trouble without you laying this kind of delusional garbage on her. There's no possibility she could stand up under the strain of a major role."

"I think I should be the one to decide that," Tatiana said. They both turned and Michael leaned toward her, concerned.

"Tats, please don't get sucked into this. I know how much you want to dance again, but Dan is way off base."

"Michael, tell me, is it true that if I danced in a movie you could cut around the bad parts?"

"In theory, yes, but what Dan *isn't* telling you is that you'd be standing under hot lights and working twelve-hour days."

Tatiana sat still for a moment, trying to digest what she'd just heard. She had never, not in her wildest dreams, imagined herself in movies. But it made sense. It really did. If she took the part she'd be working with Michael; she'd be dancing again—true, not with the City Ballet, but how much chance was there she'd ever be able to perform again on stage? Where else but in films could you dance for only ten or fifteen minutes at a time and still be seen by hundreds, no, make that *millions*, of people? But the real question was was she strong enough to survive the strain? She could hardly get herself into the middle of a film and then back out. Not only would Michael never forgive her, she wouldn't ever forgive herself if she wrecked his first chance to direct something he really cared about. For a moment Tatiana weighed all the negatives against the opportunity of dancing professionally again. *Fight this thing*, Mama had said. Well, if dancing in a film wasn't fighting polio, what was? What had all those sessions with Kate been about? All those hot packs, those endless repetitions—all those weights, knee bends, bicycle rides in the rain, those gruelingly boring classes at the Palms? For months now she'd been fighting to get back up on *pointe* and dance. For what: So she could entertain Alysa in afternoons or impersonate the Sugar Plum Fairy for Michael the next time Christmas rolled around? Sometime she was going to have to take the plunge back into the real world, and what better way than in a film where the plunge could always be repeated if she did a belly flop.

"Michael," she said quietly, "I want a chance at that role." Dan let out a whoop. "But I only mean a *chance*. I want you to let me try, but I swear to you if I can't do it, I'll get out of your hair so fast you won't even know I was there."

"Tats, are you absolutely sure?"

"Absolutely."

Michael took a deep breath and sat back in his chair. "I've stood in your way too many times and I'm not going to do it again. Frankly I'm worried about your physical endurance, and even more worried how you're going to feel if this doesn't work out, but if you really want to take a stab at the part and we can work out the script problems, well, Tats, it's yours." Tatiana had an urge to throw herself in his arms and give him a hug, but she settled for squeezing his hand. She felt so shy around Michael these days, so out of touch, but maybe that, too, would change for the better.

"Thank you, Michael."

"Don't thank me, honey. God knows you deserve a chance to come back from this thing." He turned to Dan. "Since this was your idea, suppose you set up the screen test. I know Tats is going to look great on camera—she looks great everywhere for that matter—but we have to be sure before we get too involved in this project."

Dan grinned from ear to ear, and gave Michael a mock salute. "*Oui, mon capitaine*, I'll set it up for tomorrow around noon, no, make that Wednesday; I want to have time to get her a real hairdresser, makeup, a good cameraman. Too bad Gregg Toland's no longer among the living, but there's a guy at Warner's named Todd Richter I think we can rent for the day. That reminds me, if this thing works out we're going to have to give her a new name. Tatiana Macks sounds like a brand of Russian potato chips."

For the next half an hour the three of them sat around the pool trying to decide what Tatiana's name should be. By the time she and Michael left Dan's apartment, Tatiana had been unofficially rebaptized Tatiana Trey.

"Turn your head a little to the right please, Miss Trey," Todd Richter said, 'I want to get another light reading." Obediently Tatiana turned her head while Richter's assistant stuck some kind of meter in front of her face and called out a string of numbers. Although she'd watched Michael work dozens of times, Tatiana had never imagined what a strain it was for an actor to stand under hot lights doing nothing while sound levels were set, shadows hunted down and banished, scenery and costumes rearranged.

Cautiously Tatiana lifted one leg and scratched the back of her knee with the toe of her *pointe* shoe. Her legs were already shaking, but she tried to ignore the fact. If she moved out of position, they'd probably have to readjust the lights again and that wasn't something she was up to at present. Would she fall when she actually tried to dance? She tried not to worry about the possibility, but it gnawed at the back of her mind. Michael had reassured her over and over again that if the worst happened he'd simply call for a retake.

It was going to be strange to perform in front of cameras instead of people, she could tell that already. There was something missing, something Tatiana couldn't quite put her finger on. Already she could feel it, a kind of blank where the energy should be. This was only a screen test, of course, but she could see it must be necessary somehow to convince yourself that a great, silent audience was sitting in the shadows watching your every move.

"Quiet on the set," Michael called out, settling down in his chair. There was a sudden silence. Another assistant appeared in front of Tatiana with a pair of clapboards, bringing them together with a smacking sound that made her flinch.

"Whenever you're ready, Tats."

Tatiana looked at the snarl of cables, the lights, the camera staring at her like a cyclops. She was supposed to deliver some lines about an imaginary telegram she'd received informing her that her lover—the tap dancer—was missing in action, and then perform a short sequence from whatever ballet struck her fancy.

"I only heard about Johnny this morning," she began. She could hear her own voice, speaking the lines woodenly, without conviction. Tatiana tried to summon up some emotion, but it was impossible to feel anything under these lights. Feeling increasingly ridiculous, she stumbled through to the end, and then began to dance a part of the Princess's role from *The Hundred Kisses*—a nice blend of character and technical dancing that suddenly seemed totally inappropriate. In the middle of a fairly complicated sequence the worst happened: she fell hard, bruising her knee. For a moment she lay on the cold concrete on the verge of bursting into tears. This wasn't going to work. She should have known better than to try it. Her legs were shot—macaroni.

"Get up, Tats," Michael yelled, "and we'll try it again." Biting her lower lip, Tatiana pulled herself to her feet and turned to face the camera. The crew was looking at her sympathetically. "What the hell are you all staring at," Michael yelled. "Let's get on with it."

Three takes and two hours later, Tatiana still hadn't gotten it right. Damn film. Dancing in front of a camera was like having a bucket of cold water thrown over you in the middle of making love. Every time she started to feel the rhythms, it was time to stop and start over. At least she hadn't fallen again, but her legs ached like crazy. On the fourth take Tatiana decided to do something different. Closing her eyes she imagined what it would be like to receive a telegram telling her that Michael was dead—not only Michael, how about Alysa, her mother, Winn, everyone she'd ever known or loved. A horrible sensation crept over her, a mixture of loneliness, disbelief, and grief. Opening her eyes, she mumbled her lines into the camera without really hearing them, concentrating only on the pain. Then, in a sudden burst of inspiration, she began to dance a bit of the mad scene from *Giselle*—that awful moment when Giselle, learning that her lover is engaged to another woman, stabs herself. By some miracle she got through a good minute and a half before she missed a step.

"Cut," Michael said. "That's better, Tats, but you've got to try to hold on longer before you, uh," he looked uncomfortable, "before you trip."

"It's not working, is it?" She felt a stab of disappointment so bitter it left her mouth dry.

"I'm not saying that. It's just if you can't give me a longer sequence, I'm not going to have any material to work with. The shots can't be too short, you know."

"Tell me frankly, Michael, do you want me to stop?"

"Not unless you want to."

"I'm not giving up until you tell me it's hopeless."

"Well, it isn't hopeless. You had a nice bit going there. Let's do another take and this time a little more umph on the part where you mention how much you loved the guy."

"More umph?"

"Right—and don't start the dance bit so soon afterward. You've got to give the audience time to get their handkerchiefs out."

One of the wardrobe people ran up and began to dab the sweat off Tatiana's forehead. Makeup was reapplied to her chin and nose. Someone handed her a glass of cold water. They did six more takes after that, and by the end of the day Tatiana was so drained it was all she could do to stumble into her street clothes, drive home with Michael, and fall asleep on the living room couch.

*　　*　　*

"That can't be me."

"But it is, Tats, every frame."

"I look..."

"Beautiful," Michael supplied, with a grin. "Nice job, if I do say so myself."

"Beautiful? Tats looks like a goddamn angel." Dan reached out in the dark theater and gave her a friendly slug on the shoulder, then turned in his seat and put his hands to his mouth. "Run that over again will you," he told the boy in the projection booth.

The boy nodded and the projector hummed into action, catching motes of dust in a beam of light. Once again Tatiana appeared on the screen five times as large as life. Her skin, skillfully covered with makeup and photographed through filters, was as smooth as Alysa's, her lips tinted and glistening, her eyes an impossible shade of violet. For some reason all the things she had always thought of as flaws in her face were transformed by the camera into assets. Her slight overbite was suddenly pouting and passionate; her chin, which had always seemed a little too round on the end, caught the shadows in a way that made it look like a smooth oval; her high Russian cheekbones gave her a slim, clear profile; her hair was a mane of auburn touched with gold highlights.

But it was her body that came as the biggest surprise. Tatiana had always thought of herself as having the physique of a dancer: long legs, prominent bones, a little flat-chested, pleasant-looking, slightly on the thin and lanky side—but the camera evidently thought otherwise. On screen she appeared to have miraculously gained weight. Her breasts looked rounded—not large, granted, but full and slightly lush. Her height appeared graceful, her arms delicate. Not only that, but by some act of cinematic magic Michael had turned her into an actress. Her mumbled lines, photographed in close-up, now seemed like the heart-felt words of a woman overpowered by her own grief. The mad scene from *Giselle*, filmed with heavy back lighting, looked at once chilling and ethereal. As Tatiana watched the scene unfold, she realized that Michael had cleverly put it together from four different takes, eliminating every awkwardness. No one looking at the light, airy beauty of the woman on the screen would ever suspect that she had had polio. Her legs gave the illusion of being strong and whole, there wasn't a moment's hesitation.

Tatiana contemplated her unfamiliar beauty with wonder. Michael was a genius. How in the world had he managed to transform her this way? The magnitude of the change from the self she knew to the woman she now saw on the screen was almost frightening. She watched the test three more times and still couldn't believe it.

Afterward they all went out for Chinese food to celebrate, and over the chow yuk Dan delivered a short speech. Tatiana was, he proclaimed, one of those rare people cameras love. Every studio in Hollywood spent hundreds of thousands of dollars a year combing the country for such people, so in Dan's opinion D&M had better get in gear and sign her to a ninety-nine-year contract before MGM got wise. It was all very flattering, but Tatiana couldn't shake the feeling that he was talking about someone else. Later, when she and Michael got home, she asked him to tell her the truth.

"Do I have a chance to make the film or don't I?" They were sitting on the living room couch, resting against each other in a sexless, quiet way that Tatiana found comforting. Although they had made love a few times since her illness, desire still wasn't a significant part of her life. Curling into his arms, she laid her head on his shoulder. "You might as well tell me the truth."

"I don't know," Michael played with a strand of her hair, lost in thought, or maybe not wanting to say what was on his mind. "You look fantastic in front of a camera—Dan was right about that—but. . . ."

"But what? Come on, level with me."

"You fell, Tats. You missed steps. I hate to say this to you—God how I hate to say it—but we didn't have a single unflawed take."

"Michael," it was hard for her to keep the hurt out of her voice, but she managed somehow, "I want this part."

"I know you do, but maybe you should rethink it. I'm afraid you're pushing yourself too hard. It's been less than a year since you were sick."

"Just tell me one thing. If I work out every day between now and when you start shooting, if I get into shape—and I don't mean just good shape but the kind of shape that makes it possible for me to dance at least fifteen minutes without messing up—will you let me have a try at it?"

"Tats, you know I'd give my right arm to be able to give you the role."

They sat for a moment in silence listening to the sound of the surf hitting the beach. "I'm realistic about this," Tatiana said at last. "I know you can't plan a film on a bunch of hopes, so I want you to do something else for me."

"What's that?"

"Line up someone in case I don't make it. Another dancer. Blanche Bender would be a good choice if you could pry her away from New York. Only don't sign anyone else for the part, not yet."

That night, after Michael had gone to bed, Tatiana went to her desk, dug out the list of exercises Kate had put together, and checked them over. She was relieved to see that she'd done some things right: worked out with her leg weights, pedaled all over Malibu on her bicycle, taken ballet classes at the Palms until she was ready to drop. But, to be honest, there were a number of Kate's orders she'd completely ignored. Take swimming for instance: the ocean was too cold most of the time and she hated the sticky feel of salt. Well, that was tough. Tomorrow morning she'd join a gym or country club, or maybe walk across the street and ask one of the neighbors if she could use their pool, and if the chlorine stung her eyes or turned her hair green, well, that was tough, too. She'd buy herself a pair of goggles and a wig if she had to, but from now on she'd swim at least an hour a day, just like Kate had ordered.

Tatiana reinspected the list smiling at the sight of Kate's handwriting. The letters were lined up as neatly as soldiers, every *o* a perfect circle, every *t* crossed at right angles. She thought of Kate storming into the house that first day in her yellow shirtwaist and taking over. Tatiana wondered what Kate was doing these days. Probably harassing some other patient back to health.

Run every day, Kate's list commanded, *no matter what the weather.* Tatiana felt a pang of guilt. Running was something she absolutely loathed. It was so boring, so mindless, without any of the physical complexity that made dancing interesting. But if Kate said *run,* then she'd better start running.

Tatiana batted the alarm clock into silence, crawled out of bed, and pulled on a pair of baggy pants and a gray sweatshirt that hung below her knees. Shoving her feet into a pair of dirty white tennis shoes, she staggered into the kitchen to grab a bite of breakfast before she hit the beach. The tide was out this time of day, which meant she could pad along the edge of the water scaring sea gulls. Not exactly the world's most interesting project, but it beat running on the sidewalk and getting shinsplints.

"You need a day off," Michael observed as she headed for the refrigerator. He was dressed to the nines this morning: a silk shirt, sport coat.

"Can't," Tatiana mumbled through a mouthful of milk.

Michael grinned. "I figured you'd say that so I've devised a scheme."

"No kidding?" Tatiana grabbed for a piece of toast, only half listening. All this exercise was making her ravenous. Good thing she was naturally thin. Lately the sweatsuits had been making her feel like a cross between Jersey Joe Walcott and Rocky Marciano. Too bad they didn't made anything pretty for a person to run in—silk overalls maybe, or purple tennis shoes with gold laces. She turned her attention back to Michael who was hunched over his coffee cup smiling a particularly wicked smile. "What sort of scheme?"

Michael rose suddenly from his chair. "Brace yourself."

"Huh?"

"You are about to be kidnapped." Lunging forward he caught her around the waist.

"Michael, let go." Tatiana was laughing so hard that she nearly choked on the toast. "Michael! What are you doing?"

"Taking you to my lair." He lifted her off her feet and carried her kicking and laughing into the living room.

"Michael, put me down."

"Go ahead," he said, grinning and throwing open the front door, "plead. I love it." Striding across the driveway, he deposited her unceremoniously in the front seat of the Thunderbird. "Now don't try to escape," he warned with mock seriousness as he got in beside her.

"Really, Michael, where are you taking me?"

"To MGM."

"You're kidding."

"Nope." He pulled out of the driveway. "Fact is, I've wangled an invitation for us from Arthur Freed to drop by this morning and watch Cyd Charisse working in his new musical *It's Always Fair Weather*." Michael grinned at Tatiana who was too stunned to do anything but look at him in amazement. "Now in about ten seconds it's suddenly going to strike you that you're about to meet one of the most famous dancers in Hollywood wearing a gray sweatsuit and torn sneakers, so I—your ever-loving husband—have provided a solution. Behind this seat, in a plastic bag, you will find your blue dress, a pair of stockings, the garter belt I gave you for Valentine's Day, and a pair of high heels." Michael chuckled.

"The only catch is that you're going to have to sneak into the whole outfit between here and the studio without causing a major pile-up on the freeway."

Cyd Charisse lay on the edge of a boxing ring just outside the ropes doing high kicks as Tatiana stood behind the cameras, watching in fascination. As near as she could gather, *It's Always Fair Weather* was the story of three army buddies having a reunion ten years after the war. Not a very exciting plot, but with Cyd Charisse and Gene Kelly how could MGM lose?

How indeed; Charisse was simply spectacular. Dressed in a calf-length, green pleated dress she seemed to be everywhere at once: chanting boxing statistics, imitating weight lifters, even doing a burlesque bump. Tatiana mentally compared Charisse to the ballet dancers she had known, thinking how different her body was: stronger, bigger breasted, with gorgeous legs. Everything about Charisse was sexy, and yet at the same time Tatiana could see that she had her entire body under control.

The overhead lights were hot enough to fry her eyeballs in her head, and it must have been 110 degrees on the soundstage, but Charisse seemed impervious to discomfort, repeating the same sequences over and over again without the slightest sign of boredom or fatigue, always giving the illusion that she had come upon the steps by some miracle and was performing them for the first time.

Now *there* was a woman with tenacity. Tatiana looked at Charisse, who had gone completely limp and was allowing two dancers dressed as boxers to throw her back and forth between them. Suddenly she came to life and began a chain of complicated steps ending in a dizzy series of *pirouettes*. If she'd been on the stage, the audience would have been applauding their hands off, but all Charisse got for her trouble was a glass of water and orders to start back from the beginning. *It's Always Fair Weather* was being shot in CinemaScope—a technique that was less than a year old—and evidently there had been some problem with one of the three cameras. Tatiana tried to imagine what she'd feel like if she'd put in a brilliant performance only to be told she had to repeat it becase of some technical difficulty: probably pick up one of those weights and heave it through the camera.

Charisse, on the other hand, seemed to take everything in stride. Walking calmly back to the boxing ring, she lay down and began doing the series of high kicks, her legs cutting through the air like two long blades. Lovely, absolutely beautiful. For over two hours Tatiana watched, completely fascinated.

"I need to see some movies, Michael."

"What sort of movies?" They were driving home from MGM slowly, enjoying the sunshine. Tatiana gazed at the cars rushing by in the fast lane, blurs of blue and red. That was what happened when you tried to move too fast, you lost edges and definition. All the exercising she'd been doing in the last month had been fine, but she realized now that she had been working so frantically she'd missed the essential point: endurance was nothing if you didn't have style of your own.

"I want to see every movie Cyd Charisse ever made."

"I didn't realize you were such a fan."

Tatiana smiled. "I wasn't until today—or, to be more precise, until about an hour ago when I suddenly realized that I'm totally ignorant about how a dancer manages to look good in front of a camera."

"Hence the films of Cyd Charisse?"

"Exactly."

"Mind telling me what you plan to do with them?"

"Run them forward, backward, upside down, and in slow motion. That woman's a genius, Michael. Maybe if I look at her long enough some of it will rub off."

The next day Michael came home with copies of *Band Wagon, Singin' in the Rain, Easy to Love,* and *Brigadoon,* and Tatiana embarked on a study of Cyd Charisse that changed the whole way she thought about dance.

Cyd Charisse was dancing again, only this time Tatiana was dancing with her. On the screen Charisse balanced Gene Kelly's hat on the tip of a green shoe with a heel so high it was a wonder she could walk in it, much less dance. Exhaling smoke through her nostrils, she heaved her shoulders, bent backward in angular, irregular movements, and in the dimly lit studio Tatiana imitated her: rocking, strutting, and kicking.

Jabbing the button on the projector, Tatiana suddenly brought the film to a stop, flipped on the lights, and slumped down on the overstuffed couch, exhausted. For the last week she had been concentrating almost exclusively on *Singin' in the Rain,* running "The Broadway Rhythm Ballet" sequence over and over trying to figure out exactly what gave Charisse's dancing its power.

Pulling an orange crush out of the ice chest, Tatiana opened it, tilted back her head, and let the sweet bubbling liquid slide down the back of her throat. She'd been spending so much time in the studio that Michael had helped her transform it into a miniature home away from home—cold drinks, pillows, even a hot plate in case she wanted to warm up a can of soup, though most of the time her mind was more on dancing than on food.

Cinematic dancing was so different from ballet. Take Charisse's last number in the film, the one where she and Gene Kelly performed a kind of fantasy duet in front of a purple and pink sky. On the surface it looked more or less like a conventional *pas de deux*, but the more Tatiana examined it, the more she saw that everything had to go together: costumes, cutting, music, movement. There wasn't a single element that you could cut out and leave the rest intact. The fifty-foot veil Charisse wore in the number was a prime example. Sometimes it rose up from her shoulders like angel wings; at other moments it was a puff of smoke, a trap, a cocoon. Remove that veil, and the whole meaning of the piece would be destroyed.

Interesting, Tatiana thought as she tossed the orange crush bottle into the wastebasket, very interesting indeed. Leaning forward, she started up the projector again, then got to her feet. Ultimately, of course, she wouldn't dance like Cyd Charisse at all. *Song of Love*—recently retitled *Frisco!*—was the story of a ballet dancer, not a vamp. The trick would be to come up with a style of her own by combining what she'd learned from Balanchine with what she'd learned from Charisse. Tatiana grinned, thinking how horrified most serious dancers would be at the idea of blending the two.

On the screen Charisse was running barefoot, the fifty-foot veil trailing out behind her. Tatiana closed her eyes for a moment, imagining that she was Isadora Duncan with a dash of Tanaquil LeClercq. Then, gracefully lifting her arms over her head, she let herself glide effortlessly across the floor of the studio.

"Dance!" Michael yelled. "That's it. Now put your hand on the railing. Keep coming forward, forward. Don't let the energy drop. Keep moving. Good. Good." Tatiana was dancing across the Golden Gate Bridge. Behind her, gilded by a spectacular red and gold sunset, the city of San Francisco rose up to a piece of azure sky that looked like a studio backdrop, but it was all real—every street, store, ferry tower, and cable car. Tatiana did a series of *jetés*, the soft pink chiffon of her skirt flowing out behind her. Through the viewfinger she looked like a cloud, airborne and completely weightless, a spot of color that clashed with the orange girders of the bridge.

For months she had been swimming, bicycling, exercising until every muscle in her body had screamed for relief. She had tied weights to her legs and dragged them around the house, forced herself to run on the beach, taken two classes a day at the Palms, done knee bends until she was so exhausted she was nauseous. She had seen every film Cyd Charisse had ever made—even some unreleased footage from *The Harvey Girls* that Michael had practically had to steal from MGM— not to mention every other musical she could beg, borrow, or rent, and now it was all paying off.

"Dance!" Michael yelled, and Tatiana danced without missing a step. She wasn't fully recovered, of course—she never would be—but she had the strength and endurance to go on as long as the camera rolled, and, more than that, she knew what she was doing. Film was part of her now; she knew how her dancing would look to an audience; she could imagine the way the sequence would be cut, what the final sound track would be like, even what kind of color corrections they would have to make to give her costume maximum impact.

It didn't matter that between takes she threw herself down on the sidewalk exhausted and panting to grab a few precious moments of rest. The audience would never see the pain and effort, only the beauty.

Five months later Michael and Tatiana sat on stools in front of a Moviola editing *Frisco!*. The studio they had rented was a stuffy, barren place made of cinderblocks, windowless, and too cramped for comfort, but neither of them was particularly aware of their surroundings. Their attention was completely captivated by the film in front of them.

"I liked that last shot of me better," Tatiana observed, taking a sip of cold coffee. "Definitely."

"Forget it, Tats; the light's not right." Michael ran his hand through his hair, relieved Tatiana of her coffee cup, and took a drink himself.

"What do you mean not right? I like the way the sunlight

hits my face. Like a shower of gold. The classic happy ending."

"Too symbolic."

"Roll it back anyway, Michael, and give it a try."

Michael pressed the reverse button on the Moviola and Tatiana suddenly appeared, trapped in a little square of celluloid, moving backward. Today they were cutting the last scene of *Frisco!*, or rather trying to. So far they had come up with half a dozen endings, none of which worked. Tatiana brushed her hair out of her eyes and concentrated on the tiny image. For weeks she and Michael had been shut up in this dark studio, editing and reediting *Frisco!* until they were ready to scream with frustration. At first they had disagreed over virtually every frame, but then, almost miraculously, a partnership had developed. Tatiana, almost without noticing it, had discovered in herself a sixth sense for rhythms and pacing. Michael had proved brilliant with plot, light, visual effects. One morning they realized they had arrived at a common vision, that they were, as filmmakers put it, *in sync*. Now, between the two of them, they were actually creating a film they were both happy with.

"Cut in that other shot," she suggested, "and let's try it again." Michael replaced one strip of film with another and rolled the machine forward. Sunlight flooded frame after frame. A miniature Tatiana danced in front of a golden bridge, the color of her costume flashing against the girders then merging for one perfect moment with the sunset. "That's it!" Tatiana yelled, nearly knocking over her coffee cup.

Michael squinted at the film critically and then broke into a grin. "You know, I think you're right." He rolled the film back, then forward again. "Yeah, you're definitely right. It works." He grabbed Tatiana by the waist and lifted her up into the air. "We did it!"

Without thinking, Tatiana threw her arms around his neck and gave him a kiss. He kissed her back—gently at first, then with more intensity. Tatiana felt something in her break, as if a barrier inside her had suddenly fallen. A whole combination of emotions flooded her: relief at having finished the film, happiness at having done such a good job, but most of all the simple joy of knowing she was a dancer again.

That night she moved out of the spare bedroom back into the big double bed and, after a little more than a year, she and Michael made love with a desire that was equally matched. Michael held her very close, kissing her and stroking her hair. After a while, he pulled back the flowered sheets and deliberately ran his hands over her legs, moving from her ankles to her knees, from her knees to her thighs. It was a tacit blessing of sorts, an acknowledgment that she was whole, that he found her beautiful.

"Dearest Tats," Michael whispered as he drew her body toward his. He entered her and they moved together, a little awkwardly at first and then eagerly, with the kind of passion that is one of the surprises marriage sometime holds in store.

A few months later *Frisco!*—every frame of which had been edited by Michael and Tatiana working together—was premiered at Grauman's Chinese Theater in Los Angeles, and the next day the film critic of the *Los Angeles Times* wrote the following review:

FRISCO! IS THE KIND OF FILM THAT MAKES YOU WANT TO KICK UP YOUR HEELS AND DANCE IN THE AISLES. CHOREO-GRAPHED AND DIRECTED BY MICHAEL MACKS, PRODUCED BY DANIEL DOBBS, WITH MUSIC BY RYAN LARKIN, AND A SCRIPT BY AGNES KARLYLE, IT IS THE STORY OF A TAP DANCER, A BALLERINA, AND THEIR LOVE AFFAIR WITH THE CITY OF SAN FRANCISCO—QUITE SIMPLY ONE OF THE BEST ORIGINAL MUSICALS TO APPEAR ON THE SCREEN IN RECENT YEARS.

MICHAEL MACKS HAS TAKEN A NUMBER OF CHANCES, ALL OF WHICH SEEM TO HAVE PAID OFF, THE MOST DRAMATIC BEING HIS DECISION TO SHOOT THE ENTIRE FILM IN NATU-RAL LOCATIONS: ON CITY STREETS, IN REAL RESTAURANTS, IN THE LOBBY OF THE ST. FRANCIS HOTEL, AND, ON ONE PARTICULARLY MEMORABLE OCCASION, FROM THE INSIDE OF A CABLE CAR THAT ACTUALLY APPEARS TO BE CAREENING DOWN ONE OF SAN FRANCISCO'S FAMOUS HILLS.

MACKS, WHO HAS OBVIOUSLY BEEN TAKING LESSONS FROM GENE KELLY AND BOB FOSSE, KEEPS HIS DANCERS MOVING FORWARD INTO THE CAMERA, GIVING THE AUDI-ENCE A SENSE OF THREE DIMENSIONS WITHOUT FORCING THEM TO RESORT TO WEARING CARDBOARD GLASSES. . . .

THE PLOT OF *FRISCO!*, LIKE THAT OF MOST GOOD MUSI-CALS, HARDLY BEARS DISCUSSING, SUFFICE TO SAY THAT IT PROVIDES AMPLE OPPORTUNITY FOR MACKS AND HIS PART-NER (AND WIFE) TATIANA TREY TO DO THEIR STUFF WITH THE KIND OF ÉLAN THAT MOST OF US HAVEN'T SEEN SINCE GINGER ROGERS STOPPED DANCING WITH FRED ASTAIRE.

MACKS, WHO HAS BEEN A FAVORITE OF MOVIE FANS EVER

SINCE *DANCE*, IS IN TOP FORM HERE, BUT IT IS TATIANA TREY, A NEWCOMER TO FILM, WHO REALLY STEALS THE SHOW, PRESENTING US WITH A COMBINATION RARELY FOUND IN HOLLYWOOD: SPECTACULAR BEAUTY, EXCELLENT ACTING, AND SO MUCH TALENT THAT YOU WONDER WHERE SHE'S BEEN HIDING HERSELF.

DAUGHTER OF THE GREAT BALLERINA NATASHA LADANOVA, AND HERSELF FORMERLY WITH THE NEW YORK CITY BALLET, MISS TREY BRINGS A VIBRANCY AND SHEER PHYSICAL EXUBERANCE TO HER NUMBERS THAT HAS TO BE SEEN TO BE BELIEVED. FRANKLY, AFTER WATCHING HER IN *FRISCO!*, I INTEND TO GO TO ANY MOVIE TATIANA TREY CARES TO DO IN THE FUTURE—EVEN IF IT'S A MUSICAL REMAKE OF *NANOOK OF THE NORTH*.

REAL STARS JUST DON'T COME ALONG THAT OFTEN.

18

Sorrento, Italy, 1958

The Hotel Celeste was famous for its unusual architecture.
Set into the side of a steep cliff, it hung like a wasp's nest
hundreds of feet above the Bay of Naples, a fantasy of stucco
parapets and red-tiled balconies dripping with flowers and
miniature orange trees. Tatiana stepped to the balcony rail
and looked down at the beach where Alysa was playing
happily under the watchful eye of an Italian nursemaid. From
this height Alysa was only a tiny pink spot running between
the waves, the foot of the cliff, and an even smaller red spot
that was undoubtedly her Mickey Mouse sand bucket.

"It's a beautiful view, Miss Trey," Grace Lyons said politely,
"but frankly it makes me a little nervous." She laughed
apologetically. "I'm afraid of heights. In fact, to tell the truth,
I don't even like to fly. If you weren't one of my favorite stars,
wild horses couldn't have gotten me on a plane to Europe."

"I'm flattered." It was a relief to discover Grace had human
emotions. Half an hour ago, when the reporter had first
arrived, she had projected an almost alarming aura of efficiency. A small, alert woman in her mid-twenties, dressed in a
dark, neat suit, Grace had introduced herself with a firm
handshake, settled down in one of the wicker chairs, and
begun a barrage of questions, taking furious notes in a
minuscule script that, from where Tatiana was sitting, looked
like copperplate.

In the last four years Tatiana had learned a lot about the
press—much of it the hard way. Most journalists could be
relied on to be fair and at least moderately accurate, but not
all. Tatiana still shuddered to remember the time she'd
innocently admitted to a reporter that she and Dan had been
friends in college. The reporter had jumped on the story,
manufactured a torrid love affair between the two of them,
and written it up, complete with carefully doctored photos of
her and Dan staring soulfully at each other. It had been

312

embarrassing, to say the least, to go to the supermarket with Alysa to buy a quart of milk and find her own face plastered all over the front page under the headline: TATIANA TREY'S SECRET PAST.

After D&M's next film, *Kyra,* things had gotten even more complicated. *Kyra* had been Tatiana's brainstorm. Based loosely on her mother's life, the film told the story of a Russian ballerina who fell in love with a Grand Duke and died trying to save him from the Bolsheviks. Natasha, who had flown out to California for the shooting, had been amused by Michael and Tatiana's attempt to resurrect her past. She found the extras—all of whom spoke only Ukrainian—hilarious, and the sight of St. Petersburg re-created among palm trees had made her nearly sick with laughter. The public, however, hadn't known the difference. *Kyra* had broken all records at the box office, and almost overnight Tatiana had gone from being a minor star to a very major one indeed. By the time she was nominated for an Academy Award, it was no longer possible to go to the supermarket for milk. Even though she lost out to Ingrid Bergman (who ironically won for her role in *Anastasia*—it was a big year for films with storylines about Russia), Tatiana's face had become so well known that privacy had become a thing of the past. Even here in Italy everyone seemed to have heard of Tatiana Trey, which was a pity really. Like all of Michael's films except *Kyra, Give My Love to Napoli* was being shot on location, which meant that when Tatiana walked—or, worse yet, danced—down the narrow streets off the Piazza Marigliano, she attracted such crowds that if they hadn't shelled out thousands of lira for police protection every scene would have looked like a parade.

Tatiana glanced up and saw Grace bent over her notes, silently rereading them. A good sign. Most reporters weren't that careful, but then *World* wasn't just any magazine. Tatiana sighed and permitted herself to indulge in a full two minutes of total self-pity. Fortunately Michael's mother lived only an hour or so away in a villa so stocked with priceless antiques that there probably wasn't a museum in Naples to rival it, a huge rambling place surrounded by a high stone wall where Tatiana could kick off her shoes, tie an old scarf around her head, romp in the garden with Alysa, and forget that Tatiana Trey even existed, but still it would be nice to be able to sit in a café and drink a *late caldo* without looking up to find twenty cheerful, noisy Neapolitans jockeying for autographs.

The wind was blowing from the city, bringing with it the

...ell of dust, smoke, and summer flowers. The heat was thick, soothing, like a soft blanket. Tatiana sank lazily into it, lost in her own thoughts, which today, because of some rather special circumstances, were of an extremely personal nature. Gradually her self-pity evaporated, and she smiled, amused at herself. Actually she had to admit that on some level at least, she enjoyed the fame. As much as she might complain about losing her privacy, there was something about knowing you had the largest audience of any dancer in the history of ballet that more than made up for it all, and there was no denying that being a star gave you more choices in life. Take *Kyra* and *Frisco!* for example. If those two films hadn't been so successful, she and Michael probably wouldn't be working together. How many other couples got a chance to create something that meant so much to both of them?

"It almost sounds too good to be true," Grace Lyons observed. Tatiana opened her eyes, startled to hear someone else voicing her thoughts. Pencil poised in midair, Grace was giving her a quick, almost envious smile. "Money, fame, a happy marriage, a beautiful daughter, a career doing what you love to do." Grace consulted her notes. "You even give money to good causes—Civil Liberties Union, March of Dimes, Cedars of Lebanon Hospital—and your hobbies are ridiculously wholesome: cooking, swimming, going on fishing trips with your husband. Frankly, Miss Trey, it doesn't make for a very exciting story. Now if you were in the middle of breaking up your sixth marriage, an alcoholic, or given to flings with younger men. . . ." Tatiana smiled as pleasantly as she could and took a deep breath. "Come clean," Grace leaned forward, woman to woman. "Isn't there any *scandal* in your life?"

"Nothing I can think of offhand," Tatiana shrugged and smiled. "Sorry." Actually she did have a secret of sorts but she wasn't about to share it with Grace Lyons—in fact, she even intended to wait a few more weeks before she told Michael. It wasn't scandal, far from it. Tatiana smiled to herself wondering what the reporter would say if she were suddenly confronted with the news. Not much probably. It was hardly the kind of thing that would sell magazines.

"But you've played such passionate roles." Grace was saying. "Like that scene when Kyra sneaks past the guards to spend one last night with the Duke. Positively sizzling—it was a miracle it got past the censors—but at the same time so romantic. I must have cried for half an hour, and I wasn't the

314

only one. How does a married woman with no past worth talking about come up with such *passion?*"

"I have a good imagination." Tatiana grinned, thinking of Michael. Grace obviously had a limited idea of the possibilities of marriage.

The interview went on for another ten minutes or so, and then Grace closed her notebook, shook Tatiana's hand, and promised to mail her an advance copy. Tatiana's picture would be on the front cover of the magazine, and maybe Michael's, too—it all depended on how the photographs came out.

After she left, Tatiana went straight to the closet and pulled out a conservative black bathing suit, a large floppy hat, and a terry cloth robe big enough to disguise an elephant. Ten minutes later she was down at the beach happily building sand castles with Alysa, ignoring the stares of half a dozen sunbathers, all of whom were, fortunately, too polite to approach her.

Give My Love to Napoli was a demanding film. For the next three weeks they continued to shoot mainly in Naples itself, and then, packing Alysa off to her grandmother's villa, Tatiana and Michael began a grueling four-day stint on the Isle of Capri. Over the years D&M, Inc., had changed from a small independent company with one cameraman and a handful of technical assistants to a huge international operation, employing hundreds of people—all of which made the logistics of moving the crew to an island in the middle of the bay something roughly parallel to transporting a small city. Although Michael's stepfather had invested heavily in the film and had excellent local connections, the Italian side of the operation still involved two hundred extras, five translators, three location scouts, two full-time public relations specialists, and a transportation coordinator whose sole job was to see to it that no one got left behind.

By the end of the fourth day both Michael and Tatiana were completely exhausted. The Blue Grotto sequence had been nothing but trouble from start to finish. In the first place it had proved almost impossible to film the Grotto and actually see it at the same time since the lights needed to register color destroyed the eerie phosphorescent effect of the water. When Michael had solved that problem by suggesting—rather brilliantly, Tatiana thought—that they do the entire scene in silhouette, the weather had suddenly changed for the worse, making negotiating the narrow passageway into the Grotto a kind of aquatic slalom course, the result being boatloads of soaked and disgruntled actors, hundreds of feet of ruined film, and at least one expensive camera that would probably never run again.

But somehow, at the end, everything miraculously came together and at three in the afternoon on the fourth day, Tatiana and Michael returned to Sorrento, tired but satisfied. That evening they were scheduled to drive out to Michael's mother's villa in Palazzo to collect Alysa and enjoy a celebration dinner with Anya and her Italian husband, Signor Marconetti—one of those monumental Russian-Italian banquets complete with blintzes, fettuccine, and Stolichnaya vodka.

Meanwhile, after a long boat ride in the hot Italian sun, it was a relief to get back to the Hotel Celeste. Their room was cool, rather like a cave, the tiles on the floor polished to an icy sheen, fresh flowers in all the vases, the windows thrown open to catch every breeze. As Tatiana tossed her straw sun hat onto the bed and kicked off her high-heeled sandals, she was pleased to see that room service had gotten things right for once. There on the dresser, just as she'd ordered it, stood a silver container of ice topped by a bottle of wonderful dry white wine grown on the slopes of Vesuvius that the Neapolitans called Lachryma Cristi—a sentimental touch perhaps, but she'd felt pretty romantic about this particular afternoon when she called from Capri to make the arrangements.

"Have a drink, Michael," she said casually.

Michael spotted the wine and did a double take. "What is this? Some kind of celebration?"

"I guess you could call it that." Tatiana located the silver-plated corkscrew, opened the bottle, poured out two glasses of chilled wine, and handed Michael one of them. Outside on the balcony a hummingbird was buzzing away at one of the orange trees, its tiny wings flashing like chips of stained glass. Tatiana stood near the railing for a moment, admiring the deft way the bird managed to hang suspended above the void; then she settled into one of the chairs and looked out across the Bay of Naples. She had something to tell Michael but she wasn't exactly sure where to begin. On the other hand, she wasn't in any hurry either.

"Correct me if I'm wrong," Michael observed drawing up a footstool and straddling it, "but our anniversary isn't until October, right?"

"Right." Tatiana smiled and then she grinned.

"Okay," Michael said, "out with it."

"Out with what?"

"You can't fool me. When you start looking like a Cheshire cat, I know there's something on your mind. Well, what is it? Come on, don't beat around the bush, I can take it. You think the Blue Grotto scene still doesn't work and you want me to get everyone back there for another day of shooting, right?"

She shook her head.

"You've decided to turn into a temperamental superstar and you're about to inform me that you're going to get an agent, demand a raise from D and M, and buy yourself a silver Rolls Royce."

"Nope. That's not it."

"Well, what is it then?"

Tatiana took a long, slow sip of wine, and then looked up at Michael, her eyes dancing with mischief. "We hit pay dirt."

"What?"

"Think, Michael. What is it we've been trying to do for the last three years?" It was all she could do to keep from laughing at the puzzled look he gave her. "Come on, think. You can do it. Begins with a *b* ends with a *y*, wears a size one shoe and padded pants. . . ." A look of revelation suddenly spread over Michael's face.

"You're pregnant!"

"Bingo."

"Tats that's great, that's absolutely wonderful." Michael hugged her impulsively nearly spilling both their drinks. They had both wanted another child for such a long time. For a minute or two they simply sat there, holding each other, perfectly content, not needing to say another word. Then Michael took Tatiana by the hand and led her back into the room. Sunlight cast dappled shadows on the white bedspread and the gauze curtains billowed. Tatiana had a sense of peace, beauty, and contentment so intense it made her dizzy. Sitting down on the edge of the bed, she drew her cotton dress over her head and turned to Michael. He was naked, slim-hipped, his shoulders strong and solid. She was glad to be having another child with him, glad to be carrying something inside her that was part of them both. She drew her fingertip around his waist at the juncture where tanned skin met pale, felt the tautness of his muscles, inhaled the fresh smell of his flesh. It was amazing how she went on wanting him and wanting him. Of course, like every other couple, they'd had

317

their hard times, but unlike so many of their friends they seemed to have survived them. A line from Shakespeare came to her, something memorized long ago in the middle of a cold Cambridge winter, and she rephrased it in her mind to fit Michael: Age cannot wither him, nor custom stale his infinite variety; other men cloy the appetites they feed; but he makes hungry. . . .

Leaning back against the pillows, Tatiana drew Michael toward her and for a long time she thought about nothing at all. Afterward, after the hunger was fed and they were both at peace again, he put his hand lightly on her stomach, and they fell asleep that way, shoulders and hips touching, breathing together rhythmically as the shadows on the balcony lengthened and the hummingbird, having exhausted one orange tree, moved on to the next. They woke just in time to realize that they were going to be late for dinner at Michael's mother's.

Alysa stood stubbornly in the marble entry hall of the Marconetti villa, her tiny fists clenched to her sides. "But Mama, I don't *want* to leave."

"Alysa, please, it's getting late and Daddy and I have to get back to Sorrento."

"But I'm having so much fun here. Granpa said he'd take me to see the circus tomorrow."

"The circus?" Tatiana turned to Signor Marconetti. "What's she talking about?"

Signor Marconetti smiled pleasantly and ran one hand across his balding head as if polishing it. "I'm afraid when I told her about the old Roman amphitheater, I called it a circus."

"With elephants," Alysa said excitedly, "and clowns."

"No, darling, no elephants," Tatiana explained gently. "It's just a lot of stones, a ruin."

Alysa's face fell, and then brightened suddenly. "Okay then, Granpa can take me to the beach."

Tatiana turned to Michael. "She really wants to stay."

"Well," Michael said, putting on his coat and leather driving gloves, "why not let her? We've got a lot of loose ends to tie up and there's no reason why we can't come back and get her day after tomorrow. That is, if she's not wearing you out, Giuseppi?"

"On the contrary," Signor Marconetti said, "it's a pleasure

to have the little one around." He smiled at Alysa and she beamed back at him and slipped her hand into his.

"Looks like we've got some real competition here, Tats," Michael bent down to give Alysa a good-bye kiss. "Now you be a good girl and do what your Granma and Granpa tell you."

"Yes, Daddy." Alysa threw her arms around him and gave him a hug and then ran over to hug Tatiana. As they left, Signor Marconetti picked the little girl up in his arms and carried her out on the veranda to wave good-bye. And so it was that, thanks to a casual arrangement conceived at the last minute, Alysa wasn't with Michael and Tatiana in the Hotel Celeste on the night of July 26, but rather in Palazzo dei Cesari sleeping calmly in a small study just off her grandparents' bedroom.

"Tats."

"Hmm?"

"Wake up." Michael's voice was urgent.

"Hmm?"

"I said wake up." Michael was shaking her shoulder but it was hard to open her eyes. Tatiana's throat stung and there was something heavy on her chest like a pile of bricks. Michael carried her into the bathroom and began to throw cold water in her face. Suddenly she was awake, coughing and sputtering, annoyed at Michael, and then—when she saw the smoke, blue and thick as fog—terribly frightened.

"I think the hotel's on fire." Michael's voice was level, but she could feel how much it was costing him not to show any panic. He walked over to the tub and turned the tap on full force, his hands trembling slightly. Cold water gushed out for a moment, then suddenly trickled to a stop.

"What are we going to do?" Tatiana pushed her own fear to one side, knowing that it was absolutely necessary to be calm. Thank God Alysa was at her grandmother's. Thank God Michael had awakened in time. Her mind whirled, creating and discarding escape possibilities. She thought for a moment of the view from the balcony: no fire escapes, no handholds, only a sheer cliff face dropping hundreds of feet to the beach. And then there was the elevator—an elaborate brass cage that ran five stories through a tunnel of sheer stone that would instantly turn into a chimney. Were there stairs? Any other way out? She swore silently to herself. Why hadn't she had the sense to look?

319

"We're going to get out of here; that's what we're going to do." Michael took two bath towels, soaked them in cold water, and handed her one to put across her face. The smoke was getting worse by the minute and she could hear a kind of muffled roaring. Michael took her hand and pulled her gently to the floor. "We have to stay low, Tats. They taught us in the army that hot air and smoke rise; the trick is to stay under it." He kissed her quickly. "Scared?"

"You bet."

"Me, too." He gave her a quick hug and she could feel his heart racing. "Here we go." They crawled on their hands and knees across the bedroom carpet to the door, and Michael put his hand to the wood to feel for heat on the other side. "Cool," he announced. Tatiana was so relieved that only the thought it might upset Michael kept her from breaking into tears. Thank God they weren't trapped in the room. Once again she thought with a shudder of the dizzy drop from the balcony to the beach.

Michael edged open the door cautiously by the lower corner, then flung it wide. Suddenly they were out in the smoke-filled hall. It was an odd sensation to crouch there on the plush carpet staring up at the gold-framed oil paintings through the bluish haze. Looking down the hall Tatiana saw there were stairs—how could she not have noticed them!—a whole flight to the left of the elevator. A giddy feeling came over her, triumph mixed with relief. What a story this was going to be to tell Alysa: how Mama and Daddy escaped in the nick of time. Michael spent a few precious moments pounding on doors, trying to rouse other guests, but if there was anyone inside they didn't respond.

"Hurry, Tats," Michael urged, but there was no need to tell her to hurry. She was already crawling with him down the hall, feeling the carpet beneath her hands and then the reassuring coldness of the tiles. The stairs plunged straight down, took a sharp turn to the right. Rounding the corner, Tatiana and Michael stopped abruptly. In front of them was a set of elaborately carved double doors.

"Stay back, Tats." Michael rose cautiously and pushed one of the doors open and suddenly they were face-to-face with an inferno. A wall of fire filled the stairwell, licking its way up the railing, producing a heat so intense it made Tatiana feel as if the skin on her face were being seared. "Damn it," Michael slammed the door, "we're cut off."

"What are we going to do." There was real fear in her voice

now, but she couldn't help it. If the stairs were on fire, and the elevator couldn't be used, what was left?

"Come on." Michael grabbed Tatiana's hand. "We'll go back to the room and tie some sheets together. Maybe I can lower you to the balcony underneath ours." He pulled her back up the stairs, but the hall was no longer a sanctuary. Fire had taken over, blackening the oil paintings, turning the rug into a dangerous corridor of flame.

The heat was terrible, singing their eyebrows, racking their throats. Coughing they struggled on their hands and knees back to the room and shut the door behind them. Tatiana looked at Michael and her fear turned to near panic. His face was smeared with soot, his shirt full of tiny holes where cinders had fallen on it. On his left arm was a nasty burn where he had touched something hot.

"Michael, are we going to die?"

He grabbed her, shook her. "No, we're not going to die. Do you hear me, Tats? We are not going to die. Now get over to that bed and start tearing up sheets." They worked frantically, stripping off the covers, tearing the sheets into strips, all the while trying to ignore the smoke pouring in under the door. How long could they go on like this? Tatiana tried not to think of the newspaper accounts of fires that she had read, how most people died from inhaling poisonous fumes. She tried not to think of the paintings in the hallway shriveling, of the terrible heat that must be building up on the other side of the door.

"There," Michael grabbed the makeshift rope, "that should do it." He ran out to the balcony, tied it to one of the posts, and dropped it over he edge. "Damn, it's too short." He hurried back into the room. "What else have we got?"

"Our clothes." She pulled her dresses out of the closet: cotton, chiffon, a long-sleeved blouse, Michael's slacks, a wool shawl that she had bought in the market on Capri. Scooping them up, Michael made some attempt to braid them together and then tied the whole mess to the end of the sheets.

He threw the rope over the balcony a second time. They could hear sirens now. Maybe someone would rescue them or maybe the fire would be put out. Tatiana had a momentary picture of long hoses spouting water, of the flames retreating.

"It's still too short, but it'll have to do. Hurry." Michael helped her over the rail and put the rope in her hand. Tatiana took one look at the terrible, dizzy drop to the beach below and then, resolutely turning her back on it, she began to climb down the tangle of sheets and blankets. The linen was slick and slipped under her hands. At one point she lost her grip and for a second she was plunging out of control, sliding out toward the vast emptiness of the cliff face. Using all her strength, she caught herself. The weight of her own body jerked her arms painfully, and her hands began to cramp. The rope swayed like a giant pendulum. Then suddenly she was at the end, her legs kicking against empty space, and there was nothing else to hold on to.

"Let go," Michael yelled. His face above her was an unbelievably tiny circle. "Let yourself drop. You've only got a few feet to go." Closing her eyes, Tatiana let go of the rope. There was a horrible moment as she fell through the air, an infinite space of pure timeless fear that sent her heart into her throat, and then with a jolt she hit the tile balcony one floor beneath their own.

"Are you okay?" Michael leaned out over the edge of the balcony, his body suddenly outlined by flickering red light. The fire must have broken through the door, must this very minute be burning up their bed and the rest of their clothes.

"Yes, Michael, for God's sake hurry." She watched him as he stepped over the railing and began to climb down the rope. It was awful to see him swinging back and forth up there, to know that if he did anything wrong, if one of the knots came apart, if the sheets began to tear, he would be thrown over the side of cliff. Tatiana got to her feet, grimacing with pain. She had evidently twisted her ankle. Well, there was no time to think about that, not now. She had danced through far worse injuries. Standing on her toes, she reached for the end of the rope and tried to steady it, but she was to short. Michael slid down a few more feet until he was hanging on to the very end of the rope. Catching at his legs, Tatiana pulled him in, away from the edge of the balcony. He fell on her, knocking the wind out of her lungs and for a moment they lay in a tangle, both dazed.

"Come on." Michael got up first, pulling her to her feet. The door to the room below theirs was closed and locked; Michael kicked in the glass and a cloud of smoke billowed out at them. Gasping and choking, they backed away.

"It's no better down here." Michael looked at Tatiana and for the first time she saw real despair in his face.

"Michael, it has to be better."

"Tats, there's no use kidding ourselves anymore." He slumped against the railing, tired and defeated. "The fire must have started on the ground floor."

"Michael, listen, there are more sheets in that room. We could tie them together, make another rope."

"There isn't enough time, Tats." Even as he said the words, she could hear the sound of beams crashing overhead. A shower of sparks fell suddenly, pouring over into the blackness beyond the balcony like a waterfall. "We have only one chance. We have to try the stairs again." They stared at the smoke pouring out the broken window.

"We'll suffocate," Tatiana said grimly.

"Maybe," Michael said, "and maybe not. If the hall is full of smoke, too, then we've had it. On the other hand, there's always the possibility that the fire has burned up through the floor of one of the other rooms in the suite, which would mean that when we got the outer door open we'd have a clean run for it."

"We don't have any choice, do we?"

Michael put his arm around her and drew her to him. "No," he said softly, "we don't. Either we go into that room; or we stay out here. . . ." He couldn't finish the sentence, but his face told her all she needed to know. For a moment Tatiana thought of the child inside her, and she was filled with a fierce desire to survive at any cost.

"Let's run for it, Michael." She tried to say the words gamely, but her voice trembled. Michael squeezed her hand.

"You've got guts, Tats, you know that? Now listen, once we get inside we aren't going to be able to see. What I'm going to do is try to head in a straight line from the balcony to the outside door and hope like hell that this room is set up like ours. Grab on to my hand and hold your breath. You might as well close your eyes for that matter, but whatever you do, don't let go of my hand. Got it?" Tatiana nodded. "Okay then, let's go."

Throwing open the door, he tightened his grip on her hand and pulled her into the smoke. Tatiana closed her eyes and held her breath but she could smell it anyway. The acrid thick odor of burning carpet, slick and heavy as oil, filled her nostrils and stung her skin. Half running, half stumbling behind Michael, she fled across the room, and then suddenly Michael flung open the door, pulled her out into the hall and, miracle of miracles, the smoke was gone—not completely, but thin enough so they could breathe without choking. Tatiana was so relieved she felt like laughing hysterically.

"It's okay, Tats," Michael yelled. He pulled her toward him and gave her a hug, "we're going to get out of here." It was an intense, ephemeral moment of triumph for even as he said the words, fire exploded from the elevator shaft, obliterating the far end of the corridor. The stairwell instantly became a chimney, drawing up the cooler air from below with an eerie moan. "Oh, God," Michael's face turned pale despite the heat. "Oh, no."

They stood for a moment, trapped beween the smoke-filled room and the burning hallway, knowing there was nowhere left to go. Tatiana looked at her husband and all the love she had ever felt for him rose up in her in a single wave. At that instant there was another explosion and the whole hotel seemed to shudder. Hunks of plaster rained down from the ceiling as the fire gave a great, bestial roar. Frightened, Tatiana flung herself into Michael's arms just as the entire floor gave way beneath them.

Palazzo dei Cesari, located some fifty kilometers from Naples, was a small country town with an illustrious history. First a Roman then a Norman stronghold, Palazzo boasted a Trojan arch, a ruined amphitheater, a Norman citadel, and a royal villa that had become by various twists of fate the residence of Signor and Signora Marconetti. Nestled snugly in a bend of the Volturno, the Marconetti villa was a miniature paradise, surrounded by a huge English garden, fragrant with camellias, dwarf mimosas, and cedars, but as Natasha and Winn drove through the heavy iron gates and followed the long winding driveway, they saw little of this beauty. Exhausted from a long transatlantic plane ride, and overcome by grief, they sat grimly in the front seat of the rented car each enclosed in her own private fog of misery and pain.

Each had learned of Tatiana and Michael's death in the most shocking way possible: Natasha from the evening news, and Winn from a distant acquaintance who had announced it innocently in the midst of a dinner party. Already today they had driven to Sorrento to see for themselves the charred remains of the Hotel Celeste, a skeleton of burned beams listing crazily over the edge of the cliff, its ashes punctuated by memorial wreaths and baskets of fresh flowers in honor of the twenty who had perished in the fire. There could be no funeral in the ordinary sense. Only twelve bodies had been recovered, and Tatiana's and Michael's had not been among them. As Natasha and Winn left the grim scene, volunteers were still sifting through the rubble but it might take days, even weeks, for them to find anything identifiable. The memory of that sight combined with the initial shock made ordinary conversation impossible.

Silence occupied the seat between them like a weight. After what seemed a very long time the villa finally appeared at the end of the driveway: a mass of soft yellow stone surrounded by fig and apricot trees. Pulling up in front of the entrance, Winn brought the car to a stop and set the emergency brake.

"We're here, Mama."

"Yes, we're here." Natasha looked at Winn, dressed in an expensive Chanel suit, a string of pearls around her neck, her blond hair meticulously caught up in a tortoiseshell comb: blunt, reliable Winn who had never done anything in her life but be a good, dutiful daughter, and her heart suddenly ached for Tatiana's passion and unpredictability. They'd been so much alike, she and Tatiana. Why, if she had to lose one of her daughters, couldn't it have been Winn? But that was a terrible thing to think; the shock of Tatiana's death must have unsettled her mind. Ashamed of herself, Natasha reached out and impulsively squeezed Winn's hand.

"Oh, Mama," tears filled Winn's eyes; her face was like a cup upturned, waiting to be filled with appreciation. It occurred to Natasha that perhaps Winn had been jealous of Tatiana, and that now she, too, was suffering from guilty thoughts. It was hard sometimes, when your own grief was so total, to remember that other people needed comforting.

Getting out of the car, they walked arm in arm up stone stairs and across the wide veranda past miniature lemon trees in clay pots, and half a dozen marble statues that looked convincingly classical. But, of course, Anya would have only the best. Natasha remembered the old house on Sutton Place with its authentic oriental rugs and the silver samovar Countess Belinskaya had brought all the way from St. Petersburg. Anya had been born to be wealthy; it was comforting, in a way, to think that after years of scraping along with Sergei she'd finally found a husband who could give her what she needed. Rumor had it she'd met him in a fancy Swiss sanatorium—not exactly the place Natasha herself would have looked for a husband, but for Anya the marriage had been a stroke of luck. Natasha paused for a moment, trying to remember exactly what kind of cars Signor Marconetti manufactured. Tatiana had probably written about it in one of her letters, but at the time Natasha had been more interested in details about Anya. It had been odd to hear that Anya was a devoted, affectionate grandmother. Natasha had even felt a little jealous that Alysa got along so well with her.

"Natasha." A strange apparition was walking quickly toward them from the other side of the veranda. On first glance it seemed to be a young girl dressed entirely in white—white lace dress, white shoes, white eyelet lace stockings, even a white lace parasol—but as the figure drew closer it became evident that it wasn't a girl at all, but an elderly woman. The face underneath the parasol was a monument to ruined beauty: thin and skull-like with a slack chin line and flesh as pale as paper.

Natasha looked at the woman, dumbfounded. It had to be Anya. But it couldn't be. Anya was her age exactly—sixty-three—this woman looked eighty if she looked a day. "Natasha, *preevyet!*" The woman enfolded Natasha in a stiff embrace, holding her away from her body as she deposited two dry kisses Russian style on Natasha's cheeks. Her bones were thin like bird bones, and she smelled of talcum powder, wine, and expensive French perfume. Natasha looked at the gray hair done in the same coronet of braids that Anya had favored nearly half a century ago, at the china blue eyes staring out from a face furrowed by time and misery. Only one person had ever had eyes like that.

"Anya." Natasha hugged Anya with sincere warmth, forgetting for the moment that they had ever been rivals, remembering only that they had been schoolmates who now shared a common sorrow. There was something about the moment that brought her almost to the edge of tears, an odd irrational sense of loss and reunion. If only she could know for certain that someday she would embrace Tatiana again the way she was now embracing Anya.

"To think," Anya observed in Russian, pulling back, "that after twenty-five years we'd meet again under such terrible circumstances." She shook her head sadly. "I suppose you expected to find me dressed in black like an Italian widow. Well, you see I don't believe in that kind of mourning anymore." Anya pointed to her dress. "White is the color of the great light that unifies us all, that light your Tatiana and my Mihail have entered together. A great yogi named Mahesh Ananda taught me that death is only the door to another life." Anya sighed, extracted a white lace handkerchief from her sleeve, and dabbed at her eyes. "We're sojourers on this earth, Natasha. Only sojourners."

For a moment Natasha was put off by the melodrama of Anya's mourning, not to mention its implied moral superiority. Why in the name of God did Anya always feel obliged to compete with her, even to the extent of grieving in a more enlightened fashion? But she was too full of her own sadness to be annoyed for long. Maybe the white outfit and the mystical mumbo jumbo were just Anya's way of avoiding the pain of losing her only son. The thought that Anya, like herself, was truly suffering touched Natasha, and her heart went out to this shell of a woman who had once been so beautiful, such a fine dancer. How terrible to grow old knowing you would never again have a child to comfort you.

"Excuse me, excuse me," Anya switched to English. "I'm being a terrible hostess. You," she turned to Winn, "must be Natasha's eldest daughter." There was an awkward moment while all three of them contemplated the fact that Winn was now the only daughter as well. "I think we met in London years ago when you were a little girl, but I'm afraid I don't remember your married name."

"Winn—Winn Compton," Winn supplied. "My husband Drew Compton is a banker. I think he's had some business dealings with Signor Marconetti. My sister, as you know, had a lot of investments and Drew handled most of them." Winn managed to speak of Tatiana without flinching, and Natasha was instantly grateful. If there was ever a time when Winn's blunt New England common sense seemed appropriate, it was now.

"Compton, of course." Anya managed a wan smile. "How could I have forgotten. You must come in and meet my husband, Mrs. Compton. He was so fond of your sister." Putting the handkerchief back in her sleeve, Anya led the way into the villa where Signor Marconetti waited to welcome them: a handsome, balding Italian gentleman of seventy or so whose subdued, sympathetic manner instantly won Natasha's gratitude. Quietly, with a great deal of tact, Signor Marconetti talked of how much he had enjoyed knowing Tatiana, how happy she and Michael had seemed together, what a personal sense of shock he had experienced when he learned of their deaths.

"Such a waste, Signora, so much youth and talent."

"Thank you." Natasha sat down beside Winn, not trusting herself to speak. Every reference to Tatiana, even the most well intended, was like a wound. To sit in this room, on the same couch where perhaps Tatiana had sat, was so painful it was all she could do to keep from putting her face in her hands and crying like a baby. She wondered dimly if she would ever feel whole or happy again. People recovered from tragedies all the time, at least they seemed to, but how? Did they forget the people they'd loved, or did they just go through the motions of being alive?

"... so Alysa hasn't been told yet?"

Natasha looked up, realizing she was missing something important. Winn was talking to Signor Marconetti in that calm, unflappable way of hers that at least had the virtue of putting a damper on people's emotions. "Such a young child and such a great shock." Signor Marconetti sipped a bit of seltzer water out of a heavy Florentine glass and cleared his throat. "Alysa is spending the day at the beach with Lucia, her nurse. We thought it best she not be here when you arrived, at least not until her future's been decided."

"Enough," Anya tapped her parasol on the floor like a crotchety old ballet mistress. "We'll talk about *that* after lunch."

Talk about what after lunch? Natasha suddenly became aware that there was something going on, something she'd been too upset to sense before now. But what in the world could it be? Perhaps Anya wanted custody of Alysa. Well, if she did, why didn't she just come out and say so, and then they could discuss it like reasonable human beings. The present situation was painful enough without making things worse.

Anya rose abruptly, indicating they should follow her into the dining room. It was obvious that, for all her fragility, she ruled Signor Marconetti with a firm hand, but then her mother, Countless Belinskaya, had been the same: silk on the outside; underneath, a soul of industrial grade steel.

Lunch, although consisting of a prodigious amount of food, was an awkward event. Signor Marconetti sat looking sadly at his plate as Anya downed glass after glass of wine. Neither Natasha nor Winn had much of an appetite, and everyone seemed relieved when the servants finally brought in the fruit and coffee. After the last pear had been cut and the last bit of sweet, heavy coffee drained from the tiny cups, Anya suggested, with a hint of melodrama, that the ladies all adjourn to her study. She had something to show Winn and Natasha: something she was sure they'd find interesting.

To Natasha's surprise the ominous *something* appeared to be a group portrait of the students of the Imperial School taken by the official photographer of the Maryinsky Theatre sometime in the late summer of 1915. Bending over the glass-encased print, Natasha began to pick out familiar faces, experiencing as she did so a mixture of pain and nostalgia.

"Why there's Madame Laurier. I'd forgotten how tall she was! And Katyrina Gorina. Good old Katya. Did you know, Anya, that she wept when you and Darya were suspended?" Natasha shook her head sadly, thinking how many of the bright, hopeful faces in the photo were dead—victims of the Revolution, emigration, or old age. A whole era of ballet had died with them. She knew she was being unnecessarily gloomy. Many of the girls were still alive, some perhaps even giving lessons or running their own schools, but she couldn't help thinking how quickly the years had passed and how much they'd taken with them.

Anya sighed as if in sympathy, and sat down on a small chair upholstered in petit point flowers. "I was really hoping not to have to do this but," she shrugged, "as the Italians say *che sera, sera.*"

"Do what, Anya?" Natasha reluctantly put down the photograph. In the back of her mind an alarm went off. *Here it comes*, she thought, *what Anya's been setting us up for all afternoon*. She looked around the study, a virtual museum of priceless antiques: maidens on a Greek vase whirling in a circle; a marble faun from Pompeii cavorting to the tune of a broken flute, and, most prominent of all, a huge framed poster of Anya herself eternally on *pointe*. A small voice at the back of her mind suggested this might be a good time to walk out. She was in no condition to have an argument with anyone, least of all Anya. But on the other hand, there was Alysa to consider. If there was going to be some kind of fight over her future, then it was probably better to get into it as soon as possible.

Anya took a deep breath, and fingered the cameo at her throat uneasily. Her cheeks were an unhealthy red now, flushed with the after effects of the wine, and her eyes were slightly glazed. "First," she coughed and began again. "First, I have to say I forgive you, Natasha."

"Forgive me, for what?" Natasha's sorrow turned to irritation. Couldn't Anya see that this was no time to play games?

"I used to think you were the cause of all my problems, well, at least most of them, the drinking, the fights—I was terribly jealous." Anya opened the top of her desk and took out a large battered manila envelope. "I can admit that now, because I don't care about him anymore, but at the time I was furious; I think, God help me, that I would have killed you if I'd had the chance. But then when I found out he was sleeping with anything that moved, I began to have more perspective."

"Anya, whom are we talking about?"

"Why Sergei, of course. You had an affair with him, yes? I don't mean back in Paris. Everyone knows about that. I mean in London in thirty-three."

Winn got up abruptly. "Maybe I should leave."

"No," Natasha said, "stay. You're old enough to hear this. Anya's telling the truth. I did sleep with her husband, only what I don't understand is why, after a good quarter of a century, she's picked this particular occasion to bring it up."

"Because of this." Anya handed the manila folder to Natasha. "It arrived the day before the fire; I was saving it to give to Tatiana. She and Mihail used to get all their mail here because the hotel was always losing it. After they died I opened it, thinking it might be something important. Go ahead, Natasha, have a look. Only brace yourself."

Natasha undid the metal clip, opened the envelope, and slid out a sheaf of papers. It was an advance copy of an article for *World* magazine, scheduled for publication some two weeks hence. Turning to the first page she read the title: THE HAPPIEST COUPLE IN HOLLYWOOD: HUSBAND AND WIFE OR BROTHER AND SISTER?

"Oh, my God."

"Read it."

Natasha skimmed the article, a brilliant Machiavellian piece, full of half truths and insinuation. Everything was here: her affair with Sergei, his opposition to Michael's marriage. The reporter—someone named Grace Lyons, who had evidently interviewed Tatiana only a few weeks ago—had managed to quote her in such a way that she appeared not only hypocritical but blatantly dishonest:

Q: ISN'T THERE ANY SCANDAL IN YOUR LIFE, MISS TREY?
A: NONE THAT I CAN THINK OF OFFHAND. SORRY.

*   *   *

Natasha was so furious it was all she could do to keep from ripping the article to shreds. She turned to Anya, her face pale with anger. "Tatiana never knew. Michael and I discussed it all before they were married, and we agreed that if she knew it would only hurt her. The past was over with; there was nothing anyone could do about it, and I told Michael—as I'm telling you, Anya—that there was a good chance he and Tatiana weren't even *related*."

"Calm down, Natasha." Anya retrieved the article, holding it between the tips of her fingers as one might a dead rat. "It's only an advance copy, and Giuseppi and I have already taken steps to see that this trash will never be released."

"Steps?"

Anya shrugged. "Giuseppi has some connections in New York. You'd be surprised how effective the threat of a multimillion dollar libel suit can be—especially when coupled with a great deal of money."

"You bought them off?" Natasha was so relieved she had to sit down.

"Let's just say that yesterday I had our New York lawyer call the editor-in-chief at *World*—a Mr. Kirchner—who fell all over himself assuring us that, considering the tragic circumstances, they have no intention of distributing this unmentionable bit of filth. It seems that Tatiana Trey and Michael Macks have become something of an institution now that they're dead and no editor in his right mind would risk slandering them. Interestingly enough the reporter—Grace Lyons, I think she called herself—has also lost any desire to take the story to another magazine."

"Where did this ... this *woman*," Natasha spit out the word, "get her information?"

"I thought that was fairly obvious." Anya put the article back in the manila folder and pushed down the metal catch with the abrupt motion one makes when crushing an insect. "You didn't tell her. I'm sure Michael didn't tell her, and that, by my calculations, leaves only my dear ex-husband."

"Even Sergei wouldn't pull a filthy trick like that."

"Not on purpose, perhaps. But Giuseppi called New York and made some inquiries. It seems that this Miss Lyons is a rather beautiful young woman whose morals lie somewhere between those of Agrippina and Lucretia Borgia. I can just imagine Sergei confiding in one of his Dostoyevskian post-coital moments the tragic reason why he no longer considered Mihail his son."

"The bastard."

"My sentiments exactly." Anya put the folder back in her desk and closed the wooden top with a click.

"Why did she do it? Why would anyone want to hurt Michael and Tatiana?"

"Greed, envy, a desire to make a name for herself; who knows? The question now is what are *we* going to do about our granddaughter? There's always a chance that some day it may all come out, and I hardly think we want Alysa growing up with the kind of publicity that dogged the children of Oedipus. Antigone and Ismene, as you may remember, didn't come to particularly pleasant ends."

"If Sergei tries to get custody of Alysa, I swear I'll kill him."

"I don't think we have much to worry about on that score. Sergei's never much liked children, and as far as I know he's absolutely refused to recognize Alysa's existence. Giuseppi and I, on the other hand, would love to raise her—we both adore the child—but frankly neither of us is well." Anya smiled bitterly. "I wrecked my liver on cognac some years ago, and Giuseppi has a bad heart. If we both live another five years, it'll be a miracle. You, however, appear to be in great shape. How do you do it, Natasha? Sometimes I swear you've got a picture aging in a closet like Dorian Gray—you danced at least fifteen years longer than anyone should be able to dance, and the hell of it is you still look good. What bargain did you strike with the Devil for your soul?"

"Anya, for heaven's sake."

"I'm sorry, the habit of sarcasm dies hard. The truth is, I want Alysa spared all this, and, as much as I hate to admit it, you're the only one fit to raise her. God knows I'd rather keep the child myself, and under other circumstances I'd fight you tooth and nail for her, but then you always did get everything I wanted."

"Excuse me," Winn interrupted, "but I have another idea." Natasha and Anya, who had forgotten she was in the room, stared at her blankly. "I'll raise Alysa." Winn took in their looks of incomprehension without flinching. "Well, why not?" she said with her usual bluntness. "Drew and I have always wanted a child, you know, but we can't seem to have one. Some of the doctors say I'm to blame because my tubes are probably blocked or something and others tell us Drew's sperm count is too low, but no one knows for sure. Sorry if I'm embarrassing you with the details, but the point is, Alysa would be perfect for us. In the first place Drew and I are a lot

332

younger than either of you, and in the second place we have a huge house back in Cambridge that we just rattle around in." Winn's face softened in a way Natasha had never seen before. "I love children. I really do, and so does Drew. We've both wanted a baby ever since we got married. This isn't some kind of spur of the moment decision. He and I talked it over when we heard the news about the fire. We even agreed that if no one had any objections we'd like to adopt Alysa legally and change her name to Compton." Winn folded her arms across her chest and set her chin firmly. "Now I know I haven't seen her too much—only the time she and Tats came back to Boston for Christmas—but I know she's a lovely little girl and, well, you just can't *imagine* how happy it would make me and Drew to have her. So what do you say?"

There was a long silence while Natasha and Anya digested what Winn had just said. Natasha was at a loss for words. Never in her life had she heard Winn made such an impassioned speech about anything. She looked at her daughter with new respect. It made sense, it really did. Winn was the right age to be a mother, and it would be good for Alysa to grow up in a house with two parents like any normal child.

"I think it might be a good idea," Anya said at last, "but I'd only be willing to consider it on one condition."

"What's that?"

Anya got to her feet dramatically. "You must promise that Alysa never, *never* know that Sergei Maximov is her grandfather."

"Under the circumstances," Natasha said, "I agree completely. Alysa's never seen Sergei; he doesn't give a damn about her, and the less she's associated with him, the less likely some reporter is to draw information from him. Actually, it shouldn't be all that difficult. Hardly anyone knows that Sergei is Michael's father—in fact, as Anya is no doubt aware, the studio concocted a biography for Michael years ago according to which he was born of a Russian princess and a British war hero who died in a Japanese prison camp in forty-three. Sheer claptrap, of course, but no one's challenged it yet, except this Grace Lyons woman. How *she* managed to ferret out the real relationship between Michael and Sergei is beyond me, but I'm sure we can continue to take steps to ensure it doesn't happen again."

"Oh, yes," Anya observed grimly, "we can indeed continue to take steps." She turned to Winn, steely and stubborn, her eyes narrowing with pure Slavic determination. "You'll agree then? You'll promise to keep my granddaughter away from that man?"

"Well," Winn said, "in principle I believe in total honesty. I'm not much good at keeping the truth from people; in fact, as Mama will tell you, I'm a perfectly rotten liar. But from what I've heard this afternoon, I think we have a special case here. Maximov sounds really unpleasant to say the least, and as you said, he could be dangerous to Alysa in the future. So given the circumstances, I'm willing to agree that as far as Drew and I are concerned he'd be completely out of the picture." Winn held out her hand to Anya. "That's a promise."

"Your word of honor?" Anya swept a strand of hair out of her eyes and confronted Winn with a look intended to convey that she still wasn't completely convinced.

"Winn never gives anything but her word of honor," Natasha said. "A promise from her is like money in the bank. Go ahead, Anya, shake her hand, and you'll be able to count on the fact that Alysa won't ever know Sergei's her grandfather unless he tells her himself."

Seven months later, in the spring of 1959, Drew and Winn signed the final adoption papers, and Alysa Macks legally became Alysa Compton.

Book III

ALYSA

19

Boston, 1972

Seeing *Quetzal* changed Alysa's life. She was sitting in the audience, waiting for the curtain to rise, bored and a little impatient, wondering if she was going to like the ballet or not, and then all at once music exploded from the orchestra—hot and Latin and not at all proper—and the stage was suddenly full of dancers wearing crowns of feathers. For a moment there was a hush so deep you could hear the audience breathing, then a rush of wings, glittering purple, blue, green, and gold—costumes so lavish and dancing so passionate and complex she could barely believe she was watching something ordinary and mortal.

Alysa leaned forward in her seat, willing herself up on the stage with the dancers. She imagined herself wrapped in a cloak of feathers, a bird, flying and boneless. The story unfolded: a religious ceremony, a love affair, the final tragic sacrifice of the Aztec Princess stretched on a stone altar, flowers woven into her hair, while the Evil Priest chanted over her, stone knife in hand, bending down to take the heart from her body just before the curtain closed.

By the end, Alysa was crying and clapping so hard her hands were raw. Maximov was a genius, a complete, utter genius. For years Nana had told her his work was trite, shallow, not worth looking at, and for years, out of loyalty to Nana, Alysa had purposely refused to watch the Manhattan Ballet. But Nana had been wrong. An amazing thought. How could Nana, who knew everything about ballet worth knowing, not have recognized Maximov's brilliance? Maybe Nana hadn't ever seen *Quetzal*. No, she must have; she must have seen the snakelike motions of the corps imitating the bird-snake god Quelzalcoatl, and the amazing *pas de deux* in the second act that had made Alysa's mouth go dry with excitement. Nana must have seen it all and rejected it, but why?

Alysa didn't have the faintest idea. She only knew that she

wanted to dance with the Manhattan Ballet—no, more than wanted it, *craved* it with every particle of her being. In fact, by the time the evening was over, she was already trying to figure out how to get an audition with Maximov.

The big yellow house on Salem Street in Cambridge had been in the Compton family for generations, ever since the Reverend Elijah Compton had parted ways with Cotton Mather in 1692, gone into the shipping business, and founded the family fortune. Huge and sprawling, the house was a hybrid of styles, complete with Cambridge's longest white picket fence, a formal garden, and enough turrets, cupolas, and dormer windows to stock a castle. This spring, as usual, the front yard was a mass of honeysuckle, liliacs, and daffodils, all planted lovingly by Aunt Winn, who liked nothing better than to get down on her hands and knees and poke around in the dirt.

The scent of the flowers rose up to the second story, drifting in the window of Alysa's bedroom, filling the air with a sensual, nostalgic perfume that clashed with the piles of blue jeans, muddy shoes, rock posters, and empty cottage cheese cartons. Alysa, who was in the middle of trying to write a letter to Maximov, sighed, pushed her long black hair out of her face, and finished off a can of Tab, tossing the empty in the general direction of the wastebasket. The can clanked to a stop somewhere in the region of the closet, losing itself in a heap of worn out *pointe* shoes whose bedraggled ribbons spoke of endless, grueling lessons.

The Tab can was one of about six hidden around the room like red-and-silver Easter eggs. Although Alysa had many virtues, neatness wasn't one of them, and Aunt Winn, to her credit, had recognized that long ago. Downstairs the house was immaculate: the rooms full of antiques, some of which had been brought back from China on whaling ships in the 1840s, the rugs pale orientals, priceless swirls of pink and light blue that showed every footprint. Inlaid tables were polished to a sheen, brass fire irons glowed discreetly, the floor was so slick it was like ice-skating just to negotiate from the entry hall to the dining room.

But upstairs, in Alysa's bedroom, other rules applied. From the age of four, when Aunt Winn and Uncle Drew brought her home to Salem Street, Alysa had been allowed to have her own private place to mess up as she pleased. Alysa, who had been very upset by the death of her parents, had always been grateful to Aunt Winn and Uncle Drew for understanding that she needed a room that was absolutely her own.

Over the years a routine had developed that left Alysa a maximum amount of privacy without totally abandoning her among the rubble. About once a week Mary, the Comptons' Irish maid of twenty years, came in to change the sheets and shovel out the debris—Tab cans, yogurt cartons (Alysa practically lived on Tab and yogurt), not to mention gathering up the index cards that Alysa left everywhere: shedding them like a tree sheds its leaves, Mary often teased her. Alysa had noticed long ago that neither Mary nor Aunt Winn ever read these cards on which Alysa recorded ideas for ballets (she had aspirations of someday doing choreography) as well as her most intimate thoughts—a bit of New England conscience that made her respect Mary, of course, but Aunt Winn all the more, especially since so many of Alysa's friends reported that their parents constantly pried into their private lives.

Alysa bit her lower lip and reread what she had written so far:

May 13, 1972
Dear Mr. Maximov:
   Last Friday night I saw your ballet Quetzal *and I realized that you are the one choreographer I want to work with. Mr. Maximov, you are a genius. I am only eighteen, but I have been studying for twelve years with my grandmother, Natasha Ladanova, who tells me I have great potential. I have danced professionally with the National Ballet of Canada in Toronto . . .*

Alysa paused for a moment, caught up in memories of the convent school she had attended for two years in Toronto: the nuns in their black wool robes getting French toast in the mornings while the pupils got cold oatmeal; being forced to take a bath in a cotton shift so she wouldn't get a glimpse of her body; around the school grounds a wrought iron fence so high and pointed at the top that any boy who'd tried to climb it would probably have been eviscerated. Ostensibly, Alysa had been there to learn French, but in reality she had gone to Toronto to dance with the National Ballet, which Nana had helped found. It was Nana herself who had sent her away, saying she needed another perspective on dance, Nana, too, who had insisted she go to Stuttgart last summer to work with Cranko. Nana: grandmother, teacher, mentor—the person

339

Alysa loved and respected more than anyone else in the world—who had specifically said yesterday, when Alysa timidly broached the matter, that Maximov's *Quetzal* was as trite as one of those cheap calendars you found in shoddy Mexican restaurants.

The memory of Nana's disapproval didn't make writing this letter any easier. Alysa let the paper flutter to the bedspread, put her chin on her elbows, and surveyed her room. How could she convince Maximov he should give her an audition? How could she put her whole life down in a way that would make him realize she was completedly devoted to ballet, no, more than devoted, *obsessed*. Her first toys had been ballerina dolls, her first pleasure watching Nana give lessons. The first movie she remembered with any clarity was *Kyra*. It had come on television late one night when Alysa was supposed to have been in bed. She must have been five or six at the time, and she remembered watching her mother skim across the stage of what she later realized was intended to represent the Maryinsky Theatre in St. Petersburg. It had been a terrible, wonderful experience to see her beloved mother, whom she remembered with such love and pain, suddenly resurrected from the dead, frightening enough to give her nightmares for weeks. But it was the image of her mother dancing that had stuck most in her mind, and because of it she had come to Nana the next day, stubbornly demanding lessons—five years old and already knowing without a doubt what she wanted to do with the rest of her life.

How could she put all that in a letter to Maximov without sounding completely crazy? Alysa looked around her room: at the mat on which she did her yoga; the poster of her favorite comedian Goldie Hawn; the original Degas that had once belonged to her mother and grandmother. There were so many pieces of her life she'd have to leave out of the letter. Her fencing foils hung on the wall, souvenirs of the months she'd fenced to improve her balance, only stopping when she realized she was developing the wrong muscles; her ice skates were piled up near the stereo along with her bicycle. Would Maximov care that she loved speed and forward motion, or was that one of those irrelevant things you never mentioned in a letter?

And what about her personal life outside of ballet? Alysa looked at her bulletin board, a mess of posters, notes, cartoons. She loved people, made friends easily and kept them forever. There was a note from Vicki Wright, whom she'd known since the third grade, inviting her to a party; a letter from Marie DuBois, who still wrote her regularly from Toronto; a postcard from Eric Schwartz, a dancer from Stuttgart whom she'd had a romance with last summer—kind, considerate Eric, who had relieved her of her virginity with infinite European patience. Would Maximov care that, although she liked men, ballet came first in her life? Would he want to know that she was sociable, cooperative, easy to work with, or would he only be interested in how many *fouettés* she could do before she fell flat on her face?

Alysa picked up the letter and surveyed the blots, scribbles, and erasures. Only last week her freshman composition teacher at BU had commented that she wrote as if she were running away from words. Say "dancing away" and you'd have it. Alysa shook her head as she examined the scrawl. She'd never had much patience with the printed page. Her life was quick and rhythmic; she took information in through her ears and body rather than her eyes: listening to Jim Morrison and watching a rock ballet unfold in her mind, sensing her spine vibrate to steel drum music from Jamaica, hearing Mendelssohn and feeling her feet twitch through Balanchine's *Midsummer Night's Dream*. A wonderful talent for a dancer to have maybe, but not when that dancer was trying to write the most important letter of her life.

Wadding up the paper, Alysa tossed it into the corner to join the Tab can. She might as well face facts: writing Maximov was impossible. The only thing to do was go see him in person.

Going over to her dresser, Alysa began to root through index cards, balled up leotards, and mismatched socks. It was Sunday, all the banks were closed, and she wanted to catch the first shuttle the next morning, mainly because the idea of walking in and demanding to audition with Maximov was so scary that she knew if she put it off a single day she'd never be able to do it. At last she came upon some money: about thirty dollars—enough to get her to New York but not enough to get her back. Alysa made a quick decision: what the heck, she'd go anyway, take a backpack with her jeans in it, stash it at Port Authority while she was seeing Maximov, and hitchhike back to Boston. Too bad she couldn't get Nana to call ahead and set up an audition for her, but that was obviously out of the question.

Stashing the money in her purse, Alysa walked over to her closet, plunged in, and began a protracted attempt to locate the mint green suit Aunt Winn had bought her for the trip to Stuttgart. Green was a great color on her, not that she herself cared much about clothes, but it wouldn't hurt to make a good impression. With cheerful stubbornness, Alysa kept at the task until she had assembled a complete outfit including, by some miracle, a white blouse and a pair of pantyhose without runs.

Ten minutes later Mary, the Comptons' maid, came on the unprecedented sight of Alysa standing in the kitchen ironing her own skirt.

"You want to see whom?" the receptionist at the Manhattan Ballet's front desk regarded the slender, dark-haired girl with mild suspicion. For over ten years she had been sitting in the foyer deciding who went through the door and who didn't, a task she performed with the relish of a dragon protecting a treasure trove.

"Mr. Maximov." The girl tugged at the hem of her green suit jacket nervously and lifted her head. Her eyes were a startling blue—intense intelligent eyes, with ridiculously long lashes poised above a cute slightly turned-up nose and a decidedly stubborn mouth.

"Do you have an appointment?"

"Not exactly."

The receptionist sighed and put down her pen. "I'm sorry, but half the city wants to see Mr. Maximov, and without an appointment, well, frankly, you'd have a better chance of getting in to see *Jesus Christ Superstar* without a ticket."

"But I'm a dancer, and I admire his work immensely, and I want to audition for him."

The receptionist laughed. "Well, I have to say one thing for you: you've got guts. Not much sense though. Do you have any idea how many dancers would like to audition for Maximov?"

"Are there lots?" The girl looked taken aback. "I mean lots who come in person?"

"Every day two or three of you kids walk in here."

"Oh," the girl's face fell. She couldn't have been over eighteen if she was a day. Still at the age when disappointment took you by surprise. The girl stood for a moment her brow furled in thought. "Would it make any difference if I said that Natasha Ladanova sent me?" she offered at last.

"Natasha Ladanova?" the receptionist was suddenly all attention. "My God, Ladanova hasn't sent us anyone as long as I've been here. The last I heard, she retired." She looked

342

at the girl, taking in her slender arms, the small breasts, the well-developed legs that were the sure mark of a serious dancer. "How do you happen to know Natasha Ladanova?"

"She's my grandmother."

"You've got to be kidding."

"No, it's true." The girl smiled and for an instant her whole face lit up. "I didn't mean to shock you."

"Shock me?" the receptionist reached for her coffee, nearly knocking over the cup. "You just about gave me a coronary."

"Could you call Mr. Maximov and tell him I'm here."

"Well, maybe under the circumstances, but . . ." the receptionist paused, hand poised over the receiver, "are you *sure* you're telling me the truth? I mean if I call up Mr. M. and tell him Natasha Ladanova's granddaughter is here, and then you turn out to be some hick kid from Jersey, he'll skin me alive." She shuddered. "Mr. M. angry is not a pretty sight."

"Oh, I'm Ladanova's granddaughter all right."

"Well, sit down over there," the receptionist pointed to a chrome and teak bench padded in black leather, "and I'll give him a buzz. By the way, what's your name?"

"Alysa Compton."

"Well, Alysa Compton, Mr. M. is in the middle of a choreography session at the moment, and the last receptionist who interrupted him during one of those lost her job on the spot, so you may have to wait a while."

"That's okay," Alysa went over to the bench, started to fold her legs in a full lotus, and then remembering she had on a skirt, abruptly crossed them at the knees. Too bad she couldn't just lie down on the floor and do some yoga, but from the looks the receptionist kept shooting her she could tell this was no place to look anything but as straight as Queen Elizabeth. She gazed around the foyer with growing nervousness, wondering from which door Maximov was liable to emerge. The walls, painted a stark, silvery gray, were covered with huge posters framed in chrome. Most of the faces she recognized: Pavlova, Diaghilev, Nijinsky, Carmen LaGuerra, Lydia Winters. . . .

"So you're Natasha Ladanova's granddaughter?" a heavily accented voice said sharply.

Alysa nearly jumped out of her skin. Sergei Maximov was standing in front of her, hands on his hips. He was different from the pictures she'd seen of him, his face thinner and more finely chiseled, his jaw tighter, his whole body as taut as a wire. Dressed in a black turtleneck and black pants, he

343

gave the impression of a jaguar poised on the balls of its feet, ready to spring.

"Yes, sir." Alysa didn't know whether to stand up or go on sitting down. Maybe she should shake his hand, or maybe he'd think that too forward. She tried to smile to indicate goodwill but the smile froze on her lips. Why in the world was he looking at her that way?"

"Who am I?"

"You're Sergei Maximov, sir." What a question. Of course he was Sergei Maximov. There probably wasn't a dancer in the United States, in the world for that matter, who wouldn't have recognized his face on sight.

"That's all?"

"All?" Alysa suddenly had the feeling that she'd missed part of the conversation somehow.

"Come now," he looked her up and down, "there must be more."

"Uh, well," Alysa tried to think fast. "You and Balanchine are the most famous choreographers of the century, only your works are less abstract and more dramatic than his; you're the creator of my favorite ballet, *Quetzal*, you're—"

"Enough," Maximov held up his hand. "So, Natasha sent you down her to audition for me, did she?"

"No, sir."

"What?"

"Mr. Maximov," Alysa took a deep breath, "I have a confession to make. I *am* Natasha Ladanova's granddaughter, in fact I'm her student, her only student at present since she's more or less retired. She's taught me everything I know about ballet. She's a wonderful teacher, maybe the best in the world, but she definitely didn't send me down here to see you, because she doesn't like your work."

A ghost of a smile flickered over Maximov's face. "Oh, she doesn't, does she?"

Alysa took the smile for encouragement and plunged breathlessly on. "Mr. Maximov, as far as I'm concerned you're doing the most innovative choreography in the United States. I more than admire your work: I'd give my right leg to dance with you, although come to think of it you probably wouldn't have much use for a one-legged dancer," she knew she was starting to sound ridiculous, but she persevered stubbornly to the end. "But the truth is my grandmother, for some reason, doesn't even like me to mention the Manhattan Ballet in her presence. I think she's crazy about Balanchine or something because my mother once danced with the City Ballet. The fact of the matter is, I sneaked down here without her knowledge hoping you'd give me an audition. I figured that once I got into your company, she might listen to reason."

"Into my company, just like that," Maximov snapped his fingers. "So what if you're Natasha's granddaughter? What makes you think a few ounces of genetic material equips you to dance with the Manhattan Ballet?"

"I'm good," Alysa persisted, "really I am."

"So, if you're so good who have you danced with? I've never heard of you."

"I danced in the corps of the National Ballet of Canada when I was in school in Toronto, and in the Boston Ballet this past year. Also I spent a summer in Stuttgart working under Cranko. I danced in *Carmen* and *Taming of the Shrew*."

"Any solo roles?"

"Not yet, only the corps."

"Only the corps," Maximov raised his eyes to the ceiling. "I need more dancers in my corps de ballet like I need a hole in my head. Only last week I let three girls go, shooed the little chickens out the door and told them to go eat at Balanchine's table if he'd take them." He turned to the receptionist. "If any more granddaughters of Natasha Ladanova walk in here this morning, tell them to walk out. Got that?"

"Yes, Mr. Maximov," the receptionist seemed to diminish, her whole body folding in on itself like a Japanese fan.

"Mr. Maximov," Alysa stood up, "I don't know how to convince you to let me dance for you, but I think if you don't, you're going to be sorry. I've spent the last twelve years studying with my grandmother, learning everything she had to teach and frankly there's no one who could teach me more than she could—not even you." Alysa's eyes flashed and color came to her cheeks. For a moment she was not just pretty but beautiful, a beauty magnified by the fact that she was so obviously unconscious of it. "Suppose, just once, a really fine dancer did walk into your office unannounced and you missed her because you wouldn't even give her a chance to show you what she could do. You'd regret it, Mr. Maximov, believe me."

"Well," Maximov looked at her with renewed interest, "so you're a little fire-eater just like your grandmother used to be. Maybe the strain *does* run true after all." He paused for a moment while Alysa held her breath. "I'm a Russian and we

Russians like deals; if I let you dance for me, what do I get out of it?"

"Technical precision," Alysa said quickly, "dedication, *dusha*."

"*Dusha*, eh? Sounds like Natasha's been teaching you Russian." He looked at his watch and then turned to the receptionist. "How much time do I have before my next appointment?"

"An hour, Mr. Maximov."

Maximov inspected Alysa for a moment with an odd look on his face, one she didn't altogether appreciate. She'd seen that look before, but mainly on the faces of much younger men. "Get out of those heels and into your *pointe* shoes inside of five minutes," he said, "and you're on."

Alysa tried to thank him, but he stopped her. "God knows why I'm doing this. I must be getting soft in the head." He looked at his watch again. "I'll meet you in the small studio after you've had, say, fifteen minutes to warm up. After that you're going to have precisely seven and a half minutes more to show me what you can do, so it better be good."

"Is this the music you intend to dance to?" Maximov turned the record over, inspected the label on the other side, and arched his eyebrows. "*Mohammad Akbar Plays Thumri*. Thumri?"

"It's a raga, Mr. Maximov." Alysa folded her arms across her white chiffon tunic and tried to look confident, feeling anything but. Back in Cambridge it had seemed a good idea to do something original for the audition, but here, face-to-face with Maximov, her self-assurance was shrinking fast.

"What do you think I'm running here?" Maximov waved the record in the air dramatically. "A school for hippie folk dancers? You couldn't audition to Tchaikovsky? Do *Swan Lake* like the last five hundred girls who tried out for this company?"

"Mr. Maximov, if you'd only let me explain."

"So explain."

"This piece is based on an erotic religious poem by an Indian woman who lived in the middle of the fifteenth century." Alysa noticed that at the mention of the word *erotic* a glimmer of interest appeared in Maximov's eyes. Encouraged, she continued. "It's a love song to Shiva, the dancing god, and it describes how Shiva danced the universe into being—the stars are the sparks from the lashing of his hair, the earth the hem of his robe, things like that."

"And you intend to perform ballet to this piece of drivel?"

Alysa bit her lower lip and tried to contain her anger. "Yes, sir."

"And who, may I ask, did the choreography for this whatever you call it? Some Hari Krishna with a prefrontal lobotomy?"

"I did the choreography, Mr. Maximov."

"You what?" Maximov looked at her with amazement tinged with contempt.

"I put the dance together after I saw *Quetzal*. It was such a daring ballet, so wonderful, completely amazing. I thought the man who'd created that would hardly take a second look at a girl who came in with a conventional piece . . . I imagined . . ." Alysa found herself blushing, stuttering, angry, and embarrassed all at the same time, ". . . so many girls audition for you, and I thought if I did something original you might pay more attention to me, and. . . ."

Maximov's face went red, his lips twitched, and suddenly to Alysa's profound humiliation he began to laugh. "*Boje moy!* Will Balanchine tremble when he hears he has such competition. A baby, wet behind the ears no less, and she comes in here with her own ballet. Oh, you're Natasha's granddaughter, no doubt about it."

Alysa snatched the record out of his hand, her eyes filled with angry tears. "I'll go," she said, "okay, I'll just go and you can pretend I was never here."

Maximov reached out and caught her arm. "Such a temper. You should learn that when you want something from someone it pays to be patient." He chucked her under the chin paternally. "Come now; do your little dance for me." Dropping the record lightly on the turntable, he set it in motion.

"You mean you still want me to audition?"

"A written invitation she needs? Quit the yammering and get out there and show me what you can do, that is, if you can do anything. And quit looking like someone just hit you over the head. A pretty girl like you should smile."

Alysa walked to the center of the room, adopted the opening stance, and tried like fury to smile, although in point of fact she felt more like gnashing her teeth. Was Maximov always this hard to work with, or had she just caught him on an off day?

A few seconds later the opening notes of the raga filled the room, swelling until it seemed the very mirrors were vibrating to the undulations of the sitar. Nervously at first, and then with increasing confidence Alysa began to dance. As Shiva, she emerged slowly from the void, one arm stretched forward and upward, the other crooked at the elbow, advancing on *pointe* with rhythmic pauses. Every posture was classical, yet the spirit was alien and exotic. For a moment Alysa was like a flower, graceful, sensual, her legs filled with the tensile strength and tension of stems stretched to the limit. Then suddenly, as the raga built toward a crescendo, she propelled herself across the room, turning in a dizzy series of *pirouettes*. For a minute, two minutes, she danced furiously—Shiva throwing out sun, stars, and planets, sowing the universe with energy the way a gardener sows seeds. At the end she executed a *grand jeté*, and then dropped to one knee, her arms outstretched.

"Is that it?" Maximov said. Alysa nodded, out of breath. Maximov lifted the arm off the record and the raga stoped abruptly. There was an interval of silence. "You know," Maximov said at last, "you have absolutely no future as a choreographer. That whole little bit you just did was a pastiche from start to finish: Massine's *Les Presages*, Fokine's *Firebird*, some *Swan Lake* thrown in for drama. And that *grand allegro* had the Queen of the Wilis written all over it. Oh, the idea was original enough, I suppose, but if you want to carry something like that off you need talent, not just an encyclopedic memory. Your dancing, however, wasn't bad considering the circumstances." Maximov frowned. "I don't really need any new girls in the corps, but who can tell; I might get back to you."

Alysa stood up feeling hurt, disappointed, and insulted. The message was clear: don't call us, we'll call you. Get back to her—fat chance. Walking over to the player, she snatched her record off the turntable, shoved it into its cardboard cover, stuck it under her arm, and headed for the door, head down, not daring to look at him. "I'm sorry I wasted your time," she mumbled as she fled from the studio. In the dressing room she threw the green suit on over her practice tunic, not caring that the result was a lumpy mess.

"You should leave us your phone number," the receptionist called out as Alysa passed through the foyer.

"Forget it," Alysa took one last look at the silver gray walls, the plants, the posters of famous dancers. "You won't need it. I blew the audition."

It was raining outside, the weather had turned cold, and hitchhiking out of New York was no picnic. For over an hour Alysa stood by the highway, thumb outstretched while cars roared past her, the occupants too afraid or to indifferent to do anything more than give her curious stares. Just when hypothermia was about to set in, a trailer truck finally rescued her. The trip north seemed endless despite cups of hot coffee and meaningless conversation with the driver, and the Alysa who finally straggled into Cambridge late that same night was a bedraggled, tired, very subdued version of the optimistic Alysa who had set out in the morning.

Some ten hours later Alysa was curled up in a pile of sheets and blankets trying to sleep off the aftereffects of the trip when Aunt Winn knocked on her bedroom door.

"Alysa."

"Um?" Alysa half opened her eyes and saw Aunt Winn standing in the doorway in a tweed skirt and blue cashmere sweater, a strand of pearls gleaming discreetly at her throat like a chain of soap bubbles. What time was it anyway? On the night table the hands of the small clock she had bought in Stuttgart last summer pointed to ten-fifteen. Good grief, she'd overslept her morning lesson with Nana, missed her first class at BU, and was well on her way to being late for the rehearsal of the Boston Ballet. Leaping out of bed, Alysa tore off her nightgown, and began getting dressed, pulling clothes at random from the pile on the back of the chair; jeans, a plaid shirt—wrinkled but clean—tennis shoes. Socks. She needed socks. Surely they must be somewhere.

"There's a phone call for you," Aunt Winn observed.

"What?" Alysa turned, surprised to see her still standing in the doorway, but Aunt Winn was like that: patient, well organized, and so neat that sometimes Alysa suspected her of re-ironing her clothes before she put them on in the mornings. "A phone call for me?"

"Person to person. From New York."

"New York?" For a moment Alysa drew a complete blank. Whom did she know in New York? Then, suddenly, it hit her. With one tennis shoe on and the other in her hand, she raced out of the room and down the stairs.

"Hello."

"Hello, Alysa Compton?" The voice was familiar, pleasant but a little officious. Alysa clung to the receiver, trying not to hope and doing a poor job of it.

"Yes, it me. Alysa."

"The dancer?"

"Yes."

"Well, Miss Compton, you certainly weren't easy to find. I

349

really wish you hadn't run out yesterday without leaving your phone number. There are twenty-three Comptons in the Boston area and this makes the twelfth I've called this morning, but never mind all that, I've found you and that's what counts. This is Betty Clay from the Manhattan Ballet. Mr. Maximov has asked me to contact you to see if you're still interested in joining the company."

"Interested. Oh, yes. Oh, my God, yes." Alysa jumped up and down, dropped her tennis shoes on the rug, and nearly knocked over a lamp. "I'm interested, yes, thank you."

"Mr. Maximov wanted me to tell you specifically that you'd have to come in at the apprenticeship level, which would mean you'd be taking company classes but not performing until he'd had a chance to observe you more thoroughly. Also, of course, you'd be learning the repertoire, things of that nature."

"I understand." She'd do anything to work with Maximov, sign over all her worldly possessions, stand on one toe until she turned blue. So he'd liked her dancing well enough to ask her to come into the company. The thought made Alysa giddy with happiness. For a second she had an image of herself dancing the Aztec Princess in *Quetzal*. Nothing like a little megalomania to spice up your life. She'd probably be lucky if Maximov let her stand around imitating a piece of scenery.

"Mr. Maximov would like you to come in next Monday morning, it that's not too short notice."

"No, that's fine. I'll be there."

"Say nine o'clock. I'll have your contract typed up and you can sign it, and then go to the company class at nine-thirty."

"Nine o'clock. Yes. Thank you Miss Clay. I'll be there."

Alysa hung up the phone and sat down on the stairs—mainly to keep herself from doing cartwheels across Aunt Winn's oriental carpets. In five, no make that six days she was going to have to drop out of BU, quit the Boston Ballet, pack up all her things, move to New York, and find an apartment, not to mention convincing Aunt Winn and Nana to let her go. Her mind began to buzz with plans and she had an exhilarating sense of forward motion, as if her entire life had suddenly shifted into high gear.

"No, absolutely not. I won't have you going to New York." Aunt Winn's usually placid face was red and she was, of all things, actually pacing the room.

"I agree completely," Natasha said. She lit a cigarette and

leaned back in her chair as if trying to look relaxed, but Alysa could tell from the nervous way she was tapping her foot that she was anything but. Nana was transparent, like a window, and on this particular occasion she was very upset indeed.

"What's so wrong with New York?" Alysa simply couldn't believe it. Here she was, facing the chance of a lifetime, and the two people she loved most in the world were acting as if she'd just threatened to run away and join the marines or something.

"It's dangerous," Natasha said. "Girls your age get mugged all the time."

"Dirty," Aunt Winn chimed in, "unhealthy. Trash all over the streets, derelics, pollution. Not to mention that, as your grandmother just pointed out, th crime rate is incredible. Rapes, murders, horrible things."

"You make it sound like Viet Nam."

"You have a good home here. Friends. A comfortable life. I can't imagine why you'd want to leave all that."

"Aunt Winn," Alysa said, trying her best to be patient. "Let me explain one more time. I want to go to New York to work with Sergei Maximov. Sure, plenty of people do good choreography, but what Maximov does is exactly what I respond to. It's dramatic, not abstract, original, great to watch, fantastic to dance. I know you may not understand all this, but I'm sure Nana does. Maximov could make me into the kind of dancer I want to be. How could you even think of asking me to give up a chance like that?"

Aunt Winn folded her arms across her chest. "He's a terrible man."

"What do you mean terrible?"

"Well, for one thing," Natasha snapped, stubbing out her cigarette abruptly, "he's been married an endless number of times, and for another, in case you aren't aware of the fact, he has a reputation for seducing his dancers."

"Nana, I'm eighteen years old. I'm not a virgin. I can take care of myself."

"You're not a virgin?" Aunt Winn's eyebrows shot up.

"Please Winn," Natasha said, "let me handle this. Now Alysa, I know you can take care of yourself under ordinary circumstances, but Sergei Maximov isn't an ordinary circumstance by any means. I've known him, on a personal basis, and I can tell you that he's a devious, difficult man who will very likely make your life hell."

"Nana he hardly knows I exist. The chances of him noticing me, much less bothering me, are next to nil."

Natasha and Winn exchanged a strange look. "I wouldn't count on that," Natasha said. "After all, you're my granddaughter and I think you can bet that Sergei knows very well who you are."

"Look you two," Alysa gazed from Nana to Aunt Winn, feeling increasingly upset by their resistance, "I don't know what's going on here, but we've always been straight with each other, right? So it there's some real reason you don't want me dancing with the Manhattan Ballet tell me. I mean is Maximov a dope addict? Does he run guns? From my point of view he's a genius. Oh, sure, he's hard as hell to get along with, but a genius nonetheless. And how many geniuses are there in the world anyway? I just can't understand why you've got it in for him."

"We've already told you our objections," Aunt Winn said quickly.

Natasha closed her eyes for a moment and took a deep breath. "Listen, *solnyshko*, if it's genius you want, go back to Cranko. Or if you insist on New York, I can talk to Balanchine."

"Uncle Drew and I would be happy to send you to London," Aunt Winn offered, "Paris, Copenhagen, anywhere you want to go."

"Thanks for the offer, but I'm going to New York," an obstinate expression came over Alysa's face that wasn't lost on either of them.

"Alysa," Aunt Winn said, "you aren't being reasonable."

"I'd say you're the ones who aren't being reasonable. I get the offer of a lifetime and you act as if I'm about to commit armed robbery or something."

"In case you've forgotten, you don't come into your parents' money until you're twenty-one."

"Exactly what does that mean, Aunt Winn?"

Aunt Winn looked embarrassed but she went on. "It means," she said bluntly, "that Uncle Drew and I don't have to support this . . . this folly of yours."

"Are you saying that if I got to New York you won't give me any money to live on?"

"Alysa, please," Natasha leaned forward, her face filled with pain and concern. "Don't be so stubborn. Listen to us. I swear we have your best interests at heart."

"I don't believe this. I don't believe you two are saying this to me." Alysa got up, went over to the fireplace, and stood for a moment with her back to them, resting her forehead against the cool stone of the mantel. When she turned to face them again her mouth was set stubbornly. "I love both of you very much and I hate to go against you, but I want you to know that in two days I'm leaving for New York whether you agree or not. I'm eighteen so there's nothing you can do legally to keep me here, and if you don't want to support me, well then I'll just have to support myself. Plenty of dancers live on practically nothing. I'm sure I can find some roommates, maybe even a part-time job, although that's going to make dancing hundreds of times more difficult. But I'll live; I'll eat. I'll even write you letters—unless you want to turn into a set of Victorians and tell me never to darken your doorstep again—and when Maximov gives me a big part in one of his ballets a couple of years down the road, I'll send you both tickets," her eye brimmed dangerously with tears, but she held them back, "and you can come see me if you want to. But I'm going to New York to work with Maximov—with your blessing or without it."

There was a long silence. Natasha looked at Winn, Winn looked at Natasha, and then both of them looked at Alysa. For a moment something hovered in the air, as if a revelation might take place that would change everything, but the moment passed.

Natasha sighed and shook her head. "Your aunt and uncle and I will have to talk this over." She got up slowly, looking, Alysa thought with a stab of guilt, suddenly older. Alysa had an urge to give in, throw her arms around Nana and tell her that she wouldn't leave after all, but she stubbornly held her peace.

For the next two hours Nana and Aunt Winn sat cloistered in Aunt Winn's bedroom together, their voices rising and falling behind the thick oak door like the humming of bees. Finally Nana left, looking distressed. When Uncle Drew came home, there was another hushed conference, and then he and Aunt Winn suddenly left—no doubt to join Nana for another summit meeting. Alysa, meanwhile, tried to concentrate on her packing. No matter what they decided, she was leaving in less than a week, and it was going to be hard enough even to find all her clothes in that brief a time, much less cram them into two medium-sized suitcases.

"A promise," Winn said firmly, "is a promise."
"Even to a dead woman?"

"Especially to a dead woman."

Natasha shook her head. "I'm not sure of that. In fact, to tell you the truth, I'm not sure of anything." She rolled a half-smoked cigarette between her fingers and contemplated the glowing tip as if lost in thought. "What a mess."

"My sentiments exactly," Drew observed from his seat next to the fireplace. "A first-class mess; a kind of balloon payment in the moral hemisphere, if you see what I mean, come due without warning."

Winn stood up, spots of color burning in her cheeks. "Call it whatever you want, Drew, but all I know is that I shook Anya's hand; I *promised* her Alysa would never know that horrible man was her grandfather. I gave my word."

"Any chance Maximov might have changed?" Drew unbuttoned the jacket of his suit, then buttoned it again as if he had no idea what to do with his hands. "Any chance he's become a reliable human being?"

"In the words of the old Russian proverb," Natasha observed, "Sergei will become reliable when shrimps whistle."

"Well then, we just have to keep her from going to New York," Winn walked from fireplace to window, from window to couch. Natasha's living room suddenly seemed too small to contain her anxiety. "She simply can't have contact with Maximov. For one thing, he's an evil man."

"Winn, you must be one of the last people on earth to see people in terms of good and evil," Natasha stubbed out her cigarette. "Besides, how do you propose we stop her? Lock her in her room? Tie her up? You know how stubborn Alysa is; if we try to keep her from going to New York, she'll go anyway and probably resent us for standing in her way."

"I love that child," Winn said bluntly. "I want her life to be clean and decent and normal, and . . . oh, hell," Winn collapsed into a wing-backed easy chair, "we never should have lied to her in the first place, but now that we've started how do we stop? What will she think of us if we tell her? What if she hates us for it? Maybe I could stand breaking my promise to Anya, but I couldn't stand it if Alysa hated me. I know I'm not her real mother, but I've always thought of her as my, my. . . ." Winn's voice broke and she began to cry, not softly but in big gulping sobs, wiping her eyes roughly with the back of her hand.

Natasha and Drew were stunned. Winn crying; an incredible sight. Natasha thought with a quick pang of guilt how much more upset Winn would be if she ever learned that she, too, was Sergei's daughter. Thank God she'd been able to spare Winn that at least; thank God there were some secrets that could be buried forever.

Drew walked over and put his arm around Winn's shoulder. "There, there, dear," he said, "it'll be okay."

"No," Winn shook her head, "it *won't* be okay. I'm going to lose Alysa's love and respect." She stopped crying, sat up in the chair, and looked at Natasha and Drew with fierce determination. "I'll tell you both something: that child's the center of my life. I may not show it much, but she means everything to me. Don't you people read the papers? Don't you know what kids are doing these days? They're leaving home and never coming back. There's a song the Beatles put out a few years ago; I'm not much of a rock and roll fan, but I noticed that one all right. It's called 'She's Leaving Home.' Well, if Alysa leaves us for good like the girl in that song, I don't know what I'll do. I suppose I'm too sensible to die or waste away or anything like that, but it will hurt a lot and forever—so much I can hardly bear to think about it."

"Wait a minute," Natasha stood up, "let's not panic." She wrinkled her forehead as if following a complicated chain of thoughts. "Let's think this thing through."

"What's to think about?" Winn said grimly, gripping the arms of the chair with both hands. "We have a no-win choice in front of us here, and we might as well face it."

"I'm not so sure of that."

"You mean you have an idea?" Winn's eyes briefly filled with hope again.

"Maybe."

"Well," Drew observed mildly, "don't keep it to yourself, Mother. Pass it around."

"The key to the whole thing is Sergei."

"You mean he's the problem."

"Yes and no. Problem yes, no doubt about it, but at the same time he's the solution."

"Mama," Winn snapped impatiently, "this is no time for Russian mysticism. What do you mean Maximov's the solution?"

"Well, in the first place," Natasha lifted the index finger of her left hand, "if Sergei were going to tell Alysa who he was, then he would have done it when she went down to audition for him. I know how Sergei's mind works; he watched her dance without a word. Given that, I think I can assure you he probably couldn't care less that Alysa's his granddaughter. Sergei has a way of being indifferent to the people's he's

355

related to unless they can help his career. Look at the record: fourteen years and he hasn't made the slightest attempt to contact Alysa. And if you need any more proof there are all those ex-wives of his that he ignores as if they'd never existed. Sentimentality over close relations is hardly Sergei's weak point."

"And in the second place?" Drew prompted.

"Well, in the second place," Natasha added a finger to the series, "there's his temper to consider. Sergei's famous for treating his dancers as if he were Nero and they were a bunch of Christians who'd just refused to sacrifice to Jupiter. He yells at them, criticizes them publicly, drills them until they drop—all in the name of art. Personally, given Alysa's temperament, I can't imagine her taking something like that for more than a week, two weeks at most."

"You mean you think if we let her go to New York, she won't stay?" Winn's voice was level, but there was an eager edge to it that didn't escape Natasha.

"I think there's a decent chance." Natasha shrugged. "Of course I can't guarantee that Sergei's temper will drive Alysa away, but from my own experience I can tell you that it's no easy thing to take."

"If she left his company of her own free will, then we wouldn't have to tell her about him," Drew observed. "Two birds killed with one stone and all that."

"Precisely," Natasha sat down again, picked up her cigarette, and smoked it thoughtfully. "We could risk letting her go to New York; play it by ear, as it were."

"It's an idea," Winn said, "but chancy."

"Maybe we could think of another alternative," Drew suggested, looking uncomfortable, "something that was a sure bet." He smiled wanly at Natasha. "Not that it isn't a good idea, Mother, but we bankers like better odds."

"Fine," Natasha crushed the empty cigarette pack and tossed it at the wastebasket. "Let's try to invent a better plan." And try they did for the next forty-five minutes, always coming back to the decision that the only sensible thing to do was to let Alysa go to New York and hope Sergei would make it so unpleasant that she wouldn't want to stay.

Alysa had been sorting through her things for over an hour, making a pile of clean clothes, semi-clean clothes, and things that absolutely had to be washed. The third pile unfortunately dwarfed the other two, and she surveyed it for a moment with dismay. Most of this stuff would have to be done by hand if she didn't want to run the risk of shrinking half the things she owned to a Munchkin size 3. Going into the bathroom, Alysa extracted one leotard after another from the pile, washed it in warm water, wrung it out, and hung it on one of the glass shower doors to dry. The dripping fabric made patches of color all around the room: blue, red, green, off-white. She was just starting in on a pair of black tights when she heard Uncle Drew and Aunt Winn pulling up in the driveway.

Drying her hands, Alysa hurried downstairs to meet them. They were standing in the hall when she got there, taking off their coats, and Uncle Drew was saying something in a low, comforting voice. Aunt Winn looked up, her eyes red as if she'd been crying. Why did they have to take it this way? Why couldn't they just be sensible. Alysa felt pity, guilt, and then a spark of resentment.

"Well, what's the verdict?"

Uncle Drew cleared his throat. "We just came from your grandmother's and. . . ." He seemed reluctant to continue.

"And what?"

"Well, dear," he said, tugging at his tie the way he always did when he was nervous, "we all love you very much so we've decided that under the circumstances it would be best—"

"For heaven's sake, Drew," Aunt Winn said, "don't beat around the bush. Just tell her the answer is yes."

"Yes?" Alysa could hardly believe it. "You mean you'll give me the money to go to New York?"

"Well, dear," Uncle Drew cleared his throat awkwardly, "we could hardly have you sleeping in Central Park, now could we?"

"We want you to get a safe apartment," Aunt Winn smiled bravely, "a nice place in a good part of town in a building with a doorman and a good security system."

"Oh, Aunt Winn, Uncle Drew, thank you," Alysa ran forward to hug them, relieved beyond words.

"And we want you to take Mary along," Aunt Winn continued, "because you'll need someone to pick up after you, and she has a sister in the Bronx and would like to be there anyway, and oh, my dear," she hugged Alysa, "we'll miss you so much."

"I'll miss you, too."

"Well," Uncle Drew patted first Alysa and then Winn on

the back with awkward affection, "if you two are through being sentimental, why don't we go into the kitchen, make some popcorn, and figure out exactly how much this young lady is going to need to keep herself in yogurt and toe shoes."

On the following Monday at nine in the morning, Alysa appeared at the Fifty-seventh Street office of the Manhattan Ballet, signed her contract, and was officially taken into the company.

20

New York, 1973

"One and two; one and two." Maximov clapped his hands and obediently 103 right legs extended to the front in precise *tendus* and returned to second position—50, 100, 150 times. In the seventy-five feet of mirrors that lined the central rehearsal room of the Manhattan Ballet, 103 dancers moved with the precision of the Rockettes over at Radio City Music Hall, spines erect, eyes straight ahead. "*En arrière*," Sergei called out, and the legs all shot back. "*A la seconde*," and 150 times each leg stretched gracefully to the side.

"No," Sergei yelled over the music, "no, no, no. How many times do I have to tell you. Lightly, lightly." He was dressed all in white this morning: white shoes, white pants, a white silk shirt, white scarf at his throat, but his blue eyes were as sharp and merciless as ever. They saw everything, those eyes: every hesitation, every pause, every failure to do the exercise exactly as it should be done.

Alysa, standing at one of the seven portable barres, couldn't help but think what a great drill sergeant Maximov would have made. For a moment she indulged herself in a vision of him dressed in khaki, yelling "Okay you dogfaces, hit the dirt," and the dancers going down, crawling through the mud, humping under the barbed wire while live machine gun fire crackled over their heads.

Not a bad analogy. If anyone could get you to run through machine gun fire, Maximov could. Over the last year and a half Alysa had gradually come to the conclusion that he didn't teach these company classes so much to train dancers as to retrain them, purge them of any remnants they might have of their own personalities, replace their egos with his own. If you joined the Manhattan Ballet, you soon learned that you didn't work *with* Maximov, you *became* Maximov, and a very small part of Maximov at that—a minor appendage, something he could manipulate or ignore as he chose.

The process might be brutal, but the results were spectacular. Alysa took a deep breath and plunged obediently into the next set of exercises. Despite occasional bursts of rebellion, she knew she had never danced so well in her life, and because Maximov was giving her this, because he was making her into the artist she had always wanted to be, she, like all his dancers, was willing to tolerate nearly anything.

"Lightly, *légèrement*," Maximov's voice had an edge to it that Alysa found ominous. When he started calling out the directions in English *and* French, it was always a sign they were in for trouble. Summoning up her strength, Alysa tried with all her might to move more lightly, but the more she tried the more she felt the heaviness of her body pulling against her. Taking a deep breath, she closed her eyes and tried to forget what still lay ahead this morning: the endless *jetés*, the exhausting series of *grand battements* that always made her heart feel as if it were about to burst in her chest. She thought of light things instead: of clouds, cotton threads, motes of dust dancing in the sunlight.

"Stop, hold it," Maximov raised one hand, and the music stopped instantly. He gazed around the room, his blue eyes flashing with annoyance. "Don't you people know the meaning of the word *lightly?* You want to be circus elephants, you go to Barnum and Bailey. You want to be dancers, you pick up your feet. Is this too much to ask?" He suddenly pointed to Alysa. "You over there, come here."

Alysa's heart sank. Oh, no; not again. For the last six months, ever since he had promoted her from the corps to important supporting roles, Maximov had been alternately ignoring her in class and singling her out for searing public criticism. Today was obviously going to be one of the public days. Trying to look unconcerned, Alysa made her way toward him, fear prickling at the back of her neck. You never knew what was coming with Maximov.

Maximov put his hands on his hips and surveyed her, head to foot. "She's walking like a cow," he announced loudly. Alysa bit her lower lip angrily and tried to move with more grace. "Look at her: a penguin waddling to its feed." Maximov did what she had to admit was a rather brilliant imitation of a penguin: chest thrust out, feet together, arms flapping like tiny useless wings, and the class broke into uncomfortable laughter.

Alysa tried to hold her tongue, and, as usual, failed. "I'm

not like that, Mr. Maximov," she protested. She was hurt, humiliated by the laughter.

Maximov lifted one eyebrow. "Oh, so now we have a new judge of what's going on in this class. So excuse me. In Russia the old dancing masters at the Imperial School would have sent her to Siberia for this, but here in democratic America the student teaches the teacher, yes?" His voice was light, mocking, with a cold undertone. No one laughed this time.

Why was he doing this to her? Alysa stood looking at Maximov dumbfounded, not able to believe anyone could be so cruel on purpose. He had criticized her in front of the whole class on numerous occasions, but today he seemed deliberately trying to make her break down into tears. If he'd changed his mind about having her in the company, why didn't he just dismiss her?

Maximov made a mock bow. "Could the great *prima ballerina assoluta* perhaps honor us with some dancing?"

Alysa set her mouth stubbornly. Now that was just plain nasty. Everyone knew the last real *prima ballerina assoluta* had been Mathilda Kschessinskaya. By calling her that, Maximov was implying she was being an arrogant prima donna, but that wasn't fair. She was more than willing to take instruction, if Maximov could just offer it in a semi-civilized way. Well, she'd be darned if she'd give him the satisfaction of breaking her in public. She'd dance for him, and then she'd... she'd ... walk straight out and maybe not come back at all. She'd had enough of this unreasonable persecution. Let Maximov pick on someone else. There were limits to what a person could take, even from a genius.

"Play the Aztec Princess's *pas seul* from *Quetzal*," Alysa snapped at the startled pianist, knowing she was out of line but frankly no longer caring.

"I ask for exercises and I get a performance," Maximov shrugged with exaggerated indifference, "so go ahead." He waved at the piano. "Give Mademoiselle *Quetzal* if she wants it."

As the pounding Latin rhythms filled the main rehearsal hall, Alysa gritted her teeth and started dancing. Officially, she wasn't even supposed to know the role of the Aztec Princess since Maximov hadn't taught it to her directly, but, like everyone else in the company, she had seen it performed dozens of times. Maximov had often said the trick of the piece was to imagine that you were a snake and a bird both at once. As Alysa plunged into the *pas seul* she concentrated on

361

keeping her legs supple, her body weightless. With secret spite she imagined herself a winged snake flying up in Maximov's face.

The trick worked. Channeled through her body, her anger was suddenly transformed into an elation that lifted her halfway to the ceiling in one effortless movement after another. For five minutes Alysa danced for herself alone, not even caring that Maximov was in the room, virtually oblivious to the fact that the entire class was watching her. When she finally stopped, it was almost shocking—like stepping into cold water.

"Good," Maximov observed, "very good indeed." He was beaming at her, smiling as if his face might break. Alysa stared at him, unable to believe her eyes. "So," he addressed the class, "this morning you got to see how the Aztec Princess *should* be danced. Perhaps the performance could have been more polished, but Pavlova herself couldn't have done it with more feeling." He turned back to Alysa. "Thank you, my dear. You may return to your place."

Alysa walked back to the barre, so confused she could hardly think straight. Evidently she had done something right for once. For the rest of the hour, every time she looked up, Maximov was nodding at her approvingly. It was unnerving really, like having a tiger invite you to lunch.

During the year and a half she had spent in New York, Alysa's life had fallen into a fairly predictable routine: morning classes, afternoon rehearsals, and evening performances with just enough time sandwiched in between for eating, sleeping, and sewing ribbons on her *pointe* shoes. On Mondays, however, the entire company took the day off, and so Sunday nights always had a special holiday quality. After the final performance, the dancers of the Manhattan Ballet habitually threw parties for one another in their tiny apartments, went out together for a late dinner, or took in a midnight movie knowing they could sleep in uninterrupted luxury the next morning. And so it was that on the Sunday after Alysa danced the Aztec Princess in class, she and her friend David Harper were still up at the unlikely hour of one o'clock in the morning, sitting in his apartment on the five-inch piece of foam David called his bed, eating pizza and watching a televised performance of the Kirov Ballet.

David lit another cigarette and let the smoke drift out of his nostrils in a lazy stream past Alysa's face. He was a good dancer but careless about his health in ways Alysa could never understand. Tonight, for example, David had already gone through half a pack of Camels. Alysa coughed discreetly, waved the smoke out of her face, and reminded herself to take more vitamin E when she got back to her apartment.

On David's minuscule television screen two wonderful dancers were doing a *pas de deux* in a papier-mâché garden of Eden, all lovely and light and satirical. Too bad they'd lost the *TV Guide*, or she might have been able to find out who they were, but David wasn't any neater than she was.

"Want a beer?" David inquired, getting to his feet like a basketball player jumping up for a dunk shot.

"Sure." Alysa grinned. Of all the dancers she had met at the Manhattan Ballet, David was the only one who moved like an athlete—offstage only, of course. When he was dancing David was amazingly graceful, able to leap spectacularly and come down on the balls of his feet as lightly as a cat, but there was always something about him that suggested he'd be happier hitting the beach with a surfboard tucked under one arm.

David came back with two beers, and they sat drinking them in companionable silence until the ballet was over and the credits rolled across the screen. Alysa read them to the end, and then, stretching out one bare foot, she tapped the button with her big toe, turning off the set.

"Nice trick," David observed, putting one arm around her and drawing her close. Alysa relaxed and let her head fall on his shoulder, wondering lazily what, if anything, would come next. Four times in the past few months she and David had drifted into making love, and four times Alysa had enjoyed it thoroughly, but for the most part they were just buddies, hanging out together with no expectations of a more serious commitment. Except for the fact that he took her to bed every once in a while, David was like all her friends at the Manhattan Ballet: someone who lived and breathed dancing, someone whom you could talk to about things like inflamed tendons and all-bran diets without putting him to sleep.

His body was warm and smelled pleasantly of hard work. Earlier in the evening they had performed in Maximov's romantic fantasy *Baba Yaga*, an elaborately costumed spectacular that involved most of the company.

"Tired?" David inquired amiably.

"Yeah." Alysa yawned and then grinned. "My legs feel as if someone put them through a wringer."

"How's the ankle?"

"Fine. No problem." She'd twisted her right ankle about a week ago, right in the middle of a performance, not seriously but enough to make her wince. How like David to remember.

"Want a foot rub?"

"Sure." Alysa unfolded her legs and leaned back against the overstuffed corduroy cushions, thinking that she wanted to do something really nice for David—take him to dinner maybe, since he seemed to live on pizza.

As David picked up her foot and began to massage the instep, Alysa felt the muscles gradually loosen and relax. He gently pulled at her toes, popping them; pushed his thumbs carefully into the mound of her heel, squeezed and pulled and kneaded until the tension thinned and disappeared. Placing her right foot gently on the bed, he started in on the left. "You know," he offered suddenly, "people are talking about you and Maximov."

"Huh?" Alysa sat bolt upright, jerking her foot out of his grasp. "What people?"

David put one hand lightly on her arm. "I didn't mean to upset you, but I really thought you should know. Everyone in the company is saying that Maximov has some kind of really weird thing for you."

"That's ridiculous." Alysa snapped her legs under her, her eyes flashing. "You talk as if you think I'm his girlfriend or something. Good grief, I know the man's got a rotten reputation, but he's almost eighty years old, and besides, he doesn't even *like* me. You've seen how he pounces on me in class."

"That's just what makes people talk, the way he singles you out: one minute telling everyone you've got two left feet and the next saying you're Pavlova reincarnate. Frankly, it's not normal."

"Okay, you're right, it is weird." Alysa shrugged helplessly, her irritation dissolving into the kind of muddy confusion that always came over her when she tried to figure out why Maximov paid her so much attention. "I don't understand it either, but David, I swear to you, I don't do anything to provoke it."

"How does he treat you outside of class?"

"That's the really crazy part. He talks to Toni, to Chrissie, to every other dancer in the company, but as far as I can tell, *my* existence ends for him as soon as I take off my *pointe* shoes. When I see Maximov in the street outside the studio, he barely gives me the time of day."

David sucked in his cheeks and contemplated her with a concerned expression. "I don't know, Alysa; I mean, if I were you I don't think I'd let him get away with it."

Alysa spread her hands, for a moment looking exactly like her grandmother. The gesture was pure Russian resignation. "So what am I supposed to do? Quit the company? Let's face it, David: at the Manhattan Ballet, Sergei Maximov is God. He may be on my case, but the fact is I'm a hundred times better a dancer than I was when I first came to New York, maybe a thousand times better."

"I still say he's got it in for you for some reason."

"Sure, but *what* reason?"

"Beats me," David observed. "Your really are one of the most talented dancers in the company. Okay, I'll be honest: you're a little uneven; you have your on days and your off days, but on your off days, as far as I can see, you're not that much worse than anyone else. Still, the way he picks on you all the time does make people talk.

"Let 'em talk," Alysa grabbed the pizza box, opened it, extracted a piece of crust, and began to munch on it stubbornly. "Maximov's the only person who's ever given me what I needed professionally, so if that means putting up with his craziness, then I'll just have to put up with it." She swallowed the last of the crust, rolled off the bed, stood up, put her hands on her hips, and glared around the apartment as if inspecting an invisible ballet company. "*En arrière*," she barked, "lightly, you miserable elephants."

David doubled over with laughter. "That's a wonderful imitation. You look just like him."

"Really?" Alysa collapsed back on the bed.

"Really, especially around the eyes, just like Maximov. It was almost eerie for a moment—like actually having him in the room."

At nine o'clock on Tuesday Alysa was hurrying through the foyer of the Manhattan Ballet when Betty Clay waved her over to the reception desk.

"Mr. M. wants to see you," Betty informed her.

"When?"

"Right now, in his office."

"What does he want?"

Betty shrugged. "How should I know, but if I were you I'd get in there on the double. The last girl who made him wait ended up dancing with a civic ballet in Columbus, Ohio."

Ten seconds later Alysa was standing on the threshold of Maximov's inner sanctum, looking across an expanse of blue carpet at a walnut desk roughly the size of a boxcar. Behind it, dressed in an immaculate blue silk shirt, Maximov sat: spine straight, eyes crackling with energy, sipping tea out of a silver filigree-encased glass.

"You wanted to see me, sir?"

"Ah, yes, Alysa, come in." Maximov put down his tea glass. "Have a seat."

"Thank you." Alysa lowered herself into a chair, her mind racing. There were only two possibilities: either Maximov was going to promote her to principal roles, or he was going to dismiss her from the company. It said a lot about the confusion she had felt working with him that she didn't know which to expect. Was he angry with her? Pleased? She scanned his face, but she might as well have been looking out the window.

Maximov cleared this throat. "For the last few months I've been watching you, and yesterday I finally came to a conclusion."

Dismissal. Alysa could feel it in her bones. She braced herself with the thought that this wasn't the end of the world. Nana could help her get into another company. She could leave New York, go abroad: Paris maybe.

"Well," Maximov leaned forward.

"Well what, sir?"

"Well, you might show some interest. For example, you might be asking 'What kind of conclusion has the old monster come to.'" Alysa felt herself blushing like an idiot. "Ha, you see I know what's said behind my back. Maximov the tyrant, Mr. Monster Maximov. A fool I'm not."

"Mr. Maximov, no one ever—"

"Spare me. So you want to know my conclusion or don't you?"

"Yes," Alysa swallowed hard.

"Why the long look? Smile, my little Alysa. Out of this cloud, as my uncle Gregor used to say, fish are falling." He rubbed his hands together happily. "Do you know the story of Tristan and Iseult?"

Alysa wracked her brains. "You mean Wagner, the opera?"

"No, Maximov, the ballet. Not Massine, not Ashton, not Charrat, but Maximov. I'm doing a new version as a showcase for the talents of one of my most promising dancers. Can you guess which one?"

"Chrissie Peters?"

"Ha, guess again."

"Toni Weld?" Toni had danced the lead in *Baba Yaga* so it was only natural that Maximov would be doing something more with her. But why call Alysa in to tell her Toni was going to be the recipient of a custom-made ballet?

"You're an extraordinarily bad guesser." Maximov suddenly leaned further forward and pointed a finger at Alysa. "I'm creating this ballet for *you*. You'll dance the part of Iseult on the stage of the Met at Lincoln Center."

Alysa looked at him, too stunned to speak. If she'd heard Maximov right, he was creating a major ballet especially for her first principal role.

"So what's wrong? You don't like the idea?"

"Mr. Maximov, thank you. Thank you very much. I don't know what to say." She was thrilled, shy like a child who had just been given an elaborate Christmas present—not to mention stunned that Maximov, who had been harassing her for weeks, had suddenly turned into Santa Claus. "I had no idea you thought my work was that good."

Maximov shrugged. "If I'd let you know you were good, you'd have stopped working, gotten lazy. So now you'll have to rehearse twice as hard, you understand? No late nights, no boyfriends, and you should stop drinking all that Tab. Caffeine isn't good for the body."

"Yes, of course." Wasn't there *anything* Maximov didn't know about her?

Maximov got up, walked around his desk, and confronted her, hands on his hips. "I don't expect you to give just a good performance; I expect you to give a great one. Is that understood?"

"Yes, sir."

"The critics will be sitting out in the audience like cats waiting to pounce on a mouse, but my little Alysa will dance beautifully for them, won't she, like an angel." He caught her under the chin, and tilted her head up so that she was forced to look into his eyes. "This is the kind of opportunity you don't mess up." Swooping down on her suddenly, he gave her a full kiss on the mouth. His lips were smooth, like old leather. Alysa held her breath, trying not to flinch, telling herself he was Russian and Russians kissed each other all the time, trying to convince herself he wasn't coming on to her, that the kiss meant nothing. To her infinite relief, Maximov released her and stepped back. "So we have a bargain?"

"Yes, Mr. Maximov." Putting her hands behind her back

she clenched them together and faced him. Inside she was shaking with elation, confusion, and a hundred other emotions, but she knew better than to let him suspect it.

"Good, so tomorrow instead of going to the company class you come to me in the small studio and I start teaching you and Ron the parts."

"Ron?"

"Ron Dieter, the one who's going to dance Tristan to your Iseult. I'd do it myself, only I'm much much too old." For a moment there was a sort of banked fire in the room, like the ghost of an old lechery, and Alysa got the distinct impression that if all this had been happening ten or fifteen years ago the role of Iseult would have come with many strings indeed. Then, all at once, Maximov was completely businesslike again—discussing schedules and costumes and all the million and one trivial details that went into the production of a new ballet.

Tristan and Iseult took almost twice as long to choreograph as usual, partly because they were interrupted in midstream by Christmas performances of *The Nutcracker* and partly because Maximov was absolutely fanatical about every detail. Later, Alysa looked back on the hours she spent working with him as some of the most creative and the most frustrating of her entire life. Day after day, Maximov led her and Ron through the steps of the new ballet, not actually dancing—he was far too old for that—but commanding, urging, begging, and criticizing until Alysa didn't know whether to scream at him for driving her crazy or thank him for forcing her to do her best.

It soon became clear that the best was all Maximov tolerated. From the first day he made it known that no excuse justified sloppy dancing, not even in rehearsal. The Iseult he had created in his mind was a beautiful creature: tormented, driven by passions she could hardly understand, much less control, and if Alysa ever moved with anything except fire, if her dancing ever lagged or became tepid he was on her in an instant.

"Don't dance like a student," he would yell, striding across the room. "You're married to the king and having an adulterous affair with his best friend; dance as if you knew what that meant! Your husband is about to throw you to the lepers as punishment. Lepers." Maximov would curl his lips, limp, transform himself suddenly into a deformed cripple. "The lepers will touch you here," he poked at her chest, "and here," he poked at her face. Alysa would flinch, and he would step back satisfied. "Good, now dance as if you understand what terror is; as if you know what it's like to care for your lover so much that you'd embrace a leper rather than go back to your husband."

Alysa would dance for him, again and again, until she was sure she was going to crack under the strain, and then, just at the moment when she knew she couldn't take it for another minute, Maximov would suddenly begin to praise her.

"You're a wonderful dancer," he'd say, "one of the best students I've ever had. You'll be another Fonteyn if you stick with it, another Ladanova. That's right, wonderful, perfect. Now do it again for me, Alysa my angel." Glowing with pride Alysa would go on dancing until she was ready to drop with exhaustion.

"You know," she told David one evening over dinner, "I've got this strange feeling about Maximov: when he's yelling at me, I want to take off my *pointe* shoes and pound him with them, and when he's telling me I'm good, I want to fall at his feet and worship him. I seem to love him and hate him at the same time."

"It's the old good-cop-bad-cop routine," David observed, throwing a friendly arm around her shoulder. "First the bad cop threatens you, then the good cop consoles you, and before you know it, you're doing anything they want. If you'd watch more TV you'd know these things."

After that Alysa spoke to several other members of the company and discovered, to her relief, that everyone felt the same about Maximov: he was universally resented and adored, despised and idolized, and no one, not even Betty Clay who had been with him for years, pretended to understand him.

At the end of January, two weeks before *Tristan and Iseult* was scheduled to open, Alysa flew up to Boxton on a Sunday night to celebrate her birthday. It was to be a subdued party with only Uncle Drew, Aunt Winn, and Natasha in attendance, but after weeks of working with Maximov Alysa had an expansive feeling of relaxation and freedom. All day Monday she did trivial things that had nothing to do with ballet, like riding her bicycle through Harvard Square, sharpening her ice skates, even stopping off at Brigham's for a double dip strawberry ice cream cone with chocolate sprinkles.

That night the four of them ate a roast duck dinner, and

afterward they sat around finishing off the birthday cake and drinking coffee until it was time to drive Alysa to the airport to catch the late flight back to New York. The next morning, at nine o'clock sharp, she had another rehearsal of *Tristan and Iseult* and in the evening a performance of *Quetzal* in which she danced the important supporting role of the Flower Maiden to Chrissie Petes's Aztec Princess.

"It sounds perfectly exhausting," Aunt Winn observed, helping herself to another wedge of Alysa's birthday cake, "and I for one will never understand why you put up with it. But, for that matter, I've never understood why anyone would want to be a dancer: all that work, starving yourself, and then when you're thirty-five or so they throw you out, and you've got no profession, no skills of any kind. Not that you'll ever have to worry about money of course, dear," she added quickly, "but I do think you need to look out for yourself."

"Your aunt's still hoping you'll decide to move back to Cambridge and go to work for the Junior League," Natasha smiled at Alysa. "Whereas I think a season with the Royal Ballet would be more in order: guest appearances next fall with Nureyev; a command performance for the Queen; a nice apartment with a view of the Thames instead of a view of thugs mugging innocent pedestrians in Central Park; *pointe* shoes directly from Freed's—the whole works financed by your long-suffering Uncle Drew."

Alysa grinned. "Good try, Nana, but if you're trying to pry me out of New York, the answer is still no. I love it there—not to mention that I'm eating, sleeping, and breathing Iseult these days. The ballet opens in two weeks and you can't believe how far behind we are."

Natasha's smile faded like a color suddenly mixed with water. She bit her lower lip and the delicate skin on her forehead puckered in an anxious frown. "I know Maximov's giving you an amazing chance. We're all thrilled for you, of course, but. . . ."

"But what, Nana?"

"But frankly I'm worried."

"About what?"

"About your mental and physical health, about the way Maximov goads and attacks you all the time. It isn't reasonable, Alysa, it isn't . . . normal. Ballet doesn't need to be that way. It's an art form, not some kind of savage initiation rite." Natasha tapped her foot impatiently on the carpet. "Maximov is a brilliant choreographer, nobody would deny him that, but

370

there's a cruel streak in him, and I think you're getting more than your share of it."

"Nana, you've been worrying about Maximov for years."

"And with reason. Alysa, I know I must sound like a meddling old woman sometimes, but you're a splendid, sensitive dancer with more talent in your big toe than most people have in their whole bodies. I know you. You don't need to be driven; you drive yourself—you have ever since you were a little girl. All it ever took was a word or a look from me, and you'd work until you were blue in the face. The part of Iseult sounds perfectly marvelous, but I don't like the way Maximov is pushing you to master it; I know for a fact that he doesn't have the slightest idea when to stop. The word *enough* isn't in his vocabulary."

"He pushes everyone, Nana."

"But you a little harder than everyone, yes?"

"Well, to be honest, yes. In fact, to be completely honest, I have to confess he's every bit as hard to work with as you say. But I'm tough; I can take it." Alysa shrugged and stirred her coffee. "The real question is, can the other people in the company take it? You're dead right about the word *enough* not being in his vocabulary. Maximov isn't satisfied with anything: he had them cut out my costume five times. *Five* times, can you imagine that? The costume mistress is going out of her mind trying to get the hem to hang the way he wants it. And if he doesn't let up on the stagehands they're probably going to go out on strike. Get this: the set is just a blue backdrop with a blue light. Simple, right. But no, Maximov can't just have any blue. It's got to be the same blue as the blue in the Maryinsky Theatre three thousand years ago."

"Hardly three thousand years." Natasha smiled uncomfortably, as if there were something more on her mind, but whatever it was she apparently decided to let it drop. Taking a cigarette out of a small silver box on the table beside her, she lit it and leaned back in her chair. "I danced on the Maryinsky stage, as you may recall, and I'm not quite a fossil."

"Okay." Alysa grinned. "So maybe not three thousand years, but you get the general drift. A dozen, maybe two dozen times, Maximov makes those poor guys repaint the backdrop, and then he stands around yelling at the people who do the lights until it's a wonder they don't drop one on his head."

"In the banking business," Uncle Drew observed with his

usual mildness, "you couldn't make it with an attitude lik
that."

"You're wrong," Alysa said with a chuckle, "Maximov woul
make a great banker. He'd foreclose on everyone: widows
orphans, lepers—you name it—and then he'd send then
sympathy cards."

"I think," Natasha said abruptly, exchanging a strang
glance with Winn, "we've had quite enough discussion o
Maximov for one evening." She leaned forward, intense
something glittering in her eyes that made Alysa wonder for a
moment what was going on in her mind, but Nana was like
that sometimes: mysteriously preoccupied, as if she were
listening to a radio no one else could hear. "So why don't you
open your presents?"

At the mention of the presents, the whole mood of the
room changed and suddenly things were light and festive
again. The birthday gifts were piled on a side table, swathed
in shiny gold and silver paper, tied with huge ribbons. Alysa
looked at the gaily decorated boxes with gratitude, seeing
Aunt Winn's touch in the wrapping. Nana, if left to her own
devices, was more than likely to present you with a paper bag
full of marvelous, expensive treats, but Aunt Winn alway
fussed over presents as if they were works of art.

"Go on," Natasha urged, looking unaccountably relieved
"have a go at them." She puffed on her cigarette and smiled
and color came back into her cheeks, making her look like
an excited child. Nana always loved presents, even other'
people's.

21

New York, 1974

Alysa was supposed to be eating dinner, but she was far too excited. In less than three hours she would be on the stage at the Met dancing Iseult. Her feet tapped on the parquet floor; her fingers drummed on the tablecloth; her whole body felt like a balloon tugging with anticipation at the ropes that tethered it to the ground. She was going to dance wonderfully, no, more than wonderfully: She was going to give such a performance that even Maximov wouldn't be able to find fault with it.

On the table Mary had left three tiny fillets of sole sautéed in unsalted butter keeping warm on an electric hot tray, a small tossed salad, and a glass of chilled Fumé Blanc, but as far as Alysa was concerned she might as well have left a nice pile of straw and couple of mud pies. Her mind was a hive of last-minute thoughts: of positions practiced until they had almost become instinctive; of her hands draped in a hundred graceful attitudes; of Iseult drinking the love potion; Iseult fatally attracted to Tristan; Iseult making love to her husband's best friend against all common sense, throwing herself into Tristan's arms without a shred of self-preservation.

Alysa put her chin on her hands and mentally ran through the entire love scene step by step—a difficult bit, so erotic it made her skin tingle to think about it, yet at the same time perfectly within the classical tradition. What a combination: sex and ballet, culture and passion. Only Maximov could have carried it off.

The fish grew cold and the butter congealed on the peas. Looking down at her plate, Alysa finally realized she was going to have to eat something. You didn't just step out on a stage and dance a major role fueled by three Tabs and a tablespoon of cottage cheese. Picking up her fork, she stabbed a piece of fish, conveyed it to her mouth, and began to chew dutifully. As she ate, late winter sunlight streamed in through the broad bank of windows in front of her, casting delicate shadows on her arms and hands. When she moved the shadows moved with her, running across her skin, doing the tarantella, the tango, the hokeypokey. Look at things with the right eye and you could see the dance everywhere, as elemental as the air you breathed.

My, wasn't she getting philosophical. Alysa tackled the salad, picking out the things she liked best: mushrooms, cucumbers, cherry tomatoes. Twenty stories below in the park the trees were powdered with fresh snow; beyond them, the towers of the city gleamed in the sunset, their windows molten and flawless. This apartment was an embarrassment really: three bedrooms, a small separate unit for servants, a living room big enough to bowl in—but she had to admit the view was spectacular. By staying here on his infrequent visits to New York, Uncle Drew had somehow managed to turn the whole place into a tax write-off.

Alysa took another forkful of food and tried to concentrate on the sunset, but her mind kept drifting inexorably toward what was to come later in the evening. Suddenly she realized she was beginning to get seriously nervous. The part of Iseult was difficult and taxing, full of complicated sets, *grand jetés* and *cabrioles;* what if she wasn't up to it? Suppose Maximov had made a mistake in trusting her with the role? She attempted to swallow a final bit of fish, but her mouth had suddenly gone dry at the thought of the critics, sitting shoulder to shoulder, picking out every mistake.

This was ridiculous. All dancers were tense before their big debuts; you heard stories constantly of girls who had balked at the last minute and had to be pushed out on stage. Closing her eyes, she took ten deep breaths, exhaling slowly through her mouth as Nana had taught her. Everything would be fine. She could dance the part of Iseult in her sleep. Maximov knew what he was doing. When she opened her eyes again, she felt considerably better, but there was no use taking chances. Pushing aside the rest of the food, she got up, went into the bathroom, and surveyed the contents of the medicine cabinet: buffered aspirin, dental floss, mouthwash, toothpaste, and endless bottles of vitamins—most of them the expensive time release kind—piled helter-skelter like an explosion in a health food store. Alysa contemplated her collection and decided that what the occasion demanded was calcium for her muscles, niacin for her nerves, and a good dose of B complex for general stress.

Uncapping the bottles, she spilled a rainbow of capsules and pills into the palm of her hand, and swallowed them quickly, trying to ignore the slightly bitter aftertaste. Then turning on the shower full force, Alysa stripped off her T-shirt and jeans, and threw them in the hamper. The steam rose in billows out of the pale pink tub, coating the mirror with tiny silver beads of water. Slipping out of her panties she picked up one the large Turkish towels, rubbed a clear space on the glass, and turned in front of it, inspecting her body.

Her skin was smooth and flawless, rosy at her nipples, ivory white everywhere else. The moisture made her dark hair wave slightly, tiny wispy tendrils framing her face, thick tangles falling over her breasts. Alysa gave herself a quick once-over, searching for flaws, wondering how various parts might be improved, examining every curve, not in a vain, self-absorbed way, but rather with the rapid analytical glance of an architect anxious to make sure no major problems are being overlooked at the last minute. Sometimes it seemed to her that she'd been handed the wrong bag of genes. She had her grandmother Anya's fragility without the blondness that would have made it china-doll cute; her Nana's black hair without the curls. Still, if she was stuck with being pixielike rather than devastatingly beautiful like her mother, she at least had the consolation of knowing that she had excellent coordination and enough endurance after all those weeks of practice to dance the socks off any partner Maximov wanted to throw her way. Alysa flexed the muscles in her legs, thinking how much strength it took to make Iseult look light and helpless. Then, reasonably satisfied with herself, she turned away from her reflection and let the steam coat the mirror once more.

Taking a quick shower, she did half an hour of stretching exercises, then hurried into her bedroom and began to throw her gear into her old blue-and-white gym bag. Her costume would be waiting for her at the theater, a soft puff of white chiffon, laced tightly to show her tiny waist, the tights pearl-colored so that when she did her final series of *pirouettes* the audience would see her legs as two delicate lines.

She paused for a moment in passing and contemplated the painting over her bed, an original Degas lavishly framed in gold that she had brought from her room in Cambridge. The painting had been a present from Nana who claimed it had once belonged to some Grand Duke or other back in Russia, and it had belonged to her mother as well. Against a background of what might have been blue velvet, two dancers were lacing their shoes, bent forward with a grace so perfect it was almost unnatural. Alysa rippled the muscles in her abdomen and felt the strength in her thighs. She balanced her own shoes in the palm of her hand for a moment, enjoying the coolness of the satin. She would dance well tonight, make Nana proud of her. She would be like those dancers in the painting: totally concentrated on her art, impervious to fear. Grabbing her coat from the closet, Alysa picked up her gym bag and headed toward the door, whistling the first bars of the overture.

She was already in the hall when the phone rang. For a few seconds she considered ignoring it, but you never knew. It could be anyone: Maximov phoning with last minute instructions, the Met informing her that there'd been a program change, Nana calling to say *merde*. Reluctantly she went back into the apartment and picked up the receiver.

"Hello."

"Hello, Alysa, this is Betty Clay. Thank God I caught you before you left. Can you come by the studio for a minute on your way to Lincoln Center? We have a little last minute problem."

"What sort of problem?" Alysa imagined a million things: strikes, floods, Ron being run over by the IRT. Well, if Ron couldn't make it, she'd perform the ballet with his understudy. Unless Maximov himself nixed it, this show was definitely going on.

"Mr. Maximov has changed your costume again."

"You've *got* to be kidding." She was relieved and mildly annoyed at the same time. There probably wasn't another dancer in New York who had had to stand through so many fittings and refittings. Still, when you work with Maximov you learned to expect things like this. At least it was only an inconvenience, not a real disaster.

Betty sighed. "I wish I were kidding, but no such luck. He just called to tell us he wants the shoulder straps narrowed by half an inch and another layer added to the skirt. Janet's in a complete panic, of course." Janet Patterson was the Manhattan Ballet's long-suffering costume mistress. "She wants you to come over to the studio for a quick alteration."

"Why can't we do it at Lincoln Center?"

"She says that if you make her go over there and stitch

you together at the last minute, she'll throw herself out a window. She's joking of course. Actually it's a good idea for her to be near her trusty Singer in case she runs into any problems. I remember a time, years ago, when Maximov pulled this same trick just before Carmen LaGuerra was supposed to dance Maria in *Cortez*. Janet did an alteration at the last minute, while LaGuerra was standing in the wings waiting for her cue, and before the ballet was over the whole costume had started to come apart. Mr. M. was absolutely furious."

"Say no more," Alysa looked at her watch noting that it was only five-forty-five. "I'll be right over."

"Hurry up," Betty urged, "because Janet's standing right here with the pins in her mouth, and if you don't make it in fifteen minutes she'll probably swallow them."

Half an hour later Alysa stood barefoot among a litter of thread and spools as Janet knelt at her feet, frantically basting the hem of her skirt. Janet took another stitch in the chiffon, bit off the thread between her front teeth, and stepped back to contemplate the results. She was a large women in her early fifties, wide-hipped, large-breasted, with a talent for picking up a piece of material, draping it over a dancer and miraculously transforming it into a costume on the spot—a trick she claimed to have learned from the late Coco Chanel. Usually she weathered Maximov's last-minute changes with aplomb, but tonight she looked harried. Inspecting the effect created by the extra layer in Alysa's skirt, Janet sighed and shook her head. "Well, Maximov probably won't be satisfied, but that's as good as I can do on half an hour's notice. Now get out of that thing and let me run it up on the machine before I go completely bonkers."

Alysa obediently slipped the costume over her head, and handed it to Janet. "What time is it?"

"Six-twenty. Don't stand there watching me like that or I'm going to sew the bottom of your skirt together. Get dressed, go sit in the foyer and talk to Betty, and I'll bring you this thing all wrapped up in a nice plastic bag like a baby in a blanket."

Alysa pulled on her jeans and fumbled around under bolts of white chiffon for her sweater. "You know, Janet, you're a real trouper to do all this at the last minute."

"Trouper, ha. Do you have any idea what Maximov would do to me if I said it was too late to make any more changes?"

Janet blinked red-rimmed eyes and pushed a strand of gray hair off her forehead. "Now scram."

Alysa wandered into the foyer. Betty was sitting at the receptionist's desk reading a copy of *Tinker, Tailor, Soldier, Spy*. "How's it going?" she asked. "Janet got things whipped into shape?"

"More or less," Alysa sat down on one of the benches. "Don't you ever go home?"

"Not on opening nights." Betty went back to her book, and Alysa sat for several minutes, bored and impatient, wishing Janet would hurry up and finish the costume so she could get over to Lincoln Center and start her warm-up. The seconds ticked by. Alysa crossed her legs, uncrossed them, then crossed them again. It was odd sitting here like a new girl waiting for an audition. She remembered the first time she'd come into the office, how impressed she'd been by all the famous dancers on the walls.

Pavlova. Now there was a dancer. In the poster, Pavlova was bent over her left leg, her skirt a haze of white; feathers bordered the low cut back of her costume and tiny white wings fluttered from the center of her back. A pretty outfit, Alysa thought, but a little corny. She wondered what Janet would have come up with if she'd been asked to invent something for Pavlova. Next to Pavlova hung the poster of Diaghilev, solid and slightly pudgy, a streak of gray hair mixed in with the black like a bolt of lightning. Nijinsky came next, costumed for *Le Spectre de la Rose*, looking coquettish and almost feminine but with legs like oak trees. On the opposite wall Carmen LeGuerra stood with her hands on her hips, dressed in pagan splendor as the Aztec Princess; then Lydia Winters, the ice maiden of the 1940s, so cold and perfect you'd swear her arms were made of alabaster. Alysa was just speculating on what the attraction had been between Winters and Maximov when Janet appeared with the Iseult costume.

"Here it is," Janet announced breathlessly, thrusting the plastic bag into Alysa's arms, "now for goodness sake don't wrinkle it. I'll be at Lincoln Center by seven to help you get dressed, but I want you to hand-carry this thing there yourself in case I get caught in traffic or something. I have nightmares of you going on stage as Iseult wearing your warm-up clothes."

Alysa swore a solemn oath not to let the costume come to harm, and then bundling herself into her coat, she balanced the bag on her arm and ran for the elevator catching it just as the doors were closing. Inside a tall man with a cigar was puffing away complacently. Alysa vaguely recognized him as one of the insurance agents who occupied the top floor.

"Rotten weather out," the man observed pleasantly. "Sleeting like crazy."

Alysa tried not to gag on the cigar smoke. Just what she needed before a performance. "Really?" she looked at her watch, trying to calculate how long it was going to take to get to Lincoln Center. "How's the traffic?"

"Snarled all to hell," the man said as the elevator doors opened. He stepped out, leaving his cigar smoke behind him. Bad weather and traffic; oh, great. Alysa wondered apprehensively if she'd be able to get a cab.

Outside the sleet had stopped, but the pavement was slippery. On the other side of the street a cab was discharging two passengers. "Taxi!" Alysa yelled, but the driver didn't appear to hear her. Given the fact that the light was about to change any second, there was only one alternative. Tucking the costume under her arm, Alysa ran for it. "Taxi!" she yelled, gesturing with her free hand, "Taxi!"

Suddenly her feet flew out from under her and she fell sprawling. Alysa lay dazed for a moment, trying to catch her breath. Fortunately it didn't seem to have been a bad fall although the palm of her hand felt skinned. Picking herself up, she quickly examined the Iseult costume and was relieved to see it was still in one piece. No harm done. The cab was gone, of course, but there'd be others along in a minute.

Alysa took a step back onto the curb and as she did so pain coursed through her right ankle. She put her foot down again, gingerly. More pain. Cold horror enveloped her. This was impossible, ridiculous. She couldn't have sprained her ankle, not tonight of all nights. The ankle throbbed insistently as if a small animal were beginning to gnaw away inside her boot. Alysa stubbornly shifted her weight to the other foot. Preposterous. There was nothing wrong with her, nothing at all. An empty cab rounded the corner suddenly, and she waved it down. Gritting her teeth, she walked over and climbed inside.

Lincoln Center was already beginning to fill up with its usual evening crowd, but Alysa had other concerns. Dumping another Coke down the drain, she added the ice to the plastic bag that surrounded her right ankle. It was already seven o'clock and she should have been in the upstairs studio doing her warm-up exercises; instead, she was locked in her dressing room, hunched over her foot trying to convince herself that the injury to her ankle was only minor. Beneath the plastic bag, her skin was pale blue, swollen slightly, as if someone had added a small spongy knob to the bone. Thank heavens it wasn't one of those third-degree sprains, the kind where your whole foot blew up like a balloon and you were on crutches for weeks. She'd had an injury like that once, the first month she was in Canada, in fact that was probably why her right ankle was weak. A podiatrist had told her that once you stretched ligaments they were stretched for good, like old rubber bands gone slack.

What a morbid thought. Alysa shook her head as if trying to dislodge her anxiety. This was a small sprain, insignificant. All she had to do was bring down the swelling a little, tape everything firmly in place, and she'd be able to dance just fine. The trick with injuries was not to give them too much attention. Lifting her head, Alysa looked around the room, deliberately searching for something else to focus on. The flowers, for instance. There were tons of them, a whole jungle. She was touched so many people had thought of her. Bunches of carnations and tulips, gifts from members of the company, poked out of jars, cups, and empty Tab cans; there were half a dozen calla lilies from Toni and Chrissie, a large bunch of purple and yellow iris from Uncle Drew and Aunt Winn, violets from David, a spray of pink rosebuds from Nana. Alysa took a deep breath and inhaled the heady odor of twenty different scents.

Her ankle was throbbing. Alysa tried to ignore it, but the pain rang insistently like a telephone that no one was willing to answer. It was a bad sprain.

No, it wasn't. It simply couldn't be, because if it was, that meant she wasn't making her debut tonight. Alysa contemplated her ankle grimly. She was definitely dancing Iseult, definitely, absolutely, without question. *But suppose she couldn't. Suppose she got out there on stage and limped through the ballet like a lame horse?* The question needled away at the back of her mind. If there was any doubt, she was bound by tradition and common sense to inform someone immediately so her understudy could be called. Understudy. That was a laugh. Chrissie Peters, who had also learned the part of

Iseult, could hardly be considered *under* anyone. She was the best-known dancer in the company. Alysa liked Chrissie, but Chrissie didn't need a chance like this. Maximov's new ballet had been designed for her, Alysa.

At the thought of Maximov, Alysa's courage began to falter. If she did poorly in this ballet he'd... well, who knew what Maximov would do, but you could bet it wouldn't be pleasant. Leaning down, Alysa removed the plastic bag and poked at her ankle trying to will it to be okay. Somewhere far away a violin played a fragment of a waltz. There was a knock at the door. Alysa jumped, thinking it might be Maximov.

"Alysa." Ron's voice. "Have you got your makeup on yet?"

"No."

"Well get at it," Ron sounded anxious. "We go on stage in less than an hour."

Alysa said something—she wasn't sure what—that made him go away. Possibly she promised to put on her makeup. She could hear the whole orchestra now, tuning up—pure cacophony. Shoving her fingers in her ears she tried to consider what her options were: she could dance the ballet in her present condition and take the chance her ankle would hold up; she could confess that she'd sprained it and let Chrissie take over. She could. . . .

She tried to think of other alternatives, but nothing even remotely satisfactory presented itself. What an idiot she'd been. *Why* had she run for that cab? She'd known the street was icy. In her imagination Alysa went back in time, waited for the light, and crossed the street all over again at a leisurely pace, feet planted firmly on the ground.

There was another knock at the door. "Who is it?"

"Delivery for Miss Compton." Alysa quickly shoved the plastic bag of ice out of sight, limped over to the door and unlocked it. A boy in a blue uniform was standing in the hall with a big pink box in his arms. She stared at him blankly. "Well," he said impatiently, "do you want this or don't you, assuming you're Miss Compton, that is?"

"Sure, okay, yes, sorry." She fumbled in her pocket, found a couple of dollars, and shoved them in his hand. The boy beamed.

"Good luck, lady."

"It's bad luck to wish a dancer good luck before a performance," she snapped, immediately regretting the tone of her voice. The boy's smile crumpled, and he turned on his heels and stomped off without another word.

Sitting down on the couch, Alysa retrieved the ice bag, elevated her ankle on a pillow, and tried to convince herself that everything looked a lot better than it had ten minutes ago. The box was big and unwieldly, tied with ribbons of the heavy, satin variety. Alysa pulled idly at the end of one of the ribbons, wondering what in the world was inside. Suddenly, as if in response to some invisible cue, the box began to tremble. Startled, she dropped it on the floor where it continued to vibrate. What the hell was it? A bomb? Oh, great, just what she needed—the final touch. The box jumped and twitched, but gave no signs of exploding. Cautiously, Alysa bent over, and lifted off the top. Inside, a dozen battery-powered plastic frogs were leaping over each other, kicking and flopping ridiculously.

Alysa laughed despite herself. No question who this was from. When the frogs stopped hopping, she pushed them aside and found a card in a gold and pink envelope with a frog doing a *grand jeté* drawn on the flap.

Dear Alysa,

the card read,

> *Tonight you go from polliwog to frog. Leap into the future, and don't forget to smile at the critics. Merde, darling.*
> *Love, Nana.*

Alysa read the card and then read it again. Everything about it reminded her of her grandmother. She imagined Nana sitting proudly in the audience, waiting for the curtain to go up. In some ways this was as much Nana's debut as it was hers. She was Nana's last and best student. Nana had fed her on stories of dancers who performed despite broken ribs and dislocated shoulders. She had told Alysa of Tatiana's incredible struggle back from polio to *pointe*. *Dance through the pain* Nana had always said. But how much pain was too much? How did you decide when you were injured so seriously that if you went on with the show you'd fail the very people who were depending on you?

Alysa picked up one of the frogs, a ridiculous hunk of rubber and plastic, and balanced it on the palm of her hand.

The present was a message of love, a token of faith. Alysa thought of the Degas on the wall of her bedroom, of the family tradition—her grandmother dancing with the Imperial Ballet in St. Petersburg, her mother working with Balanchine—well over half a century of dancers dedicated to their art. What part of that tradition was she, Alysa? A little wimp who gave up as soon as the going got tough? What would Nana do if she'd just sprained her ankle hours before her debut? She'd dance, that's what she'd do. No doubt about it: if she could still walk, she'd dance.

Alysa sat for a long time, torn between her feelings for her grandmother and her own doubts. Could she go on tonight or couldn't she? Could she dance Iseult the way Iseult was meant to be danced, or would her ankle give out in the middle of the ballet? Finally she realized there was no way of telling in advance. She could walk on her foot—she'd already tried that—and when it was taped, she could no doubt dance on it provided she ignored the pain. There was even a good, no, make that an excellent, chance that no one would even know she was injured. In an odd way being hurt might even be an advantage of sorts. Not that she would have ever wished it on herself, but still, Iseult was a character who lived on the edge, another of those great suffering heroines ballet was so fond of. If Alysa could take some of the pain and channel it into her dancing she'd be able to give a spectacular performance, although the strain might put her out of commission for the rest of the season. On the other hand . . . on the other hand was a long list of very unpleasant possibilities.

Alysa vacillated for another minute or two, then came to a decision: Chrissie Peters wasn't going to get that last minute phone call. Maximov had created a great ballet, a showcase for her talents, and she was going to dance it tonight on the stage of the Metropolitan Opera House come hell or high water, ankle or no ankle.

Setting her mouth stubbornly, Alysa walked over to the dressing table, pulled out a roll of tape, and began to reinforce her ankle, compressing the swelling into a smooth, hard surface that wouldn't show through her tights. Inspecting the results, she frowned, added another strip of tape, then got up and took a few test steps across the room. Good, excellent. Now that she actually had it wrapped, the pain was minimal. Putting on her toe shoes she cautiously rose on *pointe*. Hardly a twinge. She could have wept with relief.

Sitting down in front of the mirror, she began to apply her

makeup, drawing dark lines on her lids, rouging her lips and cheeks. Opening a box of powder, she spread it determinedly on her forehead. She'd dance for Nana tonight. For Nana whom she loved.

Ten minutes later, Alysa was in the upstairs studio, doing her warm-up exercises without a sign that she was injured, and forty-five minutes later she was in her costume and ready to dance.

On stage at the Met the soft black practice floor had been removed, exposing wooden boards dusted with rosin to prevent the dancers from slipping. Gripping the portable barre, Alysa did a final series of slow *pliés*, trying to make her mind a perfect blank. Every cell of her body was now Iseult—beautiful, fragile Iseult—who had, above all else, two strong undamaged ankles. It was a difficut illusion to maintain but Alysa was an expert at maintaining illusions. Put your imagination in the right place, Nana had always said, and you could dance through anything. Alysa bent her knees, flexed her arms; falling into her body, she mindlessly took refuge in muscle, skin, bone, in all the healthy, unthinking parts of herself.

On all sides the chaos grew as stagehands ran back and forth on frantic last-minute errands. Beyond the heavy curtain the audience was filling the theater. A winch creaked and the last of the extra flats swung out of the way, leaving the stage almost as bare as if a rehearsal were in progress instead of a performance. Someone threw a blue gel over one of the spots and everything was suddenly tinged with fake moonlight. Blue backdrop, blue shadows: the color gave Alysa an eerie feeling. She stretched over her right leg, concentrating on a small muscle at the back of her knee. When she lifted her head, the stagehands had disappaered. In the opposite wing, Ron saw her looking his way and smiled encouragingly.

The curtain started to rise, and Alysa realized with a start that the overture must have been played through without her hearing a note of it. All around her the bare stage was emerging out of the shadows, as stark and clean as an empty box. Alysa moved into position, trying not to pay any attention to the sudden sinking sensation in the pit of her stomach. She took a few deep breaths and forced herself to pretend she was back in Nana's studio in Cambridge. She had no worries, no injuries, no problems of any kind. In a minute she would dance for a few old friends—a little piece, nothing very important.

The ploy worked. Music swept out from the orchestra pit, weaving a spell around her. Alysa straightened her spine and opened her eyes. She felt such power now, as if all the tendons in her body were vibrating in harmony. The spotlight caught her, trapping her in a circle of rose and gold. Ron appeared on the other side of the stage, Tristan waiting for his Iseult. Taking another deep breath, Alysa began to dance.

She had not taken more than five steps when she felt the first twinge of pain—faint, then suddenly more intense. Alysa's smile never wavered and she danced on without missing a beat. She'd expected her ankle to hurt as soon as she started putting pressure on it. Pushing the pain to one side of her mind, she performed a perfect *arabesque*, holding it without a quaver. The injured ankle throbbed uncomfortably, then began to go numb. Relieved, Alysa realized there was a good chance she'd be able to forget about it—at least for the duration of the ballet.

And forget it she did for five, ten, fifteen minutes. The music drifted lightly from bar to bar, every note familiar and reassuring. For months she had practiced to that music, danced to it for hours at a time, absorbed it so completely that at night when she slept, it had played on in her dreams. Concentrating on the sweep and thrust of her legs, Alysa dipped toward Ron: tempted, unsure at first, skittish as a fawn. Then as Iseult's passion grew, her movements became stronger, full of desire and shame, plunging toward full-blown obsession.

The love potion *pas de deux* was sizzling, so intense it practically made the hair stand up on her arms. She could feel the audience watching with rapt attention, the silent energy streaming toward her from the blackness of the auditorium. Ron felt it, too. For a timeless space the two of them danced in perfect harmony, bringing all the passion of Tristan and Iseult to life.

Then suddenly, without warning, it happened: in the middle of an ordinary *jeté*, Alysa's ankle gave way and she stumbled. The pain was searing, so intense she nearly cried out. Collecting her wits, she immediately recovered her balance and went on dancing, but something was terribly wrong. Every time she put pressure on her right foot, fire shot up her leg.

"What's the matter?" Ron whispered.

"Nothing." An outright lie. The ankle was pure torture. Alysa gazed out at the sea of white faces, tilted toward her expectantly. It should have been comforting to know that Nana and Aunt Winn were out there somewhere, but it wasn't. Biting her lips to keep from crying out, Alysa moved toward Ron, trying desperately not to favor her right foot. There were about ten more minutes of the ballet left and she had to get through them somehow. With a tremendous effort of will, she forced herself to continue dancing, but the grace was gone. The pain was a tyrant, demanding her attention: a hot poker, a handful of pins stuck in her skin, a searing all-encompassing cuff of agony.

Gritting her teeth, Alysa plunged in fiercely, never missing a step, forcing her injured foot into the familiar positions, knowing even as she did so that at best she was performing like a top-notch student instead of a professional dancer: mechanically, without feeling.

"Lean on me more," Ron whispered. Alysa gratefully transferred some of her weight to him, and as she did so she looked over his shoulder into the wings and saw Maximov watching her, his face rigid with anger.

"Mama, are you okay?" Winn whispered. Natasha was leaning forward, gripping the edge of her seat as if she were having some kind of attack. Being of a practical nature, Winn immediately ran through everything she knew about CPR, realizing as she did so that she was being ridiculous. That was what years of fund-raising for the Red Cross did for you, made you prepared to give mouth to mouth resuscitation on the slightest notice. Mama had a constitution of iron and the idea that the excitement of Alysa's debut was proving too much for her was ridiculous. Only last fall Winn had had to stand under a sugar maple and yell at her to come down before she broke a leg. There she was, seventy-nine, wedged in the crotch pruning away dead branches like a teenager. Still, she didn't look good at the present moment, not good at all. Her face was distinctly pale and she was biting her lower lip the way she always did when she was upset about something. "Mama," Winn raised her voice just loud enough so Natasha could hear her but not loud enough to disturb anyone else. She always thought people who talked in the movies and symphonies took half the pleasure away, but this was something of an emergency. "Mama." It was a little maddening the way Natasha didn't seem to hear her.

"Boje moy!"

"Mama, what's wrong?" Winn hadn't heard her mother swear in Russian in years, and the words sent a chill down her spine.

"It's Alysa. Can't you see?"

Winn looked at the stage, at Alysa jumping around the way dancers always jumped around, looking pretty in her dress and white stockings. Ballet had always secretly bored Winn—a terrible thing to admit when your own mother was one of the most famous dancers in the world. She enjoyed the music of course, provided it was something classical, but visually she preferred opera, especially the kind of spectacles they put on in Italy, with elaborate sets and real horses and camels on the stage for the triumphal march from *Aida*. Possibly she would have liked ballet better if her whole family hadn't been so involved in it, but as things stood she always managed to feel a little left out and mildly untalented every time Mama took her to a performance.

Winn inspected the stage, trying to summon up what little she had permitted herself to know about technique. As far as she could tell, things were going along pretty much as usual except, well, now that you mentioned it, Alysa *did* look a little wobbly. The music changed suddenly and Alysa seemed to hesitate as if favoring her right foot, recovering so quickly Winn would never have noticed it if she hadn't been looking. Well what was so terrible about that? If Winn had had to go dancing around on her toes, she'd have hesitated, too. It must be confusing trying to remember all those steps. The story was pleasant, even reasonably intelligent, and the boy Alysa was dancing with was as handsome as they came.

"She looks okay to me, Mama."

"She's injured, I can tell."

"Poppycock," Winn said bluntly, "she doesn't look the slightest bit injured."

"That's just the problem. She's dancing terribly, like a student, which means there's something wrong with her, but she's so good neither you nor anyone else can tell from this distance that she's in pain. The critics are going to eat her alive." Natasha bit her lower lip and leaned farther forward, her face pale and troubled. Her body tensed suddenly and her fingers twitched. Winn looked down and saw that her mother's feet were making small, covert movements, as if she were desperately trying to dance Alysa's part for her.

*   *   *

The ballet ended with two lukewarm curtain calls followed by a spate of random clapping as if the audience didn't know whether to go on applauding or get up and go out to the lobby for a smoke. Alysa stood bravely next to Ron, bowing and smiling as the curtain opened, closed, opened, and closed again for the last time. The response was terrible. Maximov's new ballet—his first in three years—should have gotten a dozen curtain calls. People should have been leaping to their feet, pelting the stage with flowers, yelling themselves hoarse.

Gold-colored velvet dropped with finality, raising a small cloud of dust. The crew killed the lights and stagehands swarmed out to set up the scenery for the next ballet. "I'm sorry," Alysa turned to Ron, exhausted, in pain, on the verge of tears. "I blew it for both of us."

"Don't be ridiculous," Ron wiped the sweat off his forehead and patted her arm sympathetically. "You did a great job under the circumstances. You're hurt; it could happen to anyone."

Toni Weld appeared from the wings carrying Alysa's robe. Gently she wrapped it around Alysa's shoulders. "How's the ankle?" Her voice was concerned, sympathetic.

"Not so great."

"We were all rooting for you back there when we saw you were in trouble." As Alysa limped off the stage, the same scene was repeated over and over. People came up to her, asked anxiously how she was, offered their support. Alysa had never realized how many friends she had in the company. There wasn't a word of blame, not a single insinuation that she shouldn't have gone on. For almost five minutes she felt completely loved and protected, as if the entire company were an extended family that looked after its own, and then she saw Maximov and it all fell apart.

He was waiting for her in her dressing room, pacing between the mirror and the coatrack, his finely chiseled Russian face full of anger—not the anger he showed when one of his dancers missed a step or showed up five minutes late for a rehearsal, but something dark and frightening she'd never seen before.

"What the hell happened out there?" he barked as soon as he caught sight of her. "What were you trying to do, sabotage my ballet? My God, I give you the role of Iseult—the best role I've created in the past twenty years—and you dance it as if you were doing a recital for some second-rate school in Iowa."

"Mr. Maximov, please. . . ." She began to explain about her ankle, intending to admit that she'd been at fault and beg his pardon, but he rolled over her, cutting her off, jabbing his forefinger at her like a drill, accusing, blaming, yelling in a voice that turned her knees to water and made her almost physically ill. Talk to him? She would have had as much chance talking to a volcano or a hurricane.

"Do you know what they'd do to you if you were dancing with the Kirov and you pulled a trick like that?" Maximov stormed across the room and Alysa backed away, afraid for a moment he might actually strike her. "They'd send you to Siberia to teach *pliés* to Aleuts, that's what they'd do." He spied something on her dressing table and pounced on it like a tiger, scattering lipsticks and eye pencils in every direction. "What's this?" It was a small plastic pillbox full of vitamins. Maximov jerked open the lid, spilling the tablets out on the table. "Drugs." He picked up a handful of pills and threw them angrily on the floor. "So a drug addict I have in my company? So that's what made you dance like a sick cow out there?" He grabbed Alysa's arm and spun her around to face him; there was contempt in his voice. "What kind of synthetic horrors did you take before you came in here this evening?"

"Nothing," she was stunned by the accusation. He must be out of his mind. "I swear, I've never touched drugs in my life. I was injured, Mr. Maximov." She gestured at her right foot. "I sprained my ankle before the performance but it didn't seem like too bad a sprain and—"

"You sprained your ankle *before* the performance? You deliberately danced my ballet with an injury, *my* ballet?"

"I thought I could get through it."

"You thought? A dancer doesn't think." He dropped her arm contemptuously. "You're nothing, do you understand that? Nothing. You want it in Russian—*nechevo*—void, emptiness. You're just a vehicle for my art, my beautiful art that you've desecrated. *I* arrange you; *I* give you form; *I* decide when you go on and when you don't go on. When you're injured you inform me and *I* decide if your understudy is to take over."

"I'm sorry." He was right; she'd made a terrible mistake. She should have let Chrissie go on in her place. Alysa tried to swallow but her throat was tight with remorse and shame.

"Sorry!" Maximov's fist came down on the dressing table,

sending the rest of the pills scudding in all directions. "An apology is supposed to make things fine, is that it? I'm talking to an idiot, yes?"

"Mr. Maximov, I did my best."

"Your best was rotten; it stank this best of yours. With my beautiful Iseult I could have had immortality and instead tomorrow I get what? Three paragraphs in the *Times* about how old man Maximov has lost his touch." He stabbed his finger at her again as if impaling her on it. "You're just like your father; I should have known better. It's in the blood, throwing away your talent like a monkey throws away a diamond, making me into a fool. You're just like him . . ."

"Mr. Maximov, please, I don't understand. What does my father have to do with this?" Alysa was bewildered. He was talking like a crazy man. He must have gone off the deep end, had a stroke or something. He wasn't making sense. For the first time she wondered if maybe she should call for help.

". . . disobedient, blind, headstrong," the words poured out of Maximov's mouth, a Niagara of invective, "ungrateful, stubborn, irresponsible—well, I won't *have* it, do you understand? I won't go through that again."

"What are you talking about, Mr. Maximov?"

"About my son, Mihail, sent by all the devils from hell to torment me in my youth, and about you, sent by the same devils to be the torment of my old age. A great sense of humor God has." Maximov shook his fist at the ceiling. "On Him I spit. Job I'm not."

Alysa stared at Maximov, her mind skipping back and forth like a needle on a badly scratched record. If Maximov's son was her father, that made Maximov her grandfather, but that was insane, impossible. She must not have heard him right.

"Did you say my father was your son?"

"Of course, you little idiot. Did you think it was your talent alone that got you out there on that stage tonight to ruin me?"

For a few seconds she couldn't accept the truth. Then something cold hit her like a fist in the pit of her stomach, and all at once everything fell into place. She remembered Maximov's weird habit of singling her out from the other dancers; his excessive criticism; his sudden, embarrassing bursts of praise. It was clear now why Nana and Aunt Winn had fought against her going to New York; they knew that ultimately she'd discover the family secret. The thought that Nana and Aunt Winn had lied to her hurt badly. She felt betrayed: deeply, completely, as if her entire past, or what she had always thought was her past, had been a myth, a bedtime story composed to lull an irritable child. All of them, all these years, keeping the truth from her—why in God's name?

Maximov put his face in his hands and his shoulders shook. Maybe he was crying. She couldn't tell; she was too stunned to care. When he looked up again, his face was a cold blank.

"You'll leave, now, tonight."

"What?" The shock of finding out that he was her grandfather made her want to sit down. She was disoriented, as if she'd suddenly been picked up bodily and dropped into a foreign country.

"I'm officially dismissing you from the company for dancing under the influence of drugs."

Alysa's sense of self-preservation snapped her to attention. He had to be kidding. One mention of drugs in connection with her name, and she'd never dance professionally again. "You can't be serious. I had a sprained ankle. Didn't you understand? My ankle was sprained."

"Shut up. Who do you think you are, Pavlova?" His voice was cold as he counted off each syllable. "Do you know how many dancers would give their right arms for a role like the one you screwed up tonight? Life is a nasty business, my dear. Drugs, ankles—it all comes to the same thing in the end. You ruined my ballet and the critics are going to tear it apart. Unfortunately your injury wasn't obvious so we must come up with a more convincing explanation. I have a reputation to preserve. You hurt my career, and in self-defense I hurt yours, only I'm far more powerful you see. A poor trade from your viewpoint, but you should have thought of that earlier in the evening."

This was too much. Alysa's shock was replaced by outrage. "You can't do this to me. It's . . . unfair, cruel." She confronted him, her eyes flashing. "It's despicable. You may be a genius, Mr. Maximov, but you're a poor excuse for a human being. My grandfather, eh? Well, I hope to God you're not really my grandfather. I wouldn't want a selfish, egocentric *tvar* like you in the family."

"So she swears in Russian. How quaint."

"Don't you have any feelings, any sense of decency? Dancers are people and people make mistakes. How can you ruin my whole life just to save your own shirt? What are you anyway? No wonder they didn't want me to meet you." She didn't care *who* he was, he had no right to do such a comtemptible thing. "You've got the morals of Caligula, the tact of a doberman, and I'll tell you something else. If you had any feelings—any real human feelings, that is—your ballets would be a whole lot better. Balanchine's the one who's going to be immortal; not you. Balanchine can feel. He's got *dusha*. All you've got is an impotent old man's twisted desires grafted on to flashy technique. You're cheap thrills, Mr. Maximov."

"Very eloquent, my dear," Maximov's voice was level now, impersonal, as if he were talking to a total stranger, "but all that's neither here nor there." He gestured at the dressing table impatiently. "Clean out your drawers on your way out and try to get your costume back to Janet without wrinkling it so I can have it altered for Mademoiselle Peters. Betty will mail you your final check tomorrow morning. You should get it in, say three days at the outside. You do understand, of course, that you're not to come by the studio? That's clear, yes? Good. Adieu then." For a moment Alysa had the eerie sensation that Maximov was about to reach out automatically and shake her hand, but he turned instead and left, closing the door quickly behind him, and then there was only silence in the dressing room, discarded *pointe* shoes, and the scent of dying flowers.

To hell with him, to hell with all of them. Alysa tore off her costume and threw it in a heap on the floor, untied her *pointe* shoes and flung them after it. Ripping off her tights she wadded them into a ball and crammed them into the waste-basket. She realized dimly that she was having a tantrum but she didn't care. In the last half hour she had humiliated herself in front of half the critics in the city, been viciously attacked by an egocentric maniac who claimed to be her grandfather, learned that her own grandmother and aunt had been lying to her, and watched her entire career fall to pieces. Now if that wasn't reason enough for a tantrum what was?

Alysa grabbed her jeans and crammed her legs into them, wincing as she accidentally put pressure on her ankle. In a more reasonable frame of mind she might have gone straight to Nana and demanded an explanation, but she was overloaded, burned out, at the end of her emotional rope. If she talked to Nana now she'd say things she'd regret forever. When you were in this condition it was better to run and hide, put yourself on ice until you were a sane, civil human being again.

Snatching her sweater off the dresser, Alysa pulled it over her head, yanked on her boots, grabbed her purse, and limped into the hall. The next ballet was in progress and there was no one in sight except a few girls from the corps. Pushing past them, Alysa headed toward the exit. Five minutes later she was in a cab on her way to a small club in the Village that she and David sometimes frequented, a smoky, dark place where she could get quietly, thoroughly drunk.

22

Alysa moved the chiar a couple of inches closer, adjusted her purse under her swollen ankle, took another gulp of beer, and tried to sort out her feelings, a task much harder than cleaning up even the messiest room. She was upset—an understatement—angry at Maximov for attacking her, angry at Nana and Winn for deceiving her, but most of all angry at herself for not having had the sense to let Chrissie Peters dance the role of Iseult. Maximov was . . . there was no word she could think of malevolent enough to describe what he was . . . but if she hadn't been such an idiot, she'd be at a cast party right now instead of sitting here wishing she were dead. Well, not dead—there was no reason to get melodramatic— but at least invisible or in another country.

Alysa drank more beer, consumed with anger and self-reproach, knowing they were unhealthy, unproductive emotions but not able to shake them. Take David, if something like this had happened to him, he probably would have punched Maximov in the face; but he was a man and men punched. Women had a tendency to sit on their anger turning the pain inward like a porcupine crouching on its own quills. Well that was stupid, and she just plain wasn't going to do it. Suffering wasn't her line, she didn't enjoy it, and she didn't intend to tolerate it one minute longer than she had to.

Alysa finished off her beer, set the mug back down on the table, and pressed her lips together stubbornly. What she needed was oblivion, a nice temporary numbness, and this was as good a place to find it as any. Cigarette smoke stung her eyes and it was almost too dark to see. She peered through the haze and got a dim impression of bodies moving around her, pushing up against each other, of sharp currents of sexual electricity generated by the contact. On a makeshift stage at one end of the club a band composed of three men and a woman were singing a song about the total destruction of everything. How appropriate.

"Hi," a voice said. Alysa turned her head and realized that a boy leaning against the wall, dressed in a torn T-shirt and shiny black suit, was talking to her, his pelvis thrust forward, his elbows hanging loose, a cigarette dangling from the corner of his mouth, looking at her appraisingly. "How'd you hurt your ankle?"

"Skiing accident." She had a momentary impulse to tell him to get lost.

"Tough luck. My cousin broke his leg that way once." The boy's hair was dark, his skin tinted with something suggested southern climates—Italian probably. Taking a pack of Marlboros out of his pocket, he offered it to her, smiling a loose, easy smile. "Want one?"

"Sure, thanks." He seemed harmless enough. Alysa accepted the cigarette, inhaling the smoke deep into her lungs. She coughed and suddenly felt light-headed. Grimly she took another drag on the rotten tasting thing. If she wasn't going to be dancing professionally, what was the use of being a health fanatic? For a moment or two she let the boy talk to her of nothing in particular while she evaluated the situation.

His name, he told her, was Tony; he drove a delivery truck days and at night he came to the Village with his buddies to have a little fun. In his spare time he wrote songs, and there were people who were interested in his work, some big shots uptown who had connections. Some day he might make it big. Alysa let his words flow over her, trite and soothing. Fortunately no response seemed to be expected. Tony smiled warmly and touched her on the shoulder to make his point. He was good-looking, pleasant, not crazy in any obvious way. Better yet, he seemed to have no idea she was unhappy. Maybe he was high, or maybe as far as he was concerned, she was just another pretty girl waiting to be picked up. In any case it was clear that the chances of his knowing anything about ballet were slim if not nonexistent. Spending time in his company would be like stepping into another world where Sergei Maximov had never existed and dancing was something you only did to rock and roll. Yes, Tony was definitely a possibility. It was with the sense of having happened on exactly what she needed that Alysa invited him to sit down at her table.

Half an hour later they were on their second pitcher of beer and Tony had his hand on her knee; rolling it slowly up her leg. Alysa closed her eyes and allowed herself to imagine what he would be like as a lover. This might not be the most elegant way to deal with your problems, but it was definitely working. The bad memories were receding; Maximov's face had paled and dimmed, replaced by the fantasy of Tony's body entwined with hers. Alysa had read somewhere that sex was the best way of all to forget things—pure anonymous sex with no attachments, no strings—but did she really want to pick up a total stranger? She wasn't inexperienced, but she'd always been careful in her relationships: Eric, David—not exactly a long track record of lovers. Alysa opened her eyes and looked around the bar at the gyrating bodies, the flashing lights, the young people getting determinedly drunk. In theory everyone was supposed to be having a good time, but at least half of them looked depressed. The trouble these days was that there were no rules to follow, not for her or anyone else.

Tony's hand was large, his fingers blunt and heavy against her thigh. Taking Alysa's chin in his hand, he lifted her face to his and gave her a short, exploratory kiss. His breath tasted of beer and cigarette smoke. "How you doing?" He smiled at her, took off his dark glasses, the pupils of his eyes pinpoints, friendly eyes that said he was high and having a great time and that Alysa was part of it.

"I'm okay." She wouldn't tell him anything; the less he knew, the easier it would be for her to forget. She realized suddenly that she really did want to blank out completely, to stop thinking, erase her memory the way you erased a cassette tape.

"You want another drink?" Tony bought a third pitcher of beer, and poured her a glass, letting the foam slosh over the edge. Alysa drank a great deal, feeling the coolness of the beer slide down the back of her throat, knowing it was a bad idea but not giving a damn. Between pitchers, Tony kissed her.

Time passed and she floated with it, willing herself to forget, to go numb. Perhaps she drank some more, was introduced to Tony's friends—the last seemed likely because the next time she bothered to notice what was going on around her, she was sitting with Tony in the backseat of a '67 Plymouth next to a couple named Ross and Denise. Up front Tony's two best friends, Marty and Pico, were telling jokes, playing with the tape deck, trying to blast Ross and Denise apart by turning up the volume loud enough to make everyone's ears bleed. Alysa had the feeling she had been in the car a long while but she wasn't sure. All she knew was that some time that night the six of them had started out for Pico's loft in the Bowery and had gotten lost along the way.

A few inches to the right, Denise and Ross moved together in slow motion, Denise's face as luminescent as a mask, her lipstick smeared in a grimace. Outside, the streetlights hovered like flying saucers, and the pain had finally drained out of the night. Tony put his hand inside Alysa's sweater and cupped her breast in his palm, kissing her. His fingers moved around her nipple, teasing, stroking. Alysa sighed and curled closer, and things went more or less blank again.

She did, however, remember sitting on the curb outside a deli some time later, drinking Southern Comfort out of Pico's plastic flask and pulling money out of her purse. She was happy by then, laughing at the top of her lungs because she had won. There was no family legacy of pain and betrayal to come to terms with; Maximov's face was gone; she had never danced, never made a fool of herself. She had been born ten minutes ago—that was as far back as she could remember. The bills scattered in the street, and Alysa didn't even bother to bend over and pick them up. They were only paper, and she had more—a trust fund from her parents, stock in D&M, Inc.—all the money in the world and nothing to do with it. She'd never had to struggle like most dancers; she'd had it all: an apartment in the heart of Manhattan, private lessons whenever she wanted them, love and encouragement from Aunt Winn and Nana, even inherited talent—and *still* she'd blown it. But that didn't matter anymore. In the last ten minutes her whole life had miraculously dissolved and floated away, leaving her as clean as an empty stage. She tried, in a drunken, confused way, to explain this to the others but none of them understood.

"You're one crazy lady," Tony kept saying. He didn't want her money, and he kept trying to give it back to her, but she insisted, stuffing it into his pockets. Later, when she wasn't looking, he put it all back in her purse. Alysa was touched by the gesture; he could have had nearly forty dollars but he wouldn't take a dime from her, not even a couple of bucks for another six pack of beer.

They drove away from the deli and Alysa drifted back into the space where time had no meaning, that alchohol-muffled place where there was nothing worth remembering. When she came back to reality again, she found herself lying on a mattress under a tattered blue Indian bedspread in a deserted corner of Pico's loft. Tony was trying to pull off her sweater, running his hands over her breasts; she moved closer to him, trying to get warm. The ceiling was miles above them, peeling, covered with spots of mold and grease. At regular intervals tall factorylike windows let in the dingy light of the streetlamps. One of the windows was open; Marty was standing on the ledge chucking beer cans into the alley.

"I'm killing the goddamn rats," Marty yelled. His hair was braided into dreadlocks and his dark skin glistened in the light like oiled wood. Ross and Pico cheered him on, handing him more cans. In the sky the moon was a thin strip of celluloid. In the background a stereo played loudly, the music a tumble of drums and confusion.

"Ballet," Alysa heard herself saying, "is a peculiar art form." It was an odd thing to be discussing while a boy was in the process of undressing you, but the words just kept flowing out of their own accord. "You have to be crazy to go into it; out of your skull." She put her arms over her head, making things easier for Tony. "Among other things they make you starve yourself to death." She looked at her ribs protruding like the keys of a xylophone. "Maximov has this thing about thinness. He wants his dancers to look ten or fifteen pounds underweight. Sometimes the girls go overboard, become anorexic, even die. Why couldn't he just let us alone, let us look like women for Christ's sake?" She began to cry silently without making a sound. Tony mopped at her eyes awkwardly with the sleeve of her sweater.

"Hey, lighten up." His face was kind, concerned. Alysa put her head on his shoulder and tried to lie perfectly still. Her head was beginning to buzz uncomfortably and her whole body tingled as if it had fallen asleep. She decided she must be drunk out of her mind. What an idiot she'd been to let Pico persuade her to drink that Southern Comfort.

She closed her eyes, feeling Tony's hands on her body, enjoying the sure, steady caress of his fingers as they drew slow, invisible circles around her nipples. This was fantastic. She couldn't ever remember it feeling quite this way before, so intense but so slow. Tony put his mouth to hers for a moment, then slowly he dragged his lips down the length of her body, pausing to run his tongue around her navel and lick at the cup of her belly. Alysa squirmed with pleasure and laughed, excited. Tony's lips did wonderful things, lightly caressing the insides of her thighs, brushing her clitoris, teasing and withdrawing, darting to her breasts, covering her mouth in one long kiss that took her breath away. Her senses grew exquisitely sharp; smells and tastes mixed together: the dark sweet odor of his hair, the musky scent of his skin, his tongue like a ribbon of soft candy melting into hers, everything orange and red shot through with flecks of gold. Alysa floated beside Tony for what seemed like hours, weightless and drunk with pleasure.

"I feel like my bones are full of air," she told him.

"What?"

"You know, like a bird." Alysa rested her head against his chest again and looked at the Indian bedspread, fanning out over the two of them in fantastic patterns: fawns leaped over impossible flowers, swirling mandalas of blue and gold twisted across her knees. Tony turned her over gently and put a pillow under her chest. Holding her by the hips, he drew her back toward him, running his hands over her body as if trying to memorize every curve. Then lifting her long hair, he leaned forward and began kissing the back of her neck. Alysa gave a little cry of pleasure as Tony pulled her backward, his breath hot in her ear, every muscle of his body taut against her. He entered her carefully, his chest pressing against her spine.

Alysa closed her eyes as Tony pulled her closer and began to touch her gently again between her legs, rocking her in his arms. Her mind went totally blank, like a page of white paper. He moved and she moved with him; his body was squared, solid, thickboned—not like the body of a dancer. For one bitter, perfectly lucid moment she wondered why she was doing this, making love to a stranger. Tony pulled her still closer, and the question disappeared. The music went on and on; soon there was only a tunnel of sound stretching out in front of her and at the end, oblivion.

Hours later Alysa woke to a splitting headache, a mouth full of cotton, and the sight of Tony asleep beside her, snoring heavily. Struggling into an upright position she looked around the loft trying to remember where the hell she was. On the floor several people she couldn't remember having met were curled up, dead asleep. This had obviously been some kind of mistake on her part, but what kind of mistake? Alysa wracked her brain.

Who was this guy next to her? Had she slept with him, or had they just crawled naked into bed and passed out? She closed her eyes and tried to reconstruct the events of the previous night—not an easy thing to do when your head felt as if it might fall off any minute—and bit by bit the pieces began to fall into place: the club in the Village, the car ride the scene on the curb outside the deli. When she got to the point where Tony had pulled off her sweater, she put her hands over her face.

Oh, no. She couldn't have. For a moment she was consumed by guilt and regret, and then suddenly she saw the lighter side of the situation. She'd gone on a binge, that's what she'd done: gotten hurt, gotten mad, gotten drunk, and gotten laid—a really mature reaction. She deserved some kind of prize: idiot of the week, maybe. What had possessed her to do it? Maybe it was the Russian side of her character coming out—the double Russian side, she corrected herself. Drama, drinking, repentance: the holy Slavic trinity. Alysa grinned weakly and brushed her hair out of her eyes. In the light of morning nothing seemed quite as terrible or desperate as it had last night. Well at least she was now certain, beyond a doubt, that she had *dusha*. In fact, at the present moment she might validly consider herself a victim of *dusha* poisoning.

Her stomach felt as if a flock of sea gulls had taken up residence just above her navel. Getting up, Alysa limped unsteadily to the bathroom, avoiding several broken beer bottles, and took a long, hot shower, washing her hair with a battered scrap of Ivory soap she found expiring at the bottom of the soap dish. Locating a pen, she wrote Tony a thank-you note—it was the only civilized thing to do under the circumstances—and then, without waking anyone, she left closing the door softly behind her.

On the way back to her apartment, Alysa stopped off and bought several newspapers. The reviews of *Tristan and Iseult* were terrible, but they didn't devastate her the way they would have yesterday. She read them from beginning to end wincing with pain at the references to her lackluster dancing. Then she deposited the papers in the nearest trash can and caught a cab uptown thinking that it was time to come to terms with her life, face it head on, and see what was gone and what was left.

"Alysa!" Just inside the door of her apartment Alysa was ambushed by Aunt Winn and Natasha, enfolded in double hugs, kissed, cried over. "We were so worried," Winn stroke her hair.

"Frantic," Natasha embraced Alysa again, kissed her on both cheeks, and held her close.

As their love and acceptance washed over her, Alysa felt gratitude and confusion in equal parts. She'd been so angry at them for lying to her but now, in the early morning light, their faces seemed precious and fragile as old china: Aunt Winn's pale and lined with fatigue, the skin under Nana's eyes ringed with sleeplessness. The living room was strewn with coffee cups and cigarette butts, half-eaten sandwiches, magazines tossed helter-skelter on the floor. Alysa realized with a pang of guilt that they must have been waiting up for her all night. "I'm sorry," she muttered apologetically, "it was terrible of me not to call." She knew her words had a hollow ring to them, but she honestly *was* sorry. The problem was that an arrival speech was going around and around in her mind, one she'd been rehearsing ever since last night. At first it had been an angry declaration coupled to a long list of injustices, but over the hours it had mellowed into something more civilized, a request for information, a plea that they simply tell her what the hell was going on.

Disentangling herself from their arms, Alysa limped over to the couch and sat down heavily, dropping her purse on the floor. For a moment there was silence in the room, only the sound of traffic out on the street could be heard, as if all three women were holding their breath. Where to begin, where to start? Alysa looked from Natasha to Aunt Winn and any desire she had had for revenge dissolved utterly. They looked so vulnerable, so anxious she was tempted to forget the whole thing, but she couldn't do that of course.

"He told me," Alysa blurted out the words, or maybe it would be more accurate to say that the words blurted themselves out unexpectedly, like a set of glasses crashing to the floor. She wanted instantly to call them back, but it was too late. Diplomacy was definitely not her forte.

Aunt Winn flinched visibly. "Who told you? Told you what?"

"Forget it Winn, the game's up." Natasha pulled her sweater around her shoulders and sat down on the couch. "So Sergei told you?" Alysa nodded. The color drained from Natasha's face leaving it pinched and weary. "I suspected as much when you disappeared for the night." She looked away for a moment as if gazing into a space that no one else was welcome to enter. "I was always afraid he'd tell you," she said at last. "I nearly told you myself the last time you were home, but your aunt and uncle persuaded me not to. They felt you should be spared if possible, and somehow we all managed to convince ourselves there was still a chance you could be."

"Spared what, Nana?" Alysa could hear the impatience in her voice, the edge that lay behind her words. But she *was* impatient. This whole thing had been crazy, like a bad dream where you grabbed a doorknob and it turned into a snake or a rat in your hand and nothing made sense or was what it seemed to be. All she wanted from her aunt and grandmother were a few straightforward answers. "What were you trying to spare me? The fact that Maximov's my grandfather?"

"Not exactly." Natasha took a pack of Russian cigarettes out of the pocket of her sweater, lit one, and threw the match at the ashtray, missing it by a mile. She exhaled a cloud of smoke. Behind the milky veil her eyes were dark and intense, filled with pain. "Was that all Sergei told you?"

"Yes."

Natasha took another nervous puff on her cigarette. "Well, I'm not surprised. Sergei always did have a way of leaving the hard part for other people. As far as taking any kind of responsibility goes, he's always been a Class-A bastard."

Natasha got up abruptly, walked across the room, and stood for a moment with her back to Alysa. "I suppose I should start by making a confession." She turned, looking as uncomfortable as Alysa had ever seen her look. "You know, Alysa, this is embarrassing. The young are supposed to confess to the old, not the old to the young, and I suddenly find myself wondering how you're going to judge me."

"Well," Alysa said, "it's hard to say in advance how anyone will judge anything, but it might comfort you to know that after what I did last night—the details of which I'll spare you—I don't exactly feel on top of the moral superiority scale."

Natasha shot her a look of gratitude. "Thank you, dear." She walked back to the couch, sat down, folded her hands in her lap, opened her mouth then closed it, and gazed at Alysa helplessly. "I simply can't say it. You have to understand, Alysa, I'm almost eighty years old. I was born in another century, in another world—sometimes it feels as if on another planet—and in my day people simply didn't talk about this kind of thing to their granddaughters."

"Mama," Winn said warningly, "if you don't tell her then I'm going to have to, and you know how tactless I am. I always make a hash of things."

Natasha smiled weakly. "Your aunt's right. If I let her tell you, it's only going to be worse." She took a deep breath and straightened her spine, and for a moment, to Alysa at least, her grandmother looked like a dancer poised on the verge of a *grand jeté*. "I don't know any way to tell you this discreetly, Alysa, so I'll be blunt. Sergei Maximov was my lover. When I was married to your grandfather Ward, Sergei and I had an affair, and there's a possibility—only a possibility, mind you—that he was your mother's father as well as your father's father."

"What!" Alysa was so startled she stood up, nearly knocking over the coffee table. Cups jumped and cracked together, magazines fell on the floor. A water glass careened toward the edge, caught by Aunt Winn at the last moment.

"Please," Natasha begged, "sit down and let me finish or I'll never be able to get through this. I know you're upset, but there's more."

"More? You tell me that my parents were probably brother and sister and then you tell me there's *more?*"

"Alysa Compton that's no way to speak to your grandmother."

"Let her be, Winn. She has a right to be angry but she has to hear the rest of this." Natasha turned to Alysa. "Your mother never knew. I swear to you, she was completely innocent. But your father knew and Sergei knew, and when your father told Sergei that he intended to marry your mother anyway, Sergei told Michael that if he went through with the wedding he was finished with him forever. Unfortunately Sergei didn't keep that promise."

Natasha jabbed out her cigarette with a sharp, stabbing motion and her lips trembled with an old anger. "Oh, he didn't ever speak to Michael again, and he was too nasty even to send a card of congratulations when you were born, but a few years later, when you were just a baby, he revealed the entire story to a journalist named Grace Lyons, who proceeded to write it up in the most lurid article I've ever had the misfortune to read. To this day I don't know why he did it. Revenge, viciousness, pure stupidity—it's anyone's guess."

Natasha controlled herself with obvious effort. "I'm sorry. After nearly twenty years this still upsets me to the point that I can hardly talk about it, but it's vital you understand. Your parents were very much in the public eye at the time, so it had all the potential of becoming a major scandal. In fact, the story was just about to be released when they died. Your grandmother Anya found out about it, bought off the magazine, and quashed the story, but she never forgave Sergei for it, and frankly none of the rest of us ever did either. We wanted him out of our lives and yours permanently." Natasha leaned forward, pleading with her to understand. "Alysa you can't imagine what your life would have been like if the press had gotten hold of that story. That was 1958. Tatiana Trey and Michael Macks were almost as famous as Tracey and Hepburn. You'd have been treated like a freak in a carnival sideshow. We had to protect you from that."

Alysa sat back down on the couch and looked at her grandmother, at a loss for words.

"We should have told you when you got older," Natasha continued in a softer voice, "and believe me, we all regret that we didn't, but by that time hiding the truth from you had become a kind of habit. Even when you went to New York to work with Sergei, we kept hoping it wouldn't last. We knew the kind of temper he had and how stubborn you were, and we were sure you wouldn't be able to tolerate him for more than a week. So we went on deluding ourselves, and the upshot of it all was that we didn't trust you as much as you deserved, and for that we beg your forgiveness."

"If you'd told me, I'd have understood, Nana."

"I know now that you would have." Natasha reached out and took Alysa's hand. "I think the problem was that we were all afraid to tell you for fear you'd be devastated or, worse yet, never trust us again. In the end, I guess we failed you because we feared what all parents and grandparents fear: we were afraid we'd lose your love."

Alysa was moved. She held her grandmother's hand and thought of all the things she'd just heard—too much to process, take in, or even begin to understand in so short a time, but one thing was clear: whatever they'd done, they'd done it because they loved her.

Tears filled Natasha's eyes. "Can you forgive us, Alysa? Can you trust us again? I don't say that we deserve it, but can you do it anyway?"

"Dear Nana," Alysa impulsively took her grandmother in her arms and hugged her, then reached over and hugged Aunt Winn. "Who knows what's right and what's wrong, or who's to blame and who isn't. The past is the past. Maybe you made a mistake; maybe you did the best thing. I don't feel qualified or even capable of judging you. I was hurt, yes, but as for forgiving you, I can't help but do it. You're my family," her voice trembled with emotion, "and all I know is that I love you, and you could never lose that love, not in a million years." And for a long time the three of them sat there, hugging each other, letting the truth of it sink in.

What was left of the day was spent taking Alysa to a doctor to have her ankle examined, calling various friends and relations to report that she'd come home safely, and eating a dinner of barbecued chicken, potato salad, and cole slaw that Aunt Winn picked up at the corner deli. By evening everyone was exhausted, but there was a kind of excitement in the air that made it impossible to go to bed. For hours—long after the last of the dinner had been finished—the three women sat around Alysa's kitchen table, drinking black coffee and tying up loose ends.

"So you're thinking about abandoning ballet." It was past midnight and outside, beyond the windows, the city had grown still and heavy. There was a moment of silence broken by the wail of a siren heading downtown. Winn leaned back, put down her coffee cup, and smiled approvingly at Alysa. "I'm glad to hear it. To tell the truth, I've never understood why anyone would want to put herself through what a dancer goes through."

Alysa shrugged. "What choice do I have at this point? The world of ballet's so damn tiny, and news travels fast. After what happened last night, I doubt any major company would trust me in a principal role—not once they learned that Maximov had given me the boot for being a drug addict."

"Ridiculous," Winn snorted. "I wish I'd been there. If you ask me, we should sue that man for slander, and high time, too."

"Thanks Aunt Winn, but I don't think suing Sergei Maximov would exactly make me popular."

Aunt Winn folded her arms across her chest. "Then we'll just have to hire a couple of Mafia thugs to break kneecaps."

"Aunt Winn, where in the world did you get an idea like that?" Alysa giggled. "You sound positively *tough*."

"I used to be quite a Humphrey Bogart fan, not to mention Jimmy Cagney."

"This *is* a day of revelations."

"Sweetheart," Natasha interposed, "to be honest, you were at fault—at least partially. There's no doubt you made a mistake dancing with such a serious injury, but the punishment Sergei is meting out to you is way out of line. That's not the kind of misjudgment that should end your career, and if you want to go on dancing, I don't see any reason why you shouldn't. There are *hundreds* of dance companies in the United States alone, not to mention Europe. Maximov doesn't own the world."

Alysa shook her head. "I know that, Nana. You're right, in theory at least. Oh, sure, given your influence I could still probably dance with some minor company somewhere, but what would be the point? You know most of the excitement comes from working with great choreography, dancing with partners as good or better than you are. And I'm simply not going to find that kind of thing outside of New York, or London, or somewhere like that—unless of course, I defected to the Soviet Union," Alysa grinned ruefully, "and frankly, no matter how many great stories you tell me about your Russian days, I don't think I could take the winters. So, since pulling a reverse Baryshnikov is definitely out of the picture, I'm trying to take my enforced retirement with good grace. Maybe I'll give lessons to little girls, dance for Junior League benefits or something. Of course, if I really get an attack of nostalgia, I can always dance in the corps of some small local ballet during *Nutcracker* season when they'll take anything that's warm and can stand on its toes."

"Are you telling me that you'd still want to go on dancing if you could have a crack at the top again?"

"Oh, sure, Nana. If Balanchine or Tetley would have me, I'd put my *pointe* shoes on so fast it would make your head swim, but they won't, not after Maximov gets through presenting his version of why I ruined his ballet. Only Maximov could clear my name, and we all know how likely *that* is." She pushed her hair out of her eyes and smiled at Natasha and Winn bravely, but there was pain and disappointment in her eyes. "Frankly, it would be easier to believe a tiger would make friends with a nice tasty mouse than my dear grandfather would ever show mercy, or even a reasonable amount of fairness, when his own reputation's on the line. We're not just talking egomania here; we're talking the biggest case of hubris since Adam." Alysa set her coffee cup down with finality. "So that's that. Tomorrow we get out the Help Wanted ads and you two help me decide on a new career— something nice with long vacations, good pay, Blue Cross, and a pension plan to keep me in my old age."

Winn got up briskly, stretched, and yawned. There was a flurry of activity as the three women rearranged the chairs, picked up coffee cups, turned off the lights. Beds were turned down, teeth brushed, slippers lined up neatly where they could be found again in the morning. Soon the apartment was silent.

Time passed, marked by nothing more than the ticking of the clock on the wall above the stove. Half an hour later Natasha reentered the kitchen, sat down at the table, and remained for a long time looking out the window. She had a decision to make and it was keeping her awake. The clock monotonously ticked off the minutes. One hour passed, then another. It grew increasingly colder. Natasha mentally cursed the energy crisis that had caused the landlord to turn down the thermostat at night to the point where she could almost see her breath. Alexis's hut in the *taiga* had been warmer than this. At least she thought it had, but on the other hand maybe she was just getting old. Bundling a blanket around her legs, she sat a little longer. Finally, after a great deal of soul searching, she made her decision.

Winn was taking Alysa to a health club tomorrow afternoon so Alysa could take a sauna and soak her ankle in the Jacuzzi. Natasha had been invited to go along, but she would think up some reasonable excuse to stay behind. Then, when she was sure she had the apartment to herself, she would make a phone call—a very important phone call. Natasha looked at the phone and took a deep breath. It wasn't going to be easy. Reaching out one finger, she touched the buttons, feeling the coldness of the plastic, thinking how strange it was that all you had to do was tap a few times to summon up ghosts from the past. For a few more minutes she sat in silence, letting a mass of contradictory feelings wash through her. Then, getting up, she turned out the light, tiptoed into the guest bedroom, and crawled under the electric blanket, but it was a long time before she actually fell asleep.

"Sergei?"

"Yes?"

"It's Natasha." There was a long silence on the other end of the line, so long she began to wonder if he'd hung up. "I suppose you can guess what I'm calling about."

"If it's about your granddaughter—"

"Your granddaughter, too, Sergei."

"Natasha, let me save you a lot of time and trouble. I don't *have* a granddaughter." Sergei's voice had an edge to it. She heard a sound as if he might be brusquely rearranging things on his desk. "My only interest in Alysa Compton was as a dancer in this company, nothing else. She may be Mihail's daughter, she may have been sired by gypsies, she may have dropped down from the moon for all I care. She got the same treatment as any other dancer, and now that's she's gone, my interest in her has ended. At the moment I'm in the process of putting together next fall's program, and my time, to say the least, is limited. So if there's nothing else you want to talk to me about, I need to get on with my day. I've got a new set designer coming in here in fifteen minutes, an artist from Tokyo, and I need to learn how to say *no* in Japanese before he arrives."

"Sergei, I don't care whom you've got an appointment with. Listen to me; are you listening? I want you to clear Alysa's name of any association with drugs and take her back into your company to prove to the world that you believe her to have been completely innocent of anything except poor judgment."

"You're joking. April Fool's day isn't for another six weeks, Natasha."

"I'm not joking. I'm completely serious." Natasha forced herself to keep her voice level. Sergei was definitely the most infuriating man she'd ever met—and at her age that was saying something.

"You're actually serious?"

"Completely. You're the only person alive who can set Alysa's career back into motion again, and I want you to do it."

"You are serious. Well, in that case I'll give you a serious answer: it's out of the question. I dismissed a dancer who deserved dismissal. There's no excuse for the kind of performance Alysa gave. *Tristan and Iseult* was an exquisite piece, as perfect as anything I've done in years, and she made hash of it. Do you know what it's like to create something that cries out with artistic potential and then see it slaughtered in front of your eyes? I'm an old man and that kind of shock I can do without. Better she should have dropped dead on stage than have danced with that injuried ankle. At least the critics would have understood that."

"Sergei!"

"She's talented. I don't deny it. But as our dear Mardame Laurier used to tell us, talent's useless without discipline.

Sorry, Natasha, but Alysa just doesn't have what it takes. Considering that you only call me once every twenty years, I wish I could oblige you, but I'm running a ballet company here, not a charitable organization for irresponsible adolescents."

"So you won't clear her name and take her back?"

Sergei sighed audibly. "Natasha, why is it you never learned any feminine wiles? You're the most stubborn woman in the Northern Hemisphere—probably the Southern, too, for that matter. I said *no*. You want it in Russian? *Nyet*. You want it in French? *Non*. You want it in Japanese? Give me a minute."

Natasha took a deep breath. She could hear that he was about to hang up on her, which meant there was only one alternative left. "Sergei," she said, "what does the Manhattan Ballet need more than anything else in the world?"

"That's an easy one; it needs what all ballet companies need: money."

"And how do you get money?"

"A trickle from the audience—not even enough to begin to cover our expenses—donations from wealthy patrons, and grants from the government and private foundations. Why? Are you thinking of signing your fortune over to us? Touching Natasha, but I'd still have to say no. Frankly, I know for a fact that you don't have enough money to cover our electric bill for the upcoming fiscal year—unless, of course, you're planning on spending your remaining days living on food stamps, something I could hardly let you do considering how long we've known each other."

"I'm not planning to give you money Sergei. What I've got to offer is something far better."

"What's that?"

"I want to talk to you in person about it. I want you to come over to my apartment right now, and discuss the whole thing."

"Natasha, for heaven's sake, you can't seriously expect me to drop everything and come to see you on the off chance you might have something I want. I told you, I've got a set designer coming in fifteen minutes."

"Sergei, what were the three most famous ballets of the nineteenth century?"

"Why, *Swan Lake*, *The Nutcracker*, and *The Buccaneer*, of course."

"And what happened to *The Buccaneer*?"

"Natasha, I don't have time for this."

"Sergei, if you hang up on me, I swear I'll come down to

your studio this minute and camp out in the front office until you hear me out."

"You would, wouldn't you?"

"You bet I would, but there's no need for that. Just be civilized for once."

"You want to know what happened to *The Buccaneer*? Okay, I'll tell you; you could call the library and ask, but I'll tell you just to get you off my back. As you, I, and everyone else knows, it was performed by the Imperial Ballet from 1880 until 1917. It was Petipa's masterpiece. As you no doubt recall, you and I first danced together in it—sometime around 1911."

"The *pas de deux*—oh, I remember Sergei. All too well, as a matter of fact. Go on. What happened after that?"

"I don't know what you're leading up to Natasha, but *The Buccaneer*, as you well know, was lost during the Revolution." Sergei's voice was tight with annoyance. "The sets and costumes disappeared—burned for firewood for all I know. Petipa's original notes vanished, and almost everyone associated with the production either died of starvation or, like Madame Laurier, rest her soul, perished in the camps. Ballets of that sort were out of political favor for several years. You remember, of course, what Lenin called *The Buccaneer*?"

"A wanton display of something or other."

"A wanton display of aristocratic waste and bourgeois decadence, that's what he called it." Sergei snorted. "One of the most brilliant ballets of all times thrown onto the trash heap by a second-rate lawyer with a talent for demagoguery. By the time sanity set in again, no one could remember exactly how the original production had looked. Oh, there've been attempts to reconstruct it—most recently in Cuba of all places—but the results have been dismal."

"One more question. Who first danced the role of Laurissa in *The Buccaneer*?"

"What are you doing, Natasha? Revising the *Oxford Dictionary of Ballet*? You know as well as I do that it was Maria Nikolaevna Rochina. She made her reputation with that role."

"Suppose, just for the sake of supposing, Sergei, that a complete record of *The Buccaneer* still existed, all of Petipa's original choreography, sketches of scenery and costumes—everything—and that Rochina's great-granddaughter were alive to dance it. What would it be worth to a company to put on a production like that? In monetary terms, I mean? When you considered the incredible publicity that would surround the premiere, the new patrons the company would attract? When you considered the director of that company would have his pick of grants? That the NEA and the Ford Foundation would probably come crawling on their knees to him?" There was a stunned silence on the other end of the line. So it *was* possible to reduce Sergei Maximov to silence. How satisfying. Too bad it had taken her over sixty years to figure out how to do it, but the moment was sweet nevertheless. "Come see me, Sergei. Now. This minute." Natasha gave him the address and then played her final card. "You've got exactly one hour to get here, then I call Balanchine. Do you understand?"

Putting the receiver back on the hook, Natasha sat for a moment, savoring her victory. Then she went into the kitchen and set about making a tray of snacks, slicing cucumbers, scooping a jar of pickled mushrooms into a silver bowl. Locating a bottle of vodka in the liquor cabinet, she put it in the freezer to chill. She had no doubt whatsoever that Sergei was coming, and considering she hadn't seen him in over forty years, the least she could do was offer the man a drink.

"You have *The Buccaneer?*"

"Have a pickled mushroom, Sergei." Natasha speared a pickled mushroom for herself, ate it, and wiped her hands on the napkin. Now that she was actually in the same room with him, she was experiencing the most extraordinary flood of feelings—none of them particularly appropriate to her age— excitement, irritation, shyness, nervousness, even sexual desire. You'd think when a woman got to be nearly eighty she'd have outgrown all that foolishness, but that was the trouble with getting older. Your body changed, but inside you stayed more or less the same. At the core she was nineteen, twenty—maybe thirty at the most. She drank off a glass of vodka, stalling for time, trying to put her thoughts in order. Why couldn't he have gotten fat like all the other men she knew? Or shriveled up? Or at least lost his hair? She'd been prepared to be shocked by his appearance. After all he'd been burning the candle at both ends for years: all those wives, young dancers, too, if the rumors were to be believed; working eighteen hours days; and his drinking was legendary. Not to mention that he had heart problems, at least according to the newspapers. But here he was, slim, handsome, and as straight-spined as a Russian cavalry officer. Oh, he was old all right; no denying that—his hair was gray, and he had at least as many wrinkles as she did—but his eyes were still the eyes she had fallen in love with over sixty years ago, blue, clear, and surprisingly young, as if nothing had ever touched or dimmed them. She realized with a pang that she must still be a little in love with Sergei to see him this way. But it was, thank God, a gentle emotion, friendly, nostalgic, only a distant cousin of the passion that had once torn her apart.

"Natasha, I can't stand the suspense." Sergei poured himself another glass of vodka and drank it down in one gulp, Russian style. "I know I should spend the next ten minutes telling you how lovely you look—which, I hasten to add, is God's honest truth—and maybe talking about the weather, but I've got to know. Do you have *The Buccaneer*?"

"I do."

"Well?"

"Well what?"

"What do you mean 'well what'?" He got up and paced across the room. "You drop this on me like a time bomb, and you just sit there eating mushrooms. I want to know where you got it, how complete it is, what you want for it. And this thing about Rochina. I want that cleared up, too."

Natasha grinned and then laughed. "You know, Sergei, I never realized before that the way to control you was to shut up. I always spent so much time trying to explain myself to you, and now I've made the interesting discovery that the one thing you can't tolerate is silence."

"Natasha have a heart. You dangle *The Buccaneer* in front of me like a fish in front of a hungry cat. What do you expect me to do? Fall at your feet and spout all sorts of gallantries? Well, my knees are too stiff. So come clean. What did you do to get hold of the most famous lost ballet of all time? Screw Lenin?"

"Not exactly." She took another small sip of vodka, and sat back against the softly padded chair. For a moment her mind wandered to another room, thousands of miles away, a room in her old house on the Quai d'Argent. "The day before I left Russia Madame Laurier came to visit me. How she got through the rioters was a miracle in itself. I think she grabbed a sign and pretended to be part of a demonstration. Anyway, as I recall, she showed up around noon with a big bundle of papers under her arm that she insisted I take from her on the spot—papers that incriminated her politically."

"Why give them to you? Why not just burn them if they were so dangerous."

"She was a woman of great conscience. Those papers

Rochina's face, that had transformed her from an awkward little girl into a dancer.

Reluctantly she brought herself back to the present and Sergei. "I worked with Rochina from the time I was five until the time I was sixteen and never, not once, did she even hint at our relationship." Natasha leaned forward, wanting him to understand yet knowing that he couldn't. "Can you imagine how hard that must have been for her, how much it must have meant to her that no one, not even her own daughter, ever discover the truth? I know times have changed since then, but I don't think my mother would have changed with them. I kept *The Buccaneer* in a box because I knew that to expose it would be to expose my mother. There was no way I could have produced her notes without having to explain the truth."

"But now you're willing to?"

"My mother's dead and Alysa's alive and I've had enough of keeping secrets to last me for all eternity. You give our granddaughter the part of Laurissa and I'll talk to anyone you want—The *Times, People* magazine, you name it. I may even be able to persuade Alysa to adopt the stage name of Rochina if you like—I can't promise that, of course; it's up to her. But I'd say there's more than a good chance she'd be open to it."

"Natasha, remind me not to ever bargain with you again." He stuck out his hand.

"It's a deal then?"

"A deal." He picked up the bottle of vodka and filled their glasses. "Let's drink to it. Today, after almost sixty years of hostilities, Natasha Ladanova and Sergei Maximov sign a peace treaty. To us."

"And to our granddaughter."

Sergei paused, glass in midair. "Okay, you want me to drink to our granddaughter, I'll drink to her. Only don't expect me to take up the role of grandfather. I'm too old and set in my ways to start buying teddy bears for Christmas."

"Alysa's hardly at the age where she needs teddy bears, Sergei. Just give her the role of Laurissa and we'll call it even. And, oh, yes, you might try acting a little more civil when you work with her because she's definitely not going to take any bullying from you, and if she walks out, the deal's off. Agreed?"

"Agreed."

"To Alysa then."

"Alysa Rochina." They clicked glasses and drank. "Well,"

Sergei said, "that's that. I still have that Japanese set designer coming in, so I should get back to my office." He picked up his coat. "Send Alysa around tomorrow morning about nine, and get me *The Buccaneer* as soon as you can. If it's anything like I remember, it's going to take hell's own amount of work to pull off."

Natasha thought of all the things she still wanted to ask him. Time and blood had bound her to this man; in some ways her whole life had revolved around him, yet in the end she hardly knew him any better than the day they first met. She supposed they were friends now, but friendship with Sergei, like love, was a chancy proposition.

"Good-bye," she said. She held out her hand, and Sergei bent over it for a moment, kissing it lightly in the European fashion. What had made him do that? Affection? Politeness? Habit?

"Good-bye, Natasha. *Dosvydanya.*"

"*Dosvydanya*, Sergei." He walked quickly down the hall, an elderly man in an expensive top coat who still moved like a dancer—part of her life, a mystery she'd never solve. "*Dosvydanya*, Sergei," Natasha called out again, waving. Sergei smiled, waved back, and then the elevator arrived, opened its doors, and swallowed him up.

Epilogue

Seven months later, in the fall of 1974, Sergei Maximov presented the greatest ballet of his career: a reinterpretation of Petipa's *The Buccaneer* with Alysa Rochina dancing the role of Laurissa. Five weeks after that, almost to the day, he developed severe chest pains during a rehearsal and was rushed to Mount Sinai Hospital where he died a few hours later. Natasha mourned for him, of course, but her life went on. She had the pleasure of seeing Alysa's career blossom, the joy—three years later—of attending Alysa's wedding (to a defecting Russian dancer named Petyor Zaytsev), and ultimately, in the late spring of 1980, the pleasure of holding the great-great-granddaughter of Maria Rochina on her lap. She would have said, if anyone had taken the time to ask her, that she had had a good life.

Chronology

1738 Imperial School of Ballet founded in St. Petersburg
1832 Marie Taglioni, who popularized dancing on *pointe*, appears in *La Sylphide*
1862 Marius Petipa becomes ballet master in St. Petersburg
     Petipa's *La Fille du Pharaon*
1878 Grand Duke Alexis born
1880 Petipa's *The Buccaneer*
1892 Ivanov's *The Nutcracker*
1893 Death of Tchaikovsky
1895 Natasha born
     Sergei born
1900 Isadora Duncan dances barefoot in Paris
1909 Diaghilev organizes his Ballets Russes
1910 Fokine's *Schéhérazade* and *The Firebird*
1911 Natasha enters the Imperial School of Ballet
1912 Natasha promoted to the Maryinsky corps de ballet
1913 Nijinsky's *Le Sacre du Printemps*
1916 Ballet du la Cité founded by Emile Fouchier
1917 Bolshevik Revolution
1920 Les Ballets Sudéois founded by Rolf de Maré
1921 Natasha dances in Cocteau's *Eurydice in Hell*
     Isadora Duncan founds school of dance in Moscow
1924 Balanchine defects from Russia
1929 Stock market crashes
     Balanchine's *Prodigal Son*
     Diaghilev dies in Venice
1930 Camargo Society founded in London
1931 Death of Pavlova
     Sadler's Wells Ballet founded in London
1932 Ballets Russes de Monte Carlo founded with "baby ballerinas Baronova, Toumanova, and Riabouchinska
1933 Tudor creates *Les Rendezvous* for Markova and Idzikowsk
     San Francisco Ballet founded

1934 Tudor's *The Planets* for Ballet Rambert
Balanchine comes to the United States at invitation of Lincoln Kirstein and founds School of American Ballet
1936 Manhattan Ballet founded
1939 World War II
Natasha leaves London
American Ballet Theatre founded in New York
1941 Natasha retires from the stage and founds Ladanova School of Classical Ballet
1942 Death of Fokine
1945 Ballet de Champs Elysées founded in Paris
1946 Sadler's Wells Ballet moves to Covent Garden
1948 New York City Ballet founded
1950 Death of Nijinsky
1951 Canadian National Ballet founded
Maximov's *Quetzal*
Fred Lewis musical *Dance* goes on tour
1956 Sadler's Wells Ballet becomes the Royal Ballet
The film *Kyra* wins five Academy Awards
1961 Nureyev defects from Russia
1963 Ford Foundation announces $7,756,000 program to "strengthen ballet in the United States."
1964 New York City Ballet moves to Lincoln Center
1965 Balanchine's *Don Quixote*
1967 London Contemporary Dance Theater founded
1973 Baryshnikov defects from Russia
1974 Alysa makes her debut in Maximov's *Tristan and Iseult*

SPECTACULAR ENTERTAINMENT ALL SUMMER LONG!
SUMMER SPECTACULAR FREQUENT READERS SWEEPSTAKES
WIN *A 1988 Cadillac Cimarron* Automobile or
12 other Fabulous Prizes

IT'S EASY TO ENTER. HERE'S HOW IT WORKS:

1. Enter *one* individual book sweepstakes, by completing and submitting the Official Entry form found in the back of that Summer Spectacular book, and you qualify for that book's prize drawing.

2. Enter *two* individual book sweepstakes, by completing and submitting two Official Entry Forms found in the back of those two Summer Spectacular books, and you qualify for the prize drawings for those two individual books.

3. Enter *three or more* individual book sweepstakes, by completing and submitting—in one envelope—three or more Official Entry forms found in the back of three or more individual Summer Spectacular books, and you qualify not only for those three or more individual books but also for THE BONUS PRIZE of a brand new Cadillac Cimarron Automobile!

Be sure to fill in the Bantam bookseller where you learned about this Sweepstakes . . . because if you win one of the twelve Sweepstakes prizes . . . your bookseller wins too!

SEE OFFICIAL RULES BELOW FOR DETAILS including alternate means of entry.

No Purchase Necessary.

Here are the Summer Spectacular Sweepstakes Books and Prizes!

BOOK TITLE	*PRIZE*
On Sale May 20, 1987	
ACT OF WILL	A luxurious weekend for two (3 days/2 nights) at first class hotel, MAP meals—(transportation not included) Approximate value: $750.00
MEN WHO HATE WOMEN & THE WOMEN WHO LOVE THEM	Gourmet food of the month for 6 months N.Y. Gourmet Co. Approximate value: $750.00
VENDETTA	Schrade Collector's Knife set Approximate value: $750.00
On Sale June 17, 1987	
LAST OF THE BREED	Sharp Video Camera and VCR Approximate value: $1,600.00

| WHITE DOVE (available in US only) | Lenox China white coffee service |
| | Approximate value: $750.00 |

THE MOTH (available in Canada only)

| THE BE (HAPPY) ATTITUDES | Set of DP workout equipment |
| | Approximate value: $1,000.00 |

On Sale July 15, 1987

| THE UNWANTED | Bug Zapper and Samsonite Chairs— Table—Umbrella—Outdoor Furniture |
| | Approximate value: $1,300.00 |

| A GRAND PASSION | Cake of the month plan |
| | Approximate value: $800.00 |

| 110 SHANGHAI ROAD | $1,000 American Express Gift Certificates |
| | Value: $1,000.00 |

On Sale August 12, 1987

| HIS WAY | Disc Player with library of Sinatra discs |
| | Approximate value: $1,000.00 |

| SUSPECTS | Home Security System |
| | Approximate value: $1,000.00 |

| PORTRAIT OF A MARRIED WOMAN | Minolta Auto-Focus Camera Kit |
| | Approximate value: $750.00 |

OFFICIAL RULES

1. There are twelve individual sweepstakes, each with its own prize award. There will be twelve separate sweepstakes drawings. You will be entered into the drawing for the prize corresponding to the book(s) from which you have obtained your entry blank, any one or up to all twelve. Submit your completed entry on the Official Entry Form found in this book and any of the other participating books . . . mail one or up to all twelve completed sweepstakes entries *in one envelope* to:

Frequent Readers Sweepstakes
PO Box 43 New York, New York 10046

2. NO PURCHASE NECESSARY TO ENTER OR WIN A PRIZE: Residents of Ohio and those wishing to obtain an Official Entry Form (covering all 12 sweepstakes) and the Official Rules send a self-addressed stamped envelope to: Frequent Reader Sweepstakes, P.O. Box 549, Sayreville, NJ 08872. One Official Entry Form per request. Requests must be received by August 14, 1987. Residents of Washington and Vermont need not include return postage.

3. Winners for each of the 12 sweepstakes will be selected in a random drawing to be conducted on or about October 19, 1987, from all completed entries received, under the supervision of Marden-Kane, Inc. an independent judging organization. If any of the 12 consumer winners selected have included completed Official Entry Forms from three or more books, or have included completed Official Entry Forms from three or more books, or have entered 3 or more sweepstakes on the Alternate Mail-In Official Entry Form (See Rule #2) they are qualified to participate in a separate BONUS DRAWING to be conducted on or about Oct. 19, 1987 for a 1988 Cadillac Cimarron. In the event that none of the twelve individual sweepstake prize winners qualify for the BONUS PRIZE, the bonus prize will be selected from all completed sweepstakes entries received. No mechanically reproduced entries accepted. All entries must be received by September 30, 1987 to be eligible. Not responsible for late, lost or misdirected mail or printing errors.

A GRAND PASSION
OFFICIAL ENTRY FORM

Please complete by entering all the information requested and
Mail to: Frequent Readers Sweepstakes
P.O. Box 43
New York, N.Y. 10046

NAME _____

ADDRESS _____

CITY _____ STATE _____ ZIP _____

BANTAM BOOK RETAILER WHERE YOU LEARNED ABOUT THIS SWEEPSTAKES

NAME _____

ADDRESS _____

CITY _____ STATE _____ ZIP _____

Completed entries must be received by September 30, 1987 in order to be eligible.

ISBN-0553-26658-6